LYCAON'S FIRE

A novel from The Saints universe
by
Jeff Schanz

This is a work of fiction. Names, characters, businesses, places, events, locales, and incidents are either the products of the author's imagination or used in a fictitious manner. Any resemblance to actual persons, living or dead, or actual events is purely coincidental.

CHAPTER 1

Panicked feet churned the low-hanging mist along the ground as the woman scrambled up the mountain slope in the dark.

Just one more hill, thought Espy. Only one more hill before she could see the valley and maybe a road. Or a river. Anything that might offer a chance of flagging someone down. She hadn't seen anyone for miles – no one human – and the despair made her want to lay down and submit to the death that stalked her. Despite the unspeakable things they would do to her, she was too exhausted and too mentally drained to keep going. Death was preferable to struggling through this nightmare any longer. But she wouldn't stop. Not just for her, for the baby she carried. She couldn't let them get the baby.

Them. Whatever they were. Unholy things ripped from a movie or book. Humanlike beasts, sometimes on two legs, sometimes on four, hunting her, soulless, relentless. Ravenous. Hungering for more than her flesh. Intent on tearing her living essence out of her body through her screams and tears. Craving her terror. Consuming some piece of her body while she watched. And when there was no more fear to draw, no more frightened beats of her heart, then she would die lost and alone.

She had watched her fellow inmates be torn apart, the monstrous things picking them off one by one like it was a game. A sick game played with fear, pain, and blood. Twelve captives had been taken into the woods and set free as prey. Soon after, there were only eleven. Then ten. Minute by minute, victim by victim, the hunt progressed. Esperanza was the only one left. Her cellmate selflessly sacrificed herself so Espy could gain a bit more distance. A few more minutes. Maybe it would be enough to get her to the valley road.

The peak of the hill was within two more strides. She stumbled as her ears caught the faint sound of growling behind her. *Dios mio.* Perhaps there was a steep slope behind the peak that she could slide down once she got over the top. The beasts were faster than her, she knew that. But if she could slide…

Scrabbling up the rocky ledge, she expected to look down onto the valley. What she saw was a brief descent, then another peak. A chasm and another slope followed that one. She was not close to the valley like she thought. No road, no river. No passersby. Just more running.

She wanted to cry, but the tears, and strength to produce them, were long since gone.

The growling came closer.

Espy heaved herself over the edge and rolled two feet into a woody shrub. There wasn't enough slope to slide, and too much brush and trees to navigate a clear path. Even if she got to her feet, she may not have the energy to stay upright while she ran downhill. She stood anyway, pushed through the bush that snagged her, then gained momentum. Her feet couldn't keep the pace. She tumbled into another bush. Catching her breath, she looked up to gauge the distance she had gone. Ten feet. At this pace of standing, falling, and getting back up again, it was slower than walking.

Feet or paws were crunching ground debris behind the rise she had just come from.

There was no way to outrun them anymore. Nowhere to hide, nowhere to go, nothing to fight them with. *Well…* One thing so small, it would accomplish only minimal damage to her attackers before she was torn apart: a handmade shiv made from a sharpened spoon handle and wound with tape. Barely sharp enough to penetrate flesh, it was nearly useless as a cutting weapon, and it would only serve to piss the beasts off. That wasn't its intended purpose. Her cellmate had created the tool for her own suicide so that when the time came that no avenues of escape were left, the shiv could be stabbed into either her neck or heart to die before the beasts got her. However, in a moment of pity, the cellmate handed the shiv to Espy, then sacrificed herself to slow their pursuers down.

Espy held the crude item in her palm, steeling herself for the inevitable. She thought all she'd have to decide is whether to kill herself or not, but she hadn't counted on a third option.

Will my baby die as soon as I do? She didn't think so. Soon after perhaps. Not soon enough. The sounds of snapping underbrush and

4

dry pine needles were coming from the opposite side of the tiny peak, no more than twenty feet away. Would they cut the baby from her womb and eat it alive? Though the fetus may not have enough awareness to understand what was happening to it, the possibility of them tearing into her live infant sickened her more than the thought of them cutting the dead baby from her body as she watched. On the other hand, could she stand to see them rip open her abdomen and feed on her child despite it being dead? She doubted she had enough time and strength to kill both herself and her child, and she shook with indecision.

The tips of long, pointed, lupine ears crested the rise. Moonlight silhouetted fur backs and trailing tails.

Make the choice. Now!

She pressed the shiv point to her belly, the handle gripped tightly with both hands. One final moment to draw a last breath and close her eyes. She wished she could say a prayer her mother had taught her to tell God to welcome her and her baby, and ward off evil on their journey. There wasn't even time for that. She gritted her teeth and tensed to pull the shiv into her.

Something like a vice clamped onto her wrists, stopping the shiv from penetrating her flesh. She screamed and tried to pull free of the beast's clawed grip. It had an iron hold and her frantic twisting and wrenching accomplished nothing. The beast spun her around until she was face to face with one of the things that had been hunting her all night.

Its head was dark, canine-shaped, layered in moonlit fur, with two glowing amber eyes that bore into her. It raised its clawed hand and struck.

The claws ripped deep gashes in her forearms, beige bone showing before the blood welled over the cuts. When she dropped the shiv, screamed again, and pulled away from her captor, she was abruptly let go. Her sudden release lurched her backward with uncontrolled momentum. Nothing was nearby to grab and balance herself. All she could do was force her head and torso to spin around and see what she was about to fall against.

The broken trunk of a slender tree stuck out of the ground. Its edges were torn and sharp. *Is it enough?* There was no doubt she was going to land on it, the only question was what part of her body would be hit. Leaning a little one way and it would maim her side. However, if she could just lean enough the other way...

The broken trunk speared her chest, driving all breath and muscle control from her. She had no idea how far it went through her because she couldn't bend her head around to see it. All she knew was that her face was inches from the ground, her whole body felt like it was consumed in fire, and there was the strange sensation of liquid rolling over the surface of her back.

It was the most excruciating thing she had ever felt, and yet she was at peace. There were no other decisions to make, no worries she could entertain, nothing else to do. Except die. As the blackness overtook her, she felt a momentary tug on her leg and something like a prick. Then nothing more.

CHAPTER 2

– One year later–

The squeak of accordion doors was muted by the hiss of the bus suspension lowering to deposit its passengers onto the sidewalk. Work boots and sneakers stepped off the threshold onto pristine pavement. The last set of shoes to exit were a pair of faded black hiking boots, lingering near the bus as it shut its doors and reset its suspension to drive away.

They were the only shoes Merrick Hull possessed and they served him well. He owned very little of anything, including only one other set of clothes. His entire estate was stuffed into an olive drab duffel bag hanging from his shoulder.

Merrick pulled up the collar of his Army surplus jacket to brace against a sudden burst of cold wind funneling through the street of the tiny Montana town called Templeton. According to the map, this was the main drag of the 'ville, yet there wasn't much to see and not very far to look for it. If the road was dirt (which it was not), this place could pass for a Western movie set. In several places, wooden posts stood in front of the shops to imply that horses had once been regular transportation here, or perhaps still were.

The other bus riders had already drifted off, many of them angling toward the side street that led to a lumber mill. Merrick had done a little research and discovered that Templeton had only one main industry which was a small yet productive lumber mill. The only other notable draws were motels and cabins rented to adventurers who wished to hike the abutting national forest, or fish the various streams and lakes. It wasn't his plan to make this town his destination, but it became his plan when he could only afford a ticket this far.

He didn't actually have a destination. Just "somewhere else." *As good a place as any.* Anywhere that he wouldn't be easily identified. Small, rural places like this were preferable, closer to wilderness than city, with no security cameras to be seen.

He hadn't eaten anything since he boarded the bus, and his gurgling stomach made him audibly aware. *Yeah, explain that to my wallet.* Though he didn't need to check the wallet again to discover what cash remained, he went through the motions anyway to see if two dollars might have magically spawned more bills. *Nope.* Two lonely dollars still there. Added with the seventeen cents in his front pocket, it might get him a cup of coffee, or a soda. Neither of which were worthy nutrition. *Candy bar at a convenience store?* That, at least, technically counted as food, though not by much. No convenience store was currently visible, however.

The only business representing food was a throwback style diner two blocks away. Not typically the kind of place that $2.17 would buy an adequate meal, yet there wasn't much else to do but go check. He hefted his duffel bag onto his shoulders and headed toward the diner.

Very few folks were wandering the streets. Granted, the air was chilly, but residents of Templeton, Montana would not only be used to the cold, they probably sought it out. This far north, close to the Canadian border, the kind of people that lived here were hardy souls that wouldn't be at home in tropical climates.

Templeton was a lone bastion of civilization on the long expanse of highway connecting two tribal reservations separated by forested mountains. The fact that any buses ran here was surprising, though welcome. Main Street, Templeton was perhaps designed for the occasional traveler, showcasing a diner, gas station (one pump, no store), sundries shop, a variety of clothing stores, antique stores, hardware, leather goods, bar, post office, library, and sheriff's station. With tidy sidewalks, freshly painted store exteriors, and the picturesque backdrop, Templeton seemed to embody the ideal small-town setting one might see on a greeting card or an old TV show. But in Merrick's experience, looks can be deceiving, and nothing is ever the same behind the façade.

Keep your pessimistic 'tude to yourself, bud. After all, he had made a long journey here and didn't have great options for going anywhere else for the time being, unless it was via walking or hitchhiking. Might as well hope the town was as pleasant and serene as it appeared.

Merrick stopped in front of an A-frame sign advertising the diner's daily specials.

"Meatloaf plate, $6.99"

No thanks. He had yet to have a craving for meatloaf, ever. It was edible, that was all.

"Chicken club sandwich w/ fries, $5.99"

There we go. Damn, that sounds good.

"Soup du jour, $3.99"

You had me at chicken club.

Merrick sighed, knowing full well the chicken club was not a realistic option, and he prepared to embarrass himself with a request for whatever was available with his paltry funds. It wasn't his first rodeo. Wasn't his thirty-first. Regardless, it never felt good to explain his situation and hope no one angrily kicked him out the door. "Beat it, freeloader!" they'd yell. *"I'm not freeloading. I just can't afford your regular menu items. Look, I have a little money. See? I'll be glad to pay you, I just need to know what I can afford."* In some places that may mean a half serving of something, or maybe an unsatisfactory order taken back to the kitchen, earmarked as eventual trash. Not always above board, but a decent meal is a decent meal. Towns with fast-food places were the easiest because a lot of them had dollar menus, or cheap options for late-night snackers. Unfortunately, in Templeton, no such luck. He entered the diner.

The inside was exactly how he pictured it. Booths with laminate tables, checkered floor, two TVs broadcasting news hung near the ceiling, a carousel of metal clips clenching paper orders, mounted in a pass-through to the kitchen. Two waitresses buzzed about in pale yellow uniforms. One was a middle-aged woman, heavy-set with a piled-up hairdo, and the other was a trim woman in her twenties. Only about a dozen patrons were eating, and most of them sat at the counter. Plenty of booths were open.

Merrick picked one closest to the door and sat down. The paper placemat doubled as a menu and he scanned it for affordable items. The closest thing he found was a cup of cream of chicken soup for $2.79. Still 62 cents too expensive. *Super.* He withdrew all the cash he possessed and flattened it under his palm. After several minutes, the young waitress came over.

The sticker on her nametag displaying the word "Kat" was partially peeling from the base. Despite no makeup and a frizzed hair bun behind her head, she had the kind of facial structure that many

9

women kill for. Full lips, prominent cheeks, and caramel eyes that momentarily made Merrick forget why he was there. Her tanned skin was from prolonged outdoor exposure, not a tanning bed.

"Good afternoon, sir," she said with a practiced smile. Her voice was pleasant and hospitable, with a distinct southern accent. *A long way from home.*

Before he could respond, she leaned over and presented a well-used towel. "Excuse me," she said, then began to whisk the moist rag over the table. He raked his money off the table into a cupped hand so she could reach the whole surface. She smiled again and said, "Sorry, we don't have busboys, so…" She shrugged in finality to the statement. Holding a pen poised over a spiral pad, she said, "What can I get you?"

The money in his cupped hand felt even more pathetic than he previously imagined it was. He held it up, unfurled his fingers, and tried to give her a kind grin.

"Hi, Kat," said Merrick. "My apologies. I have very little cash, and I promise I'm not looking for handouts and I don't want to waste your time. Is there by any chance something here I can afford with two dollars and seventeen cents?"

Kat stared blankly at her pad for a moment, a vague expression that didn't tell Merrick whether she was annoyed or just thinking. After a brief grimace, she met Merrick's eyes.

"Ehh, nothing except coffee," she said, then shook her head, anticipating his response.

Merrick smiled and matched her head shake. "Yeah. More awake doesn't equal less hungry."

She wiggled her jaw around for a moment and pocketed her pad. *Not a good sign.*

"Uh – I'm probably wasting your time," said Merrick. "I'm sorry. I'll just g…"

She held up a firm palm. "Now, hold on. I didn't say nothin' like that." She rubbed her chin with her knuckles and gazed into space for a few seconds. Without breaking her posture, she asked "You here to work at the mill?"

"No, ma'am."

She seemed surprised. "Not too many new folks come here that ain't headed to the lumber mill."

10

"I don't know anything about lumber mills. I'm just –." He wasn't sure what he was "just." He waggled his head. "I just planned on passing through. Kinda ran out of bus fare." He was going to add that $20 had fallen out of a hole in his jacket, but that felt like a sympathy ploy. Despite being the truth, it just sounded like a put-on, so he just shrugged and said, "It's ok. I thought I'd ask. Didn't want to bother anyone." He glanced out the window at the one-pump gas station. "Maybe the station has a candy bar or some chips inside. Thanks for…"

Again, Kat held up the palm. "Bill don't sell nothin' at his station. Patsy's got a few snacks in her shop, but they won't tide you over for long." She shook her head. "You sit tight, I'll be right back."

Kat strode back toward the kitchen.

Merrick had been through this situation many times. A helpful employee seeing if there was an exception that could be made for a hungry drifter. Most people genuinely wanted to help, though they couldn't always swing it. If it was a no-go, then he'd make do. When he didn't have restaurant options, he shot small game and cooked them over a campfire in the woods when there were woods to be had. Around here was an abundance of woods. He could either hike his way through the mountains to another unknown destination, hitchhike, or hold up here for a little while. For a long time now, he had lived day to day, foraging for food, or hunting it himself. Meals on plates were preferred, but not always available. He did the best he could, stayed alive, kept safe, and moved on.

A moving target is harder to catch. And even in this technologically advanced, "eyes everywhere" world, a man who doesn't use bank cards, or a cell phone, or sign his name to things is hard to find. They'd have to comb through hours and days of footage from every security camera in this corner of the globe to locate him. He wouldn't put it past them to try, but he liked his chances if they did. The bus ticket was bought with cash and came from an automated ticket machine that hadn't asked for ID. This particular bus line didn't care about anything other than collecting the fee. If they had required ID, he would've opted for hitchhiking.

Kat returned carrying a tray with a bowl, a drinking glass, and a pitcher of water. She placed the bowl in front of him. Steam rose from what appeared to be chicken noodle soup. Though the noodles

11

were sparse, and the chicken minuscule, it was plainly hot, which was better than he had expected. As Merrick stared at the bowl, Kat poured water into a glass.

He flattened out the dollar bills in an attempt to make them look more presentable for payment.

"We keep a vat of soup in the back for when the deputies come in," said Kat. "We only charge 'em a dollar even, so it's easy. Just our way of bein' kind to law enforcement. It's no nevermind to me if we're kind to someone else too."

"Thank you," said Merrick. "I really do appreciate it." He scooted all the bills and coins toward the edge of the table.

She scribbled something on her pad. "It's just a dollar."

"Yeah, but I'm a big tipper. That's uh –." He separated the coins, pretending to count them. "A hundred and seventeen percent tip."

She shook her head, no indication in her expression that she thought his joke was funny. The top page in her pad was tugged off and placed on the table. Then she plucked one of the dollars and pinched up the coins, rattling them in her palm.

"Seventeen percent is fine," she said. Before she left the table, she let slip a crooked smirk.

He watched her walk to another table. She didn't sashay like prissy girls, and didn't have a clunky, masculine walk either. Smooth, efficient, feminine strides. Not showy, nor a façade.

In another life, another world perhaps, he would be interested in asking Kat out. In this world, his lifestyle prevented that kind of relationship. Plus, he didn't consider himself handsome. Slightly below average height, wiry (he preferred that term rather than "skinny" – which he was often called), dirty by civilized standards, and several points south of Chris Evans in the face. Kinda average all the way around. Good for keeping hidden in a crowd. Not so good for asking out cute waitresses. And considering a single dollar was now the extent of his fortune, that meant he was also a cheap-ass date.

He carefully sipped at the soup broth to avoid burning his mouth. Even going slow, he finished the soup fairly quickly. *Hot soup, cold day, empty belly – go figure.* Although there was no one else waiting to be seated, he felt guilty taking up a booth here, and thought it would be best not to press the restaurant's hospitality much further and skedaddle before patrons became offended by the guy with the dirty face.

He set the spoon in the empty bowl and wiped his mouth, intending to leave just as Kat happened by.

"Just a second," she said, tapping the table with two fingers as she breezed past.

Hmm? It was too late to ask what she meant because she had already disappeared behind a wall, heading toward the kitchen. He inspected the dining area, mildly surprised that nobody was staring at him, no sour faces appraising his disheveled appearance. *I guess I can hang for another minute or two.* About one minute later, Kat zipped by again with a tray of sandwiches, heading to the booth in the far corner. Done with that, she was back at Merrick's table.

"You gonna be in town awhile?" she asked.

He shrugged. "I hadn't thought too far in advance."

She looked like she had something charitable on her mind, and though he had appreciated her efforts thus far, he didn't want to impose on one person too long.

He said, "Don't worry. I'm used to roughing it, living off the land, so to speak." He tried to grin through the last line like it was a fun thing. "I'll probably make camp in the woods tonight and figure out what's next."

"I wasn't offerin' you a place to stay," she said. "But if you want to come back here around closing time, I can make a box of extra food for ya."

"I don't want to be any trouble."

She shook her head and looked annoyed. "Just stuff Burt would throw out anyway. Shame to waste it." She raised her brows, daring him to challenge her generosity.

"Well, ok, if it would be thrown out anyway. Sure. Thank you."

She shrugged. "Alright. Be at the back door around nine-thirty." Merrick raised a brow in curiosity about the early closing time, and she seemed to understand the question, adding, "It's a small town, and ain't nobody on the streets past nine. No sense in stayin' open."

He nodded and smiled his repeated thanks. She nodded back, then headed to the kitchen.

Merrick hoisted his sack and went out the door. Deciding to reconnoiter where he would be returning, he noticed an ally that went between the diner and a two-story building abutting a concrete wall behind both buildings. A limited way in and sheltered from several angles. Not a bad place to hide if he needed one. He typically made notes of paths to run, places to hide. Behind the diner would be ideal for an urban homeless man. But Merrick wasn't urban, and didn't like to think of himself as homeless. His home was wherever his feet took him, plus a tiny tent to keep the rain off. His closet was a duffel bag strapped to his back, containing the tent, sleeping bag, a change of clothes, a first aid kit, a bottle of water, an atlas, a lighter, flashlight, a compound bow, arrows, and a knife. The bow was more for hunting than defense. Weapons usually weren't necessary for his safety. He had other ways of defending himself.

Confrontations, especially fights, were avoided at all costs. The danger to everyone else was too great. When someone attempted to harm Merrick, God help them.

CHAPTER 3

Killing time wasn't something that Merrick was fond of, but the promise of a solid meal if he just waited around until 9:30 was worth the waste of a day. He wandered the main street, which was simply the highway with a couple of street lights. There wasn't much he was interested in checking out.

Templeton's little library was quaint, though sparse. Ever since he became sober, he had made better use of his time by reading a lot of free books in various libraries across the country. A college education wasn't in the cards for him, so he made do with what he could find on his own. If he had put himself on the wagon a lot sooner, he might've qualified for a Ph.D. in several disciplines. But jaded orphans with drug addictions, no home, and a truckload of mental issues don't tend to become stable and clean easily. It takes something traumatic to do that. After he cleaned up, he read constantly and was able to retain it. Libraries were a factor in regaining his sanity, so whenever available, he usually popped into a library to look around and maybe sit down with a book. Despite having the time to kill today, he felt more like exploring than reading. Still, the library was as good a place to start exploring as any.

The lobby of the library posted local notices and laminated town information placards. On the top of the bulletin board was the slogan, "Templeton, Montana: The safest town in America."

Merrick's brow went up. How often had he seen a city, town, or business claim to be the #1 of something? Truth or fiction, either way, it would be hard to prove, and he doubted there were official whistleblowers who roamed the nation searching for such claims to verify. "Best Pizza in Chicago? According to our data, your pizza is merely good. Take the sign down this instant!" Cities and towns loved to use the "safest" tag, based on crime data that was spun to discard certain neighborhoods, etc. Besides, he doubted there were too many people in this particular town that didn't know each other by first names and weren't fully aware of each other's personal business. "Bobby Taylor? Give me back my purse! Shame on you. If you need some money, why didn't you just ask me? Here's ten dollars. Your momma can pay me back when I see her at church. Now shoo!"

Having adequately learned the town's accolades, and counting the number of book stacks on one hand, he left the library. Honestly, the only thing he really wanted to do right then was sleep. Sleeping on buses was impossible, especially when you're unsure of your destination. He had figured on pitching his tent over the adjacent hill later, but he didn't want to climb all the way up there, nap, forget to wake up, and miss out on the promised doggie bag from the diner. The loading area behind the diner was fairly secluded, surrounded by concrete walls and a small alley that blocked access to everywhere except the rears of two buildings. Only employees or suppliers would use it, so it would be pretty quiet to rest for the few spare hours.

Nobody gave him suspicious looks about heading behind the buildings. *Maybe this town really is as safe as it says.* Around the corner was the back stoop of the diner. Probably used to bring in supplies or take out trash, evidenced by the pile of cardboard and paper surrounding the tall trash bins next to the stairs. Many a night he had spent using cardboard and paper as bedding, and these looked as non-offensive as any. The boxes were from canned or dry goods, and the paper was package wrapping. No blood or slime on anything. The only concern may be some wisps of steam rising from the kitchen exhaust somewhere near the trash cans, which probably wouldn't bother him. If it wouldn't freak Kat out, he could just make a comfy nest right next to the stairs and wait for 9:30 to roll around.

He waded through the recycling, satisfied that the content was as he thought, pushed a few items around for both comfort and shielding against the chilly air. A few layers of unfolded boxes and spread-out papers made a good blanket, and he was soon warm enough. He settled in wishing he had gotten a book to read while he waited.

That thought faded as he ran through old memories in his head to pass the time. Some of the memories concerned little mysteries he wanted to solve. Other memories were about larger mysteries he was trying desperately to drown out. Eventually, the long journey caught up with him, and the unexpectedly warm surroundings made his eyes droop.

He fell asleep.

Kat Seavers was on the 5th day of a 7 day work week. Burt, the owner of the diner, had promised one day off next week, and couldn't afford to give her another one until a week after that. The "busy period" always centered around the new hires and return workers for the mill. For the two weeks that the workers filtered in, the evenings were jammed and the waitresses never stopped moving. Luckily, the days were still relatively quiet.

Apparently, today was going to be an exception. First, that strange drifter came in. Strange, not because the man was a vagabond, but because those kinds of people weren't usually well-spoken, well-mannered, and funny. *Well, slightly funny*. Just unexpected all around. It didn't hurt that he was a little cute. Not so much good-looking as witty and intelligent. Kat was attracted to brains more than brawn. Even if he wasn't cute, she would've helped him. She had a soft spot for folks who ask for things nicely.

Men in general, cute or otherwise, weren't something that normally occupied Kat's mind. Romantic relationships complicated her future plans and she didn't have time for them. She wasn't a dreamer or a wide-eyed fawn when it came to the world. She knew where she was, where she was going, and all things in between. Templeton was fine for now, a step on the way to her ultimate destination. It was her father's choice to move here when she was little, and he liked the sleepy town. Though not so sleepy today.

Besides the drifter, something else was odd that afternoon (now turning evening). That oddity had pulled up in a garishly painted Chevy Suburban, adorned in bright, brazen letters announcing the arrival of "Jeremiah Gunn, Bounty Hunter." If a stranger judged the appearance of the man who had walked through the diner's door, with "Gunn" emblazoned across his chest in gold glitter, leather pants, and gold chains dripping off his shoulders, beach blonde Mohawk, plus the prominence of his name on the vehicle, one might assume "Gunn" was either a TV star or famous personality. Neither was true.

Kat had known Jeremiah by his birth name, Jeremy Gunderson, for several years, including the brief time he spent working at the lumber mill. His latest, and so far longest, venture was being a bounty hunter, and he apparently thought the profession needed pomp and promotion. Gunn had successfully captured a few small-time thieves who had melted into the reservations to hide from sheriffs who didn't have authority there. His few paychecks were promptly spent on a big vehicle and a nifty paint job. Now he stood in front of Kat grinning like a man who won the lottery and was showing it off.

"Evening, Jeremy," said Kat. "The mill rush just came in, so you may have to wait for a table for maybe fifteen, twenty minutes if that's ok."

Gunn maintained his grin. "Nah, darlin', I can't sit. Got a big bounty in the car, and a long drive to Nevada to collect."

Kat waited for Gunn to give some useful information like why he was standing there if he didn't plan to sit and eat. He just kept grinning like it was her privilege to guess.

She had no intention of doing so. "Look, it's nice to see you, but I don't have time to chat. If you'll excuse me, I've got to…"

"Now, wait a minute, darlin'," he said. "You're not going to ask me who it is?"

"No. None of my business. And we're busy, so if you…"

"Alright, alright," said Gunn. "It's only the biggest bounty anyone's ever gotten in their whole life. Just thought you'd be interested."

"No, Jeremy. Sorry, I ain't interested in criminals or bounty hunting."

"I never caught anybody like this one. He's kinda famous around here."

Gunn gave her a hopeful look and Kat ignored it.

"It's busy," she said. "You want something or not?"

Gunn sighed, plainly disappointed. "A to-go order, if you don't mind."

"'Course I don't mind." She brought up her notepad with pen poised. "You know what you want?"

"Always, darlin'."

Kat kept her eyes on her pad, ignoring the double entendre.

Gunn said, "Your chicken club special sounds good. Two of 'em. Got a deputy now." Gunn nodded like his statement was significant.

Though Kat didn't want to take part in Gunn's usual attention-getting routines, her fortitude slipped and she glanced through the window at Gunn's Suburban. Something struck her.

"He's in there?" she asked. "This criminal of yours?"

Gunn beamed. "Sure as shit, darlin'. Federal case. Murder charges. And you've heard what he did right here in…"

"He's chained up?"

"Of course. How the hell else would I…?"

"Still – he cain't be sitting in our parking lot."

Gunn's brows furrowed. "He can't get out. Besides, my deputy's got a shotgun on him."

"Don't matter, Jeremy. You've got a murderer sitting in our parking lot. Folks find out, it'll scare 'em."

"Darlin', he's chained up in the back and everything's locked."

"You want me to tell Burt?"

The owner of the diner, Burt Bosko, was a giant man, disliked people, and had been to jail multiple times on assault charges simply because humans annoyed him. He liked to appease the police officers with cheap soup and free coffee to get on their good side, but he had no time for pompous bounty hunters like Gunn, and would physically expel Gunn from the property if he thought Kat was being harassed.

"No need." Gunn cocked a curious eyebrow. "I can tell my deputy to park across the street."

Kat screwed up her mouth. "No, that's a bit far. Just tell 'em to take the car around back so nobody can see you."

Gunn made a show of holding up his glitter-encrusted cell phone, tapped out a message, then pocketed the phone. "Done," he said.

Kat nodded. She finished her entry on the pad, then asked, "You want drinks?"

"Two iced teas. Sweet."

19

Outside, Gunn's car started up, pulled away from the parking lot, then headed toward the alley.

Kat marked down the shorthand for tea, circled it, then snapped off the top sheet. "It'll probably be about ten minutes. You going to wait inside?"

"I'll be right here, darlin'," said Gunn, grinning again.

She clipped the order to Burt's carousel, then attended to her other customers.

Burt was pumping out all the specials pretty quickly, and Gunn's order was ready to go sooner than she had estimated. She still had other tables to serve, so the to-go order waited another couple minutes before she snatched it up. As he promised, Gunn was leaning against the hostess podium where she had left him.

Kat handed the packages to Gunn, donned a professional smile, and turned back toward the kitchen.

Gunn surprised Kat by grabbing her arm. She shot him a hard glance and he jerked his hand back.

"Sorry," he said softly. "It's just – you know, I thought you'd be interested cuz –," he lowered his voice, "it's Saunders in my car." He nodded like he had just shared something extraordinary. "You know, Errol Saunders?"

Kat didn't have time for this, but she did recognize the name. Probably from the news, though she rarely paid attention to news and goings-on around town. She normally kept her head down and stayed out of everyone's business.

Gunn was persistent. "Councilman here? Accused of murdering that missing pregnant girl a year back? Been hiding ever since?"

Despite her determination to avoid this conversation further, the explanation rang mental bells and the question popped out of her mouth. "You found Esperanza's murderer?"

Gunn nodded with an inflated smile. "Sonuvabitch was hiding here the whole time. Holdin' up in the loft of an old lady's barn."

Kat knew about the pregnant girl who had been mistakenly put in jail, let go, then went missing immediately afterward. Rumor had it she was carrying the councilman's baby since she had been his housekeeper and had reportedly sued him for palimony. Naturally, the mystery of her disappearance led to the public opinion that Saunders had done something with her. Then he, too, disappeared.

Kat hated news in general, it was all miserable, and this particular incident happened a year ago, but the girl who went missing was the sister of one of her ranch hands. If Gunn was telling the truth, he might have actually done something significant and was plainly desperate to crow about it. And as usual, trying to impress her.

Her shoulders relaxed and she tried to adopt a more sympathetic posture. "Well, congratulations, Jeremiah," she said, making a point of using his pseudonym. "You did a good thing, and I hope it gives you a good payday." She gave a curt nod to signal that their conversation was over, then she left to pick up an order from the kitchen. By the time she headed back to the dining area, Gunn was gone.

Good. She felt bad sometimes for ignoring his advances, despite being as brash and as tacky as possible for all the years she'd known him. She didn't wish him ill, but she did wish him gone.

She served the order to the appropriate booth, then went over to the sheriff's deputy who had been waiting inside the door for several minutes.

"Evening, Deputy Pooler," said Kat, searching the dining room for an open booth. "I think it'll only be a few more minutes for a booth if you wanna wait."

"Hi, Kat," said the deputy. "Did I just hear Gunn say he found Councilman Saunders?"

Kat nodded. "That's what he said."

The deputy put his hands on his hips. "Huh. I didn't hear anything about it."

"I thought Jeremy tells y'all when he catches someone in your jurisdiction."

The deputy chuckled. "Well, that isn't often, but – yeah, he does."

"Maybe he told Sheriff Kind and the sheriff forgot to tell you."

Deputy Pooler shook his head. "I don't get it."

"Mill shift. Everybody's busy."

Kat only meant that the sheriff might have his hands full, but the deputy lowered his head and nodded. "I hear ya, Kat. A counter stool'll be fine if you have one."

"Sure. There's one near the kitchen if that's ok."

She led the deputy to the counter stool, all the while musing a third odd thing of the day. Sheriff Kind almost never failed to take

21

either breakfast or lunch at the diner, whichever matched his shift. He hadn't come by all day. Kat didn't like the sheriff, but had nothing against him, and hoped he was ok.

Something was just plain off today, and who the heck knew what other odd things may have happened, or may happen next.

CHAPTER 4

Something triggered Merrick awake. A sound that didn't belong, a voice, or a clatter that wasn't expected.

Long ago, Merrick trained himself to keep his senses attuned while he slept, able to detect a significant change in environment or ambient noise. Living on the streets with no one to watch your back required a kind of vigilance most humans are unaccustomed to. Animals knew how to sense things while they slept, and deep in the DNA of humans, those instincts were still there if one could tap into them. Merrick had an advantage to tapping into those senses that most people didn't have, and it kept him alive all these years. Or more importantly, unhurt.

He opened his eyes, but didn't sit up right away. Slowly stretching his neck to see over the cardboard layer, he could make out a brightly painted SUV parked next to the concrete wall. A blonde mohawked man, dressed like a rock star, or perhaps a pro wrestler, had banged on the car door for someone inside to open it. The rock-star man had an armful of to-go food. Another man got out of the SUV wearing a similar shirt and jeans. Those two men talked for a moment as they sorted through the food.

Exhaust from the diner's kitchen blew out a pungent smell and Merrick grunted softly in complaint. He tensed, wondering if the rock star or his buddy had heard the grunt. Neither seemed aware. Merrick eyed the exhaust vent, noticing it was blowing onto a stack of boxes, coating them in condensation. Only one side of the stack was getting wet, causing the tower of boxes to lean slightly. He hadn't noticed when he first camped out here that the unexpected warmth was likely from the steaming vent.

Though the bounty hunter looked more laughable than dangerous, Merrick kept quiet anyway, figuring there was always a slim chance an outside professional could've been hired to find him. It hadn't happened before and seemed very unlikely. The people who were searching for Merrick had more resources than anyone they could hire, and they also didn't want Merrick arrested. Their interest in him was wholly illegal and entirely private. Outside parties like bounty hunters would bring unwelcome complications.

A muffled voice came from inside the car. One of the bounty-hunter men shouted at the car door and a muted reply came back. Another shout, another response, then a hushed conversation between the two men finally culminated in the opening of the rear door.

A disheveled man in a white undershirt, open black trench coat, and khaki cargo pants got out of the vehicle, wrenching chained handcuffs away from whatever interior thing they got caught on. Medium length salt and pepper hair twisted in all angles as if he had been sleeping. Whoever he was, he looked more sullen and perturbed than sorrowful that he was a prisoner of these two clowns. A terse conversation followed, then the mohawked man, presumably the advertised "Jeremiah Gunn," motioned for the handcuffed man to shuffle toward the far wall. Merrick couldn't read lips, but he imagined the conversation involved letting the prisoner take a piss.

The assistant bounty hunter followed the prisoner over to the wall and waited placidly behind him. Gunn leaned against the car and opened his food box. He had taken only one bite out of his sandwich before a stack of cardboard boxes next to Merrick fell over. The exhaust had weighed down one side of the boxes so much, it created an uneven distribution and toppled the stack. Not quite thunderous, but enough for Gunn to freeze mid-chew and stare at Merrick.

Shit.

Gunn squinted and cocked his head.

Merrick said nothing aloud and didn't move. He had no reason to run from Gunn despite being uncomfortable about the situation. Gunn took a long, slow chew, pointed at Merrick, then turned toward his partner.

"Hey, Jake," said Gunn.

Jake turned his head toward Gunn and said, "What?" which was the end of the conversation. Something else happened to distract both of them.

Another car pulled up. The new arrival was a late model, panel van with muffled base beats thumping inside. The passenger side opened before the car was fully stopped and a young black man got out. He wore dark grey coveralls like you'd find on factory workers. No patches or monikers indicated any company association.

For a back alley devoid of alternative exits, this was an excessive amount of traffic. Merrick was starting to regret his choice of quiet retreat. Though the rear door of the diner was only a few steps to his left in case of emergency, whoever worked in the kitchen might flip out if a vagrant came sauntering through. *"Don't mind me. Getting too crowded outside. Carry on, folks."* Not. Even if he wanted to barge in, there didn't appear to be a doorknob on the outside.

The van driver also hopped out. With naturally tanned skin and a hint of angle to his eyes, he could be anything from Asian to Hispanic, to American Indian, or a mix of any of those. He had on non-descript coveralls as well.

"Hey, man! It's Jeremiah Gunn," said the driver. "Can I have your autograph?"

Gunn stared, unblinking at the two men approaching him. Very slowly, he lowered his food box to the hood of his car. It did not look like he bought the autograph line.

Nor should he have. The rear door of the van opened and five men emerged hefting weapons. Two had bats, one had a hatchet, and two others had hunting knives. The black passenger slid a machete from his belt, and the driver raised his hand and snapped open a long, stiletto switchblade.

Merrick had no illusions about what was going to happen, though he had zero clue why, and was busy calculating his own escape strategy. The alley led to the main road, and he might make it there before one of the thugs nabbed him if the corner of the diner wasn't only feet away from the van's back doors. It had been positioned purposefully to block the alley. If he stayed put, the bins and boxes still mostly blocked their view of his position. However, if someone had the notion to check behind the trash bins, they'd find him. He swallowed quietly and decided to wait it out. There was a good chance no one would see him. And maybe when the passengers cleared the van, he'd have the chance to bolt.

Gunn put his hands up. "I'm not armed, fellas," he said. "Just tell me what you want and we can work something out."

Merrick mentally shook his head. These interlopers weren't thieves or gang members. They were assassins. *Run, Gunn.*

25

Unfortunately, there was nowhere for Gunn to run. It would have been useless advice if it was said aloud. A shotgun, if handy, would be a better play.

Gunn's partner, Jake, apparently didn't understand that sudden moves weren't the best first option, and quickly ran around the car. He was caught off guard when a hatchet flew into his chest, dropping him on his back, stunned and motionless. Immediately, the prisoner dug around Jake's pockets for the handcuff keys.

The men from the van rushed at the bounty hunters. Gunn managed a strong right cross, but that was the extent of his defense. The driver's blade drove deep into Gunn's abdomen, then, while Gunn hunched over in disbelief, the black man's machete chopped into the side of the bounty hunter's neck.

Jake faired even poorer since he was nearly dead already, not making a defensive move, and being pummeled by baseball bats, then the hatchet which had initially dropped him.

Unlocking his cuffs was as far as the prisoner got. Two of the assassins fell on him and a strangled scream was the last action he made.

Gunn was still alive when the assassins were finished with everybody else. He lifted a hand to protest the attack, achieving nothing more significant than that gesture. Blood flowed from his neck across his shirt, coating Gunn's emblazoned name in glistening red. Gurgling and coughing, he lurched toward Merrick and stretched a trembling hand toward the drifter.

What the…?

Despite the sickening gargle sound, Gunn's last words were clear: "Call – cops."

Oh, no. No, no, no. Please don't… Two of the assassins turned in the direction Gunn had just addressed. One squinted while the other cocked his head. *Maybe if I'm still, they won't be able to see…*

"Hey!" said the hatchet man. "Someone's there!"

Shit! There weren't many options available. Stand up and try diplomacy (which didn't work for Gunn), or book it fast around the corner and hope there was enough lead between him and the assassins that they couldn't catch him until he got to the street. Safety in public?

Merrick dove out of his garbage hideout, stumbled over a box that wasn't empty, got his feet under him, and started to sprint. He made it 3 strides before something took the breath out of him. It knocked him down, struggling for balance, and desperately trying to reach the thing embedded in his back.

"Got 'im!" yelled someone.

Merrick's frantic fingers touched the edge of polished wood. He got enough grip on it to pull, but pulling the object out hurt worse than when it went in. Merrick screamed, bit into his lip enough to draw blood, then yanked the wooden object out.

"Gaaawwd!" he shrieked. The pain was akin to attaching cables from a car battery to his spine. He flung the weapon several feet in front of him. It was a hatchet. Merrick struggled to regain his feet, unable to bend his back. All his extremities were jelly. He dragged a foot underneath him, ready to stand but there was no strength in any of his muscles.

Someone had a grip on his arm and yanked him upright. It was the driver.

"Well, well," said the driver. "A peepin' bum." He grinned in amusement at his analogy. The grin was replaced by a vaudevillian frown. "Sorry, my man, but can't have witnesses."

Merrick couldn't gather enough breath to plead to his attackers. Had he breathed since he was hit? He didn't remember. Cold lightning surged through his bones, a debilitating chill that he recognized well. Milky sweat beads appeared on his arms. *Please, God, no.* He tried to say, "Don't do this," to the man, yet nothing came out of his numb mouth. Maybe it was too late anyway.

The driver held up his switchblade and grinned as if it were a courtesy to display the murder weapon. He plunged it into Merrick's chest.

The pain was unbearable. It felt like his heart had exploded and caught on fire within the same beat. Merrick could do nothing except open his mouth in a rasping, wordless cry. He clenched his knuckles around the attacker's wrist, somehow managing to extricate himself from the driver's blade, then fell to the ground and constricted his body into a quivering ball. Through his watering eyes, he could barely make out the driver leaning down toward him.

Blackness encroached his vision, confirming what he feared was coming next. It was not fear of dying. He knew death was not coming. Something else was.

Merrick's eyes closed. Something else's eyes opened.

CHAPTER 5

It was a little later than Kat expected when the diner shut its doors. Not entirely surprising, just the way it was this time of season. She had already boxed up two of the leftover chicken sandwiches and a handful of cold fries, plus a chunk of cornbread, and after she slipped on her coat, she collected the to-go box, jangled her keys at Burt, and said, "Night!"

Burt nodded and grunted, his usual response, never pausing his mopping. Kat headed to the front door, then suddenly remembered who the to-go box was for. Changing direction, she skirted Burt and his mop, got a quizzical look from the man, then unlatched the back door bolt and stepped out onto the stoop.

Kat started to search the loading area for the drifter, hoping he hadn't given up waiting for her. Her eyes never moved from the first place they focused. She gasped. Not from the toppled trash bins and scattered boxes, but from the blood.

Heads, torsos, body parts, masses of things that looked like raw meat were strewn across the loading area, leaking gallons of blood onto the uneven asphalt. It was like a slaughterhouse had exploded without any building rubble.

Kat slapped a hand to her mouth and nose. The unconscious reaction might have been to stifle a scream, or might have been to block the stench of blood, loosed bowels, and shredded intestines from entering her lungs. It was simply involuntary, and Kat froze in that pose for several seconds.

Within the unfathomable nightmare, Kat noticed several other strange things. The two vehicles parked near the bodies, an old van she had never seen before and Jeremiah Gunn's Suburban, both had their doors open and streaks of blood on their exteriors. In addition, the van was still running. Knives, bats, and a hatchet were all resting in small puddles of blood. One headless man clutched a machete in his hand.

Kat recognized Gunn's clothes, though there was a lot of blood staining them. If nothing else, the blonde Mohawk made him easy to spot, plus he was more or less intact, unlike most of the other corpses. She had no idea who the other men were, or how many there were, because the body parts were scattered and hard to identify.

"Oh, God," she murmured, holding back vomit.

The diner's back door had no handle on the outside, and luckily she hadn't closed it yet. The horrific sight had stopped her before she could step past the door for it to close. She spun around and ran back inside.

"Call nine-one-one!" she yelled. "Burt! Nine-one-one! Now!"

Kat knew that the sheriff was talking to her, he had been talking to her for a while, but her brain had drifted elsewhere, tuning him out. Multiple memories were playing at once in her mind: the scene of the slaughter; picturing Gunn as he flirted with her in the restaurant; trying to recall if she had ever seen that van before; the short conversation she had with the drifter. She hadn't seen his body among the dead and she wondered what had become of him. Sheriff Quinton Kind patiently waited for her answer while holding his pen over a notepad. Kat's mind was still lost in a labyrinth of preoccupation.

He touched her arm gently. "Katheryn?"

Kat snapped out of her daze. Nobody should be calling her Katheryn.

"Huh?" said Kat.

The sheriff nodded and donned a practiced, patient smile. "I asked how well you knew Mr. Gunn."

"Jeremy? Everybody knows him. He grew up here."

"I know. I meant – did he tend to talk to you much about his life or business?"

"Oh, yeah, well – he talked a lot, but I ignored him most'a the time. Usually, he's just tryin' to impress me with his macho stories."

Sheriff Kind nodded and scribbled on his pad. "And did he talk to you today?"

"Yes."

"And what did he say?"

30

"He was all fired excited about his latest bounty. Thought it was going to be a big deal."

"Did he tell you who it was?"

"The bounty?" Kat declined her head. The name wasn't difficult to recall, it was just mixing with the sudden recollection of Jeremy's torn body lying in his own blood. She never really liked him, but nobody deserved that. Strangely, he, his assistant, and their prisoner had been less mutilated than the others.

Sheriff Kind dipped his head a little lower to catch her eye. "Miss Seavers?"

"Huh?' said Kat. "Oh, uh – he said the guy was Councilman Saunders. I didn't see him before the – um... so I just took his word."

The sheriff nodded again. "He say anything else?"

"Tried to tell me what the councilman was wanted for, but I was really tryin' to just get back to work."

More scribbling, more nodding. "Anything else?"

"I, um – took his order. That's it."

"What about his assistant?"

"Never met him."

One of the deputies came over and whispered something to the sheriff, who nodded absently. He re-focused on Kat. "What about the other people? From the van? Know any of them?"

Kat scrunched up her face involuntarily. The bodies of those people were barely distinguishable as human. All of them were shredded and strewn in a wide pattern, resembling an explosion. Not much was recognizable including their severed heads. Even if she knew them, they might be hard to identify. Despite that, she was fairly sure none of them were familiar.

"I don't think so. God, it's just that they're so... No. I didn't know them."

The sheriff was occupied with the notes on his pad for a few minutes.

Kat became lost in her thoughts again, this time musing aloud. "What'd they kill Jeremy for? Why here?"

The sheriff looked up from his pad. "They?"

Kat shook her head. "Whoever did this."

Sheriff Kind shifted and had an odd look between curiosity and suspicion. "Well, right now, we don't know if it was one or more persons, or persons at all. Bears, lightning, a homemade bomb? If you have any insight on what you saw, any detail that you noticed, it might help me."

"I don't know. It's just... I guess I keep thinking – Jeremy's guys weren't as tore up as the others. Like two different things happened. Like maybe those van guys killed Jeremy's guys, and someone – something else killed the van guys. Ya know?"

Quinton Kind exhaled and placed his hands on his hips. A reluctant smile crossed his face. "I've always said you've got a sharp eye and a keen mind, Miss Seavers."

You've told me before to mind my business and let you do your job. Not sure if that's the same, Sheriff. Quinton Kind was not a terrible person as far as she knew. He did do a good job of protecting the town, and as the flyers like to say, Templeton was normally a very safe place to live. There was just something about Kind that ate at Kat. An aura, a smell, a vibration in the air that bothered her enough to where she generally avoided the sheriff. His deputies were decent folks, and she was friends with most of them, it was just Kind that made her arm hairs tingle. He could be terse, patronizing, sexist, and grouchy, for sure. He was also persistent in uprooting evidence and chasing down criminals. A bulldog. Kat was actually glad he protected them, but as a person, he was a few degrees off. Quinton tended to treat Kat like she was a kid even though she was well into her twenties. She wasn't sure if it was because she was female, or because he had simply known her since she was a little girl. Either way, she was looking forward to the end of his questioning.

Apparently, she had missed another question. "Huh?"

"I said was there anyone else you talked to besides Jeremiah Gunn?"

"No. Don't think so."

"Who's the leftovers for?"

"Hmm?" Kat had forgotten she was holding onto the box of sandwiches. "Oh, I was, um, just taking these home. Burt had extra."

The sheriff's question seemed a little pointed, but he nodded like he was satisfied with the answer.

"For your dad?" he prompted.

Though Kat worked at a diner, she had no taste for the diner's food. She liked to cook gourmet food for herself, and would rather suffer a salad for lunch than force down a greasy burger. Why Kind knew or cared about what she brought home was a mystery to her. She wasn't vocal about denouncing Burt's cooking, though her friends understood her preferences. Have the chatty deputies been gossiping about her with the sheriff? *Why am I always the subject of conversation in this town? There's other females who live here.*

"Yeah. Easier than making him plates." Which would be true if she had really intended that. Her dad wasn't into gourmet cooking, wasn't fond of cooking for himself, and was constantly asking Kat to leave him a sandwich or two in the fridge. *Perfect reason to bring home the leftovers. Why didn't I think of it?*

"You park out front?"

"Sure. That's my car right there." Everyone knew her red Jeep, even Kind.

"Long walk around to the front from the back door. Why were you headed that way?"

Damn. She was going to use the excuse of hearing something that she wanted to check out behind the diner, but she had already told him she hadn't heard anything. And she didn't. The diner walls were solid concrete block. The fryer, grill, exhaust, and clanging of kitchen noises, plus the TVs in the dining room, added with the ambient patron conversation drowned out what little could have filtered in through the walls. If anything, Burt would've been the closest to hear something. Her best chance at an excuse would be to say she was tossing out some trash. However, she only had the food container in her hand when she had gone past Burt. She hoped they wouldn't ask Burt that question.

"Just tossing something out," she said. That was vague enough. The "something" didn't have to be a large bag of garbage, and maybe it wouldn't have been obvious to Burt. *Would you buy that excuse if you were him?* There wasn't any reason for the sheriff to be suspicious of her, and even if he was, there would be nothing worth linking her to. Just the drifter, if he finds out.

Kat didn't know why she was protecting the drifter. As far as she knew, he may have actually committed the atrocities behind the diner. The scrawny drifter didn't look powerful enough to destroy ten armed men, though she supposed it was possible. She normally trusted her gut, and her gut told her that the drifter wasn't that kind of person. *Was the murderer even a person?*

The sheriff closed his pad, tipped his hat to Kat, and turned to go. "Thanks, Miss Seavers."

"Hey, Sheriff," said Kat, touching his arm. "There any chance it coulda' been rabid wolves or bears, or something?"

Sheriff Kind appeared like he was going to give a professional answer, then he dropped his head and sighed. "I wish I knew, Miss Seavers. I really do. There is nothing good about what happened, and there's going to be a lot of scared people wondering what I'm going to do about it." He smiled ruefully, then shook his head. "So, I need to find some answers fast." Quinton put a hand on Kat's shoulder. "If you remember any detail you forgot, anything at all, you call me, ok?"

Kat nodded. "Sure. Of course, Sheriff."

Kat's preoccupation extended into her drive home. Oblivious of her unsafe speed, her Jeep Wrangler strained to hug the curves of the winding forest road that led to her father's farm. The tires groaned from the undue pressure, and the screech of rubber and asphalt finally snapped Kat out of her trance. She took her foot off the gas and focused on not being the next casualty in Templeton's historic day of deaths.

As any normal human would expect, seeing so many slaughtered people had the horrifying memories in her head playing on looped cycle. What the hell had happened? For years, she had worked at the diner and nothing scary ever occurred there, and then – right outside the back door…

And where was the drifter? He wasn't one of the corpses as far as she could tell. And despite her disdain for the sheriff's manipulative questioning, Kind did have the right to be suspicious that she was holding something back. Kat's gut feeling had rarely led her wrong, and it told her the drifter was harmless. *If he isn't, it's your ass.* Yet, if she revealed him, the sheriff would have an arrest warrant out for the drifter within minutes.

So, on top of shock and nausea, guilt about lying was added to her distractions. It was a wonder she saw the man in front of her.

What the...?

The hunched figure was walking on the road shoulder with a bag strapped across his back. The jacket collar was pulled up past his ears. Kat had never seen anyone strolling along this road. It was a long stretch with virtually no civilization for miles, and at night, it had the added illusion of being creepy from the closely spaced trees and looming overhang. Not much moonlight peeped through the thick tree canopy. Very little traffic frequented it since there were only a few farms out this way. Honestly, if Kat ran off the road due to her distracted, reckless driving, no one would find her for a while.

As she approached the man, the headlights illuminated his olive drab jacket. Only a small portion of the man's tousled hair poked above the jacket collar, but combined with the familiar ensemble and his overall slender shape, she was sure it was the drifter.

She slowed the Jeep. As she did, the drifter bolted into the woods.

CHAPTER 6

Merrick had been lost in his thoughts and hadn't noticed the car pulling up behind him. *Shit!* The headlights had already hit him, and his panic to hide from them would certainly seem suspicious. His mind raced through excuses to explain why he reacted that way as the car stopped just a few yards from him.

The driver of the red, hardtop Jeep was not the sheriff *(thank God)*, but rather a young woman.

"Hey!" she called, lowering the passenger side window. It was the waitress from the diner. "Hey, it's alright."

Her voice didn't sound angry or accusatory. Merrick stepped into the open. He offered a timid wave of his hand. She flipped a quick wave back.

He leaned against her door and peered inside. "Hello again," he said.

She squinted as she looked at him. Merrick was suddenly very self-conscious that he may have blood on him. Though he had switched out his shredded and bloody shirt and pants for his spare clothes, maybe the jacket had splatter he wasn't aware of.

"What in the world are you doin' way out here?" asked the waitress.

"Walking."

The waitress rolled her eyes. "To where? There ain't nothing for miles."

Merrick shrugged. "Figured I'd make camp after I got tired."

"It's cold out."

"I'm used to it."

The waitress – *what was her name? Kat?* – looked like she was considering something important. Then she met his gaze with a serious stare. "Do you know what happened back there?"

Oh, boy. He had fully expected the scene would be a big deal once it was discovered, but he was hoping he would be out of sight before anyone started asking questions. Especially asking **him** questions. However, just in case, he had invented some excuses, or at least believable scenarios, involving a partial truth to throw whoever might ask off his track.

"Uh oh," he said, trying to seem surprised. "I'm guessing something bad happened behind the diner?"

"You didn't see it?"

He shook his head. "I fell asleep next to the back stoop waiting for you, and something woke me up. Bunch of guys getting out of a van, talking to that Gunn guy. It, uh – looked like something bad was about to go down. I didn't want to stick around, so I bolted. They didn't chase me and I just kept running."

The waitress blinked once, the only reaction to his story. Merrick had the odd feeling that she didn't tend to get emotional and this might simply be her way.

He added, "Police don't tend to like drifters, and I haven't had too many good relationships with any of them, so – I figured I'd just keep my mouth shut and move on."

The waitress held her eyes on him like she was doing some pupil-based lie detector test. It wasn't a suspicious look, just focused scrutiny.

"Look, I'm fine out here," said Merrick. "I'm just gonna keep heading in that…"

"You still want the sandwiches?" she interjected. Her sudden question surprised Merrick a little. She held up the container of food. "The fries are cold, but –."

He nodded. "Yes, ma'am. Thank you."

She leaned toward the door, and he was about to reach in to receive the box, then he realized she wasn't stretching to offer the food. She was unlocking the door.

"Get in," she said.

"Uh, it's ok. I'm…"

The door popped open. "Get in," she repeated. "I ain't gonna hurt ya. It's cold outside. You can stay the night, then in the morning you can run off to wherever you want."

Merrick cocked his head. *Is she inviting me to…?*

"In the barn," she said with an exasperated expression. "I ain't easy and I ain't an idiot. I just don't want you to catch your death cuz I made you wait for some leftovers."

37

Oddly enough, waiting for her in the radius of the kitchen exhaust was the warmest he'd been in a while. Everything that followed was the problem.

He must have transmitted his reluctance on his face because, before he could respond, she said, "Well, alright then. Do what you want."

She held up the food box.

He swung the door open, accepted the food, then sat in her passenger seat.

"Thank you," he said. "I didn't mean for you to go outta your way, but I do appreciate it."

She shrugged and spun the wheels to get back on the road. "It ain't outta my way. I live just a little ways further on."

Though that wasn't what he meant, he decided not to say anything, and instead, busied his mouth with one of the sandwiches. *Ah, the chicken club!* With his mouth full, he mumbled a "thank you" that didn't sound like anything close to those words.

The waitress never took her eyes from the road.

Merrick finished his swallow and attempted to be a little more sociable. "So, what's your name?"

She angled her shoulder toward him to flash her "Kat" nametag.

"Ah, sorry," he said. "I figured it wasn't your real name. The, uh, tape is peeling off and there's another name undern... Never mind. Kat. Got it."

Kat darted her eyes to him, saying nothing.

"I'm Merrick," he said, delaying another bite of sandwich. "Merrick Hull. Weird name, I know."

Kat subtly bobbed her head to acknowledge she heard him. She didn't seem to be interested in a lot of conversation.

"Sorry, I'm talking too much. Just trying to be sociable." He smiled. "I'll shut up now." The sandwich was reinserted into his mouth.

Kat shook her head. "No, you're fine. There's just a lot on my mind. The, uh... well, I guess you didn't see it, but the murders were petty gruesome."

Merrick was about to nod, then realized he shouldn't know too much about what she was talking about. In truth, he never really saw what happened. Not with his own eyes.

He put the sandwich down. "Yeah, I was, uh – afraid of that. Bad?"

Her eyes went wide for emphasis as she nodded. "Never seen anything like it. Body parts everywhere. Got the town freaked out."

"Whoa." He wasn't sure he wanted to follow this much further, but it felt like the right thing to do. "What, uh – what exactly happened?"

"Nobody knows," said Kat. "Almost looked like a bomb went off." She made a queasy face. "Kinda hard to talk about."

"I get it."

"I ain't squeamish, ya understand?" she said. "I've slaughtered cows and pigs, and I'm no stranger to a fight, but – this ain't like nothing I've ever seen."

"I don't think I wanna know," said Merrick. *Not a lie.*

"Sure," she said. "And – Kat *is* my name by the way." She pointed to her name tag. "Someone else's name is underneath. Burt reused the nametag. He's just cheap."

Merrick attempted a warm smile with his mouth full. He swallowed and said, "Kat's not a nickname?"

"It's what I've always gone by. Katheryn's my given name, but I don't allow no one to call me that."

"I see. Well, nice to meet you, Kat."

They drove in silence for a half-mile. Merrick finished one of the sandwiches and Kat stayed focused on the road.

After a while, Merrick said, "Thanks again for the ride and the food. I don't get a lot of charity that extends past a hand-out and walking away. A lot of folks are scared of people like me."

Kat shrugged. "I'm not. I can take care of myself." She made a brief motion to reach between the door and her seat, then reeled her hand back. "Besides, you don't seem like any drifter I've ever met."

"Should I take that as a compliment?"

"I guess. You're polite, seem educated, kinda normal."

Merrick laughed. "Normal is the nicest thing anyone has ever called me."

"So, how come you're a drifter?"

Direct. "That's a very long story. And a lot of that story even *I* don't know."

Kat gave him a confused look.

Merrick bobbed his head back and forth. "There's things that have happened to me that I don't understand. Things I can't remember because I was on drugs, or sedated." He realized how that sounded and hastily added, "I don't do drugs anymore. That was a different me a very long time ago."

"I'm not judgin'," said Kat.

"Well, let's just say that a combination of bad decisions led to a worse result, which is something so complicated that I still don't understand, but I'm dealing with as best I can."

"You running away from it, or toward it?"

Right to the point, aren't you? "Both, I guess."

Kat shook her head. "You like to use contradictions to answer questions."

"I'm probably a walking contradiction," he said, turning to look at the dark trees as they passed. "I want to find out what happened to me, but the people involved in it are dangerous. They're trying to find me too, and I would prefer they don't." He shrugged. "It's very complicated."

"I kinda get it. Sorry, I won't ask anymore."

"It's ok. Just not a good idea for anyone to know much about me. Safer for everyone."

"Alright," said Kat. Her tone sounded both final and conciliatory.

The dark tunnel of trees and brush opened up as they wound down one side of a hill into a partial valley. That valley flattened out into farm area with the occasional solitary oak standing sentinel in vast stretches of fields. Along the edges of rolling grassy fields was the continuation of the forest, like groomed borders of a golf course.

She turned left onto a well-packed dirt road that skirted one of the rolling hills, then parked her Jeep in front of an old, wooden house that could've been the movie set for every farm film ever made. Weathered, white paint, picketed porch, slatted shutters, with a rust-colored barn about 50 yards away. In front of the house was a combination of dirt lot and open field. One set of dirt tracks led to the tree line on the opposite side of the farm. That makeshift road was flanked by a wooden fence on one side and a barbed-wire fence on the other, encompassing a cow pasture. Even in the dark, silhouetted bovine shapes were recognizable.

Merrick was about to thank her a third time for her hospitality, then noticed she was staring intently past him. As he twisted to see what had arrested her attention, she started the car back up.

"Sorry," she said. "There's a problem I need to handle. D'ya mind?"

A fire was burning near the opposite tree line. Despite the distance, which was considerable, Merrick could make out the vague figures of humans.

"Uh – no, that's fine," said Merrick. "What's going on?"

Kat had a hard look on her face as she drove down the long dirt drive bordered by fences. "Just some assholes."

As the Jeep got closer to the fire, Merrick could see it was a stacked tree-branch fire with several people gathered around it, plus a smaller fire with some kind of animal on a spit roasting over it. A Super-Duty truck was parked nearby. Kat slowed the Jeep and one of the men strode toward her.

"Tanner Fosse, what the hell are you doin'!" said Kat as she stopped the car and opened her door.

The man she called "Tanner" halted and spread his arms wide. A beer bottle wobbled in his left hand. "Pussy Kat!" he bellowed. "It's Pussy Kat, guys! My, my, my. What can I *do – for – you*, Miss Pretty Kitty?" His words were slow, slurred, and unnecessarily loud.

Kat stood up, closed the door behind her, and leaned against the car, arms folded.

"You can get the hell off my property, Tanner," said Kat.

Tanner took a drag of his beer and strolled unsteadily toward Kat. Merrick noticed that several of the men who had been loitering around the bonfire were now also moving in the direction of the Jeep.

"We're not on your property, pretty kitty," said Tanner.

She flicked a finger at the tree line. "That there's my property line. You know damned well it is."

"We're just havin' a little fun. Come on and join us." Tanner sauntered closer to Kat.

The other men were in no hurry, though slowly closing in too. Merrick was starting to think he should step in, but was afraid of what would happen if things got out of hand. *Not again. Not twice in the same night.*

41

Kat glanced over at the fire, then back at Tanner. "That one of my goats you got on that spit? You killin' my animals now?"

"Nah. S'just a deer. Come on, join us. I promise I won't hurt ya. Much." Tanner gripped his oversized belt buckle and pushed it downwards. The buckle design was a chrome silhouette of two women: one with angel wings, the other with devil horns. Both had high heels.

"It ain't deer huntin' season, Tanner."

"So? I hit 'im with my truck."

"Look, maybe everyone else is scared of you cuz your dad owns the mill, threatens people, and buys you outta trouble," snarled Kat. "But I ain't. You touch my animals and I'll make you wish that…"

"Make me what!?" barked Tanner, pitching his beer bottle at Kat's wheel. The bottle broke on the ground and splattered beer and glass shards against her rim. "You can't do shit to me and you know it. It's my word against yours, and who'd believe a cocksuckin' little waitress."

"I ain't playin' with you, Tanner," said Kat. Her tone hadn't risen despite Tanner's escalation attempt. "Pack your shit, leave the carcass, and go the hell home. Now."

"Fuck you, bitch. I'm not goin' anywhere." He reached under his coat and Merrick saw the handle of a pistol tucked into his waistband. However, Tanner didn't draw it. Instead, he slipped a long hunting knife from behind his back and started scratching his cheek with it. "But maybe if you ask me real nice." He popped the belt buckle aside and pinched his pants' zipper in his fingers. "You know, reeeeal nice? On bended knee?"

Tanner began to laugh, and his buddies, who now flanked him, chuckled as well.

Merrick opened his door and stood up. "I suggest you do as the lady says," said Merrick.

"Hey, man. Stay out of this," said one of the men.

"Who the fuck's this prick?" said Tanner. "You'd rather suck his puny cock than mine? Huh?"

"Don't, Tanner," said Kat.

"Get back in the fuckin' car, dickhead," said another of Tanner's friends to Merrick.

"Look at him!" said Tanner pointing his knife at Merrick. "You'd fuck that scrawny asshole? Nah, babe, you need to see what a real dick is like."

Faster than Merrick would've guessed, Tanner lunged at Kat. To her credit, she aimed a kick at the man's crotch, but he sidestepped it enough to where it only impacted his thigh. He yanked her around with one arm pressing both her arms to her chest and his other hand held the knife to her throat.

Merrick didn't want to risk harming her by doing something rash, and he also couldn't stand by and let this drunken maniac hurt his new friend. Looking down through the Jeep windshield, he could see the edge of a revolver handle snugged in the pocket of her door. He decided not to reach for it until he was sure there was no option left.

Tanner grinned and tried to lick the drool off his lips. "Yeah, now who's gonna make who leave?" He wiggled the knife at her throat. "Maybe after you get a good, long dick in you, you'll change your..."

Kat slammed a foot into Tanner's toes and the man immediately hunched, grunted, and froze in that order. Then she swung a hard elbow into his groin, which made Tanner release his grip on her entirely. While Tanner dropped to the ground in a ball, Kat ran to the back of her Jeep, flung open the tailgate, and retrieved a pump-action shotgun. She racked a shell into the chamber and pointed it at Tanner.

"Pack your shit," she said to Tanner. "Leave the goat carcass," she said to the other men who were slowly lifting their hands high. "And get the hell off my property."

"Bitch!" shrieked Tanner, rocking sideways on the ground. "You broke my dick!"

Kat fired at Tanner. *Jesus!* The shot exploded chunks of dirt and rock a foot away from Tanner's butt.

"Fuck!" squealed Tanner, squirming to get his knees underneath him to crawl away.

"You're crazy!" shouted one of the other men.

"Yeah, I'm crazy," replied Kat. "And I'd be doing every woman in the world a favor if I broke your dick, Tanner." She pumped another shell into the chamber. "I fire one warning shot. That's it. Next one goes in one of you. And if you reach for that pistol, I'll take that as a threat and shoot you before you can get the handle sweaty."

One of Tanner's friends shook his head and took a step back. The others just stayed still with their hands raised.

"I'll kill you!" screeched Tanner, shuffling away on his knees.

"Is that a threat?" she said. "While trespassing on my property?" She turned to Merrick and gave him a comically shocked expression. "Sounded like a threat, didn't it?"

Merrick nodded. He had never been called as a witness to anything, and assumed he wouldn't be considered a credible one, yet he somehow doubted any of this would be brought to trial.

Kat took a step towards the slowly crawling Tanner and leveled the gun at his spine. "I'd be ridding the world of a piece of shit if I shot you. All the girls you raped and your dad paid to shut 'em up? All the mill workers you ripped off?"

"Shit, Kat!" Tanner was grunting something as he crawled, sounding close to crying, choking on whatever it was deep in his throat.

"Hey!" said one of the other men. "It's ok! It's ok. We'll go. I'll get 'im in the truck and we'll go. Ok?"

"Better do it right now," said Kat through gritted teeth.

"Yeah, I swear!" said the man. "Just put the gun down. We'll go."

He put his hands on Tanner's shoulders. Tanner jerked them away and pointed a finger at Kat. "Fuck you!" He turned the finger toward the other man, and said, "And you're fired!"

"I quit, asshole. You don't want my help? Fine. Get shot." The man threw his hands down in disgust and walked back toward the truck.

Tanner watched the outspoken man march off, then searched the faces of the other men who hadn't moved since Kat pulled out the shotgun.

"God, you're all pussies," said Tanner.

One man shrugged, another shook his head in exasperation.

Tanner shakily stood as Kat kept her barrel sight on his back.

"This was a test and you all failed. Pussies," said Tanner toward the men. He turned toward Kat. "And you have no idea what you've done."

"Well, I ain't done yet unless you get in that truck and get the hell outta here," said Kat.

Tanner kept his back to Kat as he trudged toward his truck. He cocked his head toward her once to say, "I'll be back."

Kat didn't respond other than to maintain her aim on Tanner until he had closed the door on his truck.

Merrick watched the truck head down the road and disappear behind the tree line before he spoke. "Do you think he'll come back?"

"Not tonight," she answered. "But yeah, he'll try something stupid eventually." She popped the shell out of the chamber and reinserted it back into the shell tube.

They both climbed back into her Jeep and she started the engine.

"Sorry 'bout that," she said, turning the Jeep toward the house. "I wouldn't blame you if you'd rather get back on the road and get clear of here. You're welcome to the barn if you want it. It ain't much, but it's warm."

Merrick nodded. "I always try to avoid fights, but – yeah, the barn sounds nice."

The Jeep stopped in front of the barn and Kat bade Merrick get out. She stayed in the driver's seat. Merrick's confused look must've made her explain, "It's ok. Go on," she said. "I've gotta get some water and go back and douse that fire. It'll be a long night for me."

Merrick got back in the car and closed the door. "Then I'll help make it shorter. Where's the water?"

CHAPTER 7

It was late morning before Merrick woke the next day. Allowing the sun to be burning bright in the sky before he got up and got going wasn't something he was accustomed to. Since the sunshine was barely squeezing through slender cracks in the barn's wooden walls, it wasn't surprising he hadn't noticed the time. He stretched, then rolled up his bedding.

The previous evening, after he and Kat had completely snuffed the bonfire, he retired to the barn and laid out his bedding supplies, sans the tent. There hadn't been much opportunity to ponder the day's happenings, or weigh the issues he had been a factor to. He expected nightmarish thoughts to keep him awake, but his exhausted body decided differently, and he zonked out once his head hit the pillow. A straw base under a warm sleeping bag was very comfortable considering his usual options.

While working on repacking his duffel, he noticed a plate of food enclosed in plastic wrap sitting atop a nearby hay bale. Two pieces of toast and bacon were under the plastic. *Whoa.* On the rare occasions when he had bacon, it was from a discarded breakfast in a trash bin. Once his duffle was properly packed, he sat down to the welcome feast. *By the time I leave, I might have put on a pound or two.*

As he ate, he absently scratched at the place on his chest where the knife had stabbed him. New scars tended to be itchy. Partway through his meal, he heard something happening outside. He went to the doors and peeked through the crack.

A well-used, 3 axle, super-duty truck was parked outside, with three men unloading a cargo trailer. One was a middle-aged Caucasian man with graying hair. Another was a Hispanic man, thick around the waist, and wearing a folded-brim cowboy hat. The third was a slender young man, possibly late teens, also Hispanic, wearing a baseball cap. They were leading a huge bull down the ramp from the trailer. The bull shook its immense head, swinging its horns in dangerous arcs. All three men seemed adept at dodging the horns, and none of them looked overly concerned for their safety. The older Hispanic man even laughed and cracked a joke that Merrick couldn't hear, and the other men laughed with him. They led the bull to a gate in the barbed wire fence and ushered him in. Once done, they shook hands and slapped each other on the back, showing relief over the anxiety they had been disguising.

Kat came out of the house and greeted them, hugging the older white man. *Dad, I assume?* They talked for a little while, during which Kat made a gesture in the direction the bonfire had been, and all three men faced that way. Then Kat waved a hand toward the barn, followed by all three men turning to stare at the barn doors. Kat cupped her mouth with her hands and called out, "Merrick!?"

Oh, yay. Merrick wasn't fond of these moments: meeting the parents after a family member accommodated him for a night. It was sort of the equivalent of a child showing Daddy the mangy animal he found nosing around the trash and then asking, "Can I keep 'im?" Merrick wasn't planning on sticking around much longer. The havoc he had caused in town wasn't going to blow away with the wind, and whether anyone connected him to it or not, it wasn't a good idea to linger while that cloud hung overhead. It also wasn't safe for anyone who harbored him, or knew too much about him. Kat was a nice woman, and really interesting if he cared to find out more, but for her own safety, it would be best if he moved on.

Merrick opened the barn doors, blinking against the morning sun directly in his eyes. He did a low-key wave at Kat and her friends and walked toward them. The grey-haired man held out a hand.

"Howdy," he said pleasantly. "I'm Del Seavers, Kat's father."

Mystery solved. "Nice to meet you. I'm Merrick Hull. Nobody's father." That last line sounded funnier in his head and he wished he would've said something else.

Mr. Seavers shook Merrick's hand, making no obvious blanch at the terrible joke.

"So – just passing through?" asked Del.

"Kind of."

Del nodded in a noncommittal, polite way. He glanced at no one in particular, probably trying to think of something appropriate to say.

Merrick doused the awkward moment by saying, "Your daughter was kind enough to allow me a warm place to sleep, and I sincerely appreciate it. I wouldn't want to impose on your hospitality any further, so I'll get moving again very shortly."

Del cocked an eyebrow. "Well, I don't know the situation, but I'm not one to turn someone out into the cold."

"Don't worry, you're not," said Merrick. "It's the life I chose. I feel more comfortable traveling and being on my own."

"Well, every man knows what's best for himself." Mr. Seavers smiled genuinely.

Strange. Most people eventually accept Merrick's explanation, though it usually takes a few deflections of concern, or sometimes even well-crafted arguments. Mr. Seavers took Merrick's statement at face value. *An interesting family, The Seavers.*

"Ok, guys," said Kat turning toward the house. "I gotta go to work, so I'm gonna go change. There's bacon on the table when you're ready."

"Wait a minute, young lady," said Del. "We ain't finished talkin' about this Tanner Fosse situation."

"I handled it, Dad."

"You can't just pull shotguns on folks and not expect some kind of retaliation," said Del.

Merrick agreed silently, and Kat had admitted last night she'd expect Tanner to try something else at some point, yet now she seemed to be downplaying that possibility.

Kat faced her father with an exasperated expression. "If I had a dollar for every time Tanner tried something stupid, I'd have enough money to fly to Paris. I ain't one of his weepy, date-rape bimbos that don't have the balls to speak up against him. I don't tolerate nobody's bullshit."

Del interrupted with a raised finger. "Language, young lady."

"Sorry, Daddy. Anyway, I can take care of myself."

"I know, sweetie. I know," said Del in a warmer tone.

Kat seemed satisfied with Del's response. "Now finish whatever y'all are doin' and go on in and eat."

Del nodded. "Alright. In a minute." He watched Kat go inside then he shrugged at both the Hispanic man and Merrick. "She's gonna back herself into a serious corner one of these days," he said.

48

"That Tanner Fosse is an idiot, but he's a dangerous idiot. And unfortunately connected around here." He put his hands on his hips and stared at the ground for a moment.

The older Hispanic man said, "Hey, it's ok, jefe. You know I always keep an eye out."

Del smiled. "Yeah, I know, Zeus. You cain't be here twenty-four, seven though. You got your own family to go home to at night."

Zeus shrugged. "It's just me and Javi now. We don't have to sleep at home every night."

Zeus nudged his knuckles on the teenager's shoulder who nodded in response.

Del shook his head. "No, no. You guys can't…"

Zeus wasn't accepting any argument. "Seriously, Mr. Del. We can camp out in a tent, and if we see anything, we'll beat the crap out of 'em. Javi's got a baseball bat, and he's got a hard swing. Homerun hitter, boss."

Del scrunched his face at the suggestion.

Javi blanched. "I only hit two homers last year, Dad."

"See!?" said Zeus, excited. "Strong arms. And I still play a little fútbol now and then, so I can, ya know – kick 'em in the cajones."

Del was holding in his amusement well, and somehow Merrick managed not to laugh. "I do appreciate the thought, but I also need you guys bright and early tomorrow. If you get yourselves hurt, or you're exhausted from staying up all night, it won't do us much good."

Zeus looked crushed. "Yeah, I know, jefe."

Del patted Zeus on the shoulder. "We both got shotguns next to our beds if we hear anything." He then faced Merrick. "Sorry to run off, but – I haven't eaten anything since we left Great Falls. So…" He nodded once and aimed toward the house.

"Nice to meet you, sir," called Merrick.

Del waved a hand behind him as he strode to the house.

Zeus took off his cowboy hat and rubbed his forehead with his arm. He shook his head as Mr. Seavers disappeared into the house. "I don't like it, Javi."

The boy shook his head as affirmation. "Yeah, but what can we do?"

Zeus shrugged. "Camp out anyway? Take shifts? Drink some Red Bull to stay awake?"

Javi scrunched his face. "That shit's awful. Tastes like nasty medicine."

Zeus frowned. "Boy, you got no clue what nasty medicine is. When I was a kid, my mother thought Nyquil and Vick's Vapo Rub cured everything. You can't sleep with Vapo Rub on you. Can't see either. Burns the moisture outta your eyeballs." He made exaggerated blinking motions.

Merrick noticed he was out of the conversational loop and thought now was a good time to tactfully exit. Zeus apparently had other ideas.

"Oh, hey, man, sorry," he said reaching to shake Merrick's hand. Merrick halted his momentum in the opposite direction and accepted the handshake. "I'm Jesus Moreno. People just call me Zeus."

Trading one god's name for another god's name? Merrick opened his mouth to say his own name but Zeus cut him off.

"I already heard your name, Mr. Merrick," said Zeus. "And this is my son, Javier."

Javier tipped his cap.

"Hi guys," said Merrick. "Just Merrick, please."

"Sure," said Zeus. "We're just ranch hands here. It's not a big ranch, they don't need too many people, and Mr. Seavers doesn't have much money, so we're all he can afford."

Ok. Nice to know but...

"They're good people," continued Zeus. "Miss Seavers is a great lady. It's like she's my adopted daughter. I kinda miss looking after a girl since my little sister died."

"Dad." Javier pelted his father with a light backhand to the shoulder. "Nobody knows for sure Aunt Espy's dead. Just still missing."

"Well, *I* know because I just know," said Zeus.

Once again Merrick felt like he should opt-out of the conversation. And once again, Zeus wouldn't let him.

"Sorry, man," said Zeus. "Once I get going, you know – everyone's always telling me, 'Zeus, man, shut up already.' But I can't help... anyway, I wanted to ask you a question."

"Me?"

"Yeah," said Zeus, barely pausing his speaking rhythm. "Did you hear about that stuff that happened behind the diner?"

"I, uh, heard about it."

"It's sick," said Javier.

Zeus nodded. "Made me puke when I saw it. Body parts, guts, blood, poop everywhere."

"Eww, Dad," warned Javier.

"What? There really was poop. Dead people sometimes poop when they…"

"Dad." Javier shook his head emphatically.

Yeah, kid, I want this conversation over with too.

Zeus continued. "Anyway, it reminded me a lot of the wolf legends around here. And I wanted to…"

"Wolf legends?" asked Merrick.

"Yeah, man. Figured you mighta heard something about 'em. So, there's a legend that these big wolf people run around in the forest, kidnapping and eating humans. Really gross and it scares the crap out of folks."

"Wolf people? Like – werewolves?" Merrick forced a dubious expression.

Zeus shrugged. "I guess. What would you call giant wolves that stand like humans, with yellow glowing eyes, and eat people?"

"Uh – hard to believe?"

"Hey, man, I lived here a long time and I seen shit that'll make you turn white. Er – whiter. I think it was these things that took my sister."

"Dad," sighed Javier. "They said Mr. Saunders probably did it."

Zeus waved off his son. "Yeah, well, he's dead now, and that scene looks like some crazed animals tore 'em all apart. Convenient, huh?"

Javier shook his head.

"Don't shake your head at me," said Zeus with a sharper tone. "I'm not the only one who thinks the wolf things mighta done the killing at the diner. And I'm going to the meeting tonight at the courthouse. They're gonna discuss it, and I wanna be there it cuz it involves Councilman Saunders, and maybe Espy."

"I know. Sorry, Dad."

51

Zeus waggled his head, then suddenly his lighter mood was back. He faced Merrick again. "What I wanted to ask you, since you've been hiking around the woods, is if you've seen anything, you know – weird?"

"In the woods? No. Sorry. I came here on a bus. I haven't really gone very far. Just town, and then here."

Zeus reluctantly nodded and hung his head. "Yeah, ok, that's cool. Just thought I'd ask."

He snugged the cowboy hat back on his head and looked off at nowhere in particular for several awkward seconds.

"I'm really sorry," said Merrick, hoping it might help to mollify.

"It's ok," said Zeus, then patted Merrick on the shoulder. "Well, if you do walk around in the woods at night, keep your eyes on a swivel. I'm not sayin' that these wolf people are what people say, but – something weird is out there, and people go missing around here. So – you know, take care. Javi and I got work to do, then we gotta figure out how to guard the house tonight without Miss Seavers knowin'."

"Why wouldn't you want her to know?" asked Merrick.

"You kiddin'? She'd kill us if she knew we were trying to protect her."

Merrick gave Zeus a bewildered look.

Zeus held his hands up in surrender. "She doesn't like men trying to take care of her. Even friends."

"Ok, then," said Merrick.

"We'll figure something out."

Zeus slapped Javier on the arm and pointed at the scattered hay bales in the pasture. Javier looked anything but pleased.

Zeus turned back to Merrick. "Good luck wherever you're going, Mr. Merrick."

Merrick's intent to leave was both for his safety and everyone else's, but right then he felt that leaving Kat unprotected might be less safe for her, selfish, and closer to abandonment. He wasn't sure how long the window was on Tanner's grudge, but hotheads tended to carry out their vendettas while their temper was still boiling rather than wait days later when common sense might return. Maybe all Kat needed was a night or two of secret vigil to keep her safe.

Merrick could spare a night, right? Nobody was suspecting him for the diner deaths so far.

"Hey, wait," said Merrick.

Zeus halted on his way toward the pasture. "Hmm?"

Merrick shrugged. "If you guys trust me, I can keep watch tonight."

"Really?" Zeus didn't act concerned that the first line of defense for his boss's family would be a total stranger. He seemed relieved. "You don't mind?"

"Sure. I got a tent, and I can camp out in the woods somewhere behind the barn. I'm pretty good at being quiet. She expects me to be gone when she gets home, so she won't know I'm there."

"Sweet, man!" said Zeus. "Hey, look, I'll be here 'til about eight, then I'll be back about six in the morning. You can cover the in-between?"

"Yeah. I got it."

"You're all right, Mr. Merrick," he extended a hand and Merrick accepted it to shake. Zeus surprised him by spitting into his other hand, slapping that onto the two gripped hands, then motioning for Merrick to do the same. Merrick tentatively did. Zeus grinned. "That's how we did it on the Vegas streets. We're homies now."

Javier rolled his eyes at his father's inner-city reference.

Zeus ignored his son. "You need a favor, doesn't matter where or when, just ask, ok?"

"Sure."

What the hell am I getting myself into?

CHAPTER 8

Once again, Merrick's day came down to killing time. At least on the Seavers' ranch, there was plenty of things to occupy him if he didn't mind working. Which he didn't. He helped Zeus and Javi stack hay bales and a few other laborious tasks before excusing himself for a nap to prepare for the evening watch.

Numerous places he'd been had opportunities to do day labor for a few dollars, and he'd taken advantage of the ones he could do with his limited skills. Though he wasn't brawny, he wasn't a weakling either. Physical labor was perfectly fine if it wasn't lifting extremely heavy things, or requiring comic book hero muscles. He just didn't have an industrial or professional skillset. Besides an above-average aptitude for hunting with a bow and arrow (cultivated from pure necessity), and what would amount to passing grades on Boy Scout camping badges, Merrick's most marketable attribute was his mind. Years of developing faster and faster reading techniques to get through books before the library closed, and a receptive mind to retain the information he read so he could have worthwhile things to ponder when he was alone and bored, gave him enough knowledge to rival a degree or two from any top university. However, without a signed piece of paper that proclaimed he was smart, no employers were willing to take his word for it. Which was fine by him anyway. He didn't want his signature on a W2, or photo on a security badge, or any kind of identity measure that might put him on the grid. He lived as a ghost, existing in obscurity, with no practical way of locating him. And once this evening came, despite the extra day of lingering here, he would be ghostlike again, keeping camouflaged vigil over the Seavers' property by camping in the woods behind the barn.

Kat had worked a double shift, breakfast through dinner, and had gotten home after Zeus had already left. Before Zeus departed, he woke Merrick up as requested so he could make a little camp in the dense tree cover that stretched from the barn to the next mountain slope. He wanted to be close enough to be able to see the house, yet far enough that he wouldn't be spotted, or even suspected of being there. As far as Kat knew, he was already long gone down the road. Also, since Tanner Fosse hadn't said exactly what kind of vengeance he had in mind, it would be a good idea to have an eye on the pasture in case Tanner planned on doing something to Kat's cows or goats.

Merrick sat on a log that looked like it had been felled by a storm. He peered through the tree gap at the moonlit pasture. Only a few cows roamed around. Most of them congregated under a wide, barnlike shelter that had only three walls and no doors. Nothing interesting was going on, which left Merrick to random musings.

First, he imagined the cows were talking in mumbled English and he associated each sound with a word that best matched its tone. His mind wandered further and he imagined the cows standing on hind legs, spying on him through peepholes in the barnlike structure. Those mental wanderings brought him back to his old standby whenever he was too distracted to suppress it: hazy recollections of being experimented on.

Those memories felt more like mini nightmares. Snippets, images, and feelings of men holding him down, things being injected into him, a burning sensation like lava flowing inside his bones, his flesh ripping apart, and the raw edges rubbing against each other. Those memories morphed into different images, discolored and confusing, like peering through scratched eyeglasses, the wrong prescription, and tinted an unnatural hue. In those dreamlike memories, his eyes were no longer his own. He was someone else. Men in lab coats were frantically moving away from him. Every time he recalled these memories, he tried to make out any identifiable attributes of the surroundings, but nothing was recognizable. The action that followed was blurry, no details other than claws flashing, blood spraying, and screaming. That disorienting flurry led to a similar, much newer memory of claws, blood, and strangled cries. He knew that new memory was from the diner, Merrick just couldn't fully recall it, or any time he's the "other one," clearly. His last real recollection from the previous night was the mixed-race man thrusting a knife into his chest, the paralyzing pain that followed, then the familiar chilling electricity that surged through him as he "died." That's when the other one took over. And the other one doesn't let Merrick remember much, or have control. It is concerned with one thing and one thing only: the preservation of Merrick Hull's life regardless of Merrick Hull's wishes.

Luckily, the other one stays dormant unless something severely damages Merrick. Then, like an anthropomorphized survival instinct, it comes out, like it or not. Merrick lost count of how many times the other one had emerged, and every time it was over, Merrick found himself waking up in an unfamiliar place, surrounded by gore and slaughter. Even if he wasn't running from the mysterious men that wanted to capture or destroy him for what he had become, he would need to keep running to stay ahead of the investigations into the deaths the other one had caused. He had no idea if it would ever stop, or if he could somehow gain control of his other self, or at least allow it to come out on his terms, so for now, constant movement was the best course. The limits of that strategy were being tested by hanging around this town for longer than he was comfortable.

Kat Seavers wasn't going to be a part of his future life. She was barely a friend. Simply a kind soul who took pity on him and aided him for a couple days. He had met others like her, and would meet more in the years to come. Most human beings were decent animals when not being coerced by politics, religion, media, or the voice of a mob. And once he was gone from their lives, he doubted he would linger in their minds. Likewise, he tried not to lament the loss of any of their company. He'd managed to do that pretty well over the years. So, why was this diner waitress from Templeton, Montana on his mind like she was special? Why risk the trouble... No, why risk a disaster to stay here and make sure she's safe?

Because, despite the monster inside you, you're still a good man.

Pfft. You're getting all philosophical, inner voice. What's up with that?

He wasn't being a good man, he was being – *what?* Enamored? Lovestruck? Wistful for a relationship with another caring person? *Ehh, maybe.* Those feelings had been intentionally buried a long time ago, yet occasionally they still cropped up, and they did him no good. Just caused misery, loneliness, longing, and the reminder that whatever part he was supposed to play in the world, being a loving husband, father, and middle-class working stiff who barbeques at his suburban house on weekends wasn't it.

Perhaps he was meant to be a soulless killer, though so far he hadn't killed anyone that wouldn't have been a candidate for the death penalty by law anyway. *So far.* Luck of the draw? Or was it because only the shittiest excuses for humans were the ones who sought to assault him? It would be a comfort if that was always true, and if the other one would restrain itself to just its attackers. There was, of course, no such guarantee. So, keeping the other one suppressed, regardless of its necessity to be out, was the safest philosophy.

Merrick snapped out of his reflective state. Something had moved in his peripheral vision. His immediate reaction was to turn quickly to investigate, however, he knew better than to make any motions that would call attention to himself. Darkness dominated this spot of the woods, and he had been motionless and wearing his Army surplus jacket which blended into the forest colors. He slowly angled his head left, saw nothing, then slowly turned right. Also nothing. No doubt, there were animals in these woods, and most of them were probably harmless. Deer, raccoons, squirrels, birds. Although, wolves and bears lived in the woods too, they generally avoided people who didn't do stupid things to agitate them. *So, keeping still – good idea.* Wolves were crafty and could sneak around well, but bears lumbered about and you could hear them coming fairly easily. He saw neither though.

He checked his watch, one of the few personal luxuries he allowed himself. Though it didn't aid most of his daily activities, buses and trains ran on schedules, and having a watch helped for those. It was the old-school, wind-up, analog kind, and the hands said it was a little after 2 am. Darned close to the witching hour. If someone was smart and was going to try something dastardly and sneaky, 2 to 4 am was a good time to do it. Tanner didn't seem all that smart, but – *still.*

Merrick slowly and smoothly slid behind the log he had been sitting on and crouched so his eyes were just above the log's surface. He opened his duffel bag and carefully removed a bell. It was the solid brass type that probably came from something important originally, but had been sitting in a pile of discarded items in the barn. Merrick had stuffed a cloth inside to keep the clapper from making noise while he moved around, strategizing that if he saw something suspicious, he could run toward the house, ringing the bell as loud as he could to wake Kat and Del. No harm done to anyone, and maybe it would even scare off the infiltrators by itself. If not, then Del and Kat could decide what to do about the evildoers. Merrick would've done his duty, avoided a fight, and rid himself of the reason to stay here longer and dare fate to connect him with the gruesome diner murders.

He sat patiently, assuming he'd eventually see the thing that had caught his attention. It took half a minute before something finally revealed itself. A doe and her fawn. She had been virtually statuesque the whole time he'd been looking. However, her fawn wasn't as careful and took a couple of steps away from its mother to find some young shoots to munch on. *Whew*. Good news that it wasn't anything dangerous like a wolf, a bear, or a Tanner. Bad news was that he had been no more than 40 feet from them and didn't see them. Spending too much time in cities lately was perhaps making him lose his heightened senses. He relaxed a bit and the doe took that as a sign that it was safe for her to forage. Both deer munched casually on some greenery.

Yep, nothing dangerous to your fawn here, huh? Just a scrawny guy who turns into the boogieman if he stubs his toe. He knew that wasn't accurate. It usually took significant or mortal damage to make the other one…

The doe snapped her head up, then suddenly bolted with her fawn closely in tow. *Now what?* Merrick stiffened too, repeating the exercise he had done a few minutes ago. Slowly turning his head left, then right. He didn't have the same ability of animals to see in the dark (not in his current form anyway), but the moonlight was strong enough to illuminate the edges of the tree trunks. Several passing shapes interrupted the patterns of those lines. Four creeping beings if he counted correctly. They were as tall as humans, or below average-sized bears standing on hind feet. He made the less far-fetched deduction. *Showtime*.

He waited until all four figures had passed, then Merrick slunk around the edge of the log, farthest from the trespassers. Luckily, that direction was closer to the house, so Merrick was thinking that his strategy of locating the trespassers, then getting between them and the house to ring his bell, was going to work perfectly. Stepping on live foliage, or sturdy things like logs or stones, helped to reduce the cracks and snaps of his feet crunching on dry leaves and twigs. The tactic was a practiced necessity when hunting for food.

The edge of the forest was an abrupt line bordering the pasture, with a barbed-wire fence that began a gentle slope down to the cow enclosure. Moonlight muted the colors of both the green pasture and brown enclosure to gray. Enough light, though, to show the four figures clearly. There was no mistaking what Merrick saw, and yet it was like viewing a weird dream.

The four figures had stiff fur on their hunched backs, pointed, doglike ears, a thick tail trailing them, and a lupine snout. In all ways, they looked like huge wolves except for one very significant detail: they crept on two legs. Those two legs didn't have the backward knees of wolves, and were covered in what seemed like pants and shoes.

What – the fuck – is going on? Merrick couldn't justify what he saw, except that he did remember what Zeus had told him earlier that day. It had sounded like fanciful nonsense at the time. Local lore based on paranoia, superstition, and simplemindedness. Yet – there it was in front of him. Giant wolves walking around on human legs. Merrick tried to rub sanity back into his eyes, but the wolf people didn't change into anything more rational. He was fully awake, and there were, indeed, four unexplainable beings on the Seavers' ranch.

Or were they explainable? Certainly, there must be a reasonable explanation why someone wearing pants and shoes had the upper body of a wolf **besides** the Hollywood creature-feature implications.

Hey, man, I'm not saying werewolves are real, but – you **do** *realize you're not the only possible monster in existence, right?*

Not helpful, conscience.

There really was only one way to solve the mystery, and he would've preferred to avoid it. He needed to get close enough to one of them to make out their details. Real werewolf, or costume? Or maybe some bizarre illusion caused by a freak happenstance, like if he fell asleep next to a funky mushroom and snorted it as he slumbered. *Come on. That's a bigger stretch than werewolves.* A costume would be the most reasonable explanation, but – why?

As the four wolf-men approached the cow enclosure, Merrick searched the pasture for anything that might be decent cover. There just wasn't much to hide him out there. Tall grass filled the gaps between three low bramble bushes. That was about all. Most of the pasture was open field with only a smattering of trees and brush. Closer to the house was a patch of high weeds, his best destination to start ringing his bell, but only after he had a closer look at what or who these wolf-men were. Making Kat and Del run out here to face something supernatural was not part of the plan. Though he doubted the wolf-men were supernatural, he needed to be sure.

Merrick flattened out behind the patch of brambles and hoped it was enough to shield him. On close inspection, the brambles surrounded a water-pipe access junction that stuck out of the ground. The wolf-men had disappeared behind the walls of the enclosure. They certainly couldn't see him this way, he couldn't see them either. He waited for a few minutes, hoping the "creatures" would reappear outside the structure, still seeing none of them.

A low, plaintive bellowing came from inside the structure. It was definitely from a cow, and also not a normal "moo." Something was alarming the beast. Considering the wolf-men hadn't reappeared, they were probably causing whatever was upsetting the cow. Merrick had assumed Tanner and his posse would try to strike at Kat or her house directly, but it made sense to assault her cows instead. Easier, and wouldn't be noticed until the morning.

Merrick Army-crawled low and slow toward one of the walls. The wood wall was dry, cracked, and pitted, gapped enough in numerous places to see through if he pressed his eye to the surface.

Inside was dark, the roof preventing the moonlight from showing any detail of the wolf-men's bodies, and also made whatever was happening with the bellowing animal too hard to interpret. All the wolf-men's eyes glowed an amber color, easily indicating that at least three of the figures were hovering around one of the cows. A sudden movement from the cow, bucking and twisting, showed that there were horns on its head.

The bull? Uh oh. Merrick wasn't a rancher, and knew little about raising cattle, but he had read that bulls could be the most coveted and expensive of the herd, sometimes even rented out for stud services. Very possibly the same reason the bull had been gone and brought back that previous morning. The loss of something like that could be devastating to the Seavers' finances, and also made sense why these wolf-men, assuming they were associated with Tanner, might want to harm or steal it. Easy, stealthy vengeance.

Merrick had a quick decision to make. Either try to confirm who and what these wolf-men were right now, which would involve charging inside this enclosure and confronting them directly, or taking the chance that they were men in wolf costumes and just run back toward the Seavers' house, ringing his bell as loud as he could.

He couldn't risk getting hurt and inviting the re-emergence of his other self, making yet another bloody mess of shredded corpses, and creating a concrete link between himself and the diner killings. So, decision made, he tore across the pasture toward the house.

As he ran, he stripped the cloth from the bell clapper and began to swing the item hard. It clanged more than adequately loud, and since nothing was nearby to mute its sound waves, it filled the night air with its sharp tolling. If anyone in the Seavers' house was not a heavy sleeper, they would absolutely hear it. Merrick was feeling good about his chances of making this work despite the complications, and didn't bother to look back at whatever might be chasing him. If they were only men, they wouldn't be able to catch up to him easily. He had a solid lead and wasn't a slowpoke. Lots of practice chasing prey himself.

"Kat! Del! Hey!" he shouted as he ran, clanging the bell at his side. "Get up! Someone's trying to…"

Something heavy hit Merrick from behind. The bell flew from his hand as his chest hit the ground, and he skidded through the tall weeds. A sharp thing dug into Merrick's back, and for a moment, he wondered if he had been gored by the bull. Whatever it was penetrated deeper into his back, feeling more like claws than a horn, yet bigger than animal claws. More like several knives.

Merrick wasn't a weakling and had been in fights before, knowing full well that losing a fight usually meant the "other one" taking over to win it for him. So, besides avoiding the pain of "dying," he preferred to end this the human way to minimize the chance of more deaths to run from. He twisted and jabbed an elbow at whoever was behind him, a move that usually threw off attackers. It didn't work. His assaulter stayed firmly planted on his back.

"Well, if it isn't the little scrawny fuckface," said a low, feral voice. Not human-sounding, there was a strange quality like some

61

kind of technology making the tone different. "Kat isn't here to save you now," said the voice. "I only planned on killing the bull, but – no one will care if you die, and I'll enjoy doing it."

Multiple knives, assumedly like the ones in his back, touched Merrick's throat, caressing it with the cold edges of the blades.

The feral voice was closer to Merrick's ear now. "Shall I start by cutting off your balls? Or maybe your eyes? Or do you want to beg me to kill you quick? Go ahead beg – beg me to kill you fast. Maybe I will, and maybe I won't."

Tanner? With that weird, animal timbre, it wasn't exactly his voice, but who else could it be? Merrick's hand was pinned under him, next to his knife, and he had been wrestling it from the sheath as his attacker spoke. Taking a deep breath to gather all the energy he could muster, Merrick jerked to get the attacker off balance, then aimed his right elbow at where he calculated the attacker's head was. His elbow impacted a long, inhuman jaw. The move was enough to create space between the two of them, then Merrick drew in his legs and rammed them into the other man's knees. The "man" cursed and rolled to the side.

Merrick was up on his feet quickly, knife in hand, ready for a counterattack against the wolf-man-thing that had tackled him. He hadn't counted on another one running at him before he could gauge his options. There was only a half-heartbeat to see a wolf's face with glowing amber eyes as it flew at Merrick. Just time enough for Merrick to brace and jab his knife in that direction. The wolf-man collided like a freight train, driving Merrick to the ground, back-first, punching the air from his lungs. He did the only maneuver he could, jerking his knees up and catapulting the lunging attacker away using the momentum. The knife had struck soft tissue on the attacker as it vaulted away, rolling through the tall weeds, and swearing in pain.

Merrick didn't have time to appreciate his luck since the "Tanner" wolf-man had regained its feet and charged. Tanner had a similar wolf head with the same glowing amber eyes, and hands that resembled wolf paws, except each had four steel, knife-like claws aiming for Merrick's throat. Below the wolf pelt, there was also the glint of a chrome belt buckle in what appeared to be the design of side-by-side naked angel and devil women. There was no doubt who was under that wolf façade anymore. Merrick rolled just as the

Tanner-beast landed, pinning Merrick's legs, but also falling on Merrick's knife. The knife clanked against something more solid than flesh, and seemed stuck. He heard a snap, like metal breaking, then watched as the Tanner-beast raised its clawed hand high to descend upon Merrick.

The blow never came. A thunderous boom pierced the air, echoing through the pasture like a bolt of lightning hitting a tree. But it wasn't lightning. A gun had fired. Wolf-Tanner froze and looked toward the Seavers' house. Then, like a real wolf, it jumped off Merrick and started racing toward the tree border – on four legs. Merrick lifted his head, uncomprehending what he saw. He knew it had been Tanner on top of him. He knew it couldn't be a real werewolf, yet – it was running as fast and as efficiently as a wolf on four legs. Within moments, all four wolf-men had disappeared into the forest.

Merrick was about to count his lucky stars when another gunshot burst through the fading thunder of the previous shot. Pellets ripped up sod and weeds two feet from where he lay.

Shit!

He quickly got to his feet and waved his arms above his head. "Kat! Del?! It's me! It's only…"

Another shot was fired, and this time the pellets ripped into his side.

"Arrhhh!" he cried, strangling the attempted words in his throat as he doubled over. He waved his free hand. "Stop! Kat, it's Merrick! I was just…"

He could only hope it was Kat or Del doing the shooting, and he had no ability to raise his head to confirm their identity. Another shot sounded, this one ripping through his thigh. If he wasn't in excruciating pain, he might appreciate the marksmanship of whoever was about to kill him.

You know you can't die. At least, he didn't know of a way yet, which reminded him of an even more frightening concern than being shot at.

"Stop! Help!" he called as best as his gargling throat could muster.

Then he slumped onto the ground and began to feel the unwelcome, familiar electric chill surge through him.

63

No! No, no, no! Not now!
In the distance, he heard a woman's voice call, "Merrick?"

CHAPTER 9

Kat racked another shell into the shotgun's chamber as she stepped cautiously forward. She thought she had heard Merrick's voice, but couldn't be sure. Wasn't he supposed to be gone? And was he the one who had made all that racket with a bell?

She was a light sleeper compared to her father, a joke among the two of them that she'd have to carry his sleeping body out of the house if there was ever a fire. Tonight, she had been comfortably asleep when the frantic bell outside woke her up. She cursed the annoyance until she heard desperate shouts. No neighbors were within shouting range, and she couldn't understand who could possibly be clanging and yelling in the middle of the night. Then it hit her: Tanner.

Whether it was Tanner himself being an ass and ringing the bell, or someone else alerting her to an emergency, either way, she needed to get up immediately and deal with it. Grabbing the shotgun next to her bed, she threw on a robe, sweatpants, and boots, then ran out the door.

What she saw confused her. There was a man in the field being mauled by a pack of what looked like wolves. She suspected Tanner might try something ridiculous, but she wouldn't have guessed he'd let wolves loose in her pasture. How the hell did he manage that? And how stupid was he to stick around and risk the wolves attacking him? She was sleep befuddled, so perhaps if she had a clearer head to analyze it and make a decision, she would've acted differently. As it was, she had fired four times. The first one scared away the pack of wolves. The next three shots were supposed to frighten the man who stood up. She assumed he was one of Tanner's crew who had stupidly thought that appealing to her would keep him safe from her wrath. The shots weren't supposed to hit the man, just make him piss his pants. They were aimed at a nearby spot on the ground. Unfortunately, she hadn't accounted for the wide spread of the buckshot. Then she recognized the voice.

"Merrick?"

The response sounded strained and strangled, but was definitely familiar. "It's me!"

Oh, God.

She ducked through the barbed wire fence and ran to him, beating back some of the tall weeds with the barrel of her rifle. He lay in a fetal position, squeezing his arms around his abdomen. Blood streaked the surrounding weed stalks and the sleeves of his coat. A blood-smeared brass bell was at his feet. He was shivering as he looked up at her.

"Shit, Merrick, I'm so sorry," she said, lifting his head.

His tense face was scrunched, plainly struggling against the pain. Where had she hit him?

She attempted to pry his fingers up to search for wounds, but they held firm to his sides. She tested his neck pulse, finding that very strong.

"What the hell were you doing out here?" she asked and got no response.

As she shifted her hand from his neck she noticed there was some kind of slime or goo on her fingers. *What the…?* Only his hands and face were uncovered, and those were sweating a semi-opaque liquid, forming globules on his skin that seemed to be spreading and combining. His whole body began to convulse far more violently than the shivering that had happened moments before. Was he going into a seizure?

Merrick clenched a fist and slammed it against the ground.

"No! Nooo!" he snarled in a surprisingly clear and forceful voice. "Do not come out!"

Kat shook her head reflexively. "You already got me out. What are you…? Doesn't matter. I gotta get you to the car."

"Stay – away," he demanded.

"The hell I will," said Kat. "I'm getting you to a hospital."

"No," groaned Merrick through gritted teeth. "No doctors."

"What? Why? You've been shot for Christ's sake."

Despite his pinched face, Merrick rolled his eyes. "No shit."

"You can sue me later. But you need medical attention. Now, come on. Can you stand?"

Merrick shook his head vehemently. "Just leave me. Too dangerous."

"What is? Can you stand or am I gonna hafta drag ya?"

Merrick swallowed hard, either not having the breath to answer her question, or perhaps the pain was too intense. Though the wounds were bleeding, at least there was nothing torn away. Just little punctures appropriately the size of buckshot. Assuming they could get the pellets out, he'd probably recover alright.

"Come on," she said a little patronizingly. "I'll help you up. Let's at least get you to the house."

Merrick's seizures had subsided to shivering now. He nodded subtly and allowed Kat to help him stand on wobbly legs.

As Kat was aiming for the couch, Merrick slipped from her grip just before she reached it and crumpled to the floor. Luckily, there was a pillow that also fell to the floor and Merrick had something to cushion his head. When she attempted to help him back up, he waved her off.

"Ok, fine. You stay there," she said. "I'm gonna call an ambulance."

"No!" he shouted. His voice was still strained, though clearer. The weird sweating had also ceased. "Call no one."

"Damn it!" said Kat. "Why?"

"Hard to explain," he said, then paused to catch his breath. "Bad people after me. All I can say."

"Uh huh," she said with a doubting tone.

His breathing calmed. "Can't leave a trail. No records. Nothing with my name or picture."

Kat nodded. "Fine. You wanna tell me how I'm supposed to help you heal buckshot wounds?"

He shook his head. "I'll be fine. Just need..." A twinge or sharp pain must've hit because he jerked and shook for a moment. Then whatever it was passed. "Just need time and rest."

"Oh, for Christ's sake," said Kat trying to hold back telling this man he was being idiotic and irrational. "Can I at least clean the wounds?"

Merrick nodded. "Yes." He bit back another twinge. "Thank you."

Kat sighed and hurried into the kitchen. She found an old dish towel, rinsed it with warm water, and plopped it into a plastic bowl with more warm water, then carried them out to Merrick. He had pushed himself up to a sitting position, though still leaning to the injured side.

She knelt beside him and tugged aside the jacket. When she reached for the shirt, he shied away.

"Look," said Kat. "I have to clean it and get the pellets out, or it'll get infected."

Merrick seemed to consider this, then nodded. "Sorry. There's things… Yes. Please, go ahead."

Kat didn't wait for any further invitation and lifted Merrick's shirt. Considering the copious amount of blood on the shirt, she assumed there was a fair flow of blood still coming from the pellet wounds. Once she saw them, she was confused. Seven little punctures, all ringed with bright red inflammation, but none still bleeding, and all seemed to have the dark sheen of a clot. *Already?* Despite the scabs, she had to make sure they were clear of whatever dirt the wounds might have picked up in the pasture. She dabbed the wet rag on the wounds which caused a slight flow of clean, new blood. Only a little on each wound. Underneath was the welcome sight of shiny specs of metal. The pellets were shallow, which would be easy enough to dig out.

As she worked, she tried to make sense of the evening's activities. "Why were you out there?" she asked.

Merrick blanched, possibly at the water stinging his wounds, or possibly because he was reluctant to answer the question. "I suspected Tanner might come back tonight. I, uh – wanted to warn you if he did."

"I see," said Kat, trying not to meet his eyes.

"So, I camped up the hill in the woods and waited a while. Figured I'd ring that bell if I saw him, and then you could decide what you wanted to do about it."

She smirked. "That's who I thought *you* were. Tanner or one of his toadies. Weird that it was only wolves."

Merrick shook his head. "You don't…? Those weren't real wolves. It was Tanner."

"What'dya mean Tanner? All I saw was wolves and you."

"He *was* the wolves. Well, him and three others. I couldn't make out who they were."

Kat's eyes blinked rapidly in perplexity. "What the hell are you talking about?"

"They were men in wolf costumes. I couldn't see their faces, but I know one of them was Tanner."

"But – they ran away exactly like... They moved just like real wolves."

Merrick nodded. "Yeah, I saw that too. Can't explain it."

She shook her head, and as she did, brushed one of the wounds a little hard, making Merrick flinch.

"Sorry," she said. "How'd you know it was Tanner?"

"I recognized his belt buckle. Pretty clear."

"Son of a bitch."

Kat knew the local myth about giant wolf men that kidnapped and ate people in the mountains, but she wasn't a believer. It wasn't that supernatural or paranormal stories were silly to her. Things without material evidence, or that weren't seen by her own eyes, didn't concern her. If something could be proven, or she saw it herself, she'd believe it. And once she acknowledged it existed, all she needed to be concerned with was how it affected her personally. She doubted anything to do with Tanner and wolf costumes was supernatural, despite the unexplained way they could run. However, he achieved that, he was using the myth to disguise his evil intentions. It chilled her all the same.

She examined her work on Merrick's abdomen.

"Guess these are clean enough. Take off your pants."

Merrick hesitated, then began to shuck out of his pants.

There were only five pellet wounds on his thigh, and luckily as shallow as his abdomen. All things considered, he was very fortunate. They both were.

"I don't understand," said Kat. "If the wolves were Tanner and his crew pretending to be real wolves, even moving like them – how? And why? What were they doing?"

"I couldn't see perfectly, but it looked like they were trying to do something to your bull."

"My...?" Kat froze for a moment.

Good stud bulls were valuable, and theirs had been loaned out more than once to supplement their meager income. Their ranch was barely self-sustained by raising cattle to sell to dairy farms. The goats were primarily just for keeping the pasture grass level, not much good for anything else. Her father had inherited the ranch from his father, and hoped he could make it work without much effort, not willing to spend his retired years stressing over pushing the business. All they wanted was a place to live in peace. And if the bull was lost, it would devastate their budget. Kat had a lot of money stashed away, but that was for a specific purpose. The reason she worked double shifts, busting her ass, was to save up for her dreams... *No, I don't dream.* To save for what she planned to do since she grew up and decided on her future goals. Her father encouraged her to save her wages, didn't want her to support him, though she supplemented what was necessary, so she had felt good about saving the rest of her income. But if they lost the bull, she might need to help her father replace it. How much? And how much longer would it take to resave what she lost?

"What did they do to it?" she asked.

"Couldn't tell. It was dark. The bull was still standing when I started to run toward the house."

She nodded, trying to disguise the anxiety over the bull. *One thing at a time.* Merrick deserved her full attention right now, especially since she was the one who shot him.

His arms were in the way, attempting to cover his groin as she tried to clean his thigh.

"Relax," she said. "I promise I don't care about staring at your crotch."

"Sorry. Just not used to any part of me being scrutinized, especially dingy tighty-whities."

"Fine. I'll tell everyone you wear silk Calvins."

"I'd rather you tell people I was someone else entirely."

Despite their joking banter, she was reminded how odd this man was and wondered how mentally balanced he might be. "Because of the bad men chasing you?" she asked.

"Yeah. Long story."

Merrick's thigh took even less time to clean. It almost appeared to be healing as she watched. And the pellets were barely below the skin, even shallower than she had thought when she started. Almost shallow enough to pluck out with her fingernails, though she knew that was a half-ass idea and needed something more precise like tweezers.

"I'll be back in a sec," she said. "I need to get something to pull these out."

The tweezers weren't where they were supposed to be and it took a few extra seconds to remember they were next to her bed. Back downstairs, she knelt next to Merrick again and was about to set to work on his thigh when she noticed something odd. Several tiny metal balls lay on the floor next to him. Many of the pellets had blood splotches and were slightly wet from having come out of newly cleaned wounds. *Oh my god.* Had Merrick pulled them out himself?

"How did you…?" she started. "Why didn't you wait for me? Did you get them all out?"

"Huh?" mumbled Merrick. "Get what out?"

She picked up one of the pellets and examined it, then Merrick seemed to understand what she meant, and said, "Oh."

Even if he had precision tools and was a professional surgeon, she doubted he could've dug out all the pellets in the time it took her to go upstairs and return with her tweezers. The oddity wasn't bizarre enough to call Ripley's Believe It Or Not, it was just another weird thing to happen on this goddamned weird night.

"I guess they fell out," said Merrick, looking guilty.

Kat frowned. "Shot don't just fall out of a person."

She ran her hands over the thigh wounds. They had clotted again, and darned near looked like scabs already. Even the skin around the punctures had changed from inflamed red to mild pink. The same was true for the abdominal wounds. All except for one wound that still had a pellet embedded.

"I don't get it," said Kat.

She expected Merrick to offer some new excuse or explanation, but he hung his head and looked abashed.

As she aimed her tweezers at the last pellet, the little ball suddenly slipped from the wound. It bounced off Merrick's leg, then skated across the floor. Stunned, Kat watched it roll awkwardly against the uneven ruts on the wooden floorboards.

"What's going on?" murmured Kat.

She searched Merrick's eyes for some kind of indication that he was playing a trick, or maybe that she was still in bed dreaming this whole affair. Things hadn't made sense since he had shown up in Templeton, and she was a person that needed things to make sense. She didn't care if something was weird as long as she could understand it.

"Like I said – long story," he said with a fragile smile.

She had felt sorry for shooting this man until now. He had deflected and delayed, and probably lied, about every serious question she had, and she was considering poking the tweezers into one of his wounds to make him start spilling the truth.

At that moment, several loud creaks sounded on the stairs, and when she turned around, her father's pajama legs could be seen descending the staircase. He got to the bottom and rewrapped his loose robe.

"Oh, hello, Mr. – uh, Merrick?" he said.

Merrick nodded and timidly waved his hand.

"What's going on?" asked Mr. Seavers. "I thought I heard some loud clanging, then it sounded like…"

"Tanner was here, Dad," said Kat. "He and some other guys were, uh – well, Merrick saw him messing around with our bull and tried to wake us up."

"Our bull?" Del's half-asleep face morphed into a hard expression. "Is it all right?"

"Haven't had the chance to check." Kat raised a brow at Merrick, who seemed to get the hint.

"I couldn't see," said Merrick.

"Damn it," said Del. "Tanner, you said?"

Kat nodded.

Del took two steps toward the door, then took a half-step back and squinted his eyes at Merrick, probably noticing the blood. "Is he ok? What happened?"

"I shot him," said Kat matter of fact-ly.

Del's mouth twitched, unable to form words.

"He'll be fine," said Kat. "Go check on the bull, Dad."

Merrick put on a smile, then flapped his hand at Del, encouraging him to go.

The door creaked open then smacked shut.

Kat waited three seconds, then her eyes bore into Merrick's. "Alright, listen up. Before my dad gets back, you're gonna tell me the real truth. Start talking."

CHAPTER 10

There was no way Merrick wanted to risk telling Kat the whole truth. At least, not the truth as he knew it. If it wasn't him living it, he wouldn't believe it, and knew no version of it that wouldn't sound preposterous. More importantly, it was dangerous for her to know. *Yet, still...*

This woman seemed to take everything in stride. Straight-shooting (metaphorically), direct, and not easily rattled, even by his chaotic mess. He hadn't met anyone quite like her before. For years, he had wished to confide in someone, to have at least one person in this world he could trust. The problem was that sharing information about himself endangered others' lives. Whoever made him this way was looking hard for him and would not hesitate to destroy anything, or anyone, in their path. Would they also eliminate people who knew the secret even after Merrick was gone?

There were only three options available in response to Kat. He could just refuse, pack his crap, and run away. That was his safest move and his usual solution. He could lie his ass off, though he might forget what he made up later and then have to make up new lies to cover previous lies. Or he could try to explain the actual truth and hope she might be his first real ally. There was something about Kat that made him want to try, but the danger to her was a distressing unknown.

Kat's eyes burned into his. "Let's go, mister," she said. "I don't like it when things don't make sense, and nothin's made sense since you showed up."

Merrick grimaced. He had never practiced how to explain his condition because he never figured on doing it.

Kat wasn't allowing delay tactics. "I ain't stupid, and I know you've been bullshitting me since that thing at the diner happened. So, you better start explaining things, or I call the sheriff and tell him I forgot to mention that you were behind the diner the other night. Hmm? Maybe you'll tell **him** the truth."

Merrick held up his hands in surrender. "Alright, alright. Just gimme a second. This isn't easy to explain. It'll sound crazy."

"You got 'til my dad gets back. After that, I might not be willin' to listen anymore."

"Yeah, ok. I get it," said Merrick. "Alright, here goes."

He folded his legs into a better sitting position first, figuring the story was uncomfortable enough. Then he started. "There's things that change in me, things I can't control, when I get injured. Something inside of me comes out and – protects me. Allows me to heal pretty much anything, makes me very strong and – is dangerous to anyone around me."

He met her gaze to see if she was rolling her eyes or making outward signs of disbelief. Her eyes remained fixed on his.

He continued. "Something happened to me when I was younger. Back then I was living on the city streets, high on whatever I could find. It's hard to recall details because I was usually in a daze twenty-four, seven. Somehow, I hooked up with doctors running an experiment. Claimed I'd get paid and maybe give me any drugs I wanted if I just let them do these experiments on me. They were probably looking for easy marks, people with no ties, folks nobody would miss if something went wrong. I fit that bill pretty well. I had been a ward of the state since I was a teenager because my mother was a prostitute and a heroin addict. She died from an overdose, and they never found my father. No adoption came, and I just got more bitter. No one wanted a half-grown kid with a bad attitude. When I aged out of the system, I just took off, got into trouble, and stayed there. This experiment thing sounded like easy money. I had no idea what I had gotten myself into.

"What happened next is still a blur. No matter how I try, I can't remember exactly what they did. I do remember a lot of drugs. A lot! Every time I was cognizant enough to look around, I got shot up with something. I also remember the pain. Excruciating pain. God knows what horrifying things they were doing if I was drugged to near unconsciousness and still in agony. There was a weird machine that looked like it was from a sci-fi movie, and whatever it did, it felt like it was turning me inside out. This went on for days. I'd be unconscious, wake up to this crap, somehow not die while they were

75

doing it, then they'd put me back to sleep to keep doing it. I was stuck in a nightmare, awake or asleep.

"Then one day, something new happened. It's one of the few memories I can recall. I woke up from one of these sessions and noticed I wasn't tied down anymore. I guess I broke free. The men around me looked scared and were scrambling to back away from me. I must've gone on a rampage, smashing things, hitting people – I'm not really sure. The way I saw things was like looking through a fuzzy video feed. Watching from somewhere else. Not my own eyes. Somehow, I escaped, got outside whatever facility they had kept me. Security men followed me. I remember gunshots and dogs barking. The bullets hit me. Bunch of times. They weren't trying to subdue me, they were trying to kill me. It still felt like I was watching somebody else doing all these things instead of me, a bystander watching me attack the guards. I don't remember what I did to them, I just remember they were gone, not following anymore. And then – ," Merrick shrugged. "Back to black. Don't know how I wound up in the woods next to a highway ramp, no clothes, no nothing. At least whatever drugs they gave me had finally worn off and I was able to function and think for the first time in a while. I remembered I'd been shot earlier, but when I checked my body – nothing. A few scars on my chest. That's it. I was fine."

"Thankfully, it was dark out, not that many people around, so I stole some clothes, broke into a vending machine for food, then started moving. No destination, just getting far away from whoever did this to me."

Merrick looked up to see if Kat was still engaged, or if she was finding his story ridiculous. Though her expression was blank, her eyes still bore into him. *So, keep going I guess. Maybe think of a way to skirt around the monster issue?*

"I tried to stay off the main highways. Away from people. I had no idea what lingering effects I might have, and I didn't want anybody to ask questions, so I kept to the woods as much as possible. Catching food wasn't easy, but I learned. I needed better provisions, so I occasionally did some day work where folks show up in a truck and take you to do stuff like clearing brush, or hauling trash, or picking fruit, or whatever. I saved some money, bought some of the things I needed, and thought I would do ok. The experiments had scared me sober, so no more chemicals in my body, and I'd taken to dropping by public libraries to start giving myself an education. All in all, things were improving. That's when everything went bad.

"I had camped out under an overpass one night because it was raining. Two teenage girls were hurrying by, probably scared of that section of town. For good reason. Not too far away from me, the girls were mugged. I might have done nothing about it if the assaulters didn't start raping them. I'm not a hero, but I couldn't let that happen right in front of me. I stood up and yelled at the guys. Hoping that a witness would be enough of a deterrent, I ran toward them shouting for help. One of the guys ran at me. Luckily, neither one had a gun, just big knives. My self-defense skills are kinda basic, and I only managed to dodge and trip the first guy up. The other guy surprised me and stabbed me in the back. I'd love to say it missed anything vital but I'm pretty sure it didn't. I fell to the ground and started to slip into unconsciousness. Before I did, strange sensations started happening to me, weird sweating, tingling, convulsions. I felt like I was being pushed out of my body, as if someone else was claiming it. At first, I thought this was dying. Obviously, I didn't die. I'm not sure I *can* die anymore. The last thing I remember is blacking out.

"I woke up in the hospital with several people around me. One was a police officer, and also one of the girls I saved. According to their statements, the policeman found me and the unconscious girls with the two assaulters dead nearby, and me with their blood on my clothes. The girls had been knocked out before I was stabbed and didn't see what happened to me. They just assumed I had rescued them. My picture was in the news even though they didn't know my name. I was glad the girls were all right, but every fiber in me told me I should get out of there. I excused myself, said I was sorry and had to go.

"My clothes were shredded and bloody except for my shoes, so I just took off in my hospital gown and ran toward the exit. I hadn't made it out when I saw two bald men that looked like fictional secret agents, with expensive suits and sunglasses, entering the hospital. They drew their weapons when they saw me. Weird-looking guns, too big for normal pistols. They both shot me with things that looked like technologically advanced trank darts. I was completely caught by surprise and had no idea what to do. The darts were easy enough to yank out, but I could already feel their effects inside me. I sank to the floor thinking it was all over, these guys would take me back to wherever they experimented on me, and either kill me there or do more nightmarish things to me. One of the hospital security guards saw what happened and yelled for them to stop. The agent guys pulled out different guns and shot the guard with regular bullets. Two uniformed police officers came running and drew their weapons, and they were shot too.

"While all this was going on, I was close to paralyzed, with only enough strength to press the elevator button and drag myself inside. Whatever was in those darts was both making me incapacitated and also stopping whatever comes out in me from taking over like it had the last time I was injured. I don't remember what floor the elevator opened to. Two nurses saw me and hauled me into a wheelchair, then rolled me to a nurses' station to figure out where I belonged. The whole place went on lockdown because of the shooting downstairs, and folks were running around crazy. I was kind of left alone. Luckily, the agents looking for me never figured out where I went. Maybe they thought I ran out of the hospital and they went searching for me elsewhere. Eventually, the tranks wore off and I could move enough to stand up. When no one was looking, I ducked into a supply closet, found a set of surgical scrubs, and then took a different elevator down to the ER side and walked out the back door like I was an employee, not a patient."

Kat was still staring with calm interest as he spoke, not appearing to be confused or incredulous, so he continued. "I'll try to hurry things along. I made my way back to the place the girls had been attacked, collected my stuff which was luckily still where I hid it, then I tried to disappear. As much as I was glad to have helped the girls, I placed too many other people in jeopardy. People got killed because of me. Innocent people like the cops and guards just doing their job. I couldn't risk that anymore.

"I've been on the road for years now. I know I have to keep my name and picture away from being posted anywhere, or those agents may show up again. It took only hours to find me once I was exposed, and they've found me before even without any exposure, so

I have no doubt they'll find me again. It's not safe for me to be anywhere too long, or for people to be around me. That's why I keep to the woods when I can, not engage anyone too long, and keep moving. It's all I know how to do.

"And I've probably stayed here too long as it is. You and your father might already be in danger."

Merrick wasn't sure if he was finished, but the basics had been said, and it seemed like the right time to find out if Kat was going to call bullshit, or believe him. So he waited for her to respond.

She squished her mouth around, an unconscious reaction to whatever she was contemplating. Finally, she said, "This is what I'm supposed to believe?"

Yeah, I didn't think she'd buy in immediately. "I swear, it's the truth." *As much as I'm willing to divulge.*

"Uh huh," she said. "You do realize that even country bumpkins like me have heard of The Incredible Hulk before, right?"

"Uhhh, I don't understand what that…"

"It sounds like you're trying to pass that story off on me like I'm an idiot."

Merrick wasn't prepared for this reaction. "I never thought… Sure, I guess there's some similarities to Hulk, but – it's not like I made this up. I'm real, Hulk's not. Uh, he's also a physicist, and an Avenger, and helps people. I'm just a hobo who did too many drugs, got caught up in something really bad, and now I'm stuck this way and trying to stay alive without getting other people killed. That's something else too – Hulk doesn't murder people, I do. And nothing happens if I get angry. It's only if I'm hurt and my life is in jeopardy. I'm probably closer to a werewolf than Hulk. Except for the moon thing."

"So, now you're telling me you're a werewolf?" Her tone was sarcastic.

"No. No, it' just… I'm trying to relate… Never mind. I should've never told you. I thought maybe you'd be the one person in the world that might understand."

Merrick tried to stand up but was roughly shoved down by Kat.

"We're not finished," she said. "I'm not saying I don't believe something bad's happened to you, or that you can't do – uh, weird, violent things. But you gotta understand that your story sounds pretty fishy."

"I've never told it to anyone. Sorry you don't believe it."

He again tried to stand, and again he was pressured to sit. This time, he allowed himself to return to the floor.

She shook her head. "Alright, if that's all I'm going to get outta you, I guess I'll go along with it. For now." She emphasized the last two words as something that sounded like a threat. "Can you at least level with me about one thing?"

Merrick sighed. "If I can."

"Were you responsible for what happened behind the diner?"

Oh, boy. Merrick closed his eyes, took a much too long breath, then nodded. "Some of it. The bounty hunter, his partner, and the prisoner were killed by those guys from the van. They saw me, I tried to run, then they stabbed me. I don't know exactly what happened after that, but – I know it was me. The other me."

"Stabbed you? Where?"

Merrick lifted his shirt higher and fingered a wide scar across his chest.

"Here, I think," he said. "I've got scars everywhere. Hard to keep track of them all."

"Holy…" started Kat. Her chilly attitude to him seemed to warm a degree seeing the scar. "If that's a knife, it should've killed you."

"Should've. Certainly isn't the first time."

"Dear Lord," she said, tracing the thick scar tissue.

A loud smack of the front door interrupted their conversation. Del Seavers walked into the living room, hands on hips, a smear of blood across his robe.

"They tried to cut the bull's throat," said Del. "Botched it. He's still alive, but not in good shape. I need to get the vet down here, pronto. And then call the sheriff."

Though Merrick tried not to react like a guilty person at the mention of calling the sheriff, he was fairly certain Del noticed him blanch a little.

"You sure it was Tanner?" Del asked Merrick.

Merrick nodded. "I didn't see his face. Just his belt buckle under the outfit."

"Well, that's not going to convict him in a court of law," said Del.

"You said you heard Tanner's voice too, right?" asked Kat.

Merrick knew where this was going. Unfortunately, he wouldn't be able to testify even if he was dead certain. He considered lying, then ended up nodding to Kat's question.

"Yeah, but it was altered somehow," said Merrick. "And even if it wasn't, it would only be my word claiming it."

"Yep," agreed Del.

"I'm sorry, sir. I wouldn't be able to testify even if I had concrete evidence."

"Why not?" said Del.

Kat answered for him. "Because it's dangerous for Merrick to stay here. There's gangsters looking for him, and he doesn't want anyone to get hurt if they find him."

A little simplistic, but – nice save.

Del didn't look so convinced. "Uh huh. Well, we can take care of ourselves around here, but – I understand your worry, and I wouldn't want to hold you here against your will."

"Just call the vet, Dad. We can decide what to do about Tanner later," said Kat.

Del nodded and walked away, presumably to find a phone.

"Thanks," said Merrick.

Kat didn't nod, rather had a faraway look on her face as if responding to him was less important than the other things she was thinking about.

Merrick took the moment to reiterate his position. "I should leave before the sheriff sees me and I get on his radar."

Several seconds later, Kat snapped out of whatever thing she was preoccupied with. "I think it's too late."

"Huh?"

"He knows someone else was behind the diner that night," she said. "I don't know if he's seen you directly, but he suspects I know who you are. He knows I held something important back from him."

"Oh."

Kat's eyes were once again looking far away. "And I'm pretty sure he's holding something important back from us."

CHAPTER 11

There wasn't much time for Merrick to lament having to leave his new confidante. He had stayed longer than he should already. Despite finally being able to tell someone the truth (part of it), he wouldn't be able to stick around to develop that relationship. *What else did you think was going to happen?*

About an hour later, wearing borrowed clothes from Del, Merrick felt strong enough to go back out to the woods and collect his gear. As he trekked to the woods, his mind churned with arguments and excuses as to why he spilled the beans to Kat if he just planned on running away afterward. The case for confiding in Kat (despite her disbelief) was pretty thin, yet he still felt good about it, and didn't really know why. His shoes were crunching through leaves and twigs loudly as he approached his camp, and he didn't hear the other man moving nearby.

"That's far enough," said a male voice.

Wha...?

Merrick froze. At first, he assumed it was Tanner or one of his wolf posse. That might have been preferable to who it actually was.

Sheriff Kind stepped out from the shadows. The moonlight made him look like a grey-skinned apparition. He hadn't drawn his weapon, but he appeared ready to. "You wanna tell me who you are and what you're doing here?" asked the sheriff.

"Oh, uh – I, uh…"

Merrick was plainly stunned and was totally unprepared to invent an excuse for what he had been doing here. He had assumed he would be on his way before the sheriff arrived. Del had promised to wait to call the sheriff once Merrick left. Yet, here he was nonetheless, and Merrick hadn't bothered to prepare for that contingency. About as sloppy a two days as he had ever been a part of.

He cleared his throat and thought fast. The truth (an edited version of it) was his best option. "I'm a friend of Kat's, and I was trying to help the Seavers last night by watching over their field. I had reason to believe that – uh…" He didn't want to say Tanner's name. Something in the back of his mind told him to avoid naming names yet. "…To believe that someone planned to cause damage to the Seavers' property, and I was hoping to alert them if that happened. I had a bell and I rang it when I saw trespassers. Kat can attest to that."

Though the sheriff didn't relax his posture, he did take his hand away from his holster and placed it on his hip. "Just out here helping Kat and Del, huh? I see. And they knew you were out here?"

"Well, they do now. I, uh – Kat isn't fond of people helping her, so her ranch hand, Zeus, and I came up with this plan."

"So, you're friends with Zeus too? How come I've never seen you before?"

"I only got here a couple days ago."

The sheriff's blinks were the only movement on his stony face. He scanned the little camp area. The duffel bag with all Merrick's gear had been opened, presumably by the sheriff, who pointed to it. "And the bows and arrows? Those for personal protection?"

"No, sir. Food. I travel a lot in the woods and use it for hunting."

The sheriff looked a little disappointed with that answer. "Are you aware of the license restrictions on hunting game around here?"

"I have not read them fully, but I only shoot small game, sir. Squirrels, rabbits, possum. Nothing on the usual game lists."

The sheriff continued to look disappointed as he nodded and waved Merrick forward. "Alright, son, come collect your gear and put it in my car. We're going to ride down to the Seavers' place and confirm your story."

"Yes, sir."

As Merrick repacked his duffel bag, he mulled some things over. Kat had said the sheriff suspected she lied about who might have been behind the diner. Likewise, she suspected the sheriff was holding something back from her. Del hadn't called the sheriff yet, yet here was the sheriff snooping around the Seavers' property anyway. Either he suspected Tanner had done something, or had heard about it. Who would he have heard about it from? A limited number of people knew: The Seavers; Zeus and his son; Tanner and his three buddies. It was possible Zeus gave the sheriff a heads up last night, but it seemed unlikely. If Kat found out he had gone behind her back to the sheriff, he'd be in deep doo-doo. No, the only person who could've spoken to the sheriff was the infiltrators themselves. *Why the hell would they do that?* Unless they were trying to switch the focus onto the mysterious and guilty-looking drifter? Based on the sheriff's noticeable disappointment, he already had Merrick in his sights and was looking for an excuse to bust him.

Sitting in the back seat of the patrol car, Merrick wondered if he was even going to be let out again once they got to the house. The answer came when they stopped and Sheriff Kind opened the door, smiling politely, not warmly.

"Please remain with me for the time being," said the sheriff.

Merrick was only technically a free man, being passively required to stay at the sheriff's side until dismissed. Not much else to do but go along with it.

Kat and Del came out and talked with the sheriff, backing up Merrick's claim, at least the parts he had told them about. Del relayed what he knew about the bull, and Kat talked about what she saw. She conveniently forgot to mention that she shot Merrick, and Merrick didn't offer to correct it. The only real reaction from the sheriff came when Kat mentioned the wolves.

"Wolves?" said Sheriff Kind. "I thought you said it was Tanner Fosse."

"It was. Him and his friends. Dressed as wolves."

The sheriff gave Kat a hard stare before he wrote something down in his report booklet. "If they had on disguises, then – how did you know who it was?"

Kat darted her eyes to Merrick. She had been doing well to keep him out of the spotlight thus far, but this question couldn't be answered by anyone but him.

"I got a clear look at his belt buckle," said Merrick. "And it was his voice when he threatened to kill me."

Sheriff Kind's hard look switched to Merrick. "How can you be sure it was his voice?"

"Well – the sound of it was altered by – I don't know what. It was more the things he said. His words. Referencing things from the other night."

That wasn't exactly proof, and certainly not enough to warrant an arrest. All the evidence was circumstantial and subjective.

"We figured it wouldn't stand up in court, Sheriff," said Merrick.

Sheriff Kind shook his head and tapped his report pad with the butt of his pen. "Unfortunately."

"It's why we hadn't called you yet," lied Kat. "But since you came anyway, we figured we'd tell you everything." The last sentence had a suggestive undertone to it, almost imperceptible.

The sheriff didn't seem to notice. "Well, Tanner said that you shot at him the other night. Said he was minding his own business and you got out of line. Knowing Tanner as well as I do – I figured he might have been the one out of line. But since no one got hurt –." The sheriff put his report book in a jacket pocket. "Well, I thought I'd just do a drive-by since I was in the area."

And happened to know exactly where my camp was? Merrick intentionally made his camps far enough from the road that they wouldn't be noticed. Kat had expressed suspicion about the sheriff and Merrick could see why.

"Maybe I can't prove who it was, sheriff," said Kat. "But I have a right to protect my property, and they tried to kill our bull and attacked my friend."

The sheriff held up placating hands. "I understand. I'll send some deputies out here to do a sweep of the field and see if we can't locate evidence that will hold up in court, alright?"

Everyone was in agreement with that, and the sheriff nodded like the conversation was done. Unfortunately, it wasn't done.

"I'm afraid I have some other business too," said the sheriff. "The reason I was out this way." The group became still as Kind prepared his next statement. "As you know, there's been a gruesome scene in town behind the diner. We have dismissed other theories like an animal attack. We are, in fact, treating it as a murder case."

Uh oh. Here comes.

The sheriff continued. "Though we have no eyewitnesses at the moment, we do have reports that someone meeting your description…" Kind's eyes lit on Merrick. "…Was last seen in that area." His eyes shifted to Kat. "And that he was seen in the diner as well, conversing with you, Miss Seavers."

Like a literary detective milking the room with a pregnant pause, Sheriff Kind turned to stare out at the pasture, appearing like he was examining it in the dark.

Del took a half-step forward. "Quinton, you know damned well Kat had nothing to do with that."

The sheriff turned leisurely back toward the group. "Didn't say she did, Del. Not saying anyone here did. But I do have some more questions for you, Miss Seavers, and for you, Mr. –?"

"Chaney," said Merrick quickly. "Frank Chaney."

"Mr. Chaney," said the sheriff with practiced courtesy. "I'm sorry to insist, I will need you both to come down to the station and answer a few more questions later today." When he turned to Merrick, his professional smile was as thin as it could get without being noticeably sinister. "I hope you hadn't planned on leaving our little town anytime soon."

"I have no appointments, Sheriff," said Merrick, attempting to sound at ease.

"Good," said Sheriff Kind.

Kat was not so easily rolled over. "Whatever you've got to ask me, you can ask me right here, Sheriff," she said. "I ain't got nothing to hide. And I *do* have things to do. Burt's got me on the morning shift today."

"I understand," said the sheriff. "And I do apologize. But I'm afraid I can't stay longer. There's pressing police business elsewhere. You can come to the station after your shift, Miss Seavers. Mr. Chaney, you can contact one of my deputies who can drive you if necessary. I assume you don't have transportation."

He tipped his Stetson sheriff's hat and turned toward his car.

"You ever gonna do something about Tanner Fosse?" called Kat. "Or do you only shake down his victims?"

Ouch.

The sheriff slowed his stride and turned to present a moonlight-rimmed profile. "Tanner will be dealt with," he said. The tone didn't sound like lip service. It honestly sounded a little cold.

The dust had barely settled from the departing sheriff's car when Merrick noticed a truck lumbering down the dirt road toward the house. Kat explained that the local vet, Dr. Levy, made emergency house-calls at any hour as long as he thought the circumstances

86

warranted. He pulled a covered trailer behind his truck as it came to a stop in front of the Seavers' house.

Merrick was excusing himself to pack when Kat grabbed his arm.

"You're not going to run away are you?" she asked.

Merrick didn't like the way Kat put it, but the answer was essentially *yes*.

He grimaced. "The sheriff looks like he expects me to be guilty of something. He's focused on me. I can't stay."

"You gave your word," said Kat, sounding hurt.

No, I didn't. I said I had no appointments. Wasn't a lie. "To quell the panic, Kind needs to arrest someone fast. A drifter who has no ties to anyone or anywhere would be the easiest to frame for murder."

Kat's gaze hardened and she stepped closer to Merrick, whispering in a hard hiss, "Frame? Merrick, you did it."

"Just the assassins, and that was self-defense. Sort of. The other three were dead before I – you know."

She lowered her head and adopted a softer expression. "I get it. And I'm sorry," she said. Placing her hands on his shoulders, she made him meet her eyes. "Look, I know Sheriff Kind and he can definitely be a bag of hammers, but when he's suspicious of someone and that someone runs, he's a rabid bulldog. He won't ever stop. He'll hunt you down and probably shoot you before you hear the word 'freeze.'"

Merrick tried to lighten her mood. "Well, getting shot definitely sucks, but I'll live." No indication from Kat that his humor worked. "Listen, I've been in trouble before. I keep moving, intentionally stay off the grid, no documents, no pictures, no technology to track. It's near impossible for anyone to hunt me down if they don't know my real name, or fingerprints, or anything other than seeing my face once."

Kay shook her head. "Is there any real evidence tying the diner to you?"

"I don't think so," said Merrick. "I'm never sure what happens when – the other one takes over, but I didn't leave anything behind, everything is still in my bag, and my DNA isn't on file anywhere, so – probably not."

"Probably not," Kat agreed. "If Kind had evidence, he wouldn't be harassing you, he'd be arresting you. You said it yourself, he's looking for a reason. I wouldn't put it past him to have you watched."

Merrick didn't have a good response for that. She made reasonable points. However, he had been using the "run away" strategy for years and had survived without deviating from it.

Kat wasn't letting up though. "If you run and he catches you, you give him a reason to throw you in jail, and he'll have leverage in court."

Merrick wanted to assure her that, though her argument was valid, the sheriff wasn't the only person hunting for him. Dangerous people had been hunting him for half his life.

A voice announced from the driveway, "Alright, show me to the bull." The vet had his kit in hand ready for work.

To Merrick, Kat said, "We'll discuss this later."

Del and the vet walked by Kat and Merrick on their way to the pasture. The vet clapped the men on their backs and said, "I'll need both your help to get the bull loaded up after we sedate him."

Swell.

CHAPTER 12

The deputies arrived soon afterward. Sunrise was in its infancy and neither deputy looked wide-eyed or bushy-tailed. Extra-large cups of coffee and a box of donuts accompanied the sheriff's yawning team. Though the box was passed around to both Kat and Merrick as a courtesy, neither was in the mood for the sweets.

Merrick wanted to essentially disappear and avoid any kind of further contact with authorities, but once again that wasn't in the cards. The deputies required his presence as they combed the pasture for evidence.

The two deputies took turns shaking Merrick's hand as they led him into the field.

"Simon," said the deputy with *S. Pooler* on his name tag.

"Frank," said Merrick. "Nice to meet you." The other deputy extended his hand and Merrick read the name tag. *M. Yellow Feather?*

"Just call me Max," said Deputy Yellow Feather, noticing the curious stare at his name tag. "It's a small town. Nobody uses our last names. Mine's too long anyway."

"Your *first* name's too long too," said Deputy Pooler. "Your Indian one. Maxie – Maxie horny ho?"

Max shook his head and rolled his eyes. "Ma'xehonehe."

Deputy Pooler smirked. "That's what I said."

Max sighed with a hint of a grin being held back.

"What tribe?" asked Merrick.

"Cheyenne," said Max. "I've never been out to the nation, though. My folks were from Missoula. Raised Christian. But my dad gave us Cheyenne names, wanted us to remember the old ways. I tried but – it's not really for me."

Deputy Pooler chuckled momentarily. "He's scared of horses."

"I don't like anything that can trample me," corrected Max.

Merrick nodded. "I prefer buses and walking myself. Mainly walking."

The two deputies were near the area where the bull had been attacked. Max knelt and examined the pressed down grass.

"The vet take the bull to his place?" asked Max.

"Half hour ago," said Merrick.

Max ran his hands along some of the larger stalks that were stained with blood. "Only a little blood. It going to be ok?"

Merrick nodded. "The vet said they missed the artery. So, I think so."

Simon scoped the immediate area and didn't find anything worth investigating. "Just you and the bull got attacked?"

"As far as I know."

"Show me where the wolf guy attacked you," said Simon. Merrick didn't hear any mockery in the deputy's tone, although it felt like something else might be in there.

It took a while to recall where he had been, especially since it had been dark. He went to the only recognizable thing, the water outlet pipe, and slowly worked back toward the house.

"Hey," said Simon. "Found something."

All three men stopped and looked near their feet.

Simon snapped a picture with his cell phone, then donned a white glove and lifted up a broken knife. He examined it for several seconds, then held it up for Merrick to see.

"Looks like mine," said Merrick. "I used it in self-defense and it got caught on something. Then he ran. I wasn't sure what happened to it."

Max walked over with a plastic bag and Simon dropped the knife in it. "Procedure," he said. "You can collect it later once we clear things up."

Merrick shrugged. "If it's broken, I don't want it back. I'll need to get a new one."

"I have a bunch from my uncle if you want one," said Max. "Cheyenne ceremonial design. He makes them himself, mostly just for tourists, and he gives me some of the good ones."

"Sure," said Merrick. "But I don't have any money to pay for it. I wouldn't want you to…"

"Nah," said Max. "I have like twelve. What am I going to do with them? The least I can do for a friend of Kat's."

Merrick thanked Max for the offer, outwardly showing a grateful face, knowing the comment was more than a friendly statement. It was a deceptive probe. Kat hadn't told them anything about Merrick, nor had Mr. Seavers, and the deputies hadn't asked Merrick any formal questions so far. Either they had no interest in his background or they were being sly and trying to coax information out of Merrick with friendly banter. He found it safer to assume people he was talking to were smart rather than dumb.

"She barely knows me," said Merrick. "She's just a kind soul helping a drifter out. And I was repaying her by watching the property last night. That's all."

Max nodded and looked satisfied with the answer. Simon shook his head.

"Don't mind him," said Deputy Pooler chuckling. "He's got a crush on Kat and just wants to know if he's got competition."

Merrick shook his head. "Don't worry. Once your sheriff decides I'm not a dangerous criminal, I'm heading out. So – just friends. That's it. No threat."

Max laughed. "Nah, man, it's cool. Half the town has a crush on her. You'd just be on the waiting list like the rest of us."

Deputy Pooler raised his hand and smiled. "Hey, I knew her in first grade. I already took a number and I'm in line ahead of both of you, so – no cutting."

"Man, that's just sexist," said Max while examining a broken grass stalk.

"No it isn't," said Simon.

"It's not right, whatever it is," said Max.

"You're just jealous cuz I saw her naked."

Max guffawed. "When you were both like five!"

"Counts. Kissed her too." Simon's mischievous grin made it clear his intention was goading Max rather than legitimately claiming a conquest from first grade.

"You're weird even for a white man," said Max.

"Stop," said Simon.

"Why? You started…"

"No – stop walking," said Simon. "Take a step back. Something's under your foot."

Max lifted his foot and set it down behind him. In the pressed down grass was a dirt-covered piece of metal. Simon snapped a photo of it, then picked up the object. He rotated it twice in front of his eyes before brushing it off carefully. It was a belt buckle.

"Yeah, that's it," said Merrick. "That's the belt buckle I saw. I think my knife might've struck it. Didn't know it came off."

"The loop on the back snapped off," said Simon. "Could be what broke the knife."

Max nodded at the object. "Yeah, that's Tanner's belt buckle alright. Probably not enough for an ID though."

Simon shrugged. "Eh, I dunno. I've seen people get ID'd with less." He dropped the buckle into another plastic bag then stood up.

A few steps later, Max found a tuft of gray fur stuck to a tangle of grass. Not cow, not human hair. That got bagged too.

"So far, everything corroborates your story, Frank," said Simon.

Max got in a squatting stance and moved a few steps from where the fur had been found. "Yeah, some heavy footprints along here too," he said. "No clear sole marks, but the indentations are big enough for a man."

Merrick stood up to see the supposed tracks. He didn't see any footprints, just some areas of grass slightly less straight than others. "You can really see all that?"

Simon snorted. "Him mighty Injun tracker."

Max looked up. "You really can be a dick sometimes, Simon." He stood and brushed off his knees. "I grew up reading detective books and got interested in learning how to study details like footprints. I wanna make captain or maybe sheriff someday."

Simon waggled his head. "Look bud, mad respect for mastering those skills, but good luck kicking the 'ol grizzly bear outta his sheriff throne. He's been here longer than I've been alive."

"I didn't say here," said Max. "But, yeah, nobody's gonna bother running against him."

Max slowly crept through the pasture, following what Merrick assumed was tracks. They eventually came to the rise that entered the woods. Max stopped near a bald patch of dark dirt.

"Close to a full imprint here," he said.

Merrick leaned over to see. "My camp was just a little further up there. It could be mine."

92

Simon snapped a photo, then said, "We gotta upload it all to the sheriff and we'll sort it out later. Lemme see your shoe for comparison."

Merrick tipped his shoe up to show the sole. Simon snapped another picture of that. Walking further north, Max stopped again next to a sandy area.

"Bunch of tracks here," said Max. "Three or four people maybe. No full imprints though. One clear heel of a boot."

Simon took pictures.

"All going toward the house or pasture, so far," said Max. "Haven't seen any going the other way yet."

"They were in a hurry when they left," said Merrick. "Kat had shot – a gun to scare them."

Max nodded. "Longer strides, pushing off hard, prints would be smeared and farther apart. You remember where they were as they left?"

Merrick shook his head slightly. "Hard to say. Seemed close to here. They were also running – uh, on all fours."

Simon had an amused look. "On all fours? Like – actual wolves?"

Merrick slowly nodded. "It was dark, but – yeah, that's what it looked like."

Though Simon was trying not to laugh, his face was losing the battle of concealing it.

Max brushed off his hands. "It's ok, man. I've heard weirder things from townsfolk. I even found wolf tracks once where someone said these wolf people were seen."

Simon closed his eyes and huffed. "Aw, come on. Not again. It's just a myth, Max. All bullshit. The stupid werewolves don't exist."

"I don't know," said Max. "A lot of Indian tribes believe in similar things. Like the wendigo from the Algonquian: manlike with animal faces; they eat humans too. Or the Navajo Skinwalkers, which are pretty much straight-up werewolves. Witches who can turn into craven animals. I don't know any werewolf myths from my people specifically, but there's a few man-eating ones."

"Your *people* are from the suburbs," Simon scoffed. "You were born in a city and lived in a condo until you came here."

Max wasn't listening. His focus was locked onto the ground as he walked past Merrick. He stopped a few paces south, knelt, and

93

brushed the ground with his fingertips. Without looking up, he held the pose for a dozen seconds before anyone spoke again.

"Lemme guess?" said Simon. "You think you see wolf tracks?"

Max nodded. "Maybe."

"Real wolves live around here, Max. It doesn't have to be your werewolves."

"Didn't say it was," said Max. "But these're bigger than normal wolves. Claws longer."

"Bears make big prints," said Simon. "Claws are longer. Probably that."

Max shook his head. "No. Bears have more digits. These are canine."

He slowly walked up the slope and into the woods, staying low to the ground. Simon made only a couple of sighing noises, saying nothing further. Eventually, Max stooped and pointed.

"Get a shot of this," said Max.

Simon shook his head as he snapped the picture of what Max pointed at: a scarred rock.

"What did I just take a picture of?" asked Simon.

"Four claw marks. They scraped against this rock as it ran."

Simon pocketed his phone and folded his arms. "Max, buddy, I don't give a crap if you believe in werewolves, but you can't have me send this bullshit to Sheriff Kind as evidence. Even I know claws don't cut through rock. Those're made by something else."

"You're right about that. Normal claws are too soft to cut through rock." Max's face was a mixture of perplexed and disturbed. "These were metal."

CHAPTER 13

Kat was driving distracted again. At least this time she wasn't screeching tires like she had been the previous night. Her preoccupation was mulling over the things from the three-ring-circus morning that had finally ended and appeared to be under control. Their bull was being taken care of by the vet, evidence had been gathered to hopefully indict Tanner for his attempted murder of the bull, and the sheriff was off her back until 4 pm. She had made Merrick agree to accompany her to the station after her shift was up that afternoon. He promised he'd stay at the ranch, then have Zeus drive him to the diner that afternoon, so she felt comfortable heading to work.

She liked the early shift better than the late shift. Sleeping in wasn't in her nature, and she disliked driving the long mountain road home at night. You never know what you'll run into on that drive: deer, raccoons, wolves. She saw a bear once, though it never ventured onto the road. And two nights ago, she picked up a man who had brought nothing but trouble.

So, why are you so interested in his well-being? He wasn't handsome, or muscular, or magnetic. At best, he had a dorky, bookish charm, but for the most part, he was a strange, paranoid drifter shrouded in mystery. Maybe it was the mystery she liked? It would be easier to believe that everything his body was able to do, like expelling and healing those shotgun pellets, was a trick, or some explainable oddity that didn't have to do with his kooky story of abduction, experimentation, and Men-In-Black intrigue. That said, she wasn't the kind of person who denied what she saw just because it was weird or supernatural. *More like superhuman.*

She believed something scientifically explainable had happened to him. Who caused it and why hadn't been adequately answered, despite his story. In the real world, there aren't mad scientists who create monsters in their labs, then let them escape into the wild to murder and cause mayhem. *Are there?* Doctors that inject people with formulas to transform them into superhuman beings are comic book creations. Despite Merrick's earnestness, his story simply had to be fiction.

He said he was being chased by sinister agents, and she was certain he believed that. That doesn't mean it's true. She knew a homeless man once that swore his deceased wife was still with him, talking to him every day. Kat witnessed the homeless man asking questions to thin air, answering other unheard questions, even arguing with himself. There was simply no one there. But the man absolutely believed his dead wife was with him. The mind is a powerful thing.

Could the brain be powerful enough to produce the effects she saw on Merrick's body? Whatever occurs when he becomes injured is apparently beyond his own understanding. *Like a split personality?* He may genuinely not know what he does in those states. And yet, it wasn't necessarily evil. From what she understood, a bunch of assassins were hired to kill Jeremiah Gunn and either kill or liberate Councilman Saunders. And Merrick killed the assassins. Or – the other Merrick did. Probably in self-defense. And even if it wasn't, not exactly a terrible loss. If the assassins had been arrested by the sheriff, they would've received the death penalty by law. She wasn't going to shed a tear for them. They should have been brought to proper, legal justice, that's all.

Someone obviously feared having Saunders in court. Hiring people to bust Saunders out of custody isn't a good way to set him permanently free. It's better for covering something up and keeping it from being discovered, especially if Saunders died in the attempt. Maybe he would've implicated someone else in his crime? Or a different crime that no one else knew about?

Kat's imagination was getting the best of her. There wasn't much else to do while driving except think, and her mind was spinning circles within circles at the moment. It was a relief when she got to the diner, donned her apron, and clocked in. Work stuff would occupy her mind.

She buzzed around the customer's tables, trying hard to be extra attentive so as not to give her mind time to interject its conspiratorial musings. Unfortunately, the early shift wasn't the diner's busy time, and there were only so many things she could distract herself with before her imaginative contemplations wormed back into her head.

She noticed that Sheriff Kind hadn't been there. He wasn't always a breakfast man but especially when he was up early, which she knew firsthand he had been, he rewarded himself with a plate of bacon and pancakes. Burt, the diner's owner and cook, didn't make amazing pancakes but he did put a lot of them on the plate. Worth the price, and Kind got the special "sheriff's discount" on top. Regardless, Kind hadn't come by. Though not necessarily something to be suspicious about, her overcooked imagination planned on storing that info just in case.

He could be out arresting Tanner, ya know. Unlikely. Even though his deputies picked up some legitimate evidence on her property that could be linked to Tanner, it probably wouldn't be enough to do anything official yet. No, Kind said he had other police business, a statement which might normally be a joke since significant crimes haven't happened in Templeton for a long time. It had been almost a year since Zeus's sister, Esperanza, disappeared and Saunders was implicated. But after what happened two days ago, having new police business might be a legitimate excuse. She assumed Sheriff Kind suspected Merrick of being involved in the murders, and might even be hiding in wait for him to skip town, but that seemed paranoid. Only somebody unbalanced would be sneaking around in the bushes for who knows how long, just waiting for the opportunity to nab a suspect who may or may not be walking away from his promise to come in for questioning. Far-fetched. Nevertheless, her mind toyed with the notion.

Why did she even care? She normally gave no shits about what Sheriff Kind was up to, and she had only known Merrick a couple of days, and kept him appropriately at arm's length while he had been here. Of course, Tanner's sortie into her cow pasture and Merrick's help in thwarting their murderous plan (yes, killing a bull was murder to her) had altered that casual acquaintance strategy, but still, it's not like she had so much as hugged the man since he'd been here. She was just being a kind human, that's all. And so was he.

Mentally, she shook her head at her flimsy excuse. There was something else about Merrick that attracted her, and not necessarily in a sexual way. Once she stopped denying it, it was easier to understand what it really was. She was jealous.

Merrick was a free spirit, traveling anywhere he pleased, doing whatever he wanted, no ties, no barriers. *Well, money is a barrier.* He saw much more of this world than most people did and certainly more than she ever had. His wanderings were a stateside version of the very thing she was saving to do herself. All the money she had put away, all the plans she was making, all her ambitions led to the kind of life Merrick was leading, but for her, it would be Europe. A continent of incredible history, culture, and awe-inspiring sights would be her destination as soon as she had enough money. She was close now, but she was scared there could be expenses she hadn't counted on. If she got stuck in Europe without any money... *So what? Merrick has no money either.*

Yeah, and he hunts for his own food and sleeps in a tent.

So?

Kat wasn't squeamish about camping and hunting, but it wasn't her strong suit. She had imagined a life of country inns, B n' Bs, and hospitality from the locals, trading labor or favors for a bed and a roof. That was her travel ideal. *Still...* Merrick found a method that worked for him and was living a life that intrigued her.

He wasn't a hobo either. Smart, friendly, perhaps a scholar to a degree, studying the world. *And running from people trying to kill him.* Yes, there was that aspect. Certainly not similar to her in that regard. All she wanted to do was experience new things, new people, new cultures, then perhaps write a book or two. She thought she'd like to be a historic fiction novelist.

"Miss?" called a patron.

Kat snapped out of her daydream. She approached the table. "Yes, Ma'am. What can I do for you?"

The woman pointed to the sausage links on her plate. "This sausage isn't vegetarian."

The woman talking was definitely no one Kat had ever seen before. Likely a traveler stopping off for a bite.

"No, ma'am," said Kat, somewhat confused. "It's just regular sausage."

The woman rolled her eyes. "Well, why does it say vegetarian?"

Kat wanted to respond kindly but had no idea what to say. She shook her head, flummoxed.

"Right here," said the woman pointing to the placemat menu. "What's that little green symbol then? Doesn't that mean vegetarian?"

"Oh," said Kat, suddenly understanding. "It just means it's local. Bill Pardo raises 'em. His ranch is just a few miles away."

The woman harrumphed like a soap opera star. "I don't eat meat. It's barbaric and cruel to animals. Throw this away, please."

How does this help the pig that's already been cooked? "I'm sorry, ma'am. Can I bring you something else?"

"More coffee. And the check. I suggest you label your menu better in the future."

"Yes, Ma'am."

Kat walked back to the coffee dispenser wondering if she might "accidentally" slip and pour hot coffee in the woman's lap. *No, I wouldn't, but –the other me might.* She thought she was being funny in her own mind, but all it did was remind her of Merrick's predicament. He needed help and wasn't going to admit it. She was his only chance. It was important to her for some reason. *Dang, girl. You're acting like he's family.*

No, it wasn't that. But something.

Merrick hoisted the bag on his shoulders and strode toward the truck. Zeus was unpacking something from the bed and hadn't noticed Merrick approach.

"Oh, hey, Mr. Merrick," said Zeus.

"Hi, Zeus."

Zeus held his gaze on Merrick's duffel bag. "I guess you're not stickin' around like you said, huh?"

"I can't," said Merrick.

"You're not worried about the sheriff?"

Merrick shrugged. "It's not optimal, but I've been chased by worse. I can't get my name or picture posted anywhere or the, uh – mobsters will find me."

Merrick had tried to explain that mob hitmen were searching for him because he witnessed a mob murder. It wasn't as dire as his real circumstance, but it was the best lie he could think of that Zeus might believe.

"And you can't tell the police or nothin'?" asked Zeus. "They can't protect you?"

Merrick shook his head. "It was cops that got murdered by the mob. And it was at a safe house where they were trying to protect me." That was a new twist he invented just that instant. It hadn't been thought through, and he hoped it didn't contradict anything else he had said. He wasn't used to explaining these things to people.

Zeus whistled and shook his head slowly. "Dios mio. That's some serious shit. I wish you luck, man." He slapped a callused hand on Merrick's arm. "Thanks for helping Miss Kat out last night. It took some cajones to stand up to Tanner like that, so – you're all right in my book." Zeus squeezed Merrick's arm, then let go. "Mira, güey, you need anything, you call me, I'll be there. Neta. Ok?"

"I will," said Merrick, knowing he would never do that despite the good intention.

"You know Miss Kat's gonna be mad at you for breaking your promise."

Merrick nodded. "Yeah, I know. I don't have much of a choice. It's for her safety too. Take care of her, ok?"

"Don't worry. I always keep an eye on her," said Zeus. "We all do, you know, when's she not looking." He grinned.

"I'm sure," said Merrick returning the smile.

Del had come out of the house as the two men were talking, and Merrick was surprised by Del's hand on his shoulder.

"Leaving?" asked Del.

"Yes, sir," said Merrick.

Del hung his head and put his hands on his hips. "I ain't going to pry into your business, and I'm sure you got a good reason for running out on the sheriff, but – forgive me if I'm a little worried for ya."

"It's ok," said Merrick. "And thanks. I appreciate anyone who worries about me. I don't get a lot of it."

Merrick suddenly recalled that he was wearing Del's old clothes. He examined his pants and shirt, remembering that all his own

100

clothes, except for the jacket, were torn and bloody, wadded up in his bag. He needed to throw all of that away somewhere.

Merrick apologized, "I'm afraid I'm still wearing your clothes. I don't have replacements."

Del smiled and shook his head. "Keep 'em. They don't fit me anymore. It's the very least I can do. You saved our bull and helped us out. I wish I had a better way to repay you. You refused the money I offered for your work the other day."

"I told you, it was my idea to stick around. You shouldn't be obligated to pay me."

"Then I definitely owe you a much bigger favor than just the clothes."

Merrick shook his head preparing to tell Del that no favor was owed, but then he got an idea. He dug into his duffel bag and pulled out the plastic bag of torn, bloody clothes.

"Well, if you don't mind, I'd appreciate it if you could discard these for me. You got a trash can?"

Del smiled and took the bag. "No, but we have an incinerator."

"Oh. Ok, even better." *Wow. What in the world do they need to burn so frequently?*

Del seemed to notice Merrick's curious reaction. "We're kinda on our own out here. Once a month, a waste truck comes around and we pile the big stuff and a few bags on the road. But for the rest, we just incinerate it. Easier."

"Thanks."

It struck Merrick a little odd that Del had gone through the trouble of building an incinerator for trash. Incinerators weren't a common item in most places, and operations like morgues or waste plants were generally the only ones that needed them. Still, he had never lived somewhere like this, so it actually may be the norm.

Del held up the bag. "I still owe you. This isn't that big a favor."

It is to me. Merrick smiled and waved a hand as he began to walk up the dirt road. "Tell Kat I'm sorry."

Del shook his head. "Oh, no way. I'm not gonna get hollered at for lettin' you to skip out. I didn't see squat. Write her a letter yourself when you get somewhere safe."

Merrick laughed and nodded, then waved again. It occurred to him that he didn't know the address here and decided to squint at the house number next to the door. "1800." Then he'd get the road name from a street sign or his map later. It had been forever since he'd written anyone a letter.

Up at the edge of the road, he looked right, then left, seeing no cars. No patrol cars were hiding behind trees like he was suspecting there might be. Technically, he wasn't disobeying his directive yet. Even going for a walk with his bag packed didn't constitute ditching his promise to stay in town. He had studied a map earlier and figured he had to walk a few miles along the road before he got past the mountainous region enough to head west through the woods. He'd hit an Indian reservation there, cut through that, then decide where he wanted to go afterward. Once he got to the reservation border, then he would be technically ditching. Technicality or not, Merrick knew full well that Sheriff Kind was looking for an excuse to arrest him, and if he was caught wandering the road, he'd have to make his excuses in handcuffs.

The road ahead was built alongside a high hill connected with a mountain, and was steep on both sides: one tilting down, the other tilting up. Walking on the slopes would be a pain until he got past the hills, so he'd need to stay on the road for the time being, careful to keep a keen eye open and duck into the trees if necessary.

At the entrance to Kat's dirt drive, the road didn't have a sign to indicate its name. He'd just have to figure it out from his map later. He turned left, crossed the street, and got on the right shoulder, the easiest position to hop onto the downward slope and hide from passersby. No cars went by for several minutes, so he simply walked and took in the lush pine mountains and valley. Pretty country. It was too bad he couldn't stay longer. *Yeah, too bad.* He knew full well that it was less the pretty scenery and more the pretty company that was making him reluctant to go. *Get over yourself, dude.*

His mental wanderings were probably the reason he wasn't paying close enough attention when something glinted around the edge of a bend. He blinked and held up a hand to shield his eyes from the morning glare. The thing that glinted was something metal, maybe chrome, obscured by a thick bush. Nothing chrome should be on the side of the lonely road through mountainous woods. Merrick squinted and looked harder, trying to make out details. Then he saw some dull black rubber next to white paint.

Oh no. A sheriff's car. Had to be. Who else would park in a random spot on the road and hide the vehicle behind brush?

Merrick scrambled behind a tree and tried to think. Had the deputy seen him yet? No voice called out so far. Maybe he had ducked out of sight soon enough. He surveyed his immediate area for a discreet exit. Below him was a steep drop through tangled bushes and pine straw. No chance of descending quietly. Staying on the road and running back past Kat's entrance wouldn't be a good option either. This was a trap and another sheriff's car would likely be parked in the opposite direction. No, down was the safest play, and even if they followed him, he was more adept at traversing and navigating woods than anyone he knew.

He ducked down, then extended a foot, resting it against a little gnarled bush, hoping it wouldn't crack under his weight. It creaked a little but didn't break. He slunk down the slope, using the woody trunks of bushes as stairs. One solid slab of rock was a good place to gather his balance, and once his feet were firmly underneath him, he leaped out to get distance through the air, planning to slide down an open area of the hill that only had one slender tree to maneuver around. He landed near the tree, braced against it with his hands, not expecting the tree to break. It had looked like a healthy trunk, but when his momentum and weight bent it, it snapped, making a loud crack that echoed through the woods. No longer having the tree for balance and a speed brake, he tumbled down the hill crashing into a dry bush that made further snaps and cracks, echoing like a pinball through the formerly silent woods.

Though he was being poked and pricked in several places, he was all right, being supported by the brittle bush he landed in. Just unfortunately tangled, and any movement to free himself would snap more little branches. He stayed still and quieted his breathing so he could listen for anything happening on the above road.

Several seconds passed. No motors revved, no car doors squeaked or slammed. Maybe the racket he made falling hadn't been suspicious enough. Animals moved through these woods too. It could be any number of...

A dog barked from the road above. It sounded close. Pebbles and sand crunched in slow rhythm like boots stepping on pavement. *Oh, no*. The dog barked again, this time long and continuous. It was closer.

Merrick had two choices: Hurriedly extricate himself from the bush, run like hell, and hope the deputy didn't release the dog, or stay quiet and hope nobody sees him here. The dog would smell him but…

"Stay where you are," said an amplified voice. *A bullhorn?* "Do not try to run! The dog is trained to take you down, if necessary."

Shit, shit, shit.

The dog's head appeared over the road edge above. He sniffed the air, then looked straight down at Merrick. A big German Shepherd. Though Merrick was normally a dog lover, he wasn't a fan at that moment.

The deputy appeared an instant later, removing his sunglasses and staring directly at Merrick. A wad of spit went down Merrick's throat hard as he stared up at the man he least wanted to see. Sheriff Kind's grin looked more feral than the dog's.

CHAPTER 14

Merrick sat in the sheriff's office waiting for Quinton Kind to return. It felt like it had been an hour sitting there alone, though he hadn't checked his watch. He was too busy stewing in his anger. Some of it was directed at Sheriff Kind, most of it was at himself. At every step during the last few days, he had reminded himself not to get comfortable, not to tempt fate, not to do things that would risk his anonymity, yet here he was sitting in a sheriff's office, probably about to be arrested, and even worse, having his prints and picture processed and entered into a police database. He might as well have gone on television, sent a formal invitation to the agents who hunted him, and announced his address.

He wasn't too concerned about a possible murder charge. Evidence was circumstantial, no eyewitnesses, so an indictment wouldn't hold. In previous times, when his other self created havoc, there had been nothing left behind that could be matched to Merrick. The other self didn't leave fingerprints or recognizable DNA, and the few times there were eyewitnesses, no one described a human, much less Merrick. He wasn't afraid to talk to Kind about it, in fact, he had a fair story to tell when asked, but he knew the visit to the sheriff's office, especially without an ID, would culminate in all sorts of documents signed, pictures taken, and information processed. A big, fat, hairy footprint for the agents to follow. And he might wind up waiting for them from inside a jail cell.

Just fucking great.

The door to the office opened and Kind walked in, a stack of papers in his hand that Merrick was forced to fill out earlier. Though the name he printed was for his new alias, Frank Chaney, fingerprints and a mug shot were still taken. At some point, the data would reach those who were looking for him, and proper name or not, they would come. How soon was anyone's guess.

Kind sat down at his desk, folded his hands, and donned a smug, Mona Lisa visage. Comfortable in his little kingdom. Though Merrick had been on the outskirts of it before, now he was trapped within the king's walls. Arrested or not, jailed or not, Merrick was exactly where the sheriff wanted him.

"Mr. Chaney," said Kind with an unnerving smile. "Probably not your real name. Very convenient that you have no ID or birth certificate, or any records to verify. No data came up from your picture. You've managed to stay completely off the grid for a long time. So, for the sake of sanity, we'll just go along with the name you supplied."

Merrick said nothing, focusing on being immune to any baiting the sheriff might try.

The sheriff unsheathed a pair of photographs and laid them before Merrick. He spread them out evenly on the desk.

"Do you know what these are?" asked the sheriff.

Merrick examined them. "Footprints."

"Specifically boot prints," said the sheriff. "The one on the right is a photo of your boot's sole taken by Deputy Pooler this morning. The one on the left is an imprint in blood from behind the diner. They're a match, Mr. Chaney." The sheriff paused, probably to see if Merrick was going to react, but no reaction came. "It places you at the scene. We had our experts confirm the match, and it would stand up in court. So – now are we clear about the trouble you're in?"

Merrick said nothing.

The sheriff leaned back in his chair, still playing the man holding all the cards. He wasn't wrong, though his hand wasn't as strong as he portrayed.

"Playing silent isn't going to help your case. It just allows us time and motivation to place your puzzle piece in all the places that we don't have good fits for yet, then see what connects. Maybe you're a man who already has a past he's running from, or maybe he's trying to stay hidden for other reasons. Either way, you could become the prime focus of all our investigations, and your picture and prints would be sent out to every law enforcement agency in this nation unless you decide to start telling me things that might change my mind. Hmm?"

That was cop-speak for *"I'll make your life hell unless you give me what I want."* And once again, the sheriff wasn't wrong. And had improved his hand.

Merrick had prepared a story that was partially true and addressed most of the points. There was also a rogue element he was hedging to introduce. He needed more time to consider it. But he may have to think while he talked. Continued silence was going to push the sheriff into vindictiveness.

"I was there," said Merrick flatly.

The sheriff nodded. "Finally. Some sense from you." He interwove his fingers and seemed to settle himself for a long story. "Alright, go on. Tell me about the murder of Councilman Saunders."

Saunders? There were at least 10 people that were killed in that place. Kind was singling out the convict?

"Saunders was killed by the men from the van," said Merrick.

Kind's eyebrows went up slightly and he wiggled his interwoven fingers. "You saw this clearly?"

"Yes. That part of it."

The sheriff nodded and seemed to be processing this. "Where were you and why were you there?"

Time for Merrick's constructed story. He still debated whether to introduce the rogue element. Hopefully, there was time to decide while he spoke.

Merrick cleared his throat. "I went behind the diner to check out their trash. Maybe some food they had thrown out. Restaurants sometimes discard perfectly good food and other things that can be salvaged."

His eyes darted to Sheriff Kind who seemed content to listen for the time being. Merrick continued. "There wasn't any food, but there was a warm exhaust coming from the trash area and it felt good, so I sat down near it. I guess I fell asleep. Some noises woke me and I saw the bounty hunter and his assistant back there talking. Their prisoner got out of their car to take a piss."

Kind was still sitting quietly, attentively. Not scowling or showing outward signs of hostility. *So far, so good.*

Merrick continued. "I was behind a lot of boxes and things, so I'm pretty sure the bounty hunter didn't see me. I don't like to draw attention to myself, so I kept still. Then they were all surprised when the van pulled up. There were seven guys…"

Sheriff Kind held up a hand. "Could you hear their conversation? Between Saunders and Gunn?"

Still concerned with Saunders? Merrick was starting to form a picture in his head of what this was all about. A very fuzzy picture, but there was a form taking shape. "Not well, sir. I only heard what was said once the van arrived. They were all talking louder and clearer then."

Sheriff Kind considered something again, then bobbed his head at Merrick to continue.

Merrick did. "The men in the van got out carrying weapons. Gunn tried to negotiate with them before the men attacked him. I was scared and ducked down, trying to stay hidden."

Sheriff Kind had an impatient expression and held up a hand again. "If you were hiding so well, how did you see what happened to Saunders?"

"I could see clearly between the trash bins. Several men from the van got him. First, they threw an ax at the assistant. Then stabbed Gunn. Then several guys stabbed, hacked, and beat Saunders to death."

Kind seemed interested in Merrick's abridged tale. Though it didn't mean the sheriff bought it straight up, it was a good sign that he was looking for real information rather than a scapegoat.

It was time for the decision whether to deliver a really farfetched, invented story, or to plead ignorance. He obviously couldn't say the truth: *The van leader stabbed me, I turned into a monster which I can't control, then killed the rest of them and booked it for the woods.* Would a spun version of that same truth work? Given all the myths and legends in this area, would something similar pass muster?

"Go on," prompted Kind.

"That's when things got weird." Merrick decided to tell the farfetched tale. He was already in pretty deep with Kind, and since the mysterious agents were likely revving up their car now to come find Merrick, he needed to deflect focus from him pronto to be let go. "I heard something that didn't sound human. Like an animal growl. I've lived in the woods a long time and I recognize a lot of dangerous animals and I never heard one like that before. I couldn't tell if it was only one or more, but I didn't want to find out. Even though the men didn't see me, animals could probably smell me. Maybe the stench from the trash heap would help, so I carefully

108

pulled a few more pieces of trash over me and ducked down further. I couldn't see much of anything that way. As long as it saved my life, I didn't care."

Sheriff Kind leaned forward on his elbows. "Animals suddenly showed up?"

"I don't know what it, or they, were. But it didn't seem human."

"You're telling me animals killed all those men from the van?"

"I couldn't see it," said Merrick. "I was trying to keep my head down. I heard snarling and screaming. And I saw – glimpses of – of – fur and claws."

Sheriff Kind leaned back, jaw clenched, his demeanor no longer patient. Merrick was taking a big risk spinning this yarn. Still, it was the closest he could come to the truth without implicating himself. And as he was dreaming it up, he supposed he'd toss in the wolf-people descriptions as part of his vague recollection of what the killers looked like. At worst, the sheriff wouldn't believe him and Merrick was no worse off than he had been. Kind may think Merrick was drug-addled and hallucinating. Or maybe it would throw suspicion at Tanner and his wolf-men buddies to hammer the nail in their coffin. Merrick had hopes for that one, but it seemed more like wishful thinking than a legitimate outcome.

"Fur and claws," said the sheriff, his tone skeptical.

"Yeah. I've heard weird stories from some of the residents about these giant wolves that kill people, and since I saw men who pretended to be wolves at the Seavers' – well, I don't know if it's the same, but it coulda been, I guess."

"You think this is funny, Mr. Chaney?"

"No, sir. No – I, uh, just don't know what to make of what I saw."

"Mm hmm." The sheriff rubbed his face with his palms. "So, you see men with wolf costumes in the Seavers' field the other night, and you just happened to see them behind the diner too?"

"I know it sounds preposterous. But whatever they were, they were more than just men in costumes. They – tore those men apart. It was terrifying."

Sheriff Kind was visibly irritated and quickly losing the ability to suppress his temper. It was unknown if that irritation was with Merrick or the situation. "And I guess since you were behind the trash the whole time, you never saw any of those other guys actually get killed?"

Merrick nodded.

"I don't suppose these wolf people talked? Said anything?"

Hadn't thought of that. "Not that I understood."

"And you never got a good look at any of them?"

"No, sir. I was scared, keeping my head down. When I hadn't heard any noises for a while, no more screaming or growling, I lifted up my head and peeked out. All I saw was blood, and body parts, and – well, you know. I freaked out and tried to run. I slipped on something immediately, probably blood, and got blood on my clothes. I got up and starting running. I don't even remember where I ran to. I just ran. When I got into the woods, I stopped and tried to relax. I changed my clothes and headed northwest on that mountain road. Kat drove by and offered me a ride to her place to rest for the night, she had no idea where I'd been. She was just being nice to a tired traveler. Then you know the rest."

"These bloody clothes – do you still have them?"

"No, sir. Threw 'em away. They freaked me out."

The sheriff nodded solemnly.

Merrick was a little surprised that his tall tale wasn't being rejected. He assumed that these local myths had a base in some sort of reality, and maybe Tanner and his crew were mimicking the legend, or maybe those costumes were part of the source. Impossible to know which, but Merrick figured it wouldn't be dismissed offhand. It was still a pleasant surprise that the sheriff was acting invested in the story.

"I'm sorry, sheriff," said Merrick. "I should've told you everything immediately, but I think you can understand why someone in my position would be frightened that he wouldn't be believed. Vagrant stranger, happens to be in the place where murders happen, blood on him, and apparently leaves a boot print in blood. Pretty damning. And I don't have eyewitnesses or proof to back me up. But..." Merrick gestured to his slender frame. "Do I look like a guy who could do all that against armed men? Trained killers?"

The sheriff gave Merrick a chilling look. "I've seen men scrawnier than you capable of a lot worse. Nobody really knows what a man can do if he really wants to." His eyes bore into

Merrick's. "It's awfully convenient that the description of the killers is also the description of the men you saw in the Seavers' field. It's also awfully convenient that you only heard certain conversations." The sheriff forced an expression change to something more ambivalent. "Maybe if you had some information to give me from something they said, it might serve to exonerate you. You sure you heard nothing else?"

There was no doubt that the sheriff was angling for something specific, some detail he needed to satisfy his suspicions. Unfortunately, Merrick didn't know what it was.

"I don't know. The van driver talked the most, but he only asked for Gunn's autograph, invited himself closer, then that was it. He didn't have a distinguishable accent either. Nor did the other guys. They only talked to Gunn for a second, then they killed him."

"You didn't hear Saunders say anything else?"

"Uh, I – don't – think so."

"And these wolf people? Or whoever these 'killers,'" he made air quotes, "were that you saw – they said nothing understandable? You sure? I haven't heard a reason to believe your story yet."

Merrick was confused. The sheriff's objection to his story was the lack of overheard conversation, not the claim that cryptid wolf people came and wiped out the assassins. He considered making up an overheard conversation, then decided against it.

"Sorry, sir," said Merrick. "Just what I said. It sounded like animal noises and screaming. Then the – whatever they were, left. And I ran."

Sheriff Kind's face was stony and tense. He took a deep breath, then another. After several seconds of staring into space, the sheriff slowly gathered the photos of the boot prints and slid them back into a manila folder. He popped that folder on the desk like it was emphasizing some decision he had just made.

"Mr. Chaney," said the sheriff. "You have lied to me, broken your promise, and generally been deceitful since you got here. There's not a reason in the world to trust anything you told me. So, why the hell should I?"

Good question. The answer was, of course, that he shouldn't. But Merrick was a keen observer, a skill he needed to stay alive in unfamiliar surroundings, which was an everyday occurrence, and he had been calculating who this Sheriff Kind person was with every question he posed. One thing was for sure, the sheriff knew something significant he wasn't sharing, and wanted to know if Merrick knew it too. The real question was if knowing this information would help Merrick's case or bury him deeper under the jail cell.

"You're still my number one suspect for the murder of Councilman Saunders," said the sheriff. "So I'm gonna need a damned good reason why you shouldn't be."

Merrick had taken a risk in spinning the wolf-people story, and it hadn't cost him anything, but also hadn't gotten him off the hook. He was down to one more possible ploy if he wanted to stay outside of the jail cell.

"Because Saunders knew those men were coming to kill him," said Merrick. "I'm pretty sure you know that too. And I think you even know who they were."

Sheriff Kind's eyes narrowed, seeming almost reptilian as he regarded Merrick. He leaned forward just enough to give the sense that he could jump over the desk if he chose.

"And why exactly do you think that?" said Kind with honey-coated menace.

"I don't think it benefits me to say right now."

"You're playing a dangerous game, Mr. Chaney," said Kind.

"Well, I don't have a lot to lose since you keep telling me you're going to put me in jail on murder charges."

The corners of Kind's mouth curled ever so slightly like he was fighting against a grin. "There are far worse things than going to jail, even on a murder charge. Far worse."

Like what? What's worse than being sent to the electric chair? Merrick had already crossed the point of no return, so he might as well play all his cards and see what happens. "You know I didn't kill Saunders – or any of them – because you know who did. And you're worried I heard something that you're afraid other people might find out. So, you don't wanna let me go until you know for sure. Am I going to stick with the official deposition, or would I say something different by the time it got to court?" Merrick raised a brow to say that the ball was in Kind's court.

The sheriff said nothing, continuing his serpent's stare, unflinching. There was cold fire behind that stare. Something burning with blinding intensity, yet without consumption. Merrick felt like he was staring into power. A much greater force than what was represented by the sheriff's patch on Quinton Kind's sleeve. Indefinable, unnatural, and possibly irrational, but it was there. Whoever Sheriff Kind really was under his small town, middle-aged sheriff façade, he was not a person to take lightly.

Further contemplation on the subject was interrupted when a knock came on the office door. The blinds were drawn so Merrick couldn't see who was there.

The sheriff grumbled and faced the door. "I'm busy!"

A voice from outside the door said, "You are illegally interrogating my client without counsel."

Sheriff Kind's eyebrows went up. "Excuse me?" He shifted in his chair. "Who the hell are you?"

"I am Mr. Chaney's attorney, sheriff. Open the door and allow me to talk with my client."

Kind's eyes darted to Merrick, questioning when the prisoner had magically called for a lawyer. Merrick was equally confused.

The sheriff stood up and opened the door, filling the doorframe as an imposing barrier to letting the "counsel" in. Merrick leaned back enough to make out the face of the man claiming to be his lawyer.

Zeus Moreno stood at the door in a dusty, ill-fitting business suit, with Kat standing behind him.

"Mr. Moreno?" said the sheriff as both a surprised exclamation and an invitation to explain himself.

"May I come in please?" asked Zeus in a professionally amicable manner.

"No," said the sheriff. "Unless you changed professions that I'm not aware of in a day."

Zeus shook his head. "My client is allowed counsel of his own choice, regardless of your objections. Right, Mr. Chaney?"

Now what? Zeus had adopted a put-on, formal accent like a movie lawyer, with a hint of televangelist. Merrick wasn't sure what was going on, but Zeus was very plainly waiting for Merrick's blessing to legally come in. Besides being unexpected, there didn't seem to be much to lose.

"Yes, Mr., Moreno," said Merrick. "Uh, I asked him to be my counsel if anything bad should ever happen, sheriff."

Whether the law allowed an unlicensed lawyer to sit in on an interrogation or not, the sheriff didn't shut the door. He shook his head as Zeus walked in.

"Where the hell is this game you're playing leading to?" said the sheriff to no one in particular. He gave an unwelcoming stare to Kat, then held up a hand to forbid her entry.

Kat put on an innocent, confused face. "But you told me to come by at four o'clock to answer questions."

"You won't be needed," said Kind. "I wanted you to confirm that Mr. Chaney was behind the diner. We've already established that. So – go home."

Kat scrunched her mouth and darted her eyes to Merrick first, then Zeus.

"Uhh," muttered Zeus. Miss Seavers is my assistant," said Zeus. "She will be taking detailed and accurate notes of everything being said."

"Of course, she will," groused Sheriff Kind, stuck somewhere between blowing his top and laughing at the absurdity.

"Now," said Zeus, sitting down. "What are your charges against my client?"

The sheriff took a moment to expel a long breath, then said, "Resisting arrest, perjury, withholding evidence, and vagrancy."

"I see," said Zeus. Zeus's wooden expression slipped for a moment, probably indicating that he was expecting more serious charges.

"Buuuut," said the sheriff, "the chief issue here is that he is a person of interest in the murder of Councilman Saunders."

"And can you tell me what you have discussed?"

Sheriff Kind smiled and turned to Merrick. "Mr. Chaney claims he has harmed no one, and was an unwitting witness to parts of the crime, which he conveyed to me in unconvincing detail."

"I see," repeated Zeus, clearly looking confused. "Do you have evidence against my client?"

The sheriff held up the envelope of photos, "His boot print places him at the scene, and he will remain a murder suspect unless we receive information that implicates someone else. *If* there is someone else."

"What kind of information?" asked Zeus.

"That's up to Mr. Chaney. His recollection of things has been conveniently fuzzy on the important parts, and incredulous on the rest. So, I would highly suggest he greatly improve his memory, as soon as possible. I hear jail cells are good places to think." The sheriff donned a patronizing smile that was plainly intended to provoke a reaction.

"Are you inferring that my client is lying to you about what he witnessed?"

"Mm hmm," said the sheriff.

"Oh," said Zeus. He gave Merrick a quick, questioning glance which Merrick didn't know how to answer. "Well, uh, since I don't know what was said, I would need to…"

Sheriff Kind held up a palm. "Ask him yourself. We're done here." *We are?* "Mr. Chaney is free to go with all the lesser charges dropped under one condition. He is still a prime suspect in the murder case, so he must remain in town and be available for further questioning and possible arrest as things develop. Since he already went back on his promise once, I must insist he wear this."

In the sheriff's hand was a thick metal ring with a device attached, resembling a giant's watch. He shook it and grinned.

Kat straightened and dropped her pen. "That's a house arrest anklet."

The sheriff nodded. "It's this or I put him in jail and set bail at a couple hundred thousand. Got a credit card?"

Kat's face became dark with anger. "You can't do that without a formal charge."

"I can charge him with all the stuff I mentioned before," said the sheriff. "Then you can test Mr. Moreno's attorney skills in a real court of law. Hmm?"

Zeus waved his palms at the sheriff. "Nobody needs to do any of that. Let's all just calm down here."

Kat wasn't being subdued so easily. Never moving her eyes from Kind, she said, "You ain't foolin' me, sheriff. You know somethin' you ain't sayin'. Just like the shit with Tanner, you're just gonna cover it up and blame someone else for it cuz it's easier."

"That so, Miss Seavers?" said the sheriff with unnerving calm. "I suppose it *was* easier not to submit the assault with a deadly weapon charge against you. And possibly an aiding and abetting a fugitive charge. And Mr. Moreno impersonating an attorney to gain access to a confidential police interrogation. So, maybe I should do my job a bit more thoroughly, huh?"

Kat's face was reddening. "You know, sheriff, I always thought you were an asshole. I didn't know why before, but now I do."

The sheriff reached down, clapped an iron hand around Merrick's foot, then locked the steel cuff around his ankle.

"And I always thought you were smart, Miss Seavers. Now we all know better."

Kat stood up, her right hand balled in a fist. A combination of obscenities were rumbling in her throat as she raised her fist with one finger extended.

Zeus sprang up and blocked her bodily from Sheriff Kind's sight. "Oohhhkay!!" said Zeus in an almost singsong tone. "It's time to go. The anklet'll do fine. We thank you for your time sheriff and we'll be taking Mr., uh – Chaney with us and be going now. Thank you for your understanding, and not throwing him in jail, and not – uh, throwing me or Kat in jail, and – have a nice day." He waved a frantic hand at Merrick to get up before the sheriff got madder and changed his mind.

Merrick, however, was lost in gloom. His pictures and fingerprints were in a police database, and he had a GPS tracker attached to his ankle that would instantly alarm the sheriff if he tried to cut it off. With minimal effort, the dark agents could find exactly where he was at any time. The target on his back was now a neon sign, with a searchlight in the sky and GPS navigation to it. Two days ago, he was untraceable, untrackable, a ghost. Today, he was a walking dead man.

Merrick met the sheriff's cold eyes with a frigid stare of his own. "You have no idea what you've done."

"Neither do you," said the sheriff.

CHAPTER 15

Kat kept her eyes on the road, only occasionally peering at the rearview mirror's reflection of Merrick sulking in the back seat. In contrast, Zeus was animated and jovial in the front seat.

"Man, if I only went to college," bemoaned Zeus. "Maybe I could be a rich lawyer right now." He winked and pointed to something imaginary in the windshield. "I object! No – objection, your honor. Object – ob – objectionnn," His voice was changing pitch and tone with each iteration of the word, like he was attempting to decide what character voice he should adopt as a lawyer.

"What're you doing?" asked Kat.

"What sounds cooler? You know, if I became a real, serious lawyer? Ooobjection! Or – objectionnn, or…"

"Zeus, stop. It's not funny," said Kat.

Zeus gave her a disappointed look and shrugged. "Hey, I did ok pretending to be a lawyer act back there."

Kat shook her head. "Sorry. That's not what I meant." She sighed. "It's just that I think we got Merrick in deep trouble."

From the back seat, Merrick murmured. "No." He sat up a little straighter. "No, you didn't. You guys didn't do anything wrong. I'm the one who got myself into this mess."

"And we'll help you get out of it," said Zeus. "Maybe I can call my cousin for help. He's a lawyer in Vegas. Kinda shady though. I used to work for him when I was in high school. It's how I knew enough lawyer stuff to fake it today. A lot of his clients are like – you know, no questions asked."

"Probably wouldn't help, Zeus," said Merrick. "But thank you."

Kat interjected, "I don't know. Maybe Zeus's right."

"How's a lawyer going to help?" asked Merrick.

"Well," Kat started. She seemed either uncertain what to say, or hesitant to say it. "We gotta get the sheriff off your scent and get him onto someone else's. And since…" She stopped suddenly, aware that Zeus wouldn't know the real story. "Since, uh, the sheriff might be trying to cover up something, we may have to get Merrick off the hook an unusual way."

"Like what?" asked Merrick.

"I don't know. But maybe something like a shady lawyer is what we need. You know, for pressure or leverage."

"Leverage?" said Merrick. "You mean like – blackmail?"

"Well, not exactly," said Kat. "Or – I don't know. The son of a bitch is hiding something he doesn't want anyone to know, and maybe people got killed because of it. There's gotta be a way to use that."

"Oh, Miss Kat, I don't know about blackmailing Sheriff Kind," said Zeus. "He scares me sometimes. I think he's like one of them evil spirits that's all normal on the outside, and all –," Zeus made snarling noises trying to imitate a vicious monster, "– on the inside." He shook his head. "You know?"

"Yeah, Zeus," said Merrick. "I do know. And I think you're right."

"I am?"

"Not literally a monster in there, yet there's something inside him that's more than the sum of his parts. I can't put my finger on it, but – yeah, there's something else there."

Zeus shrugged, looking surprised.

"Can your cousin sorta – intimidate Kind?" asked Kat.

Zeus shook his head. "Hey, he's not that kind of lawyer. I meant shady like he doesn't care if he works for the mob, or criminals, or whoever. I don't know nobody like you're talking about."

"What about your sister's ex-husband?" asked Kat. "The mob guy? He's powerful down in Nevada, right? Would he be willing to do a favor for you?"

"No way. He'd kill me if he found me. I took Espy away from him. She couldn't divorce him, couldn't do anything to get away from him. Except just leave for real. He owns people. Cops, you know, county officials. That's why we came here. I took her as far away as we could get that didn't have no networks, nobody that he could make a deal with to find her." A somber cloud seemed to hang over Zeus's head. "Then she gets killed anyway. I don't care what Javi says, I know she's dead."

"I'm sorry, Zeus," said Kat. "I didn't mean to bring it up."

"It's ok," said Zeus. He forced a relaxed smile on his face. "It's been a year now. I should be over it. Guess it's because Saunders got captured then killed, and he's the only suspect in Espy's disappearance. If I didn't know better, I'd think that her gangster ex-husband is the one that sent those goons here to kill Saunders. Except – who the hell killed *them*?"

Kat shook her head a little too enthusiastically, realizing she overcooked her attempt to feign ignorance of who killed the "goons." *My acting chops need work.* Luckily, Zeus didn't seem to notice.

Merrick sat up straight in the back seat. "Hey. You may have something there."

"Have what?" asked Zeus.

"Someone sent those guys to kill Saunders," said Merrick. "It was a hit, I guarantee it. I just couldn't figure out motive. But – if your sister's ex wanted revenge for her murder, then maybe."

"All the way from Vegas?" said Zeus. "That's a long damned way to drive to go looking for a guy that nobody knew how to find – until Gunn... Hey, how'd they know Gunn had him?"

Indeed.

Kat glanced at Zeus. "I talked to Jeremy just a little while before it happened. He said he had a long way to drive. I wanna say he was driving to Nevada."

Zeus nodded. "Yeah, the call for extradition mighta come from there since Espy was still listed as a Nevada resident. We never changed it 'cause we didn't want nobody to know where she was. So, I guess they'd bring Saunders back to face trial there."

"I don't know if it works that way," said Merrick. "But maybe."

"So, basically, someone in Nevada knew Gunn had him," said Kat.

"Looks like," said Merrick.

"Maybe your gangster somehow heard about it from his cop connections, then hurried to send guys up here," she added.

Merrick scratched his chin. "Don't recall seeing Nevada plates on the van though."

Kat shook her head. "I didn't notice. But they coulda stolen the car."

"Probably. No tracing it that way," said Merrick.

"That still doesn't answer how, a year later, Gunn gets commissioned to find Saunders," said Kat. "And the call comes from Vegas? How does anyone there even know who Saunders is? And why would Vegas police care, especially if they didn't even know your sister was up here?"

Zeus blew out a big held breath. "No idea."

"The whole thing's fishy," said Kat. "Weird and fishy."

She parked in her usual spot under a huge, ancient tree next to the house. Zeus was greeted by Javier who had finished his chores for the day. Kat invited them all in for dinner, but Zeus and Javi declined, saying they had something to take care of at home.

Though Merrick tried to excuse himself and set up his tent away from the house, Kat wasn't allowing it. "Until that anklet comes off, you're our guest. Sheriff would expect you to stay here anyway."

Kat deflected Merrick's protests and warnings that the bad men could find the anklet signal and come any minute to kill him, or kidnap him, and probably wouldn't hesitate to kill her and Del. She dismissed his concerns and demanded he take the spare bedroom. One or two more protests went by during dinner, again deflected.

"Don't make me shoot you again to make you stay put," said Kat.

Merrick spit out part of his food in laughter.

The dinner she had made was simpler than she preferred. Del wasn't a fan of her gourmet cooking, so when they ate together, she kept her culinary creativity mild. Tonight was half-assed, retread chicken parmesan. Chicken she had already baked for Del's sandwiches, linguini she had made herself and refrigerated, and homemade marinara with fresh tomatoes she got from her friend's garden. Though the sauce had been made last week, it still tasted fresh enough. Semi-gourmet, slapped together from stuff she had already made.

Del liked it fine, and Merrick looked like he might have an eating orgasm. Kat did a mental headshake to rid herself of that imagery. *Get your head out of the gutter, girl.*

Her father excused himself from the table once he was finished, claiming he had an early morning appointment with the vet to go over the bull's treatment, and wanted to get some sleep. Kat was tired too, especially since they had been up since the wee hours, and that wake-up alarm had been abrupt to say the least. Despite her tiredness, she stayed up and talked with Merrick at the kitchen table for two more hours. The mystery of Sheriff Kind and the weird assassination of Councilman Saunders wouldn't let her brain rest anyway. At least she finally had a day off tomorrow and could sleep in a little if she wanted.

She set down a cup of coffee in front of Merrick, then sat down herself. "I've been here since I was in first grade and never saw nothin' like this happen before."

"Well, obviously something happened at least a year ago to Zeus's sister," said Merrick.

She sipped at her coffee. "There was that, but she just disappeared. There was nothing freaky to see. Since she was pregnant, and she was Saunders' housekeeper, the rumors flew that he did something. Maybe to avoid scandal and shut her up. No one knows. But it wasn't long after she disappeared that he disappeared too. I heard stories that the sheriff went to arrest Saunders and the guy ran. I also heard rumors it was the FBI that spooked him. Someone also said it was some gang members who chased him, but I think that one's only coincidence. Probably just racist cuz Zeus and Espy are Mexican – folks assume they'd be connected to the Mexican mob."

"Ironic that Espy kinda was. But it wouldn't be likely that her gangster ex-husband knew what was happening way up here back then, otherwise, he would've come after Espy sooner."

"Ok, so if he didn't know about Saunders or Espy before, then what changed that made Saunders a target all the way from Vegas?"

Merrick took a long slug of his coffee. "I don't know. But I do know, or suspect, that Sheriff Kind has something to do with it."

"Me too, but – I have no idea how or why."

"I had a hunch – and made a risky statement as a way of getting the sheriff off guard, playing it like I had info I was keeping close to the vest, and he wouldn't want me to say on the stand in court. I told him I thought he knew who those assassins were, and why they were sent to kill Saunders."

Kat's brows went up. "Why'd you do that?"

121

Merrick waggled his head. "Wasn't sure. A gut feeling. Just took a chance in his office saying so. And I think I touched a nerve. He was only concerned with Saunders' death. None of the other people. So, all he thinks he needs to do figure out that one. He doesn't seem to care about the others. He was digging for information from me because I was there and might have heard someone say something compromising about him or someone he's trying to protect, not because he thinks I did it. Despite him saying otherwise, I don't think he believes I'm capable of that. Sure, he'll pin it on me if he has to, but it doesn't look good to stand me up in court and say I slaughtered nine or ten people – armed people – with my bare hands." Merrick gestured to his physique. "Would you buy that if you were a juror?"

Kat smiled politely and said, "Sorry, but not really."

Merrick shrugged. "Me either. I'm no badass."

Kat lifted a brow. "Not this version of you."

"Right. And good luck trying to claim that in court too."

Kat considered that, and it made enough sense. She never liked Kind before, liked him even less now, and could believe that the sheriff might be corrupt enough to either order a hit or knowingly allow one. She just couldn't figure out what his angle would be.

Kat rubbed her forehead with her fingers. "You know, I just remembered something one of his deputies said."

"About what?"

"About Saunders' capture. I was talking with Simon – uh, Deputy Pooler, in the diner, and he said he had no idea Gunn had captured Saunders. Seemed odd to me. He was confused because the sheriff would usually alert his deputies to stuff like that. Maybe even order them to protect Gunn while he's in town. I don't know how it works."

"Hmm. So, you think it was an intentional omission? Keep the deputies out of the way?"

She shrugged. "I hadn't thought about it until now. But – maybe, yeah."

"Wow," said Merrick. "Seems pretty clear that the sheriff knew what was going down. Our dangerous little hunch might have legs."

They both sipped at their coffee for a moment, saying nothing. Despite the sickening circumstances, Kat was enjoying talking with someone intelligent. She had so few good friends in Templeton, no one she felt at home discussing complicated things with. And of all people, a homeless drifter blows in and now he's in her kitchen, talking conspiracies and murder mysteries over coffee. *The world's a weird-ass place.*

"So, why kill Saunders?" she said. "Why do it that way? What does Kind, or anyone else, gain out of it?"

"The key to me is why Saunders was headed back to Nevada," answered Merrick. "If he's got something the sheriff doesn't want exposed, or maybe something on Kind himself, wouldn't that be more valuable leverage here? If Saunders is going to sing, his plea bargain would mean something here, not in Vegas."

"Maybe the judges are on the take here."

"I wouldn't put it past small towns like this to have all the important men in a mutual agreement to not rat on each other. Maybe they're all on some sort of council, meeting secretly in dark rooms to conceal conspiracies."

"You watch too much TV."

"I don't watch any TV," said Merrick. "Can't fit one in my bag, and they don't make cables long enough."

"Smartass. Phones and iPads are small enough to easily carry around, and there's lots of online TV services now." She gave him a challenging yet playful stare, knowing full well someone like him isn't going to own that kind of technology or pay for a subscription to anything. Just bait for a tease.

Merrick nodded. "Yeah, well, the only mechanical thing I have is my watch. Besides not having the money to buy any of that stuff, I don't want anything that can broadcast my position to…" He cut his sentence short and looked down at his left foot. A long sigh slid through his throat as he regarded his house-arrest anklet.

"I'm sorry," said Kat, meaning it.

He nodded. "I'm more worried for you guys. Despite your kind hospitality, these men looking for me are vicious and remorseless. They'll…"

"We've been over this. You're staying here."

Merrick smiled ruefully and placed his palm on Kat's hand. It was warm and softer than she expected for such an outdoorsy guy (she couldn't think of a nicer word for homeless in her mind).

Normally, she hated people touching her, except hugs from her dad, but this felt nice. *Girl?*

"Not inside your house," said Merrick. "Don't argue. It'll eat at me every second if I put you in more danger. I'll stay in the barn. If someone comes for me, maybe it'll be far enough away from you."

Kat hated to have her edicts dismissed, but he did have a point about his conscience eating at him. Regardless of whether the bad guys hunting for Merrick were real or imagined, his belief and concern for Kat and Del's well-being would give him serious anxiety. If sleeping in the barn made him feel comfortable, then she would accept that.

"Alright," she said. With a crooked, impish smile she added, "You know you're the only man around here that's talked back to me and ain't been shot at for it."

Merrick lowered his brows and gave her a contrarian smirk.

"Ah, shit," she said and started to laugh. "Guess you ain't either."

He patted her hand then stood up to leave.

"Wait," she said. "How's long's it been since you had a shower. You know, with real soap and hot water?"

Merrick opened his mouth to answer, then looked puzzled. "Uh, I suppose dunks in lakes and washing in rainwater isn't going to count to you?"

"Nope. Get your ass upstairs and get yourself a hot shower before you run off to the barn."

Merrick shook his head, not from disagreement, rather from incredulity. "Who am I going to offend in the barn?"

"You're offending me right now. Now go on."

"Alright, alright. *Mom*." He made the last word clownishly sarcastic, then covered his rear as she raised her hand to swat at him.

Upstairs, she laid out towels and showed him how to work the shower dial. She found another set of clean old clothes that no longer fit Del, laid those out in the spare room, then she sat in her room with the door open, in case he needed anything.

Twenty minutes later, longer than she expected, he emerged pink and glistening, with a towel wrapped around his waist.

"Oh, sorry," he said, noticing her clear view of him as he entered the hall. "Didn't know you could… I'll just…" He pointed to the spare room.

She waved off his modesty. He probably had no clue she had situated herself specifically to be within easy view of him when the bathroom door opened. *That sounds creepy to me, and I know that's not what I meant.* It was just for making sure he could get her attention by leaning out the door if he needed something, not to sneak a peek at his physique. Which, by the way, was as expected: not typically her type, slender, wiry, though more defined than she imagined, athletic like a runner maybe, not brawny. *He cleaned up well though. I wonder how long it's been since he's...* She shook her head to ward off her wandering thoughts. *Ok, nosey, how long's it been since **you've** been with someone?* It took some forceful remembering to squeeze that nugget of information to the surface. *A year and a half? Christ.* She didn't need men, they complicated her life, she had no time for the nonsense most of them represented, but... *damn.*

She also noticed something else in the brief flash she got as he shuffled past her door. His wounds were completely healed. Small dots of lighter-colored skin where the pellets had been were highlighted against the heated pink tone of the rest of his skin. The other scars on his chest and shoulders that looked like they could have been knife slashes or bullet punctures dotted his torso like bizarre tattoos.

He really does have some kind of special healing ability. Despite witnessing pellets falling out of his body, she still wanted to deny it was more than a fluke. Seeing all those wounds spread across his body squelched her doubts. And for the briefest moment, her sex-starved brain imagined her tracing those scars with her fingertips. *Stop it!* She slapped her book shut and drew her covers to her shoulders.

Merrick was dressed, on his way back toward the stairs, and heard the loud clap of the book. "You ok?" he asked.

"Yep," she said quickly. "You got everything you need for stayin' warm out there?"

"Yeah, I'm good. Thank you for the shower."

"Welcome. Good night." She snapped off her lamp.

Merrick stood in her doorway a heartbeat too long for her comfort. "Good night," he said, then walked towards the stairs.

If I dream about him, I'm going to punch myself in the face.

CHAPTER 16

Merrick settled himself into the combination of straw floor and his sleeping bag. It was his second night in that configuration, more comfortable than his usual arrangements. If it was any other circumstance, he would've easily fallen asleep, however, he was wide awake. Strangely, it was not just because he worried that the dark agents who hunted him would show up at any moment. Random thoughts and images of Kat swirled around in his mind.

He had long ago given up on the concept of a love-life. Being a drifter meant usually being dirty, never staying anywhere long enough to create a relationship, and not being safe to make one even if he did linger somewhere, which all made it virtually impossible to find female companionship. Especially sexual companionship. Add to that the fact that he wasn't especially handsome, or muscular, or financially stable, and it was darned near impossible to consider the problem as anything other than a lost cause. So he stopped worrying about it. Put it out of his mind. Look but don't touch. And after a while, don't bother looking at all. Yet, there he was stewing in his barn bed about the pretty Miss Seavers.

I would do better to obsess about being caught by the agents.

It was certainly a better chance of coming to fruition. Far better odds than Kat suddenly getting a sexy hankerin' for a weird, paranoid, homeless guy, then getting out of her comfy bed, walking through the cold in her nightgown, and jumping his bones in a barn. Merrick laughed aloud, then stifled it. The thought of Kat sleeping with him was more preposterous than believing he turned into a huge, hairy beast with claws.

And there was another thing to add to the ridiculousness of the situation. She had only heard part of his story. He had neglected to mention that his alter ego was not only strong and resilient, but also a physically different being. Though he had never studied himself in a mirror before, and seeing through his other self's eyes was vague and disjointed at best, he did recall times when he had noticed his hands and arms being covered in something that resembled fur, and long claws extending from his fingers. Looking through the other one's eyes also comes from a taller perspective, so he assumed his alter self was larger as well. As far as he knew, he could be a werewolf, except that he thought those old myths were fairly silly. Full moon? Killed by silver? No basis in science or reality. Whatever happened to him was most definitely based in science, evidenced by all the lab coats who had hovered around him until he finally escaped. Nobody brought in a werewolf to bite him. *I don't think.* Anyway, none of the other myths were related to his condition, so he dismissed that. But he was indeed some kind of creature when he transformed. So, hypothetically, even if Kat could get by all the other obstacles of his lifestyle and still find him desirable, knowing he transformed into a hairy, razor-clawed beast would probably be a deal-breaker. *Sure, that's the reason.*

Still... Kat was right there in that house. He had been self-conscience as he showered, very aware that he was naked in the vicinity of a beautiful woman. Those two things didn't usually coincide, so he supposed that could be the reason why he was so preoccupied. Regardless, this fantasy wasn't helping his sleeping situation, so – *stop!*

He closed his eyes and tried to relax in the warm sleeping bag.

Think of something other than Kat.

A memory flashed of the sunglasses-wearing agents who burst into the hospital and started shooting innocent people.

Not an improvement. Try something else.

He pictured Sheriff Kind sitting in a dark room, chain-smoking a cigarette, and ordering sinister agents to cover up werewolf crimes.

Oh, for crying out loud! Merrick opened his eyes and stared at the rafters. If he wasn't going to be allowed to sleep, he might as well work on their little mystery.

Quinton Kind parked his patrol car on the side of the road and peered through the passenger window. A bonfire was burning in the

128

woods, not very far from the road, and not well concealed. In front of his car was a familiar super-duty truck. He expected to find it here, no laws were being broken by the owner being here, yet it bothered him all the same. The owner of the truck had zero respect for anything or anyone, further substantiated by him brazenly making a bonfire during the dry season, in woods filled with kindling. Just another of the countless reasons Tanner Fosse shouldn't be allowed in the inner circle. But that wasn't Quinton's decision. He sighed and pinched the bridge of his nose. It was late at night, he had long ago been done with his shift and should be home nursing a beer, yet here he was, still dressed in his uniform, having to go deal with this coddled moron because nobody else could or would do it.

Sheriff Kind crunched through the dry leaves, not bothering with stealth, and not needing a flashlight. The woods were lit well enough by the bonfire. Only when he was within the clearing did Tanner turn to face him.

"Quinton!" called Tanner, his mouth slack, a beer bottle in one hand. "Whatcha doin' sneaking up on us, big guy? Don't you ever go home?"

Sheriff Kind wanted to backhand the kid. Though Tanner was twenty-five and not exactly a kid anymore, Kind thought of him that way because he knew the boy when he was in grade school, and also because Tanner hadn't grown up at all. A dumbass in high school and still a dumbass now. Pure nepotism and ignorance were the only reasons Arthur Fosse let his son run things at his mill.

A little over a year ago, Arthur had decided to promote Tanner from a floor manager to vice president of operations. Tanner had been a piss-poor manager, more interested in petty whims and playing power games than running an efficient operation. But work still got done, probably despite him, and the oblivious elder Fosse believed his progeny was capable enough to eventually run the whole thing. It only served to bolster the little shit's belief that he was Teflon coated, and the townsfolk were his playthings. No matter what trouble he got into, Arthur Fosse always fixed it. Or more specifically, made Quinton Kind fix it.

Too many years. Too many God damned years.

The sheriff stood with his hands on his hips, shaking his head. "What the hell did you do?"

Tanner spread his arms wide, bearing an inebriated grin. "What? What's up your ass, Quincy? We can't have a little drink by a campfire anymore?"

"You know what I mean, you little shit," said Kind. "The Seavers' ranch. What the fuck were you thinking?"

Tanner kept his arms wide and took a long, exaggerated step toward Kind. "Pfft. That bitch whined I was on her property, then she shot at me. I already told…"

"No. The night after that, you moron!"

Tanner's arms slapped against his hips and the beer bottle fell out of his hand, spilling its contents into the dirt. He angled his chin up with a pursed mouth, mugging like he was insulted. "She didn't see shit. That all you're worried about? Hmm? Someone finding out?"

Sheriff Kind ground his teeth, restraining himself from drawing his gun and ending his troubles right here. Except, he was a dead man if he did. Fosse's little private army of professional gunmen would see to that. *God fucking damn it.* Those were the real enforcers of the inner circle's will, unlike Tanner's friends, currently staggering around the fire, who only played at being badasses.

Tanner followed the sheriff's gaze at the drunken posse, then turned back to Kind and snorted derisively. "Pfft. They already know. They were there." Tanner seemed distracted by something, then continued, "Except for one guy. He was a dick, so I fired him."

"You have no idea what you've done, do you? You never do."

"What the fuck? Kat doesn't know it was me."

"Actually, she fucking does," said Sheriff Kind. "Your belt buckle is in one of my evidence bags."

Tanner looked quickly down at his zipper. "Shit. So, that's where..." He shrugged. "Fuck it. Toss it away like you always do, big guy."

"And the drifter heard your voice. They know it was you."

"Scrawny dickhead." Tanner seemed to consider something, then grinned like he had just remembered where he placed a million dollars. "Hey! What if he just kinda disappeared? You know? He'd be a good one to add to the fire."

Sheriff Kind shook his head. "That's you and your father's solution to everything, isn't it?"

Tanner spit something on the ground. "Who gives a fuck how a problem disappears? As long it goes away. And you're good at it, Quinny. So just keep doin' it. You wanna keep your job, don't ya, **Sheriff**?" The last word was spoken with undisguised contempt. "Just do what you're supposed to do." He took a few awkward steps toward Sheriff Kind and slapped him on the shoulder. "Good dog. Good boy."

"The minute your father even has a doubt about covering for you anymore –," the sheriff paused for emphasis, but Tanner cut him off.

"What, sheriff? What'll happen, huh? You gonna shoot me?"

"In the fuckin' head," said the sheriff flatly. His gaze was unblinking.

Though Tanner tried to maintain a defiant pose, there was a noticeable uncertainty in his eyes.

"And one more thing," said the sheriff. "And don't fuckin' lie to me. Did you do that shit behind the diner a couple nights ago?"

Tanner looked genuinely confused. "What? Why? Why the fuck would we do that? You said that no one was allowed back..."

"Like you ever fuckin' listen to me, or anybody. Just guarantee me you weren't anywhere near the diner that night."

Tanner shook his head emphatically, an act that made him partially lose his balance.

Kind wanted to believe Tanner's answer. There'd be one less problem if it was true. Regardless, it still didn't solve the overall dilemma.

"None of you either?" he asked the hedging onlookers.

They all shook their head. One said, "Heard about it though. Sounds freaky. Wasn't you?"

Sheriff Kind gave the man a killing glare. "No. Because I'm not a sloppy idiot like you assholes. If I ever went on a killing spree, and believe me I'm considering it with you dickheads, nobody would ever find any evidence. You'd just disappear."

"Hey, nobody ever found any evidence about us before," said one of the drunken comrades.

"Because I got rid of it all, you fucking twit!" barked Sheriff Kind. "Right now I've got hair from one of your suits, and his belt buckle, sitting in my evidence locker. Plus a photo one of my deputies took of some marks in a rock, stating that they were made by metal claws from your suits. You think all that'll magically disappear on its own?"

"Oh, uh…" mumbled the drunk man.

"Fine," said Tanner. "So, we were at the Seavers'. But it wasn't us behind the diner. There's no evidence to hide cuz we weren't there."

Sheriff Kind rolled his eyes. "Yeah, well, that damned drifter was there, and he claims he saw someone in wolf suits back there too. The sunuvabitch'll probably tell the court that if I ever officially arrest him, so I gotta tiptoe around until I can get rid of that shit you left, or someone might be stupid enough to believe him. You follow?"

"But it wasn't us," said Tanner, looking genuinely confused.

Kind shook his head in disgust. "Doesn't matter. If someone in one of those suits gets fingered, whether it's you or not, everyone does." The sheriff sighed deeply, adjusted his hat, and glanced at all the men now gathered next to Tanner. He took a deep breath, then said clearly. "Do not put them on again, ever, until I say so. Understand? Ever!"

The men stood quietly regarding each other, seeing who might nod or agree to the sheriff's demands.

"Anything for you, Sheriff," said Tanner with a warped smile.

Kind once again restrained himself from shooting the idiot. *I'd be doing the world such a favor if I did.* Instead, he turned away and went back to his car. He had work to do. Work he had done many times before, and this one wasn't even as hard as many of the others.

Everything bad in this town started with the Fosses, and especially Tanner. And yet, Arthur owned everyone and everything. And the sheriff was his right-hand man, or bitch, depending on what mood Quinton was in. He had always found the weight of it heavy, and nowadays it felt even heavier with the crap that happened behind the diner. *Still a mystery how those thugs died.* He almost wanted to say "Fuck it all!" get in his car, and just drive until he hit one of the coasts. Screw Fosse. But it didn't work that way.

His life was borrowed and he knew it. The only question was whether it was worth the price. As he sat in the driver's seat, he considered the question, and not for the first time. By the time he turned the keys in the ignition, he had made up his mind. Not for the first time.

CHAPTER 17

Kat was surprised to see that breakfast had already been made when she awoke. Since it was her day off, she had slept in a little, though she planned on being up before her dad had to leave. It didn't end up that way, and by the time she got down the stairs, Del was gone and a Saran-wrapped plate of French toast and sausage links were on the counter. At first, she assumed that Del had whipped up something before he left, but then she remembered that Del had no idea how to make French toast. If the meal wasn't meat or something pre-made he could warm up, Del didn't know what to do with it. Zeus wouldn't have roamed around the house without permission, and neither would Javier. *Merrick?*

There weren't too many other possibilities unless she had breakfast-making ghosts. Culinary poltergeists aside, the breakfast was welcome, so she made herself a plate and sat down alone at the table.

As she ate, she heard a mild commotion outside. Thumping and clanging, along with familiar voices, not loud or distressed. Had her dad already come home? She figured she'd get the final bites down, then venture outside and see what's up. The door opened before she finished.

"Oh, morning, Kat," said Merrick, out of breath and in a good mood. "We didn't wake you did we?"

"Umm – no." Kat squinted, more in question than confusion. "What's going on out there?"

"Your dad came back, needed help getting the bull unloaded and put back in the pasture." Merrick ran a glass under the faucet, then guzzled down the contents. After a few deep breaths, he spoke again. "Just finished. I hope you don't mind that I cooked. Your dad was hungry, and I rummaged through the fridge and figured – you know."

"No, no. That's fine," said Kat. "Thank you. Tasted good."

"Thanks. I made sure there was enough left over for you."

"Zeus here too?"

Merrick shook his head. "No. Your dad wasn't expecting to bring the bull back so soon. Thought it was just going to be a checkup visit, but the doc needs room and said the bull was ok to return. Wasn't anybody here to help, so –." He ran a little more water into his glass, gulped that, then smiled.

Kat chuckled. "So, you're our new ranch hand now?"

"Temporarily," said Merrick. "Gotta earn my keep around here if you're stuck with me."

Merrick looked downright pleased with himself and Kat couldn't help but shake her head in amusement. After a shower last night, and despite the hard work this morning, he looked acceptably human. Hair brushed in a style other than greasy hobo, a little healthy sweat glistening on his otherwise clean, cute face.

Oh, my God! She shivered intentionally and dropped her head into her hands.

"Kat?" said Merrick, moving toward her. "You ok?"

"Yep!" she blurted. "Fine. Fine. Good. Yep."

"Ooo – kay," said Merrick.

"Sorry, ignore me," she said. "Sleep-deprived. Stayed up a little too late thinking about our sheriff problem." Not entirely a lie, and sounded good enough as an excuse as to why she was acting weird.

"Me too," said Merrick. "Hey, I got some things to talk about with you, but..." He pointed a thumb at the door. "I promised Del I'd help him with one more thing. Stay here?"

"It's my day off," she said. "I ain't going anywhere."

Merrick grinned apologetically, "Actually, I'm hoping you will be."

A few hours later, after a hurried muffin baking session, they were in Kat's jeep at the library parking lot. Kat had something complicated planned for herself, which involved acting, the muffins, and the possible use of "feminine wiles." She felt confident she could pull it off as long as nothing unexpected happened. Merrick's job was somewhat easier and only required him to nose around in the library hall of records, or more accurately in this little library, the rack of old-ass newspapers.

He requested to be given the history gathering mission, claiming he was very familiar with libraries in general (like she wasn't?). The other mission was to sneak a peek at some police records, which sounded more like something Kat should attempt anyway. She had friends in the department, or at least friendly acquaintances.

Before they had left, Kat had texted the sheriff saying that she was taking Merrick to the library. The anklet broadcasted intermittent GPS signals to the sheriff's computer system, so the text was meant to dispel suspicion where Merrick might be headed. She got no response.

Merrick got out of the jeep and nodded conspiratorially.

"Wait," said Kat. "What are you going to use to take the pictures?"

"Pictures?" He looked confused and held up a pad of paper and pen. "I'm just gonna write stuff down."

Kat grimaced. "Ehh. That'll take forever." She got an idea and dug out her cell phone. "Here. Use this." She pointed to the icon for the camera. "Touch here, it opens the camera, then just touch the little button to take the picture."

Merrick looked at the phone and darted his eyes up to her. "I think I'd rather you ask me to grow wings and fly."

"Cowboy up, Merrick," she said. "You're smart. You'll figure it out. Take a snap of any interesting pages and we'll look at them together tonight."

Merrick made a pinched face. "I'll try."

Good Lord, a four-year-old can work these things. "Ok. If you get done before me, I'll meet you here at the Jeep. If not – I'll find you in the library."

Merrick nodded. "Good luck."

Right. Into the wolf's den, I go.

As Kat approached the sheriff's station, she examined the cars in front. Sheriff Kind's car wasn't there. *Good.* Exactly what she was hoping for. She adjusted her blouse, made sure an extra button was undone from the neckline, and her hair was smoothed down. She preferred to wear her hair in a ponytail most of the time, sometimes pinned up while she worked, but rarely down. Just too much fuss to style it, and she didn't like the idea of primping. Today was different. She needed to look the way men liked her to look. Only for a little while.

As she opened the door to the sheriff's station, she reminded herself to put a little sway in her stride, careful not to bump or overturn the basket of muffins she carried in her right hand. The front desk deputy had his head down, scribbling something when she walked in. Without glancing up, he said, "I'll be with you in just one moment," and continued his writing. Kat stood in what she considered a prissy posture: ankles together, one knee slightly bent, hip cocked, hands daintily clasped on her basket in front, shoulders back to accentuate her breasts. Normally, she had no interest in playing the coquette, though she was perfectly capable of adopting the mannerisms if called for.

The first challenge was to get past the front desk. The station was designed so that the clerk's desk was surrounded by walls, a barrier to the remainder of the station, and once allowed through the side door, then all the deputy desks and rooms were accessible.

The deputy clerk finally straightened up and gave her a friendly smile. "Yes, ma'am, what can I… Oh, Kat! Nice to see you."

The deputy's name escaped her, and as she took two steps forward, she casually focused on the deputy's name patch: "L. De Garza." *Leo?*

Younger than her, she remembered he had hung around her and her friends when she was in high school. Kinda like a puppy needing attention. She had only occasionally spoken to him since they graduated, and he rarely came into the diner.

"Hi, Leo," she said.

De Garza grinned at her recollection of his name. "Hi! What can I do for you?"

"Well, it's kinda embarrassing," she started. "I came in here yesterday to help answer questions for a friend, and…"

"Yesterday? I was here yesterday. I didn't remember you coming in."

"It was late afternoon. Did you work the early shift?"

"Yeah. Yeah, that's why. Sorry. Didn't mean to interrupt. Go on."

The interruption was a mild example of why none of her high school friends liked chatty little Leo hanging around.

"Well, when I came in yesterday, I had a talk with Sheriff Kind about my friend and – well, it got heated, I got mad, and I left in a huff."

"Oh, that's too bad," said Leo. "Sheriff Kind is kinda a grouch sometimes. I'm glad I wasn't here for it."

"Uh huh. Well, I was supposed to talk to Deputies Pooler and Yellow Feather about something else and I forgot because I left all mad. I brought these blueberry muffins as a kind of apology. Would you like one?"

De Garza looked a little confused. "But I wasn't there the other day."

"It's ok. I made a lot."

De Garza shrugged and made a hesitant smile. He accepted one of the warm muffins.

Kat asked, "Is either Deputy Pooler or Deputy Yellow Feather in?"

De Garza tried to answer, but his mouth was full. Moments later, he had successfully downed his mouthful of muffin mush. "Think they both are. Go ahead, Kat."

He pressed a button on his desk and the side door buzzed. Kat kept a warm smile pointed at Deputy De Garza until she got through the door.

The inside of the station had a very simple layout. Just a single room with multiple desks in two rows and an aisle down the middle for walking. On one side of the room were glass partitioned offices. The largest was Sheriff Kind's office, trimmed in wood, with its window to the main room veiled by drawn shades. Kat glanced at it only momentarily before she searched for Simon or Max. Not exactly hard to find. Besides one other deputy busy making Xerox copies, Simon and Max were the only people in the room. Their desks were across the aisle from each other.

"Kat?" stammered Simon Pooler.

"Hi, Simon. Hi, Max." She walked over to Simon since he spoke first.

"What're you doing here?" asked Simon.

"Well, it's a little embarrassing. I was here yesterday to talk to Sheriff Kind about my friend, and –well, things got heated, I got mad, and said things I kinda regret."

"Yeah, we heard," said Max.

"You were here?" asked Kat.

Simon shook his head. "No, but we heard about it when we got in. Man, the ol' bear was in a shitty mood."

Kat grimaced. "I'm so sorry. That's actually why I'm here, to apologize. I feel bad cuz Sheriff Kind is a good man and a good diner patron. I brought blueberry muffins as a peace offering. Want one?"

Simon chuckled. "A good man? I don't know about that, but – hell yeah, I'll have a muffin."

Max shook his head at his partner. "Is there enough, I wouldn't want to…"

"Oh, I made extra for you guys. It's all right."

He smiled and took the offering along with Simon.

Simon mumbled through a cheek full of half-chewed muffin, "He's not here by the way."

Max hadn't bitten into his yet. "Doesn't like to stay at the station much."

I know. "Oh, I see. Well, I'll just drop this off in his office in a sec, but –." She bit her lip. "I was kinda hoping to get an update on the Tanner Fosse case. I mean, our bull's going to live, but…"

"Yeah, Tanner's a piece of shit for doing that," said Simon.

Max gave Simon a hard glance, then immediately blinked it away. "Well, technically, we can't say anyone did anything until they're convicted, and…"

"He did it," said Simon, still chewing.

"Aaand," continued Max, a little louder to overrule Simon, "Tanner hasn't been arrested or brought to the station for questioning since we've been here."

"Nothing happened to him at all?" said Kat, trying to act astonished.

"I'm sorry," said Max. "But I don't think so. Not yet anyway."

"Ehh, I can check and see what's up," said Simon.

"Would you please?" said Kat, almost squeaking in a girlish voice. *Geez, girl, ease up on the pedal.*

Simon turned to his computer station and wiggled the mouse to wake it up. Kat stepped behind him and leaned against his chair, her long hair falling on Simon's shoulder.

"Wow, these computers are old," she said in his ear, trying to distract him. She wasn't wrong. The terminals still used CRT monitors.

"Yeah," said Simon clicking on the database icon and tapping in his password. "Almost as old as dinosaur bones, or maybe Sheriff Kind himself."

"That's rude, man," said Max. "The guy's probably in his fifties but only looks forty. I wish I looked that good at his age."

Simon narrowed his eyes as he typed. "Max, we put up with you kissin' his ass when he's here, but when he's gone – knock it off, bud."

"Just sayin'," said Max, visibly shrinking in his seat from the put-down.

A list of names popped up and Simon scrolled through them. "Hmm," he eventually said. "No warrant for Tanner here. Kinda hoped we'd get one by now."

"Not even a citation?" asked Max. "A fine?"

Simon shook his head. "Nope."

"Oh," said Kat, putting on a somber tone. "Ok, thank you," she said as miserably as she could.

"Maybe Sheriff's gathering more evidence," said Max.

Simon made an offended face. "Come on. Kat deserves the truth, not some fantasy." He sighed and turned to face her. "He's a Fosse. We all do what we can, but…"

"I know," said Kat. "I know, and thank you both."

"If we find anything new, I promise we'll jump on it," said Max. "You know, keep it alive and on the sheriff's desk?"

"That's sweet, thank you, Max," said Kat.

Simon nodded enthusiastically. "I'd love a chance to bust his ass."

Kat smiled and touched Simon's shoulder. "It's ok. I guess I'll just leave this basket for the sheriff and go home."

Max directed his hand toward Kind's office.

"Thanks. I know where it is," said Kat. "I was there yesterday." She dabbed at her eye with her sleeve to feign crying. Men tended to

140

act overly gracious if they thought she was crying, and the awkward effect would help her do what she needed to do next. However, she worried she had laid it on a bit thick.

"The muffin was delicious," said Simon with a hopeful smile.

Max looked suddenly aware that he hadn't eaten his and picked it up.

"Thank you," said Kat. "Do you have a piece of paper and a pen so I can write the sheriff a note?"

Max got up a little too quickly and snatched up a piece of printer paper and a pen from his desk.

Kat smiled demurely and accepted the items. "I'll just be a minute. I'll leave it on his desk when I'm done."

They both nodded and Kat gave them a short wave as she strode to Kind's office, remembering to add a little extra sway so they'd stay seated and watch her instead of following.

She calmly stepped into Kind's office, noticing his desk wasn't directly in view from the door. *Perfect!*

She slipped behind the desk and took a moment to examine the items on it. A domestic disturbance report was open in front of her. Nobody she knew, which was odd. But that didn't seem important. There was a scrap of paper on the corner of his ledger containing a phone number with no name. She took the paper she had borrowed from Max and copied the number down. Might be important, might be nothing. She could decide later. Time was of the essence. The two deputies wouldn't be fooled for long.

She wiggled the mouse to bring up the sheriff's station home screen. It asked for a password. She recalled the keys Simon had pressed. Her fingers tapped: 817&tss!92. It took every ounce of concentration she had to memorize the password as he had typed it. She wanted to scream aloud when the password was accepted. *Yes!*

There was no time to play around or even carefully examine what was available. At any moment, someone might peek in at her. She clicked on "Personnel."

A display of rectangular fields came up with each deputy's name and vitals. Most she knew. She noticed Kind's profile and focused on it.

Quinton L. Kind, current address, *blah blah...* came from New Mexico, *yatta yatta... Born in '79?* Kind looked about that age, but for some reason, she expected him to be older. Everything about the man screamed old school, as if he came from the 40s or 50s. Nothing seemed suspicious to her, so she clicked out.

The criminal database looked interesting so she clicked that, knowing full well it may be the last thing she had time to do. God knows why no one had checked on her yet. The database came up with a very unfriendly UI. She had no idea what she was looking for, or where to start. There was a clear prompt for recent searches, so she tried that.

At the top of the list that opened was a name that surprised her. Not so much the name, but the address: Las Vegas, Nevada. Juan "El Sombra" Jimenez was connected with all sorts of trafficking (drugs, guns, girls). *Yeesh. Swell guy.* Three arrests, three plea deals. He also had a normal business address. *How the hell is a guy like that out and doing business on the streets of...?* She stopped and looked twice at El Sombra's business phone number. It started with "702." The number on the scrap of paper started with "702." She compared the two numbers.

What the f...? Sheriff Kind had handwritten the gangster's business number and placed it on the edge of his ledger. Why in the world would a Montana sheriff need to call a Las Vegas gangster? Her suspicious mind had an answer for that, but now was not the time for deliberating.

A thumping noise happened outside and her breath caught in her throat. *Long enough!*

Kat slapped the pre-made apology note on the desk next to the muffin basket, stuffed the notepaper with the copied number in her pocket, then stood up and acted casual.

Simon shook his head slightly as he stared at Kind's open office door. Max turned and gave him a quizzical look.

"You wanna tell me why we're letting her be in there by herself?" said Max. "It kinda seems like she's up to something."

Simon shrugged dismissively. "Oh, I'm pretty sure she's up to something."

Max cocked a brow as he eyed the office. "Well, whatever it is, it will get her thrown in jail if the sheriff finds out she's snooping around his office." He started to get up and Simon pulled him back down, thumping the rolling office chair against the desk.

"Maybe," said Simon, sounding more curious than concerned. "And maybe that's exactly what she's trying to avoid."

"What? What's going on, Simon?" coaxed Max.

Simon shook his head. "Not sure. But it has something to do with that Chaney guy. Kind is going after him, and she probably thinks he'll eventually get around to booking her for aiding and abetting. I think she's looking for blackmail dirt on the sheriff from our computers."

Max glanced at Simon, then Kind's office, then Simon's computer. Something seemed to dawn on him. "You think she was trying to learn the password?"

"Yup."

"And that's ok!?"

"No, but –." He turned his chair back to his keyboard and wiggled the mouse. "Maybe she turns up something important. Even if we find something, we can't indict him with it directly. Has to go through channels. Unless – it gets handed to us by an outside party. Hmm?"

"Jesus, Simon. Just because we don't like the guy, doesn't mean we should…"

"Max, the evidence from the Seavers' field is gone," said Simon. "The buckle, the hair, the pictures of the prints. Everything except the boot prints of that Chaney guy."

Max considered this, then looked at the page on his screen. He clicked on a few things then sat back. "Wow," he said. "Even the wolf prints."

"Yep." Simon took a deep breath. "There's been evidence missing on a lot of my cases. Kind's got an agenda. I don't know what it is, or why, but it's not right, Max. Something needs to be done."

"Simon, whatever trouble she thinks she's in will be seriously far worse if anyone finds out she's breaking into the database."

"I know," said Simon. "That's why I'm going to help her."

Max blew out a subtle raspberry. "They'll kick your ass out of the department."

"Fuck it. This town sucks."

Max shook his head. "Well, I'm not going to be a part of this. You're on your own."

Simon turned his chair to face Kind's office as Kat emerged. She flinched a little when she noticed them staring at her, then smiled, waved at both men, and quickly walked toward the lobby door.

"Good," said Simon.

Max watched Kat walk through the door to the lobby. His eyes darted to Simon, then back to the door. "Ok, I'll help her too."

Simon laughed in his throat. He rolled his chair over to Max's desk, slapped his partner's shoulder, said "Me first," then leaped out of his chair and jogged to the lobby door.

"Miss Seavers!" he called, sliding through the lobby door.

Though Kat had already exited the building, the front doors were glass, and he could see her stop and turn toward him. He bumped through the front doors and stopped a little closer to her than he had planned.

"Sorry," he said taking a half-step back. "I think you forgot this." He was talking a little too loudly, holding out a blank piece of paper.

Kat squinted at the paper and hesitantly took it.

"Listen," whispered Simon. "If you need more, let me know. I'll help you."

Kat looked a combination of shocked and scared. "More what?" she stuttered.

Simon shrugged. "I don't know what you just did, but – I can help if there's more you need."

Kat's nervous expression relaxed. A slender smile curled on her lips.

Simon gave a nearly imperceptible nod. "Max'll help too," he whispered and rolled his eyes.

Kat leaned forward and gave him a quick kiss on the cheek. "That's for you and Max both," she said. "Share, ok?" She giggled for a moment, then seemed bothered by the sound that had come from her throat. After a clipped wave, she turned and jogged across the street toward the library.

144

Simon touched the little damp spot on his cheek. *Share? Not a chance.*

CHAPTER 18

Sheriff Quinton Kind watched the headlights roll toward him. It was late afternoon, not typically dark enough for lights, but the woods were dense and the headlights probably helped the car navigate the tight path. Kind had been waiting nearly an hour, half an hour past when he had told the visitors to meet him here.

This little clearing in the woods was hard to find from the road, only a barely visible dirt path cut into the thick woods that used to be an access road to an old water tower. Leveled and moved fifty years ago, only the tower's concrete base, some access grates, and sawed-off struts remained. Since then, teenagers used this location as a nice, dark, hidden place to party and drink. The sheriff knew all about it, of course, and didn't raid the parties unless he felt things were out of hand. Oddly enough, if the teenagers knew what was really underneath the tower ruins, they would've stayed far away. Despite its secret purpose, today was just a convenient spot for a clandestine meeting. *And a little surprise party.*

The Cadillac Escalade came to a halt fifteen feet from the sheriff. He remained placid, leaning against his patrol car. The visitor's passenger door opened and a man stood up behind it. He was olive-skinned with black hair, wore a tapered leather jacket, a thick gold chain around his neck, and a gold glint to his eerie grin. A gun butt peeked out from under his jacket.

"You Sheriff Kind?" asked the man with the bored tone of someone who knew the answer.

"I am," said Sheriff Kind. "You Ernesto?"

The man shook his head. "No, cabrón. I make sure everything is ok before he comes out."

Sheriff Kind shrugged. "Suit yourself. Look around if you like."

"Maybe I will," said the man, widening the eerie, golden glinting smile.

He shut the car door and roamed around the circular clearing, staying close to the car, with his hands casually stroking his chest. A poor job of concealing his anxiety to keep his hand close to his pistol. Sheriff Kind made no sudden movement of any kind, only shifting once to ease the pressure on his feet. Gold Tooth paced around for a moment, then shook his head.

"I don't know, Sheriff man," said Gold Tooth. "Maybe I don't like this area. Maybe I don't think it's as safe as you say. Maybe you're hiding something."

"Just what do you think is going to happen here, ese?" asked the sheriff.

"You tell me, Mr. Small Town Sheriff man."

Sheriff Kind rolled his eyes. "I'm a middle-aged white man, alone in the woods, meeting several young, strong men with guns. That scary to you?"

"No, cabrón. Mira, too easy to hide men. Maybe we can't see them behind trees or bushes. Pero – ya lo sabes tú. Si?"

"Well, isn't that your job to go see if there's people hiding behind the bushes? Eh, pendejo? Your boss pays you to look around and you don't bother going farther than the car bumper? He can see the same thing you're seeing from the back seat, son."

Gold Tooth looked flustered at being insulted. Quinton guessed that few people probably ever talked back to these weasels. The wattage on Gold Tooth's grin dimmed considerably.

"You got a big mouth for an old man," sneered the gangster. "Maybe I tell my boss he shouldn't get out. He won't like it, cabrón. You waste his time."

"You're wasting *my* time," said the sheriff. "You're the ones who asked for this meeting. Your boss demanded a secluded place to talk. So here it is. You don't like it? Then go home. I have better things to do than sit around out in the woods, arguing with some greasy kid who thinks he's big shit because he carries a gun. Everyone in this state carries guns, chico."

Gold Tooth's grin morphed into a sneer. "Yeah, old man, I got a gun. See?" He pulled a mirror finish, chrome pistol from his holster, larger than an average pistol, possibly a .50 caliber Desert Eagle.

"Shiny," said Kind. "And expensive. Your mom save her stripper money to buy that for you?"

Gold Tooth's sneer stretched and he leveled the gun at Kind.

147

"Paolo! Enough!" shouted a well-dressed man who had just opened the back door. He glared at Gold Tooth, now known as Paolo, then faced Sheriff Kind. "I am Ernesto. I called the meeting."

Sheriff Kind tipped his Stetson. "Buenas tardes," he said. He hadn't moved from his leaning position on the patrol car, even when Paolo was threatening to shoot him, and Kind now straightened and held up a palm. "I'd shake your hand if your guard Chihuahua wouldn't try to shoot me with his shiny canon."

Ernesto moved smoothly and slowly toward Sheriff Kind. His head was held nearly immobile as he walked, like a pageant queen. He stopped within five feet of the sheriff.

"You have balls, Sheriff," said Ernesto. "I can appreciate that. So, I'll get to the point. I have seven of my men missing. Seven men I sent over here to help you with your little problem."

"True, it was my suggestion, but El Sombra wanted the problem fixed as much as I did. I'm not responsible for your men being careless."

Ernesto cocked his head. "So, they're all dead?"

Sheriff Kind nodded. "They didn't make sure the area was clear and got jumped by some drifter. Made a mess of 'em."

Ernesto shook his head with a disappointed expression. "One man? Just some drifter? This is what you want me to believe?"

"Obviously, I didn't see it. But I know there's ex-Navy Seals, or ex-special ops soldiers that could probably do that, and maybe this guy is one of 'em."

"That sounds like a lot of bullshit, Sheriff. And if I say I believe you, then I'd be as stupid as maybe you think all us gangsters are, huh?"

"Believe what you want, doesn't change anything."

"I see." Ernesto searched Sheriff Kind's eyes, probably for cracks in the armor. "And is this Chuck Norris, Rambo, superhero guy in jail so I can see him for myself?"

"Eh, not yet. You see, us cops have to find legal reasons to incarcerate someone, and even harder-to-find legal reasons to execute someone. But he should be soon."

Ernesto chuckled. "Seems like those legal reasons got conveniently forgotten a few days ago. Hmm?"

"That's a different matter."

"When it's your own ass, it is, isn't it?"

Sheriff Kind was tired of playing the trading quips game. "What do you want, Ernesto?"

"Restitution, Sheriff. To repay the families and widows who lost their loved ones."

Sheriff Kind was restraining a laugh but a little snort slipped out. "Distraught widows? Now you think *I'm* stupid?"

Ernesto ignored the jab. "Plus a little recompense for myself and Juan since we lost valuable employees."

"Uh huh. Exactly how valuable?"

"Ten thousand each. Seven men, so seventy thousand."

Quinton made a show of adopting a pensive expression, then pulled out his wallet. "A bit above my wage scale, so – how 'bout thirty-five?" He pulled out three bills: a twenty, a ten, and a five. "Five for each?"

Ernesto's face darkened. "Do not play games with me, Sheriff."

"No game. It's gas money to get you home. Take it or leave it."

Ernesto glowered at Kind, his breathing increasing in volume. Quinton put the bills back in his wallet and tucked that into his pants.

Ernesto brushed imaginary dirt from his sleeve, then said, "Since you insist on an insulting negotiation, Sheriff, my price just went up. Eighty thousand."

The sheriff met Ernesto's indifferent gaze with a hard glare. "If we had that kind of money to burn, we woulda spent it on professionals instead of bumblers who couldn't do their job without getting themselves killed and, by the way, alarming every law enforcement agent in the state," said the sheriff. "So, in essence, they failed. Big time. And maybe you pay for losers," the sheriff's eyes darted to Paolo, "but I don't. And those clowns are going to cost my town a whole lotta trouble, money, and blood before it's all over. So, unless you wanna contribute to *my* losses, I suggest you take your men with their shiny teeth and shiny guns, and get on back to wherever you make the rules. Because here, I do. And we're done negotiating. Comprende?"

"Yeah, I comprende, Sheriff." Ernesto calmly turned and strolled back to his Escalade. "But I don't think you do. How did you put it? One middle-aged man in the woods, all alone?"

Two other men suddenly opened their car doors and stood. A pale white man with a flat-top haircut and a bald Asian man. *Equal opportunity gangsters.* They both unholstered their pistols. Large caliber like Paolo's, though not shiny.

Sheriff Kind shook his head. "You don't wanna threaten me, Ernesto. You really don't."

Ernesto's eyes widened in amusement. "Oh? So, maybe there *are* men hiding behind the bushes? Hmm? Should we fire a few shots in there to find out? Or maybe shoot you and see what happens?"

"Just get in your car and go the hell home." The sheriff sighed and slid a cigarette from his shirt pocket. "Or – don't. You'll probably tattle on me anyway, won't you?"

"Tattle? To who?"

"Your boss, El Sombra."

"I'm the boss! Juan and I are – colleagues. But yes, I will inform him how uncooperative you were, and that you refused to pay our damages. And so, you had to pay with your life instead."

"Not smart." The sheriff produced a Zippo lighter from his pants pocket. "Either you behave and keep this stupid conversation to yourself, or we have to take drastic measures."

"You pissed me off, Sheriff. People who piss me off don't live long. Especially people who won't pay what they owe me. They get their tongue pulled through their neck before they die. But I'll forgo that part today." Ernesto walked around the man standing next to the open rear car door. "Paolo, Sacha, Kino," said Ernesto. "Prepararse."

Paolo's rapist grin was back on his face as he leveled his pistol at the sheriff again.

Ernesto slid one leg into the car and faced Sheriff Kind. "Better hurry and take some good puffs of your cigarette, Sheriff. It's the last cigarette you're ever gonna have."

"Eh, cigarettes will probably kill me someday," said the sheriff. He flicked open the Zippo's top. "But I'll still live longer than any of you."

Ernesto's other two men moved their pistols to aim. Sheriff Kind placed his thumb on the Zippo's igniter.

"Hold your fire," said a voice from the old tower ruins.

The gangsters jumped and twitched their aim around the clearing, looking for the source of the voice.

On the concrete floor of the tower ruins, a steel hatch squeaked open, and a tall man ascended to the surface with his hands raised. He had a tanned, fortyish-looking face with snow-white hair. His ensemble was an odd combination of flannel shirt, blue jeans, cowboy boots, and a long leather executive jacket. The man kept his hands at head level.

Sheriff Kind rolled his eyes and lowered the Zippo hand. "Arthur, what the hell are you doing?"

"Hey!" shouted Paolo. "Who the fuck are you?"

The newcomer smiled patiently. "Lower your aim for a moment and I'll tell you."

Ernesto took a deep breath then nodded at his men. "Talk fast, gringo."

The man slowly lowered his hands. "My name is Arthur Fosse. And let's just say if Sheriff Kind is the Secretary of Defense in our little berg, I'm the President. Nothing happens around here without my authorization."

Ernesto made a non-plussed face. "Ok, President Fosse. You gonna authorize my eighty thousand?"

"I'll consider it," said Fosse with a hint of condition to that answer. "First, may I ask how many of your guys are in the other car? I know there's another of your cars guarding the entrance."

"Why should I tell you that?" said Ernesto. "You gonna tell me how many more of your guys you have hiding around here?"

"I'll be glad to show our hand. I was just trying to come to an understanding before we do."

"No deal," said Ernesto. He spread his arms wide. "Here's all you need to understand. Pay me my money, or die with your Secretary of Defense."

Fosse faced Sheriff Kind who had folded his arms while all this banter was going on. "What's your guess?" Fosse whispered to Kind. "Two at the entrance? So, six total?"

"Yeah, pretty sure. Why do you care?" asked Kind.

Fosse gestured with a flared palm toward the gangsters. "I want them for the fire. They're excellent candidates. I could use five. If there's six, that's one too many."

Sheriff Kind shook his head in disbelief. "You take a lot of risk for your damned obsession, Arthur."

"Hey, gringos!" jeered Paolo, aiming his pistol at Kind again. "You payin' or you dyin'?!"

Kind ignored the toothy gangster. "A lot of risk," he repeated to Fosse.

He raised his Zippo to his cigarette again. Fosse lifted a single finger high. Kind ignited the lighter.

"One what?" said Ernesto.

A loud crack echoed through the woods. Paolo's head exploded in a bright spray of red and pink. Several gunshots dented the armor plating of the Escalade on all sides, and several more smashed the shatterproof windows.

Gangsters shouted and shrieked, covering their heads and ducking back into the SUV. One got a sloppy shot off at the sheriff, harmlessly passing overhead and smacking into a tree trunk. The driver kept his head low while shifting into reverse. Metal canisters crashed through the SUV windows, spewing pale yellow gas. Men in the SUV waved their arms frantically, coughing and choking. The driver gunned the motor in reverse, spinning dirt until the rear of the car uprooted a medium-sized tree, lifting the back axle a foot above the ground. Its back tires spun freely with no purchase to move the vehicle. Men inside the car slumped against seats, only getting one shot off that hit nothing. Yellow gas swirled in the SUV, billowing out of the broken windows.

Sheriff Kind gave Fosse a gas mask he retrieved from his patrol car, then put his own on. He raised his hand and circled it in the air.

Movement occurred along the ground fifty to sixty yards away from the clearing. At first, it appeared that the leaves and ground cover were coming alive, but soon, the recognizable forms of humans draped in Gillie suits began walking toward the sheriff and Fosse.

Fosse asked in a muffled voice obstructed by the gas mask, "The other team do their job?"

The sheriff plucked up a radio receiver and pressed the talk button. "Team two, check in."

"The other two are incapacitated, sir," said the voice on the other end.

Kind nodded before saying, "Copy. Good job. We're done here. Hit 'em with needles, I repeat needles, and bring the car here."

"Copy," said the voice.

Fosse opened the driver's door of the SUV and held up a syringe. The flattop-haired driver was still conscious, though unable to do much more than moan and wobble. Fosse plunged the syringe into the driver's neck. "Risks don't concern me," said Fosse. "I don't lose."

Sheriff Kind sighed and shrugged. In his mind, he was shaking his head. History was ripe with powerful men who believed they couldn't lose. They were all dead. And not by old age.

CHAPTER 19

Merrick sat at the kitchen table, scrolling through the library pictures on Kat's phone as she made dinner for her father. Although his snapshots came out fairly clear, the wording was so small, he had to zoom in to see most things, making him squint.

"You sure you don't want any?" asked Kat.

"Not hungry, but thank you," said Merrick. "I've eaten more in the last three days than I have in the last three weeks. Just not used to it."

She shrugged. "Yeah, I'm not hungry either. I had a couple of those muffins I cooked. Way too heavy. I'm not a pastry chef."

"Well, you're amazing at everything else, so…" Something in one of the pictures caught Merrick's eye. He temporarily froze his words in his throat, not noticing he hadn't finished his awkward compliment to Kat.

Kat glanced back to give a smile of thanks, then noticed his rapt attention. "What is it?" she asked.

He shook his head. "Maybe a misprint, but – I don't know."

Del suddenly entered the kitchen. "What's a misprint?" he asked, then looked at Kat. "Smells good, honey."

She rolled her eyes and smirked. "You always say that. Even when I'm making stuff you hate."

"Well," said Del, searching for an appropriate response. "I'm hungry, it smells good, and I promise to eat it, whatever it is."

Kat laughed. "Regular ol' fried chicken. Just for you."

"Then I'm definitely going to eat it."

Kat nodded and smiled, then she titled her head toward Merrick, an invitation to continue what he had been saying before Del came in.

"It's an article from twenty-two years ago," said Merrick. "Introducing Kind as the new sheriff. It says that he and Arthur Fosse were squadmates during the Vietnam War."

Kat dropped her tongs on the side of the frying pan. "Um, that's kinda impossible."

"I know. That would make Kind like seventy or eighty."

"I just saw his official birth date today. He was born in seventy-nine. Definitely after the war."

"Plus he doesn't look seventy or eighty even if he fudged the records."

"Why would he alter his birth date?"

Merrick shook his head. "Maybe he's a vampire and doesn't want anyone to be suspicious."

"Be serious," said Kat.

Merrick shrugged. "Ok, not a vampire. There are weirder things out there than vampires anyway."

"Like what?" she scoffed.

One is sitting in your kitchen. Merrick made no reply, just playfully rolled his eyes.

"The newspaper goofed," she said. "What's the point of a conspiracy like that?"

Merrick scrolled through another article and nodded. "Yeah, you're probably right. Here's the next day's edition and they printed a retraction, citing the previous day's error."

"See?"

Merrick mumbled to himself as he read. Then he said louder, "Says that they made a mistake, it was Fosse and Kind's fathers that had been in the same squad during Vietnam. Their sons were squadmates in Afghanistan. Apparently, same names, that's why they screwed up."

"Weird, but ok," said Kat. She set a plate of fried chicken in front of her father.

"Yeah," said Merrick. "Really odd coincidence though. Fathers squadmates, sons squadmates, same names, just juniors."

"Hmm," said Kat. "And I just saw his record. Didn't say junior."

Merrick shrugged. "Gets omitted in records sometimes."

He glanced up at Del who hadn't joined their conversation. Del made a hurried smile, then busied himself with his chicken. Earlier, when they arrived home, they had mentioned to him that they were investigating Kind and the strange circumstances of Gunn and Saunders' murder. Del had been against pursuing it any further. Yet, there he sat, quietly enjoying his meal as they batted around conspiracy theories.

Kat turned off the skillet and sat down as Merrick was doing a search for the Army squad number that had been mentioned in the article about Vietnam. He scrolled down the page.

"Huh," he said. "Well, they got this part right. Here's the platoon list, separated into squads – Quinton Kind and Arthur Fosse right in the middle."

Kat shrugged. "It's weird. Still doesn't mean they're vampires or something. Probably just their dads like the article said."

Merrick ignored the remark. His scrolling had come to a platoon group photo. He squinted as he reverse-pinched the picture to coax it bigger.

"Whoa," he said.

"What?" asked Kat.

"It's pretty much him. Younger, mustache, little thinner but – it's him. There. Middle row."

Kat nodded. "Wow, he really looks exactly like his dad. Hey..." She jabbed a finger at the screen. "Same for Fosse. I've only seen him a few times, doesn't like people, stays out of the public, but – he looks the same too."

Kat spun the phone so Del could see it. He seemed uninterested in viewing the picture, but humored his daughter. He waggled his head. "Yeah, they both do. Thinner, but – yeah, you're right. Apples from the same tree, huh?" He lowered his eyes to his dinner.

"Bizarre," said Kat, returning the phone to Merrick.

"Well, yeah. But I still say that gangster's number you saw on Kind's desk was more bizarre."

"I kinda wanna call it and ask the guy what's going on," said Kat.

"You can't be serious," said Merrick. "First of all, he wouldn't answer it himself. Somebody would screen his calls. Secondly, I wouldn't go playing around with this guy."

Del looked up from his plate. "Who?"

Kat shook her head. "Oh, I wouldn't. Just sayin' I kinda want to."

Del repeated, "Who?"

"Mexican gang lord from Las Vegas. Apparently, Sheriff Kind's been calling him about something. Or plans to. Sounds real fishy to me."

Del straightened up a little. "Las Vegas? Gang lord? Why would Quinton call someone like that?"

156

"We don't know," said Kat. "But he specifically looked his number up, then wrote it down on a piece of scrap paper. It was the only number on his desk. So I copied it."

Del's face pinched. "You better not go messing around with a gang lord."

"I'm not going to call him, Daddy," said Kat. "Maybe just research more about him."

Merrick nodded and touched the browser address bar on the phone. "What was his name again?"

Kat rolled her eyes up in thought. "El Something Jimenez. Um, El – El Sombra Jimenez. I think his real name was Juan."

Del's fork hit the plate, sounding like something had broken. Both Merrick and Kat jumped. Merrick sprang up and craned his neck to scour the kitchen, thinking an agent might have suddenly burst into the room. His heart was thumping like a machine gun.

"Sorry," said Del. "Sorry. I didn't mean to... I just was surprised at the name you said."

"The name?" said Kat. "El Sombra Jimenez? Why?"

Del wiped his mouth with a paper towel, appearing to need a moment to explain. "It's just that when Zeus moved here from Vegas, he told me it was to get his sister, Espy, away from her gangster husband. Said the guy murdered people, dealt drugs, trafficked women. Espy had no idea who he was until after she married him. Couldn't divorce the guy because he owned all the officials. So – she and Zeus fled and came here."

"We know the story, Dad," said Kat.

"Well, I'm, uh – pretty sure El Sombra was the name of the guy."

"Really?" Kat looked stunned. "Why would...? Dad, you sure it's the same guy?"

"Think so," said Del. "That's the name I remember, unless I'm remembering wrong. Ask Zeus."

"Ooooff. Only if we have to," said Merrick. "A touchy subject, for good reason. Who wants to tell Zeus the gangster he ran from is back in the mix?"

"Ugh," said Kat. "It's bad enough Saunders has been in the news so much. Although, Espy's murderer being dead probably isn't a terrible thing, but bringing it back up all the time, and now El Sombra getting involved, it'll just drive a dagger in Zeus's heart."

"Saunders?" said Del. He shook his head vigorously. "He didn't murder Espy."

Kat gave her dad a harsh look. "Dad, just because he was a friend doesn't mean the guy didn't do it."

Del continued to shake his head at his daughter. "I'm telling you, I don't think so."

"Dad," said Kat like the name disappointed her. "It makes complete sense. Saunders raped her, got her pregnant, she tried to sue for child support, and he killed her. He was a councilman, another one of Fosse's tight little circle of corrupt friends. If we're right about Sheriff Kind, and he's covered up other crap around this town, you can bet he helped Saunders get away with that too."

"Then why'd he let him get killed?!" Del noticed his response came across more like an outburst, so he shrunk a little in his seat and lowered his eyes. "I, uh, mean that you guys have been trying to say that Kind was in on this murder plot in the back of the diner. So – if it was him, why would he save Saunders just to let him get killed later?"

Merrick had no answer for that. Kat didn't either.

Del grimaced and tucked his chin into his chest. "Sorry. I didn't really want to be involved in this discussion. I wish you guys would drop it. I, uh – I won't get in your way anymore. I'll just…"

"No. No, it's ok," said Merrick. "And you have a good point, sir."

Kat looked unconvinced. "What if Saunders was going to make some plea deal? Spill something bigger, something that Kind was involved in, if they got him to court? Maybe that's what Kind was afraid of."

Merrick was lost in thought as Kat spoke. In a mumble, but spoken aloud, he said, "Afraid enough to ask a gangster to kill the guy."

"Hmm?" said Kat.

Del was staring at Merrick too.

"I, uh, said afraid enough to ask a gangster to kill Saunders." The theory took shape in his head as spoke. "Zeus stole his sister from this El Sombra guy, right? Even though the guy was a criminal, he might've actually loved her. Or at least, wanted vengeance if he found out she'd been killed."

Kat nodded. "I only saw her once, but she was beautiful. Really beautiful."

"Right," continued Merrick. "So, someone tells El Sombra that the guy who raped her and killed her – supposedly," he made pointed eye contact with Del, "has been found and is being brought back to Vegas for a trial. Without cop escort. Only a bounty hunter. Once Saunders gets in police custody, he's untouchable, but when he's with Gunn?" Merrick paused to make sure his train of thought was on point. "There's an opportunity to get Saunders before he can make it to custody. So, maybe Kind is the guy who alerts El Sombra. Maybe he tells him where Gunn is, what the plan is. Gunn would've been obliged to inform the sheriff of his intentions, right?"

"That's what I thought," said Kat. "And Simon told me he and the other deputies hadn't been notified, so – could be they were supposed to stay clear. Not know anything so they couldn't interfere."

Merrick nodded. "El Sombra hurriedly sends a bunch of his guys to enact vengeance, and whatever information Saunders had dies with him."

They all sat quietly for a few seconds, ruminating on what Merrick said.

Kat finally broke the silence. "So what was so important that Saunders knew that would make the sheriff want him dead rather than in jail? Was it just because Kind covered stuff up for him, ya think?"

Merrick shrugged. "Maybe Kind didn't cover up anything for Saunders. Like your dad said. Maybe Saunders was always running from Kind."

"So, we're really sayin' that Kind had Saunders hit?" asked Kat.

Merrick nodded timidly. "It's the scenario that answers the most questions."

Del sighed. "Well, *if* he did, it wouldn't be for the reasons you think."

"What reasons then?" said Kat.

Del shook his head. "I knew Saunders a long time. He sure as hell wasn't a saint. And he might have even killed people before the thing with Esperanza."

"Um – what!?' said Kat.

"Speculation," said Del, frantically waving off his daughter. "But he did love Espy. We talked about her. He really loved her."

Kat gave Del a laser stare. There was no need to interpret the intent, judging by the mention of a middle-aged man, and employer, and possibly murderer, getting his twenty-two-year-old housekeeper pregnant.

"It's not like that, Kat," said Del. "I don't think he got her pregnant. I don't think anything happened between them at all."

Kat crossed her arms and drummed her fingernails on her tricep. "She took him to court."

Del was noticeably getting more anxious, which was understandable since Merrick could feel the heat from Kat's mood. "That wasn't his story. He confided in me a little," said Del. "They did both go to court, but to testify against someone else on Espy's behalf."

Though Kat's mood hadn't cooled, her fingers stopped their tattoo. "Who?"

Del shook his head. "I was told it was best if I didn't know."

Merrick was surprised that Del knew as much as he did, and was willing to let that answer hang in the air. However, Kat wasn't in the least mollified. She leaned forward in her chair, her laser stare boring into Del without blinking.

"Who?" she repeated.

"I don't know," said Del.

"Why didn't you tell Zeus all this stuff?"

"I – it wouldn't bring Espy back."

"It could'a helped find the real killer," said Kat. Her eyes narrowed even further as she stared down her father. "Or do you know who that was too? It was the guy they took to court, wasn't it?"

Del shook his head. "They never told me. I – really don't know."

Kat was grinding her jaw and breathing louder through her nose. "You bite your lip when you lie, Dad," said Kat. "It's why everyone beats you at poker. You've lied to Zeus, and you're lying to me now. People have died because of these stupid secrets, and Merrick's going to be charged with murder, and maybe me for helping him, just because Sheriff Kind can do whatever he wants around here, and you know stuff that can help but you won't tell me. Keeping your

160

secrets is more important than helping your daughter save her friend. So, forgive me if I'm just a little ticked off. Either you tell me the whole truth…" She slammed her fist on the table, causing Merrick to once again jump up in his seat. "Right now!" snapped Kat. "Or I pack my crap and leave. You and your secrets can rot here alone in this piece of shit, lying-ass town."

Jesus! Merrick had missed the family feud aspect of this speculation and wasn't sure how to react. He sat statue still waiting for whatever happened next.

"No cussin' in this house, Kat," said Del, attempting to regain dignity.

"Then I'll leave. I'm dead serious, Dad." Kat wasn't accepting any kind of fatherly intimidation at the moment. She reiterated, "Who'd Espy take to court, Dad? You know. Who!?"

Del looked ready to cry, blinking away potential tears. His eyes dropped to his plate of chicken and he seemed ready to use it as a pillow. "We suspected Tanner," said Del. "Nobody saw it, but everything pointed to him. When we asked Espy, she refused to say. She only said she wanted to leave town. She looked scared. Like – someone had threatened her life if she spoke out."

Though Kat had relaxed a little, she wasn't making a move to comfort her obviously distraught father. "What about Saunders, Dad?"

Del kept his eyes down. "He told me he had offered her money to stay and testify with him. Bring the Fosses out into the open."

"Oh," said Kat, looking much more subdued. She glanced at Merrick. "There were rumors about money. They said Saunders tried to pay her off. Hush money."

Del shook his head and pressed on. "When they got to trial, the evidence had been altered. They had nothing to convict the Fosses. At least, that's what Saunders told me. He was scared. For both of them."

Kat reached across the table for her father's hand. He gave it to her.

Merrick interjected, "Scared of who?"

"Arthur Fosse," said Del. "He owns everything around here. People too. We all suspect Sheriff Kind does his bidding, but – there's never any evidence. Kind arrested Espy on bogus charges

161

before she disappeared. And when Quinton went to arrest Saunders for her disappearance, Saunders ran."

"So Fosse gets Kind to arrest his enemies," said Merrick. He kicked out his foot to show the blinking anklet as testament to being in the know. "But they still have to be convicted in court."

Del shook his head. "For the dangerous ones, there's no court. Fosse makes people disappear. Forever."

"More gangster hits?" asked Merrick.

"No," said Del. "I can't say."

"Dad! Damn it, how?" demanded Kat.

"It's too dangerous to say any more about this," said Del. The tears started streaming down his cheeks. "They threatened me if I ever said anything. You two stay the hell away from Quinton and Arthur. You'll end up dead."

Kat got out of her seat and walked around the table to her father. She pressed up against his back and tightened her arms around him.

"I'm sorry, Daddy," she said. "But staying away from them isn't a choice anymore. They're going after Merrick. They'll make him disappear."

CHAPTER 20

Kat worked the early shift the next day. Nothing of interest happened other than Sheriff Kind once again didn't come into the diner. Was he avoiding her? Or was her conspiracy-obsessed brain being overactive? She assumed if Kind found traces of her snooping around in his office, he'd confront her, so perhaps it was good news that she hadn't seen him.

When she got home, her body was tired, but her mind was just getting started. The men were off somewhere doing ranch stuff, so she had the house to herself. Now she had to figure out what to do with the remainder of her day. Though she wanted to dive deeper into the information they had gathered thus far, she needed more of Del's insight to make the weird pieces fit. She knew she had been overly harsh last night and couldn't ask her father for additional disclosures without an apology and a much more delicate strategy. If he even knew anything further to give.

In the meantime, she could catch up on some chores she had put off like laundry and cleaning. It's not that Del was a chauvinist, it was just that his generation didn't place enough emphasis on teaching men to take care of their own homes. He did try, he was just terrible at anything domestic. Kat preferred things were done right rather than have to go back and fix poorly done tasks. Re-folding laundry took the same effort as folding it right the first time. She sometimes wondered if Del being a simple, old-world man was one of the reasons why her mother left. *Sore subject. Move on, girl.*

To distract herself as she worked, she thought about drawing alternate conclusions to their mystery, but that seemed counterproductive. They were already making assumptions based on very incomplete data, and no great literary detective would do that. More data was needed, then she could see where the new information led rather than inventing more cockamamie theories by herself. She preferred to bounce the ideas off Merrick anyway. His collaboration felt comfortable.

She wasn't blind to the oddity that she had lived in this town roughly twenty years, knew everyone, liked some of them as friends, and hadn't found a man that lit her fire (*I'm not counting drunken hookups, and thank God none of them were Tanner*). Yet, here comes a grimy drifter, penniless (*not true, he has a dollar left*), weird, and paranoid about some shady agency that's after him (*although, after last night's conspiracy chat, shady men coming to kill us all isn't as big a stretch as it was before*), and suddenly he's invited into her home, showering in her bathroom, and making her want to... *Don't you dare think it! Stop that!*

Why? Yeah, he's not Chris Hemsworth, but he's smart, funny, worldly, resourceful, and has a genuine character I haven't seen in a long time. Plus a freaky superpower. And he's not exactly uncute.

Ugh! You're better off playing with your toy. Plus – he's going to leave. He HAS to leave! If you believe him at all, it's not safe.

How's he gonna leave? I have to help free him before he can leave.

Fine. So, help him, let him leave, then forget him.

She caught herself sitting on Del's bed with an armful of his laundry. Her intention had been to just drop it off, then her inner monologue took over and she must've sat down to let it play out. She didn't normally loiter in his room. There was an unwritten rule of privacy in a father/daughter house, and it seemed only fair not to pry into his sanctum. Fortunately, there was no one here to make excuses to. Del was outside with Merrick, Zeus, and Javi, doing something in the pasture, and even if he came back in, she'd hear the door smack shut downstairs. It was a squeaky, noisy door regardless of how many times they oiled it. She hadn't planned on snooping on anyone else (*one hair-pulling adventure in the sheriff's office is enough*), but since Del obviously knew more than he was letting on and the subject was sensitive to him, maybe a little snooping would be safer than asking.

God, you're so full of shit today.

Shut up.

She peered under the bed. Nothing but dust bunnies. The nightstand only had a book, reading glasses, antacids, and a condom. *Dad?* She shrugged. Should something unforeseen happen one night and her dad brought home some woman from a bar – better to be prepared. *Fine. Eewww, but – fine. Moving on.*

She went through his chest of drawers, bypassing his skivvies. If something important was there, she didn't want to start the conversation with, "I found this hiding in your underwear." The closet was the last reasonable target, so she decided she'd do a once over of it, then call it quits and not mess around anymore in his room.

The clothes were hung by color (her doing). His books and cases were stacked neatly on his closet shelf net to wadded sweaters. There were two shoe boxes that looked promising, so she pulled one down.

Inside were her old school projects, homemade Father's Day and birthday cards, and a few assorted items from when she was a kid. *Aww.* She wanted to go through them, but now was not the time. That box was placed back on the shelf and the other box was pulled down.

Within it were mostly letters. When Kat pulled back the edge of one to see who they were from, her breath caught in her throat. The letter was signed, "Anjie Seavers."

Mom.

Kat had been given her mother's middle name. Anjelica Katheryn Seavers was a pretty, wanna-be actress who had frequented Del's bar when they lived in Austin, Texas. Anjie was there most nights and had a running tab. Kat only knew Del's version of the story: how they met; how he was a decade older than her and was surprised when their casual flirting led to something serious; how he couldn't imagine why a young, beautiful, fashionable lady would be interested in a flannel-shirt-wearing bar owner; how Mom got restless and left when Kat was four. Kat had never really known her mother's side of the story. Maybe it was in these letters. Though Kat didn't think she had time to deal with this now, she couldn't help skimming at least one of them.

"Dearest Roy," it started. Kat recalled her dad telling her that Mom had called him Roy. Delroy was his real name, he preferred Del, but Anjie called him Roy anyway. *"I'm sorry it came to this. You're much better at this than I am. It's not what I'm built for. I never felt right staying at home, being a wife and mother..."* Kat skipped past that page to the next. Most of her life she had lived

165

alone with her dad, and she had been told her mom had cheated on Del, decided she wasn't good at raising children, left, then came back and, in a twist, tried to claim full custody to get enough child support money to live on. Del offered to sell his bar, give her almost everything he had if she just let him have full custody. She had agreed, took the money, and never saw, called, or wrote to Kat ever again. Kat had never forgiven her, and now the letters in front of her could be proof of what her dad said, or more evidence that he had kept things from her. She swallowed hard and read on.

At the bottom of the second page, *"My new apartment in New York is near Broadway. I'm hoping to try out for a few plays. If you ever make it to New York, maybe you'll see me in one."* The third page talked about her career aspirations. The fourth page was short. She claimed to have two dates for the night and had to run. *"Hopefully, someday, Katheryn can forgive me. I wish her the best."* Kat tucked the letter back into the envelope and looked at the return address. There wasn't one. Their own Montana address was clearly penned though.

Mom knows where I am, but doesn't want me to know where she is. Kat shook her head. She wanted to cry, and felt like she'd have to punch herself if she did. Her dad may have lied or concealed things from her about Templeton, but he had told her the truth about her mother. All these years, she was hoping to find some nugget of information that her mother just made a big mistake and would come back begging for forgiveness. Though her mother probably didn't deserve forgiveness, Kat wanted the opportunity to decide. This felt like a needle in that tiny balloon of hope.

In the box was a photograph of her parents, sitting at a bar counter, arms around each other. Kat had seen pictures of her mother a few times and had foregone looking at any for probably a decade. Now she examined her mother's face with scrutiny. The woman was nearly her twin. *Damn it.*

In all her years, she had never once heard her dad say, "You look just like your mother." Numerous times he had told her how beautiful she was, how more beautiful she had gotten each year, etc. Now she knew why he never said it. *I'm so sorry, Daddy.*

The urge to cry nudged at her again, and again that was not going to happen if she could help it. Instead, before the day was out, she'd give her dad an extra long hug and not tell him why. Then she'd open a bottle of Jim Beam and get drunk. And then bury her head into Merrick's shoulder and tell him she was sorry for screwing up his life. Then he'd tell her he was sorry for screwing up hers. Then maybe they'd screw each other for real.

What!?

Hey, stuff happens when I drink. I've drunk-fucked far worse.

That's a bullshit excuse. Drunk or not, you just want to fuck him.

Ugh!

She slid the top on the box and crossed back to the closet. In a hurry to leave the room and find a chore to escape her randy thoughts, she tripped on the door frame, bumped an old yearbook on the shelf which began to fall off. She lunged to catch it and tried to trap the book against the far wall. As she pressed the wall, it swung open.

Oh, shit!

The wall was on hidden hinges and opened into a whole new room. Whatever was in there was completely dark and nothing could be seen. *Oh, no. Oh, boy. Dad's been hiding weird secrets, and now there's a secret room in his closet. This isn't happening.*

Their life used to be boring. Del raised cattle on a subpar ranch. Kat was a waitress in a POS diner. They had been here for twenty years and nothing weird had happened. *Not true. You've just not cared before.* She cared about Espy, but, still... *secret murders, secret plots, secret lies, secrets, secrets, secrets.* And now a secret closet room. *Fuck me.*

Kat let the secret wall-door swing shut, tucked the book back onto the shelf, then exited the room in a jog.

Merrick had spent the entire day helping Zeus and Javi in the field. Del drove the tractor doing something unrelated. The combination of Merrick's unfamiliarity with the tasks, and the fact that he paused every ten minutes to scan the woods for spying agents, made him a far slower worker than he would like. Neither Zeus nor Javier complained, and seemed genuinely happy for Merrick's help, and claimed it took them less time than normal because of it.

Even though the woods weren't full of sneaking agents, nor were unmarked cars invading the driveway, Merrick still expected something bad to happen at any moment. Whenever it did, he planned to run into the woods, leading his pursuers far away from Kat and Del. He didn't care what happened to him as long as Kat and Del were safe.

A few days ago, you were pretty concerned about what happened to you.

Things change. The first priority was not to make the people around him victims of his circumstances. Especially, people he cared about.

He could try to deny that Kat and Del meant that much to him, but he wasn't delusional about his own feelings. He was a realist. The world was a difficult, dangerous, and deceitful place on its own without making it harder by lying to yourself. His concern for Del and Zeus was based on human decency and friendship. His concern for Kat was more than that. Despite all the effort she made in demanding people not try to take care of her, it only made people try harder to take care of her behind her back. She was something to fight for, and in his case, avoid getting into a fight for. Or at least avoid doing something that could get her hurt or killed. That was Merrick's main concern about waiting for dangerous men to track his GPS signal to this ranch, and possibly destroy everything.

One day had gone by already with no sign of them, and another was almost in the books. He had expected it would take the agents only hours to find him, yet nothing so far. Had he miscalculated? Was he giving them way more credit than he should? He had been on the run a long time – was he even worth chasing anymore? If he didn't have to run, would it be possible for him to find a place to settle, get a job, live under a roof, and just become another average, ordinary citizen?

Nope. The first time you get mugged, or have a car accident, or slip in the shower, Lord help anyone around you.

Speaking of showers – that last one felt so good. It had honestly been years since he'd had a hot shower. If Kat and Del didn't mind, he'd like to enjoy that luxury once again before anything else happened. If it ever would.

After the sun had set, Zeus and Javi got into their truck to head home. Del and Merrick walked into the house to find Kat alone at the kitchen table, a drink in her hand and an open bottle of Jim Beam next to her glass. Bowls of mashed potatoes, vegetables, and the remainder of the fried chicken crowded the middle of the table, ready for them.

"Hey, honey," said Del as he walked in. "I didn't think you liked to drink anymore."

She shrugged. "Once in a while." Her speech wasn't slurred, but there was a hint of inebriation in its slow delivery.

She stood up and crossed the room to Del. Her sudden, forceful hug took Del by surprise and he glanced at Merrick, bewildered.

"I'm sorry for before," she said in a sweet tone. "I love you, Daddy."

Del looked ready to tear up. "Aww, honey, I love you too." He patted her back as she continued to hold him to her. "I should've told you the truth," he said, "but they threatened me if I stirred up anything. I didn't want anything bad to happen to you."

"I know," she said. "It's ok."

It took a few seconds before she let Del go. He kissed the top of her head.

They all sat around the table for a while, chewing on food, chatting about cute memories from Kat's childhood. The conspiracy talk had not been brought up by either Del or Kat, and Merrick got the impression it was intentional. Eventually, Del got up and excused himself to take a shower and go to bed.

Kat had gone through half the bottle of Jim Beam, mostly by herself. And was still coherent, but noticeably wobbly. Del had partaken of a finger or two on ice, and Merrick abstained. He still didn't feel right being unprepared for agents to bust down the door at any moment. *And maybe you're as paranoid as everyone thinks you are.* Right now, his concern was whether Kat's little binge was a sign of something else wrong.

Merrick patted Kat's hand. "You ok?"

She smiled tiredly and turned her hand to grasp his. *That's new.* "I'm fine," she said.

"You just look like you could use an ear to bend."

Kat met his eyes and, for a moment, gazed deeply into his without blinking. It was like she was trying to see into his head. She frowned, then rested her head on her hand. "Why are you so damned nice, Merrick?"

Merrick blanched and straightened in his chair. "Umm – sorry? I'll try to be – meaner?" He shook his head. "What's the matter?"

"Nothing," she said, examining him like she was deciding something. "You're just too nice, and smart, and sweet, and cute for a greasy ol' drifter."

"Uhhh, ok." He reached for the bourbon bottle assuming she'd had too much.

She snatched it cleanly away. "I'm still pretty nimble when I'm drunk."

"I can see that." He held up his hands in surrender. "So, nothing's wrong? I mean besides the stuff we already talked about?"

She shook her head emphatically. "Nope. Everything's fine. But you know what? There's something wrong."

"Uhhh – huh. Ok, so tell me."

"I can't tell you," she said, turning her head melodramatically away. "But you know what?"

"What?"

"There's something I can't tell you. You know why? Cuz it's a secret."

"Right. So, what's the secret you can't tell me? It's ok, you can tell me. I won't say anything to me."

"Ok," she said and grinned. "No, wait, I can't. Cuz I don't know what it is."

"You don't know what the secret is?"

She nodded, then shook her head. "It's my dad's. He's got a secret door in his closet. It's all dark. I couldn't see anything. You know what's in there?"

Merrick raised his brows. "No. What's in there?"

She shrugged testily. "I said I don't know. It's a secret." She clanked the bottle spout against her glass and splashed more onto the nearly melted ice.

"Save some for tomorrow," said Merrick and managed to swipe the bottle away before she could protest.

"I'm tired of secrets," said Kat, downing her latest pour. "I want to trust everyone again."

"Well, if it helps, you can trust me," he said.

She smiled. "I know. I trust you, Merrick."

"Good. And right now, you can trust me that you need to get to bed and sleep this off."

"If you say so," she said. "I'm not sleepy." She cranked open a huge yawn that resembled a lion's roar.

Merrick stood and helped her up. "Then you can sit awake in bed and think of all the secrets you hate."

"Ok."

She could walk, though not straight, and not without support. Merrick slowly shuffled with her up the stairs, his arm around her waist and her arm over his shoulder.

"You better not try anything when we get to my bedroom," she said.

Merrick chuckled. "I'm not that kinda guy. I promise I won't try anything."

"Why not?" she protested. "Don't you think I'm pretty?"

"Uhhh," he stammered. "Yes. Yes, of course. Very pretty."

"Good." She leaned against her doorframe. "But I don't have sex with guys just cuz they get me drunk."

"Uh huh," said Merrick, not sure if he should correct who was responsible for her condition.

Kat's eyes were staring at nowhere in particular. "I had a lovely night. Thank you."

"Sure. I guess goodnight then."

She closed her eyes and started to slide down the door, headed for the ground.

"Uh oh. Wait…" He hooked his elbows under her armpits. "Let's get you all the way to the bed."

As long as he held her up, she had enough leg coordination to make it to her bed. She sat heavily on the bed, then proceeded to take her shoes off – poorly.

"Let me help with that," he said.

He got both shoes and socks off before he noticed she had already unbuttoned her pants and had them halfway down.

"Oh, whoa," he said. At first, he was going to try to hoist them back up, but that would place his fingers dangerously near body parts he was trying to avoid. It might be better to just yank the pants off the rest of the way. He tugged at the cuffs and the pants slipped off, which was enough undressing for his comfort, so he turned back her sheets and coaxed her under them. As she fell toward the pillow, she hooked an arm behind his head and pulled him with her.

An indiscernible word squeaked in his throat that was meant to be an exclamation. His loss of balance put him nearly on top of her, bracing with both arms to keep the last inch of distance between them. It was still a compromising position. She took it as a cue to pull her face to his. She kissed him hard and sucked on his top lip. *Oh, man.* He wanted to return the kiss – wanted to with every Y-chromosome in his body – but even weird, paranoid drifters have morals, and this was no way to make love to an incredible woman. He pulled his lip away from her suction, then gently kissed the top of her head.

"Kat, in any other universe…" started Merrick. He sighed and sat on the side of her bed. She stared at him with questioning, heavy-lidded eyes. In contrast, he was trying to keep his eyes off her. "You are the most beautiful, amazing, wonderful person I've ever known in my miserable life, and being here with you is the happiest I've been – maybe ever." He shook his foot and the anklet jiggled. "Even with this thing on. You're drunk, not thinking clearly, and you're just being sweet again to a lonely drifter. Even that mistaken kiss is the nicest thing that's happened to me in – as long as I can remember. Thank you. But I should really go and let you sleep it off. If you woke up next to me in the morning, you'd regret it, and I'd feel terrible for letting you."

He risked meeting her eyes and found her still staring at him. She had also been unbuttoning her blouse as he spoke. *Even drunk, she's nimble.*

"You talk too much," she mumbled as she started on the fourth button.

He grasped her wrists, and as he prepared to say something to her, her eyes suddenly closed and her head lolled to the side.

Ok then. Her shirt was open enough that most of the roundness of her breasts was exposed. He reached to refasten the buttons, then hesitated, afraid of what else he might see – or do – if he got too close. He retracted his hands, then drew the sheets and comforter up to her neck. *Close enough.*

She had already started to snore. It seemed safe to leave the room now.

He shut the door carefully, then steered toward the stairs to head back out to the barn. Before he descended the first stair, he stopped and thought of something. Taking a step back, he leaned to peer into the spare bedroom. His borrowed clothes from yesterday were cleaned and lying on the bed ready for him to change into.

Merrick smiled. *Well, since you went through the trouble...* Though he may not get to make love to a beautiful woman tonight (or probably ever), he could console himself with a hot shower. *I think I deserve that much.*

CHAPTER 21

The same straw floor that was so comfortable to Merrick the previous nights was about as loathsome tonight as a bed of porcupines. In a single minute, he shifted three ways inside his sleeping bag, then repeated the process every other minute. The problem was the sleeping bag didn't contain Kat's warm, naked body. The barn was not her bedroom. Despite being closer than he had been in years to someone, he was also lonelier.

He had weaned himself from wanting things, conditioned himself to be content with the simple things life offered. None of that was ok right then. A special kind of happiness was in that house fifty yards away and he had turned it down because of his gentlemanly principles. There were times when he envied people like Tanner who just took what they wanted and gave the middle finger to consequences. The irony was that, despite Merrick's gentleman's code, he still turned into an uncontrollable, craven monster from time to time. Tanner was always one, yet nobody hunted him for it. Merrick's monster-self did as much damage as Tanner, if not worse, and yet here he lay, cloaked in his morality like it canceled out both the anxiety he suffered and the chaos he caused. *Kat deserves better anyway.*

And you don't?

As Merrick thought about the glimpse of her toned, bare legs, her panties slipped low on her waist, her open shirt pushed wide by her breasts, he reached down under his shorts. Though he had left her peacefully sleeping, in his imagination, she was very awake. In fact, she was standing in the barn doorway, silhouetted against the moonlit haze, wearing the same partially unbuttoned shirt atop those perfect bare legs. Walking slowly, deliberately toward him. Fantasy Kat didn't seem to care that it was too cold to be dressed that way. The final few buttons were undone and the shirt fell open to her panties. *No. Stop.* His hand jerked away from his groin.

He had never felt guilty for masturbating before. The object of his fantasy was also not usually sleeping so close-by. It just felt wrong.

Like he was doing the very thing he had refused to allow himself to do in her bedroom despite her invitation. It was still a violation. Fantasizing and masturbating was fine, he just shouldn't use Kat. At least, not here.

He rubbed his face with his fingertips to force reality back into his brain. Perhaps his preoccupation with sex had dimmed his senses because only then did he notice a noise very nearby.

Feet crunching on crisp grass. Someone was outside, coming closer. *Shit!*

Merrick leaped out of his sleeping bag and snatched up a pitchfork. It had been placed next to his bedding specifically for this purpose. If an agent was approaching the door, it occurred to him that they would number more than one. Maybe they were surrounding the barn at that moment. Was there another way to get in? He quickly searched for alternative entrances, seeing none. Just the front door. Unless they broke through the wall, the door was their way in.

He snuck to the front wall and flattened himself behind the door hinges. When the person came in, Merrick would tackle them and then see who it was. Give himself the upper hand first, then decide if he needed to ram the pitchfork into their chest. The door creaked open. Moonlight slid through, interrupted by the shadow of someone moving. A dark human shape draped in something like a loose overcoat stepped into the barn.

Merrick dove at it, expecting to impact a man's firm body along with the sharp edges of a rifle or gun holster. The body he was pressed against was softer and smaller than a man. The person under him yelped as he fell on top. The moonlight through the door was just enough to catch the trespasser's face.

"Kat?" he choked.

She nodded enthusiastically, trying to subdue a cough.

"God, I am so sorry," he stammered. "Why…? What're you…?" He knelt above her, mouth slack, utterly stunned. A moment ago, she was in his fantasy, standing in this very doorway, and now she was actually here? The coincidence was crazy and he reasoned that he'd fallen asleep, dreaming something that just happens to feel real. Unfortunately, his erection from that previous fantasy was hyper-real and poking into Kat's stomach.

175

"That's twice tonight you've ended up on top of me," she said with a hoarse throat, warding away the last cough.

"Sorry," he said as he stood up, offering her his hand. "So sorry."

"It's ok," she said.

Straw was embedded in the blanket she had draped around herself. His hurried attempt to brush her off was doing no good. "God, you've got straw everywhere," he said. "Come over here. I've got a flashlight. I'll get 'em off."

He led her to a hay bale next to his bedding, knelt on his sleeping bag, and rummaged around in his duffel for the flashlight. The batteries were somewhat low, but it was enough light to pluck off the stray straw needles.

"I thought you were, uh, one of the bad guys, you know?" he said as he swatted at straw protrusions. "Didn't mean to... Are you ok? Did I hurt you? Why did you come out...?"

She pressed a finger to his lips and said, "Shh." Her fingers caressed his before she switched off his flashlight. The straw-infested blanket was suddenly shucked off to reveal a loosely tied silk robe open to her navel.

Merrick was stunned. *What's she doing?* "Kat? What's going...? Are you still drunk?"

She shook her head. "You really do talk way too much."

The belt was untied around her waist and the robe fell open. Only a pair of panties was underneath. A different pair, lacier, than the ones he had seen earlier. The robe slipped from her shoulders and onto the straw floor. She stood above him, naked except for the panties.

Oh – my – God. He didn't think he'd ever see a perfect body like that except on the cover of a fitness magazine. The spare moonlight sneaking through the barn cracks made her skin look luminous and silver. "Uhhhhhhh mmmm aahhh," mumbled Merrick.

She chuckled once in her throat. "It's kinda cold in here, Merrick," she said and folded her arms over her breasts.

"Yeah. Right. Sure. Ok." He unzipped his sleeping bag so it was completely open. She accepted the offer, stepped in, made a show of laying down, then smiled as he continued to stare.

"I'm warmer now, but I'm all alone," she said.

He swallowed and said numbly, "I promised I wouldn't try anything. And if I get in there, I will definitely try something. A lot."

She reached to him and brushed her fingers against the erection straining in his shorts. Just a gentle touch, yet the feeling was so alien and erotic to him, he almost lost control right there.

She chuckled again. "I'm not drunk anymore. I'd just like a simple night with you. No strings. Please get in here."

He did. After shucking off his shorts, his nervous fingers fumbled with closing the sleeping bag zipper.

"No. Just the blanket I think," she said.

His own blanket was handy and he yanked it on top of them.

She wiggled to get him in the precise position on top of her. Although he was physically ready to enter her, he worried he would last no more than ten seconds, and her gamble on him would be a huge disappointment. That was almost a worse thought than never getting to be with her at all. So, to prolong the moment, he began kissing her neck and slowly working his way down.

Her breath skipped and she moaned slightly before saying, "Mmm, that's nice, but..." she reached down and stroked his member. "It's been a year and a half. I just want you inside me, ya sweet, goofy man."

He shook his head. "I don't think you understand." He kissed her throat. "I haven't done this in *many* years." He kissed her clavicle. "If we did that first," he kissed the valley between her breasts, "We'd be done by now."

She laughed heartily. "Delay tactics, huh?"

"Yup." He kissed the top of her breast. "Now shut up and let me pleasure you." He circled her areola with his tongue. "If I can remember how."

"Mmmmm," she moaned and raised to meet him, massaging his scalp with her fingertips. "Then take your time remembering."

They had fallen asleep naked, and even after waking up, still lay quietly together. Merrick stared at the barn ceiling, or rather past it, replaying the night's memory in his head in hopes he wouldn't forget. He had expected that Kat might have thanked him for his service then trotted back to her house, but she was still there. If she had used him, she still was. And if she *was* using him, who cares? However, it didn't feel like that.

Her fingers traced the edges of the scars on the upper region of his chest.

"Do you remember where you got any of these?" she asked.

"Pretty much all of them," he said.

"Did they hurt?"

"God, yes. Just because I heal fast doesn't mean getting shot or stabbed doesn't hurt like hell. The thing that hurts the worst is when my heart stops."

She shifted so she could see his eyes. "That can happen and you still – live?"

He nodded. "Happened next to the diner, I think. Things get hazy when the other one takes over."

She took a deep breath. "Why do I always get involved with weirdos and monsters?" Her burgeoning grin told him she was trying to tease him.

"Hey, I may be a weirdo but I'm only half monster," he said.

"Half sex machine," she said, pinching his butt.

"Nuh uh. No way was I that good."

She giggled. "Ehh, how would I know? It's been a year and a half. Nothing to compare it to."

"Boy, you build me up, then tear me right back down, don'cha?"

She leaned forward and gave him a gentle kiss on the lips. "Best sex I ever had, monster boy."

He shook his head. "If I accept that compliment, you'll just tell me there's nothing else to compare it to."

"Pessimist," she said and snuggled into his chest. "Still – thanks for thinking I haven't had much sex before."

He stroked her hair and tried to refocus on the ceiling. The word "monster" was echoing in his head. He had already told her he was an abnormal being, modified in a lab, and carried around an alter ego that emerged and wreaked havoc in uncontrollable fury. *What else does she need to know?* She may think his alter ego looked human. She may picture him as just some juiced-up guy with maybe extra muscles and – *what? Green skin?* Maybe that too. Whatever her expectation, he doubted it was what he really looked like.

178

He had never seen himself in a mirror or photograph, and only had glimpses of fur and claws to gauge what he might resemble. He could be a giant cat for all he knew. Or a werewolf. *No, no. The moon and silver stuff is bullshit, remember? Yeah, whatever.* His other self wasn't a man. Man-like, along with something animal. And that brought him back to why his alter ego was important to his current thoughts. She joked about being with a monster, but –he really was one. Would that be a deal-breaker later?

What later? What deal? Are you going to stay?

The only reason he hadn't left was that the sheriff had a literal leash on him. The only way to stay out of jail was to either prove who killed Saunders (if it wasn't the sheriff), or get the sheriff arrested for corruption and accessory to murder. *Or run anyway?*

The anklet could be broken by an industrial cutter, which may even be on this ranch. Once it was cut, it would alarm the sheriff and he'd burn rubber to get here. If he was in town, it may take about twenty minutes to arrive. Since Kind had shown an insufferable obsession with keeping an eye on Merrick, perhaps he'd have a squad car parked nearby on a stakeout. Might be watching right now. At best, Merrick would have a twenty-minute head start against tracking dogs and an eventual posse. At worst, he'd be caught immediately and be put on Death Row. Maybe a few extra years spent appealing the ruling. Although, the rumor was that the judges are bought and sold here, so an appeal probably wouldn't matter in the end.

If I get conjugal visits, might be worth it. He had forgotten how good sex was, especially with an amazing woman like Kat. It was almost worth dying for. Almost. *No, but seriously, she is.*

Kat nudged him out of his mental wanderings by tapping him on the stomach. "Hey, there was something I actually wanted to talk about last night. It made me really anxious, which is why I got drunk."

"Yeah? What is it?"

"I accidentally looked in my dad's closet and..."

"Accidentally?"

She rolled her eyes. "Ok, I snooped in my dad's closet. I was looking for more information, you know, so I wouldn't have to coax it out of him like… well, that was a bad scene before."

"Yeah, I get it."

"Anyway, I found some old letters from my mother which had me freaked out some."

"Freaked out? Why?"

"My mom, uh, left when I was little. She essentially sold me to Dad, then went off to New York to be an actress."

"Oh. Wow. Ok."

Kat shrugged. "The letters just confirmed what I had been told. Which means my Dad didn't lie to me all these years. He only lied about Tanner and Kind because he was worried about my safety."

"Well, I don't know anything about your mom, but I coulda told you Del was genuinely worried about telling you those other things."

"There's been a lot a' weird shit going on and I needed to trust him. And I do. Sorta. But…" She cut herself off and breathed deeply.

"Ok, what's the but?" asked Merrick.

"He's got a secret room that's connected to his closet."

"Ooohhh," said Merrick. "I wasn't sure you were telling me legit things last night."

"Some of it was legit. Some of it… I'm a weird drunk."

"A little. And a nimble one."

She rubbed her face with her palm. "Yeah, I remember sayin' that. I remember most of the things I do when I'm drunk. Kinda grosses me out sometimes when I… never mind. Anyway, I didn't look in there, it was too dark, and I felt guilty already. I don't know if there's anything weird in there, if it's a big deal, or not. But – it's there. And it's one more secret he's kept."

"Mm hmm. Yeah, that doesn't sound good. I wouldn't jump to conclusions though."

"No, I won't." She ran fingernails over Merrick's chest. "But it'll eat at me until I know what's in there."

Merrick wasn't sure what to think about that. Whatever importance Del's secret room and personal secrets may or may not have to the mystery involving Kind and Fosse, if they poked around to find out, that crossed a line and jeopardized a father and daughter's relationship, and probably Merrick's friendship with Del as well.

Which won't matter when you leave.

180

Right. There's that too.

As if Kat read his mind, she asked, "You still think you hafta leave?"

Though he wanted to say anything else, it would be a lie. "Yeah. I do." He kissed her head. "They'll come for me eventually."

"They haven't come yet. Maybe you're not as important to them as you think?"

Maybe. He had wondered the same thing earlier. But it seemed more wishful than convincing. He said nothing and nuzzled her scalp.

"Maybe I could go with you," she said. "Travel the country for a while."

Merrick got the twinge of tears in the corner of his eyes. "That would be incredible for me and lame for you."

"You don't know me. I wanna travel. Been saving up for years to do it."

"Aww, Kat, that's… I would love nothing better. Seriously and truly, but – something will happen. They'll catch me, and they might hurt or kill you. Even if they don't, I might turn into the other one and hurt you myself. I couldn't live with that. As much as I want it – we can't."

She nodded. "You're a weird man, Merrick Hull." She kissed one of his scars. "And I'm still glad I did this."

"No regrets?"

"A few."

Merrick stiffened and bent his head to meet her eyes. She was tucking her face down to conceal her grin.

When she looked up, her grin had widened. "But there's still time to make some more regrets." She shimmied to get on top of him. "Anything left in the tank?"

"I'm just your sex slave, aren't I?"

She kissed the underside of his jaw, breathing hot on his throat as she said "You got a problem with that?"

No, ma'am.

CHAPTER 22

Kat's mind was wandering as she toweled off from her shower. She had only teased Merrick about having regrets. She didn't. The closest thing to a regret was that her plan for a once-only, casual, no-strings-attached rendezvous had not gone as expected. She wanted more. The only orgasms she had ever achieved before were on her own, not from any of the scant physical relationships in her past. Merrick had just given her three from two go-rounds. He would eventually leave, so it should be easy for her not to get attached. That was the part of the plan that failed. She wanted him around. How long? Undetermined. She wasn't in love, but... She really liked that he was here. Maybe that's all it was.

Sounds like denial.

Maybe. She wasn't interested in a romantic relationship. Didn't want anything that tied her down to a particular place, certainly not here, hooked into a mortgage, raising kids, she and her husband suffering soul-crushing jobs to pay for their growing family. Sure, kids and a husband someday, just not now. Not for a while. Merrick should've been safe, he didn't stay put, was unable to have any of that other stuff, and even if they fell for each other, it couldn't last, and certainly wouldn't lead to the mortgage in the suburbs. It all seemed perfect when she decided to offer herself to him last night. Now she had a small doubt. Would it really be ok when he left?

If he ever leaves. Then, there's that. Eminent arrest awaited Merrick if they couldn't find Sheriff Kind a suitable, alternate murderer. Unfortunately, the answers they uncovered wouldn't help their situation. The actual men who killed Saunders were dead, the man they worked for was a high-profile gangster, and the man that hired them for the hit was probably Kind. Even solely pinning the murder on the gangster would suggest that Kat and Merrick knew about Kind's involvement, so they'd be right back to the same problem. There were no options left that would compel the authorities to take Merrick's anklet off except to indict Kind. And how the hell hard would that be?

Saunders apparently tried it and died. If a high-ranking councilman couldn't do it, how could a waitress and a drifter accomplish it? So, her worries about Merrick leaving may be unwarranted since she could see him whenever she wanted in prison. The whole situation made Kat sick.

When she got down to the kitchen, breakfast had already been made by Merrick. Nothing special, just some eggs and toast, which Del was happily devouring. Merrick was just setting his own plate on the table and gave Kat a big smile. She smiled back. In her mind, she was stifling a scream.

Del reminded her he had business in Great Falls and would be gone most of the day. He and Merrick chatted while she spooned some eggs on a plate.

Her mind was elsewhere, wondering if they had industrial-sized bolt cutters that could snip off Merrick's anklet. Though she knew it would immediately alert the sheriff, maybe he couldn't get here that fast. There might be a half-hour window to put distance between them. If she packed her things quickly, put Merrick in her Jeep, they could be at the reservation border before they were caught. Though Merrick would insist she not accompany him any farther, she would be a fugitive too. Officially aiding and abetting. After she let him out, she could circle around the long way (a very long way, through Idaho), then head to the airport and catch a flight to begin her European trek. On the run instead of free and easy, though maybe it wouldn't matter way over there. Burt would expect her at work, so she'd have to call him from the road to tell him she quit.

She only had two bites of her eggs when there was a knock at the door. Kat and Merrick gave nervous looks to each other. Del calmly put his fork down and wiped his mouth.

"It's probably just Zeus," said Del. "You two are paranoid."

Del left the kitchen and Kat tried to relax. Her father was right, and despite the predicted dire circumstances, that didn't mean it would start this minute. The front door squeaked open and Kat heard a man's voice talking to Del. It didn't sound like Zeus. It also didn't sound like Sheriff Kind.

A moment later Del walked back into the kitchen followed by Max Yellow Feather. The deputy looked anxious.

183

"Would you like some breakfast?" asked Del. "I think there's still some…"

"No. No, thank you, Mr. Seavers," said Max removing his hat. "Hello, Kat. Mr. Chaney."

"Max?" said Kat. She realized she should say something more welcoming. Max had never come into their house before. There'd never been a need to. Considering current events, she feared Max may be here on official deputy business to arrest Merrick. "Um, please sit down."

"Thank you," said Max, sliding a chair from the table. "I, uh, guess you're wondering why I'm here."

Kat nodded, saying nothing.

Max was kneading his hat and struggling to force a casual smile on his face. "I'm not here on legitimate business. I don't know how long I can stay."

Kat raised her brows and looked at Merrick.

Max explained further. "I faked a report that you had seen someone suspicious around your property and I was coming out here to investigate. I just can't tell you what I need to say over the phone. I – think our phones are monitored."

"What's goin' on, Max?" said Kat, wariness in her voice.

"Ok," said Max, expelling a deep breath. "I did some research for you. Actually, Simon and I both did. We couldn't get a moment to tell you about it without being overheard. This way was all I could think of. Simon wanted to come too, but he's stuck partnering with the sheriff on patrol today. I – think Kind suspects something, wants to keep an eye on Simon."

"Max?" Kat put her hand on top of Max's to get him to focus. "What's wrong?"

"Alright. It's what we found out about Kind and Saunders. Simon called Jeremiah Gunn's secretary. Got lucky finding her because she was only in the office to pack her stuff. She said Gunn wasn't commissioned by anybody for Saunders's capture. Saunders called them to turn himself in."

"What?" said Kat.

"Saunders contacted Gunn first. Said he'd turn himself in if Gunn would take him to the Las Vegas police to enter a plea deal. Very specific about it. Gunn had to agree otherwise Saunders wouldn't give his location."

"Did Saunders say why?" asked Merrick.

"Not specifically," answered Max, "The inference is that he had something on someone here and thought all the local judges were too corrupt. Since the woman he's accused of kidnapping and murdering, Esperanza Moreno, is still listed as a Las Vegas resident, he would have been handed over to Las Vegas police eventually anyway. Using Gunn to transport him keeps him out of our system."

Kat nodded conspiratorially to Merrick who nodded back.

Max continued. "Gunn was supposed to notify the sheriff about the capture, but there's nothing entered in the database. And none of us were ever told. However, Gunn's secretary said she called Sheriff Kind herself to give him a heads up."

Everything Max said, so far, was backing up their suspicions.

Del had gotten up to pour a cup of coffee for Max, who accepted it. "Thank you," said Max to Del, then turned back to Kat. "Gunn keeps a location-broadcasting app on his phone at all times in case something bad ever happens to him and they need to send help. It's pretty easy to find him on it."

"So, if someone wanted to hunt him or Saunders down," said Kat, "not hard to do."

"Yeah," said Max. "Somebody knew where Gunn was and ordered the hit. Maybe they waited until they found a good place like the back of the diner to do it."

Kat was suddenly feeling very guilty about demanding Jeremy park his car behind the diner that day. The assassins would've killed him at some point anyway, but it wasn't a good feeling to know she had provided the ideal circumstance.

Max only paused briefly. "We tried to ID the assassins. The van was stolen in Great Falls, so no help there. None of the bodies had identification on them, so we sent out inquiries to other departments. We took pictures of the, uh – heads that were in the best shape to be identified. We got positive IDs on two of the corpses. They both came back as wanted men from Seattle. Edward Iona and Stefon Bryan. Both were suspected of working for a Pacific seaboard trafficking organization that moved kidnapped girls across the borders. Bryan and Iona were wanted for rape, assault with a deadly

185

weapon, accessories to murder, plus trafficking. When Iona was fifteen, they put him on trial as an adult for the murder of his parents, but they couldn't convict him. Real piece of work. Anyway, the traffickers are headed up by a guy named Ernesto Montoya, who's the main supplier to a drug dealer and pimp named Juan Jimenez, known on the street as El Sombra. Iona brought in the women to Ernesto, who supplied Jimenez with prostitutes. And guess who was on Sheriff Kind's search index?"

Kat obviously knew. She also wondered if she had misinterpreted that information and the sheriff was just digging into the corpses' identities.

Max answered that unspoken question a moment later. "Jimenez. Kind's inquiry didn't occur after the murders. It was the day before. Those guys in the van were triggermen for a multi-state trafficking and kidnapping organization under Jimenez's thumb, and they showed up at the most opportune time to kill Saunders. We assume Gunn was just in the way. Witnesses eliminated."

Merrick gave Kat a conspiratorial look and a quick nod. Kat recalled Merrick's story about being stabbed by the leader, possibly Iona, and being told it was because there couldn't be witnesses.

Max took a sip of his coffee, then continued. "Zeus admitted to us a while ago that he had taken his sister away from Las Vegas to escape El Sombra. And now, assassins who are associated with him just happen to show up when Gunn captures the man suspected of killing her? The only people, besides family, that knew Esperanza had come here was the sheriff's department. And the only people who knew Gunn was here were Gunn's secretary, Sheriff Kind, and Saunders. Unless Saunders ordered the hit on himself – you get the idea."

"Yeah, we get the idea," said Merrick.

"There's more," said Max. "All the evidence we collected from your ranch is gone. Everything except Mr. Chaney's footprint and boot photo. I hate speculation, but there's really only one person who's capable of dumping it without a trail. I'm fairly certain Sheriff Kind is erasing anything pointing to Tanner and keeping only what indicts Mr. Chaney. I don't have an official answer as to why."

Merrick shook his head, looking miserable. It didn't take a genius to know that the screws were tightening and Kat knew who held the screwdriver.

Max took an awkward pause to sip his coffee, then continued his disclosure.

"The rest of what I have to tell you is speculation on my part," said Max. "I feel confident about it though. I looked through all the evidence of the Saunders, Gunn murders. It's not our case, so Simon and I had to sneak looks, but – something odd happened to the knife that killed Saunders and Gunn. When we originally picked it up, it didn't have any fingerprints clear enough for an analysis. None of the weapons did. The assassins used gloves. Useless to process the fingerprints, so we didn't bother. Still – the knife had been marked as sent to the lab for fingerprint analysis. I checked with the lab and they hadn't received anything from us. But the knife is gone from the evidence locker. I feel certain that Kind is intentionally altering the record and the evidence so it can reappear and be marked as positive for somebody's fingerprints. And I think I know whose fingerprints will magically appear on it."

Merrick sank into his seat and closed his eyes.

Kat shook her head and took a deep breath. What Max was inferring seemed pretty plain. "He's going to frame Mm... Frank?"

"Seems like it," said Max.

"What the hell can we do?" said Kat, her throat tightening. "How're we supposed to go after Kind? He's too strong. Fosse'll protect him, and he's got too many powerful people in his pocket." Kat's emerging tears were unexpected and unwanted. She smeared the start of the first one with her wrist. "They're gonna kill him, Max."

Max was silent for a moment, then said. "Not if I can help it. I can't let a law enforcement officer, even my boss, get away with something this bad. I – uh, already sent a report secretly to Internal Affairs. It's probably not enough to convict him. Maybe it starts an inquiry that might impede his plans, you know, put a spotlight on anything he does from now on, and maybe those things will raise flags at IA. I had to try. Once Kind finds out we've done this stuff... Well, Simon and I are looking into moving somewhere else. Maybe find a sheriff station in Idaho if we aren't blackballed."

Kat slapped her hand on her mouth. "Oh, my god. Can't you…? You guys shouldn't do this."

"Who else is going to, Kat? You said yourself he's too powerful for you to try. And the only way to convict him is to go through the proper legal channels. Yeah, any time a sheriff is corrupt, it's risky for the deputies to report it, but it's downright impossible for anyone else."

Kat didn't have a rebuttal. Her tears were coming faster and she wasn't easily keeping up with wiping them away. "I'm so sorry, Max."

"No, Max," said Merrick. "It's my fault. Just by coming here, I ruined everyone's lives. I…"

"It's fine," interrupted Max, his tone terse. "We don't have much time. Listen, I didn't just come here to talk to you. I came to – unlock Mr. Chaney's anklet."

"What?" blurted Merrick.

Max nodded. "If I unlock the anklet, it won't alarm. It will show up as deactivated, and it won't notify the sheriff immediately. He'll only notice when he checks it later today. Maybe it will give Mr. Chaney an hour or two head start. I'll claim it was on when I visited and I have no idea how he got free. Might be enough time to get into the reservations before they catch on. So – if you're willing?" Max met Merrick's eyes. "Get your stuff together as fast as you can and I'll unlock it when you're ready."

"Oh, my…" stammered Kat. "Max why would you…?"

"Kat," said Max, then paused for several seconds before continuing. "Whether you like it or not, we all look out for you. And what Kind is doing to your friend is criminal. And even if I didn't care about that, it's just a matter of time before he gets around to charging you with aiding and abetting a murderer, or fugitive, or something like that. Once he knows that you're onto him, and he might already, he'll find ways to get at you. Eliminate anyone who can testify against him. I can't let that happen. I've had a crush on you since I was in high school, and if I can't even help someone I care about, I sure as hell don't deserve to be an officer of the law."

"I – I – uhh," mumbled Kat.

"I shouldn't have told you that," said Max, rubbing his eyelids with tense fingers. He blinked the stress away and met Merrick's eyes again. "Just make sure you get away safely, ok, Frank? I know that's not your real name. Doesn't matter. Just stay alive."

"I will," said Merrick. "Thank you. I don't know how to repay…"

"Save it. Listen, there's one more thing," said Max turning back to Kat. "I took a photo of an indentation of metal claws next to your pasture. I've been following the wolf people legends for a while. Folks laugh at me, but I still think they're real. Sheriff Kind got rid of that evidence too, and I think I know why. I confirmed something else while I was doing research. All the disturbances, all the disappearances, all the reports of the wolf people kidnapping and eating people, it was all just silly talk until about twenty years ago. We have records of random missing persons that date back fifty years and only twenty years ago did people go missing in specific numbers. Twelve people missing every year. All of them with a criminal background or formal accusations. Some were escaped convicts. Some were paroled. Some were accused and acquitted. All had been through the system. Even Zeus's sister was accused of selling drugs and acquitted. Hers smelled like a set-up though no one had any proof. Most of us assumed Saunders had it concocted, except that he was the one who put up bail. It didn't make any sense at the time. In any case, she was set free and planned to leave the state the next day. Then suddenly she goes missing. And it was around the time of year that these wolf-men sightings ramp up.

"I don't think the wolf-men are some mystery monsters. I think they're just men, like the ones you saw on your ranch. And I think the Fosses, at least Tanner and his friends, are involved. I believe they wear wolf suits that have metal claws, and they use 'em to assassinate people that they want dead. So, they amp up this legend and use the wolf disguises to do it. I don't know who runs it all, but considering the stuff with Tanner, I'd wager you're already on their list."

There was a lump in Kat's throat big enough to impede her breathing.

Max audibly sighed. "I have no idea if Kind is one of them, but I'm sure they're connected. Why else hide all the evidence I submitted? I think they're the ones that killed those assassins. The whole scene was a slaughter that looked more like vicious animals than any one man." To Merrick, Max said, "It's why I believe you

189

had nothing to do with the deaths behind the diner. Just wasn't human. And if the wolf-men had seen you there, you'd be dead too." Max shifted his eyes to Kat. "Anyway, whether you believe all that or not, I'm telling you there are people in this town that are dangerous enough to kill anyone in their way, and I don't want to see you as another victim. You, Zeus, your father, nobody's safe from these people. They'll kill all of you just because they'll assume you shared your suspicions. You – all of you need to get out of town. I'm going as soon as I can too. I never planned on staying here forever. I just figured it'd be after I built my reputation as a deputy for a while."

"I don't know what to say, Max," Kat said with a quavering voice.

"Don't say anything. Just be safe." Max was quiet for several seconds and no one in the Seavers' kitchen knew what else to say. Max finally said, "We need to get moving if we're going to do this." He leaned toward Merrick. "Mr. Chaney? You down with this?"

Before Merrick could respond, Kat reached over and grasped his hand. She forced a smile and nodded to him. "You should do it."

Merrick's eyes were wide with wonder and worry. "But – what'll happen to you? You'll be a target after I leave."

"I've been meaning to get started on my future plans," said Kat. "I guess now's as good a time as any. I'll get a few things settled here, then head out too." She placed her palm on her father's hand and smiled sorrowfully. Del nodded and smiled back.

Merrick's eyes went back and forth from Kat to Max like a tennis match. "You sure? You – you'll be ok?"

She nodded again. "I can take care of myself."

Del reached across the table and cupped her hand with both of his. "But you don't always need to," he said. "This place doesn't mean anything to me. Your grandpa left it to me. I thought it would be a safe place, just somewhere we could live in peace. If we can't be safe here – then we need to be somewhere else. I didn't have much to my name when we came here, and we did all right. We'll do all right again." He retreated his hand to his lap and said, "You can start your future in Europe now if you want, or you can save up some more money and stay awhile longer with me. Somewhere else. We should all get out of this town."

Kat smeared the last of her tears away and choked back any further outbursts. She was done being the weepy victim. "Alright then." She clapped her hands. "Come on. We got things to do."

CHAPTER 23

Merrick's possessions took a total of 10 minutes to fully pack. It would've taken even less except that Kat insisted he pack a few extra items like dried meats and preserves she put aside for extreme winters, a couple of water bottles, plus a tiny item she folded into his palm.

He scrunched his face as he looked at it. "Your nametag?"

She shrugged. "I won't need it anymore, and – it's what I was wearing when you met me. Figured it was the easiest thing to remember me by."

Merrick wanted to laugh. The memory of her body illuminated by the filtered moonlight was burned into his brain like a cattle brand. The feel of her underneath him, then subsequently on top of him, was a sensation that couldn't be purged from his memories with a lobotomy. Her nametag would be a paltry and unnecessary reminder. Kat Seavers was never ever going to be forgotten.

"Thank you," he said.

Del Seavers gave him a restrained yet genuine hug. After he was done, he re-donned his manly air, folded his arms across his chest, and nodded. "I'm sorry things got so crazy around here. You're a good man. Woulda been nice to have you around."

"Thank you, sir," said Merrick.

He opened the front door and stepped onto the porch where Max waited. The deputy was leaning against the porch pillar, staring out at the mountains.

"You ready?" said Max, turning toward Merrick.

Merrick nodded. "As I can be. I'm more worried about you guys than me. Trouble is something I'm used to running from. If Kind and Fosse are as powerful as you say, how you gonna break away?"

Max shrugged. "An officer of the law isn't as easy a target as a drifter. No offense. We have combat training, video in our cars, records of everything we do. Plus we're armed. And Internal Affairs has my report, which might raise an eyebrow or two. I don't think anyone's gonna come after me or Simon right away. Especially not without a plan."

"Hope you're right," said Merrick.

Max held up a finger and said, "Which reminds me, I brought something for you. I kinda promised it before, so…" He held out a wooden-handled knife with a beaded leather sheath. The middle of the polished handle looked like smoothed tree bark. "My uncle makes them for tourists. Some are cheap, but this one's pretty sturdy. Should work out well as an everyday knife." Max lifted the edge of his pant leg. A similar knife was strapped to his ankle. "I keep one myself for luck."

"I don't know what to say, guys," said Merrick. "Everywhere I've gone, I've been treated like vermin. People avoid me, try not to look at me. And here – just being here has caused you so much trouble, and you guys still treat me like family." He shook his head. "I thought I knew how the world works."

"Don't none of us understand the world," said Del. "You're doing good to understand yourself."

Which I don't. Not all of me.

Max tapped the watch on his wrist.

"Yeah, ok. Let's do it," said Merrick.

He tucked the knife in his duffel bag and sat down on the porch so Max could get to the anklet.

"What're you going to do after this?" asked Merrick.

Max shrugged as he worked the key. "Once Simon's shift is done, we're going to meet for drinks then figure it out. We'll be safer if we stick together, at least for a little while."

The anklet snapped open. No noises sounded, no angry red lights blinked. The anklet sat serenely in Max's palm.

"Done," said Max.

Merrick leaned forward to get a good look at the anklet. "This thing's completely off? No signals? Doesn't show up on tracking devices?"

"No, it's off," said Max. "The sheriff will eventually notice it's off the grid though. Need to get it out of their house, make it look like you ditched it. I guess – uh, I can toss it out of my car window when I leave."

Merrick nodded to Max. "Thank you. And by the way – it's Merrick. Merrick Hull. My real name."

Max nodded back and offered a subdued smile. "Take care, Merrick."

"If I can ever repay you –."

Max slapped Merrick's arm as the male-accepted gesture for *"don't worry about it,"* then tipped his hat to Kat and Del. "Folks," he said. "Good luck," he said to Merrick, then turned toward his car.

Kat ran to him. "Oh, no you don't, Ma'xehonehe Yellow Feather." Kat swallowed Max up in a full-body hug, then gave him an extended kiss on the cheek. "That's for you," she said. Then she gave him a small peck on the other cheek. "That one's for Simon if you wanna give it to him later."

Max tried to keep his chuckle silent but couldn't. He burst into a good laugh. "Somehow, I don't think I will."

He got into his car and started the motor.

Merrick took a deep breath, gave Kat and Del each a single nod, then began walking toward the pasture. He wasn't sure he could handle more goodbyes and didn't want to press Kat into one. That apparently wasn't up to him though.

"Wait!" called Kat. She caught up in a few strides. "Before you go, there's something you forgot in the barn. Come with me and I'll give it to you."

Merrick scrunched his face. *In the barn?* He was sure he had everything. "Oh, ok," he said.

Kat opened the door, went in, and Merrick followed. The moment he shut the door, Kat pounced on him. They tumbled to the floor and she buried her mouth in his. She released her lock on him after about half a minute.

"Sorry," she said. "I didn't want to make a scene in front of Max or my dad."

"You're forgiven," said Merrick. "God, I'm going to miss you. You've ruined me, ya know that? Can't be a homeless bum so easily now. All I want to do is come back to you."

"Yeah, well, you screwed me up too, monster boy."

"I know. I really did. So sorry."

She smacked his rump. "Not because Kind may come after me," she said. "I can take care of myself. No, because I didn't want any men in my life. I was just going to pack my shit and travel Europe. Write books, see sights, live life, and experience the world." Her eyes went down to the ground. "I'm not supposed to want you to stick around."

Merrick reached up and kissed her again. "And I'm not supposed to want to either. I trained myself to suppress all those desires and emotions so I could stay alive and not harm anyone else. And I've done the opposite of that since I've been here."

Kat playfully bit Merrick on the neck and let him up. "You better go before I jump you for real and the sheriff'll catch us both butt-ass naked in here."

"That's the opposite of a good incentive to leave."

"Hush," said Kat. "Go on now before I change my mind."

Merrick headed up the hill behind the barn, angling away from the house in the general direction of his old campground. He remembered the road was nearby his old camp, and if he crossed it and headed down the other side of the hill, he'd have one medium-sized mountain to traverse before he hit the reservation. Though mountains weren't fun to scale, there was a bad taste in his mouth from the last time he tried to leave via the road. Plus, crossing the mountain was also the straightest course to his first destination, and coincidentally the hardest for the sheriff to follow.

As he trudged up the hill, he was lamenting his stay with the Seavers. So many of his important rules he had broken. So many things he wished had never happened, and yet – he wouldn't have had the time with Kat if he had just moved on as he planned. The memory of her was worth being stabbed, and jailed, and having to run from people who wanted him either dead or incarcerated (which was the norm anyway). All worth it.

What wasn't worth it was the danger he had put her and Del in. That was all his fault. Though Tanner would've been a dick to Kat even without Merrick there, it wouldn't have escalated to the level it was now of trying to indict Sheriff Kind on murder charges in order to keep Merrick's scrawny ass out of prison. By leaving, he was hoping to change the game. Kind would probably be occupied with

Merrick's escape for a while, then later, he'd turn his suspicions back to his deputies and the Seavers. They'd have time to get their affairs in order and relocate themselves to somewhere less crazy.

Merrick saw the road above him. The morning sun was bright and the sky was clear, artistically blended with the pointed tops of stately pines. It really was pretty country. Probably hell in the winter, but he wouldn't be here for…

A large car drove by. Long, black SUV with tinted windows. New and shiny, not the typical scuffed up, dusty ranch variety that would be likely around here. Nothing truly suspicious about it other than Merrick doubted it was owned by any of the locals. To him, it resembled a government or FBI vehicle. The SUV went past Merrick, toward the Seavers' turn-off. Merrick hustled up the slope to keep an eye on it. His paranoia was in high gear, and he was well aware that there was no reason to suspect whoever owned the car was up to anything other than a leisurely drive toward Flathead Lake. There were plenty of reasons someone would travel this route, including the picturesque scenery.

He was about to turn away and ignore his distrustful mind when he noticed the car stop. It was a considerable distance from Merrick, and not yet to the Seavers' driveway, straddling the shoulder of the road. Nothing should be there to stop for. Doors opened and six men wearing business suits got out. Several of them looked like they were carrying long, black objects. *Rifles?*

They left the SUV behind and crossed the street, heading down the slope toward the Seavers' barn.

Oh, no. No, no, no.

Kat hurried through packing the kitchen, simplifying their family-sized collection of plates, cups, utensils, and appliances into a single box of necessities. There was room in Del's truck for plenty more boxes, but Kat thought that sudden flight should mean traveling light and not packing more boxes than could be unloaded from the car in a single trip. Her own Jeep had three suitcases which were the entire contents of her room sans furniture.

She had never been a hoarder, never lined her room like a nest with knick-knacks and pictures, etc. Twenty minutes was all it took to stuff everything she cared about into suitcases, which all fit in the cargo area of her Jeep.

Del's room and the kitchen would take longer, though she hoped not too much longer. She'd have the kitchen done within an hour and thought it prudent to be on the road soon after. No destination in mind, just somewhere for the both of them to hold up for a while until things blew over. Del was on his own for his room, which was what he was supposed to be doing when he came from behind Kat and embraced her.

She was startled for a moment, then relaxed in his arms. "Hi, Dad," she said somberly.

"Hi, honey." Del kissed the top of her head, then released her. "I want to apologize. This is all my fault," he said.

"What? Dad?! Stop. That's not helping."

Del shook his head. "I'm serious. There's, uh – a lot I've been too scared to tell you about this place."

Kat tossed a folded towel onto the counter and turned to fully face her father. "Whatever you think you've known or not known don't mean you're responsible for the mess Fosse and the sheriff made."

"For their mess, no," said Del. "But bringing you here to get all caught up in the middle of it – yeah, I blame myself for that."

"Daddy, it's ok. You couldn't have known that all this…"

"But I *did* know," said Del. He took a deep breath and dropped his gaze to the floor. "I knew a lot. And what's worse, I went along with it."

Kat pressed her fingers under her dad's chin to lift his head up. "Went along with what?"

"Just at first," said Del, ignoring Kat's question. "It was disgusting and I couldn't go along with it anymore. But that's not what I'm most ashamed of. I never spoke out against them. Never said anything."

"Dad!? Said what about – what?"

"Your grandfather told me about the inner circle. How you had to play their game in order to get by here. Until he died, I didn't think much about it. But once we were on our own, I had to understand what he meant. We should've never stayed here. Should've sold the ranch and moved on. It was never safe here."

"You're talkin' in circles," said Kat, trying to prompt her dad out of his rambling.

Del didn't acknowledge the nudge. "I just thought if we laid low, stayed quiet, kept to ourselves, none of it would matter. But now?"

"Daddy, I love you, but I'm gonna whoop you in a second if you don't get to the point."

Del gave her a reluctant smile and nodded. "Maybe I should just show you. There's – uh, a little hiding spot behind my closet where I've kept some things I never wanted you to know about until – well, until after I was gone. There's a letter to you in one of the boxes in my closet that explains it all, because I just didn't think I'd ever be brave enough to tell you what I've been involved in."

"Umm. You're talking like you plan to die soon. What's going...?"

"No, honey. No, I'm just trying to explain things in case something bad happens while you're away."

"Away? From you? I thought we were going together."

"You're packing up and getting out of here immediately. I'll catch up with you later. I've gotta stay here and get things settled with the livestock and the ranch."

Kat wanted to argue, but the truth was, she didn't have a plan for the animals and property. She had hoped they could both get somewhere safe, report what they knew to authorities, then come back in a while and try to settle everything here. By then, between Max's IA report and their disclosure to another law enforcement agency, the sheriff, Tanner, and Fosse should be under official scrutiny, and anything suspicious that they might do to her or her father would be noticed by the authorities. That plan sounded like wishful thinking to her, there just wasn't much of a choice. Where would she even go to sit around a wait for her father? And for how long? A few days wasn't going to solve it, and the animals couldn't be left entirely alone for too long. Del was right about that. God knows what would happen to them, and who might steal or kill them out of spite.

"There's gotta be another way," said Kat.

198

"I don't think so, hon. It's still our property, and it's financial security for you someday once it's sold. The people I'm talking about are going to seek vengeance for us leaving. And if I stay, they'll have to get through me first."

Kat shook her head. "Daddy, what the hell is so damned important that people need to die for it? Why us?"

"That's what I've been trying to tell you." Del motioned that they should sit down. Kat felt like she should stay standing just to make her father get to the point, but she reluctantly sat as well.

"There's an inner circle here," said Del. "A power group made of about a dozen men, headed by Arthur Fosse. Sheriff Kind is one of them, though he wasn't always. Fosse's been here a lot longer. Long time ago, your grandfather was one of them. This group decided to take law into their own hands and round up and kill criminals that either escaped the system or just committed horrific crimes like murderers, rapists, child predators. They had to find ways, of course, to make the bodies disappear, and that's where your grandfather came in. He built our incinerator to dispose of the corpses."

"Jesus," muttered Kat.

"The 'cleansing,' as I heard one man put it, changed over the years, and Fosse turned it into a ritual hunt. Made it a sick event. Even justified it as some old Greek tradition. But it's even worse than that. There's a legend about one of the mountains just over the reservation border. Restless spirits, evil energies reside there, and Fosse decided to make that spot his ritual place, build a big bonfire, then burn and bury the bodies in a fire pit. Grandpa's incinerator wasn't needed anymore, and that was his only contribution. Since he never went on the hunts, he was released from his obligation to the inner circle if he promised to keep quiet. However, he felt obligated to tell me when we moved here, so then I knew too."

Del paused and gazed into his daughter's eyes, and Kat stared back. She assumed there was more, and Del was just gauging to see if she was about to storm out of the room in disgust. She was disgusted, but far too interested. She nodded to him as a signal to continue.

He nodded back. "I was naïve when we first got here, thought I needed to be in this circle to get along here, so they recruited me. Gave me one of their suits."

199

"Suits?"

"Wolf suits. They're a real wolf pelt attached to a kind of mechanical exoskeleton that has metal claws, night vision, and stuff to make them hunt better and move faster."

"Holy shit."

"I'll get to more of that later," said Del. "And don't swear in my house. They made me take part in one of the rituals. They call it Lycaon's Fire, or just The Fire. Named after the Greek thing I mentioned. It's only once a year. They dig a huge pit, build the bonfire, dress in these wolf suits, set twelve prisoners free on the mountain, then hunt them down and kill them. The next part is the hardest to stomach. Or was for me. They take a bit of flesh from each prisoner, while they're alive if possible, eat it, then burn the rest of the corpse."

Kat held her hand in front of her mouth. She wasn't going to vomit but she didn't want to tempt fate. Once she was sure she wasn't going to puke, she asked, "Where do these prisoners come from? There ain't twelve serious criminals like that around here. One once in a while, maybe, but not…"

"They find them from all over. Sometimes they get lucky with local criminals, and sometimes Kind barters for criminals. They hide what's happening by saying the prisoners escaped, or went missing after they're released, etc," Del made air quotes for *escaped* and *missing*, "but really they're just kept in secret holding cells, for however long it takes, kept alive until it's time for the ritual. They blindfolded me once and took me out to the secret holding facility. Some underground place with iron cages. Like slaves waiting for the gladiator games."

Kat shook her head in disbelief. She had read books and seen movies about crazy things like this, never thinking it could ever be real. And sure as hell not involving her father.

"So did you – kill – any…"

Del nodded. "One. The man had raped a little girl. Went to trial but got off on a technicality from contaminated evidence. Though I didn't feel bad about him dying, I couldn't handle the guilt of killing him myself. Not that way. It wasn't right."

"My god, Dad," said Kat. "That's insane. And sick. And no, it ain't right at all. Why? Why do this? Why's it so important to them?"

Del sighed. "There's something unnatural on that mountain. The legends aren't wrong. A presence, energies, something that gets into you when you stand around that spot where they make the fire. Makes you feel stronger, younger, faster, like a different person. Like there's some other stronger spirit inside you pulling the strings. It's an intense feeling. Like you're two people. It scared the crap... it scared me. I didn't want it in me. Fosse tells the inner circle that they have to make sacrifices to appease the spirits, and it's supposed to be a part of receiving the energies into your body, but... I think it's just an excuse. When I was there, I felt it, and I didn't take part in the flesh eating. I only pretended. I couldn't do it for real. And afterward, I told Fosse I couldn't do it anymore."

"God, I'm so sorry, Dad. These people are psychotic. But – at least they're only killing other murderers and psychos, right?"

"That's just it. I don't think so anymore. I think Fosse and Kind have been using the rituals to clean up their messes. People that got on their bad side for whatever reason. Or maybe threatened to spill their secrets." Del gave Kat a knowing brow raise to see if she got the inference.

She did. "So, if we blow the lid off their twisted shit, we could be next?"

"You know better than to swear in my house. And yes, he told me that if I ever moved away, or told anyone, I'd be found and killed. And worse, you'd be thrown into the hunt."

Considering everything else she had heard, that admission didn't surprise Kat, but hearing it nevertheless made her want to scream and punch her fist through a wall.

Del reached out a hand and gently rubbed the top of hers. "That's why I kept silent. That's why I hid it. But I wanted you to know someday. I wrote it all down and kept it behind my closet with the suit they gave me."

"You have a wolf suit in your closet?"

Del nodded. "What's left of it. The pelt deteriorates. That's what I was going to show you, to prove I wasn't lying. Do you – want to see it?"

Kat wished this entire conversation was a bad dream or a joke, but there was no denying it. Her father was an honest man, and despite everything, was being honest with her at great risk to them both. She didn't need to see the suit to know it was there. *Damn it. Yes, I do.* She was curious, like passing a car wreck and wanting to look.

"Yes," she said. "But later. I need to finish the kitchen."

"I don't think there's going to be a 'later.'"

Right. It was washing over her again. Everything they knew about Kind and Fosse, everything they'd done to help Merrick. They were all in mortal danger now.

She shook her head. "I'd rather we leave it all, the suit, this house, and this whole town in the past. Let's just hurry and pack, then get the hehh… get out of here."

Del nodded. "Okay," he said and left the kitchen heading toward the stairs.

He had only ascended the first stair when there was a knock at the front door. Kat took two steps to answer it before Del stopped her.

"Wait," he said. "Just in case."

Del slowly approached the door, then opened it only a few inches to see who was outside. Kat side-stepped so she could see through the crack.

"Excuse us, sir," said a bald man in a dark business suit and sunglasses. "I'm Agent Janus from the Department of Homeland Security." The man flashed a plastic ID with his picture. "Sorry to bother you, but we're looking for a federal fugitive. I'd like to ask you a few questions, please. May we come in?"

Two other men stood behind the speaker, both had sunglasses and business suits. Only one had hair. All three looked unfriendly, and all three looked like they lived in a gym. Their arms and chests stretched the confines of their suits.

"I'm sorry, gentlemen," said Del. "I haven't seen anyone around our property anytime recently, and we're in the middle of something right now. So, no, now is not a good time to come in. I wish you luck."

As Del began to shut the door, the man's battering ram-like hand jammed the door open. "This will only take a minute, sir. We need to ask you some questions."

Despite Del putting his weight behind his push, the door didn't budge. "There ain't been no one around here. Now – please leave us alone."

The door was pushed further open, the effort barely registering on the bald man's face. "We know Merrick Hull's been here. Lying to us will not help your situation. Comply with us and you will not be harmed."

"Harmed?!" scoffed Kat. "Listen, mister, I don't know who you are, but you ain't from Homeland Security. I don't think you're from any law enforcement at all. So, you can take your lyin' ass off our porch and get the hell…"

The door slammed open, knocking Del backward, and the man stepped through the threshold. His two associates followed and both drew their pistols. The guns looked like sci-fi creations with oversized barrels and tubes above and below. Nothing any real law enforcement officer would carry.

Del swung a baseball bat that he kept next to the door. The bat hit the leader in the stomach and the man doubled over.

"Run!" yelled Del.

Kat's mouth hung open as she watched one of the agents swing his gun around and squeeze the trigger. The gun bucked and popped, shooting a metal cylinder that punched into Del. He crumpled to the ground.

Kat screamed, then ran.

CHAPTER 24

The kitchen pantry had a door that led outside and Kat darted through it without looking back. She had no intention of abandoning her dad, despite his heroic intent. Her strategy would involve appearing to run away so the bad men would be misdirected, and then she would double back. Once she hit the back step, she took a hard left.

A thick bush stood next to the rear of the house and Kat ducked behind it. She waited to see who would follow her from the kitchen. Within a few seconds, her question was answered when an agent opened the back door and stood on the step, scoping the adjacent woods. Obscured by the bush, Kat could only see the edge of his shoulder, the profile of his head, and his hand holding the strange pistol that shot metal cylinders. Probably a tranquilizer gun judging by what hit her father. Another reason she wasn't petrified at the moment, assuming her dad had only been knocked out. Her temper was still boiling, however, and she had every intention of getting her own gun and confronting these men with it. She wouldn't be shooting tranks at them.

The man on her back porch took off into the woods, exactly as she had hoped. As soon as he couldn't be seen from the denseness of the trees, Kat snuck out from behind the bush.

An old trellis was attached to the house under her window, the ornamental vines having long ago died, making the trellis useless for anything other than a late-night, stealth ladder to and from her bedroom. She had only used it a couple of times when she was in high school when her father had forbidden her to go out, taking advantage of the trellis for simple teenage rebellion. But now it was her ticket to getting into her bedroom (where she kept her shotgun) without the intruders seeing her. She grasped the first spar of the trellis. It had been a long time since she had climbed the structure, time enough for wood exposed to the outdoor elements to weaken. The spar came off in her hand.

Shit!

Before she had enough time to consider her options, a hand wrapped around her neck and something cold and hard pressed to her temple.

"Don't move," said the man behind her. "The needle of the tranquilizer is strong enough to penetrate your skull, and if the drug goes directly in your brain, it'll probably kill you. I'd prefer you stay alive to answer…"

Kat wasn't waiting around to listen to the rest of the man's droning. Probably more of a reaction than a plan, she swung the piece of broken wood and hit the guy in the head. He released her to clutch his head, which gave her time to turn fully around and swing the broken spar with full strength. The wood crashed against the bald man's skull. Her intent was to pull the spar back for a final blow to make sure he went down, but the spar wouldn't budge from the man's head. Only then did she notice that there had been a long nail at the end of the wood, currently embedded in the thug's cranium. *Oh, shit!* The man fell to the ground, limp.

Kat reached down and picked up the man's dropped pistol, then jammed it into the back of her waistband. She spun and scrabbled up the trellis, happily surprised to find the remaining spars were sturdier. Only the lowest one cracked as she climbed, the rest held her weight. At her window sill, she looked down at the man she had impaled with a nail. Still down and not moving. Kat pushed her window open, looked and listened for a moment to see if her plan had been guessed, then hoisted herself in.

Her squeaky wood floor was betraying her attempt to be silent, and for a moment, the bumping and whispering downstairs sounded like a response to knowing she was upstairs. After several anxious seconds, when no one ran up the stairs toward her, she felt she might have time to get what she came for.

The pump-action shotgun was next to her bed. She pressed her palms flat on the floor and drug her body across the floorboards, assuming the strategy would reduce the floor creaking from the pressure points of her knees or feet. It worked well enough, and she was able to reach her shotgun.

She was sure at least one shell was left in the gun, though she hadn't replaced the ones she had used recently, and may not have enough loaded to hold the intruders off. The box of shells was in her nightstand. She slid the top drawer open and fished around for the box. The top was already pulled back, so she grabbed a handful of shells and brought them to her lap. One of the shells slipped from her grip and fell to the floor. The brass cap clunked against the wood, echoing through the nearly quiet house. A heartbeat later, Kat heard footsteps running on the ground floor.

Shit, shit, shit!

Taking calm, even breaths, she loaded one shell into the tube. Then another. Feet thumped on the staircase. Another shell slid into the tube. A bald man's head breached the horizon of the stair landing along with a rifle aimed at Kat's head. Not a trank gun, she noticed – a military-style, assault rifle. The time it took to quietly scream in her head was the same amount of gut reaction time it took to jerk her shotgun toward the attacker and fire. The pellets scattered, obliterating the newel post, exploding splinters everywhere, ripping the wall along the stairwell, and spinning the attacker around so that he fell face-first down the steps. A shock of percussion shook the house from his impact with the bottom landing.

Kat ground her teeth and loaded the last two shotgun shells. She racked the next one into the chamber.

"If you fuckers don't get out of my house," called Kat, mentally chiding herself for breaking Del's in-the-house swearing rule. "It will be the last thing you see on this earth! You hear me?"

She listened for an answer. None came. The only sound was Del's labored breathing, which was actually a good thing. It meant he was still alive.

"I'm coming down these stairs," announced Kat. "If I see any of you, I'm firin'. Or you can just get the hell out now!"

She slowly, hesitantly moved to the top stair. Still no sound from below. "Alright then," said Kat in an increasingly quavering voice.

"Put it down, Miss Seavers," said a voice from below. "All it will do is get your father killed. I only need one of you alive to talk, so – up to you."

Kat wanted to tell the man to fuck off, but she was done posturing. As soon as she saw his face, she'd put buckshot into it. She gingerly took a step down the first stair. It creaked like a horror movie house. She swore silently and went down another step.

A loud gunshot sounded downstairs followed by an anguished yell. It nearly scared Kat out of her skin. The yell was from her father.

"Daddy?" The word squeaked out despite her intention to stay silent.

The whimpering that followed was most assuredly from her father. No words, just pitiful noises from his throat.

"Your father has been shot in the leg," said the lead agent's voice. "The next shot will be his head. I will not ask again. Throw your gun down the stairs. Now!"

Kat was panicking. She thought she'd be able to do this, even with her dad in jeopardy, but her courage was failing. She was on the verge of complying when a metallic click happened behind her.

"Don't move," said another voice.

Kat moved despite her intention to comply. She reacted by turning her head to see the barrel of a large-caliber pistol pointed at her head. That was as far as she moved until the man behind her tugged the trank gun from her pants, then spun her around and snatched her shotgun. It was the same man she had impaled in the head with the nail. Blood coated that side of his collar and shoulder, though the wound itself had clotted. *What the f...? They heal too?*

"I got 'er!" said the formerly injured man, calling down to his comrades. To Kat, he said, "Go," and jutted his chin toward the bottom landing.

Kat wanted to go downstairs and see her father's condition as soon as possible, which was, unfortunately, the same directive she was preferring to delay from the agent. There was still a spark of rebellion inside her brewing a crazy plan to turn the tables on the agents. She hadn't decided yet whether to act upon that spark or extinguish it when the man she had shot appeared perfectly healthy at the bottom of the stairs, aiming a rifle at her chest. A nail in the coffin of her burgeoning plan.

Fuck.

The closer agent gave her a stiff shove. She tromped down the stairs armed only with a killing stare.

Her father lay against the entryway wall, one of his pant legs soaked with blood. His eyes were squinted, his breathing rapid. The lead agent's pistol was pressed against Del's ear.

"You answer wrong, your father dies," said the agent.

"Kat, don't..." started Del.

The agent smashed his pistol butt like a hammer into Del's temple. "Any words I don't like and your father dies." The pistol was re-aimed at Del's ear. "Now – where is Merrick Hull?"

"He's not here," said Kat nervously eyeing the agent's trigger finger. "I swear! He was here, just for a little while, and he left. That's it. He left a while ago. I don't know where."

The lead agent cast an expectant look at the agent who had pushed Kat down the stairs.

That agent said, "He was here. Maybe an hour ago. The scent is still fresh."

The scent? What the...?

The lead agent nodded once. "Then he knows. He's still here somewhere."

"No!" yelled Kat. "No, I swear he left. None of us knew anyth... he didn't know you were coming. I swear. He's gone. He's..."

The lead agent moved faster than Kat thought was possible. One moment his gun hand was pointed at Del, the next it was firing at Kat's feet. The floorboard in front of her buckled and burst splinters at her shins before she registered the shot. Her feet spasmed as she hopped backward.

"Lie," said the lead agent. "He's still around here somewhere."

Kat shook her head. The tears were close to leaking out. There was nothing she could think to say that would make this man let her and her dad go.

"Outside," said the agent to his men. "Now."

With a pistol-to-his-head as encouragement, Del managed to stand. Kat was ushered outside by the bloody, nailed agent, followed by the agent who had been shot by Kat. Besides being bloody, both looked unaffected by their injuries, and neither looked happy with her. The lead agent led them all to the open area between the two pastures.

Around the corner of the house, three more agents appeared, all carrying automatic rifles. Not that Kat and Del's odds of beating any of the agents were good before (about a .001% chance of a bolt of random lightning striking them down), but those slim odds decreased to zero with the addition of three more armed agents. Whatever was going to happen, Kat was at their mercy. The tingle in her skin was the blood leaving to take cover further inside her body.

"Merrick Hull!" shouted the lead agent to the air. "We have the Seavers! Show yourself or we will kill them! You have thirty seconds to comply!"

Only the breeze rattling the leaves answered him.

Kat swallowed and shook her head. "He's gone." The words sounded closer to a wheeze since her throat was losing its wetness.

The leader ignored her. "You know we will not hesitate!" he shouted at the woods. "Twenty seconds!"

No voice answered. The wind rustled the pine branches behind the house.

The leader looked at Kat. "Which way did he go?"

She shook her head. "I didn't watch." That was the truth. Merrick had only taken a few steps toward the pasture before she turned away and went back in the house, unwilling to watch him fade into the trees. She preferred the last memory of him being their final embrace. Despite not lying about her lack of knowledge of his whereabouts, she knew the truth wasn't going to save her. She needed to give the agent something.

She flung a hand out toward the south side of the pasture. "That was the direction he was walking before I looked away." *Almost the truth.* Just a little angle misdirection.

"You think I'd believe that?" said the agent.

Then why'd you ask me, you tool?

The agent seemed to guess her thought. "That way is toward town. He'd probably head to the closest reservation. You wanna correct your answer before I put a bullet in your father's brain?"

"I didn't see him leave, ya prick!" screamed Kat.

Del grunted and straightened up. "He stole a horse," he said. "Was headed up the drive last I saw. Steep slopes around here. He'd have to stick to the road shoulder. Not sure which direction on the road, but your car would be faster, so you might…"

The leader agent landed a backhand swing with the gun against Del's face and Del fell over. As Del struggled to right himself, the agent leveled his pistol at Del's forehead. The agent's face displayed no emotion as he said, "Too late, old man."

Kat was ready to scream, expecting the shot to come, but it didn't. Instead, a different kind of shot came.

The lead agent jerked and stumbled as a razor-tipped arrow stuck out both sides of his torso.

What the...?

The other agents all spun to face the house, the general direction the arrow seemed to come from. One of the agents shot a window shutter, then seemed unsure where he should be aiming. Before he could determine his target, an arrow pierced his leg. He shrieked, clutched his thigh, and fell to the ground.

"There!" shouted one agent, pointing at the ancient tree near Kat's car.

All the uninjured agents began firing at that spot. The agent with hair began charging at the tree. Another followed him while two others fired from where they stood. A man broke from the cover of the tree and hopped over the porch railing, sprinting for the door. He had on an Army surplus jacket and a composite bow tucked under his arm as he ran.

Merrick?

Automatic rifles clanged and roared, splintering the front of Kat's house, catching Merrick in the barrage. He stumbled and jerked, trying to keep his balance. Blood splattered the house exterior.

No. Oh, no.

Merrick hit the front door with his shoulder as the two pursuing agents clambered up the porch steps. The door slammed shut, shiny and slick with bright red smears.

One agent shot the door handle while the other kicked the door open. They both ran in.

Kat swiveled her head, looking for a chance to break away from her captors, but the two standing agents both kept consistent eyes on her, with one ushering Del closer to Kat so they could be watched easier. The agent with his leg shot stood up, the broken tip of the arrow in his hand. He flung it away angrily. The man with the torso wound also stood up, albeit slower. His partner snapped off the arrowhead, then yanked the remainder through the leader's back. He grunted for a moment, then gave Kat a venomous glare.

Inside the house, several shots rang out. The momentary flash of light showed murky silhouettes moving past the window. Kat heard a crash of something like ceramics or glass, followed by a muffled thump. Then the back door squeaked open and smacked shut. *He ran out the back door?*

Kat was trembling with anticipation to see a glimpse of Merrick, assuming he was heading to the back woods. However, she didn't want to give away his position should she spot him. The thought gave her an idea. She shifted her weight, turning a bit like she was going to hide her head to cry, giving her a slightly better angle to see around the side of the house. A stumbling figure could just be seen pelting toward the woods. *Go!*

Unfortunately, the lead agent saw him too. "There!" he bellowed. He turned to his three other men and said, "Switch to tranks. Let's go."

Kat didn't understand the point of the switch since they had already shot Merrick with real bullets, and tranquilizers sounded far less substantial.

One agent was left behind to guard Kat and Del as the others ran off toward the barn. Kat knew if she attempted to try something now, the guard would be hyperaware. On the other hand, it was the only opportunity they were likely going to get.

"Um, excuse me, sir," said Kat. "My father has lost a lot of blood. I need to get him somewhere he can lay down."

"Lay down there," said the icy guard indicating the dirt below them.

"His wound will get infected with dirt," argued Kat. "I need a cleaner…"

"Shut up and sit down." The guard clicked the hammer of his pistol back. "We don't even need you anymore. It'd be easier if I just killed you both."

The argument made more sense than Kat would like. She sat down quickly.

The guard made a sour, thinking face. "Although, I think he wants to keep you as leverage. So – just shut up."

Kat rested her hand on the ground for balance and almost yelped in pain. She had leaned against the razor-sharp arrowhead the guard had tossed away. She nonchalantly felt for the length of the broken shaft and found it was about 5 inches long. Enough for a hand to grip. *And stab him through his fucking neck.* Her fingers tightened around it.

Concocting a hasty plan, she abruptly hopped up on one knee. "Oh no," she muttered with her most winning worried expression. Pretending to see something behind the house, her eyes grew wide and her left hand slapped against her mouth.

The hope was that the guard might assume she saw Merrick being manhandled or captured. The guard obliged by intently staring at the spot in the woods where Merrick had disappeared.

Kat sprang up and lunged at the guard. He turned just in time to witness her ram the arrowhead through his neck. She yelled something incomprehensible and threw an additional fist into his nose. Then she grabbed Del's hand and they both ran to the house.

On the porch, she paused to see where the guard was. He hadn't followed them yet, but was no longer down either. He was wrestling with the arrowhead embedded in his neck.

"I'll get my gun!" said Del heading for the stairs. "You find yours!"

She nodded though she didn't remember what the agent had done with it. *Tossed it – where? On the couch? There!* The chair closest to the hall had her shotgun lying on its seat. She swept it up, then knelt behind the chair for cover.

Del thumped around upstairs getting his own gun. *Upstairs!* Much more defensible. They could hold up in one of the rooms and brace the door.

Kat ran for the stairs. She had gotten midway when someone screamed outside. No gunshot, no noise, just a sudden, bloodcurdling scream. Kat paused to hear what might come after. Nothing did. She bounded up the remaining steps and met Del in the hall.

"We should hunker down up here," said Kat.

Del scanned the hall, then the stairs, anxious for a better solution.

"The spare room doesn't have anything under the window to climb!" blurted Kat.

Del's confused look was probably twofold, but he got over his hesitancy and nodded.

Father and daughter ducked into the spare room and locked the door. They shoved the dresser behind the door and went back to the bed to flip it over. The two crouched behind the overturned bed, shotguns ready, and waited.

CHAPTER 25

Agent Janus crept from tree trunk to tree trunk, keeping low, eyes scouring the shadows for movement. He knew the subject, Hull's alter ego, was a master of many things: speed, stealth, and killing. It was the perfect predator in many ways, and judging by the scream earlier, it had already killed one of the agents. Janus would not underestimate it. He was also not afraid of it. He had hunted similar subjects and killed them before, and despite this one being different, it also wasn't necessarily better. Wasn't stronger, wasn't smarter. Had no control. Just another byproduct to eliminate. Just another beast to hunt.

The tranquilizer gun he carried had darts that were specially designed to subdue the strongest animal. Each dart also carried an additional ingredient targeting the enzyme that triggered the transformation process. Janus had no interest in bringing back the subject alive, but bullets were not going to kill it unless the subject was unable to mutate its form to heal its wounds. If they hit the subject with enough darts, it would be forced back into human form, inhibited from changing back, then Janus could kill it. That, or just chop off its head.

Something was wadded up ahead of him on the ground. It looked like an Army jacket. Janus didn't bend to pick it up, didn't examine it, just moved warily forward. Several steps further, another item of clothing had been discarded. A workman's boot. The subject was unburdening itself of human clothing and leaving an easy trail to follow. Janus stepped past the boot seeing yet another boot up ahead. *Like bread crumbs.* This subject may not be as smart as the others. The agent focused ahead of the other boot, thinking the subject was probably fully transformed by now and hiding in the dark copse just ahead. And even if it wasn't, maybe there would be footprints to track from there.

Something occurred to Janus. He hadn't seen any footprints at all while he followed the supposed "bread crumbs." This hadn't occurred to him until he thought of looking for the clawed footprints

214

once he reached the copse ahead. These kinds of subjects were adept at using the trees with their strong claws, and he was suddenly aware he had been thinking two-dimensionally as he tracked the discarded clothing. He'd been smart enough to look up into the branches of the trees making up the copse ahead and saw nothing there, but he'd forgotten about the trees above and behind him. His brain went into panic mode. No footprints meant that the thing had been using the trees the whole time, deliberately dropping clothing to keep Janus's head looking down and lure him into the perfect ambush spot. The subject could be anywhere above him, even behind him.

The epiphany would never be acted upon because a clawed hand swept down and speared Agent Janus in the back. Janus's mouth opened to scream, only getting out a sharp choking sound since he had no more air in his throat. His lungs had been punctured. The single clawed hand lifted Janus into the tree as if the agent was no heavier than a ham hock. Janus frantically flailed to find something which could free him, but nothing except the long, hairy arm was available to clutch. The subject spun Janus around, bumping his head against a snarling reptilian snout. Saliva dripped across rows of wicked gray fangs, long and bent like pulled carpentry nails. Janus stared into mirror-like eyes that looked through him. Those eyes narrowed as the beast emitted a base growl from deep in its chest. Then another clawed hand slashed at Janus's neck.

As Janus fell from the tree, the last thing he saw was his body still impaled by the beast's hand. Only part of him was falling. *Just my head?* Once he impacted the ground, he rolled, eyes down, with no way to right himself. Whatever remained to happen to his body, he wouldn't be able to see it.

His mind made one last point of reason: *But I can't die.* Then he knew and thought nothing more.

No one came up the stairs, nothing crashed downstairs. Whatever was going on seemed to be happening in the woods behind the house. Kat heard muffled voices out there, unable to make out discernable words. A sharp gag had been the only thing recognizable, then just more muted noises. Kat wondered if perhaps she had enough time to grab her car keys and get in her Jeep. She simply didn't know where the agents were in the woods, and one wrong assumption could make Kat and Del sitting ducks in their vehicle, surrounded by an agent firing squad.

Someone suddenly yelled outside. It resembled a war cry, like a man shouting before he charged into battle. Then, as happened to the gagging screech before it, the sound was gone. A gunshot followed a few seconds later, then several more in rapid succession. There were popping sounds, similar to what Kat heard when the agents tranked her dad. Then more gunshots. Then silence.

Kat didn't like the silence. She preferred screams, shrieks, and gags. She assumed Merrick had made the switch to the "other one" sometime after he escaped to the woods, and she was hoping the terrified noises represented agents who were dying by Merrick's hand. And though she didn't understand the preference for the tranquilizers, she was sure the things had some kind of advantage against whatever Merrick had become, otherwise the agents would not have dropped their assault rifles in trade. Since she heard the trank guns popping, she wondered how many might have hit Merrick. Was he now lying on the ground, inert for them to do whatever the agents wanted?

She wanted to go out there and help Merrick, but her father needed her help too. There wasn't much choice at the moment.

A choked exclamation sounded outside. Was it Kat's imagination, or did it sound like someone starting a shriek, then getting it strangled into silence? That same imagination of hers was picturing Merrick crushing an agent's throat. *Please be that.*

The front door of the house banged open. "Bitch! Where are you?!" bellowed one of the agents. *Oh crap.* The guy she had stabbed with the arrow. She had almost forgotten about him. He should be dead, of course, but apparently, everyone in Merrick's world has unnatural healing abilities. The agent's heavy shoes clomped across the downstairs floor in a slow rhythm of someone cautiously searching.

216

It won't take him long. There weren't too many hiding options in the house. He'd try the upstairs in another half minute, then it would be a matter of who shoots who first. She reasoned that buckshot might make it through both the dresser and door once she heard his boots creak in front it.

A sound broke her out of her strategic musings: A growl. Not like a dog or an angry human. Something much stranger, bigger, and unknown to her. It was haunting and unnatural, like something manufactured for a movie. Whatever it was, it came from below their window. Kat listened quietly, hearing the creature move swiftly around the house. The noise softened once it was on the other side of the building, seeming to stay in that vicinity for nearly a minute. Then came something that truly frightened Kat: the squeak of the floorboards across the hall.

Someone's up here! How did they climb the stairs without her hearing? Another floorboard creaked, this time followed by the same unmistakable growl she had heard from outside. *Dear God, it climbed up!* Could it be Merrick? Despite the fact that he admitted to turning into something more bestial, Kat was imagining it was something similar to the movie *Split*: same body, different attitude and abilities. Not something physically different. Or could the thing in her room be one of the agents? They healed liked Merrick, so maybe they turned into beasts too. Whoever it was, it crept outside their door.

Del raised his shotgun, aiming at the center of the dresser blocking the door. Kat placed a trembling hand on his barrel and lowered it.

Del silently mouthed, "What!?"

Kat shook her head. Despite the absence of good reason, her gut told her not to fire at whoever was outside.

Suddenly, heavy feet were pounding up the stairs, fast. The now-familiar popping sound of a trank gun happened three times, then all hell broke loose in the hall. One of them yelled and the other roared. Bodies smashed into a wall, shaking the whole house. Wood splintered, something ceramic smashed, more thumping, yelling, roaring, snarling. The house shook again as what sounded like two bodies tumbled down the staircase, arms and legs slamming into the wall, shattering the already broken railing. One of the combatants cried, "Help!" then made a fierce yell before going silent.

Kat's legs tensed to stand up and push through the door, wondering if it was Merrick that cried for help, but the voice wasn't familiar. Though she wasn't sure she would recognize "the other one's" voice, her gut was again telling her it wasn't his. The unknown victor made a throaty rumble sound, then seemed to move away from the staircase. Not coming back up.

Downstairs, the squeaky front door slapped open and someone else ran in. More yelling, more snarling, more gun popping sounds. The walls buckled from an impact, then a table was smashed. Did one of the combatants fall on it, or hit the other with it? Glass shattered somewhere, boots shuffled and stomped, one of the combatants shouted, "Fuckin' kill you!" before he made another shout of an unrecognizable word that was cut short. The sounds of gargling liquid immediately followed before there was a softer, yet heavy, thump on the floor. Several seconds went by with no noise at all, then Kat heard a moan followed by labored, constricted breathing. One, two, three slow, heavy steps creaked on the downstairs floor, then ceased. Something huge and heavy fell to the floor.

Kat and Del remained where they were, glancing at each other in anxiety as to what may come next. For several minutes, nothing did. Kat's imagination pictured that whatever Merrick had become was lying on the floor downstairs, maybe hurt, maybe dying, and maybe needing her help. Her gut was inventing knowledge that only her ears had heard. Even if she was right, were more agents coming? At least two were now presumably dead or incapacitated after coming into the house and meeting the mystery opponent, which left four more agents unaccounted for. Judging by the gagging and screaming earlier, some of them may have died outside already. Unfortunately, that wasn't a definitive body count.

Kat scooted closer to the window. Del made frantic hand motions for her to stay put, but she waved him off. She placed her ear to the window sill and listened for twenty seconds. Nothing sounded outside. No noises from downstairs either. Desperately wanting to leave the room and find out, she fought the urge and waited several more seconds to make sure she wasn't ignoring any sounds from sheer hope.

"Anything?" whispered Del.

She shook her head. "I'm gonna go down there."

Del's alarmed facial expression didn't match his restrained whisper. "Why?"

Kat stood up and crept around the bed frame. "What if Merrick's dying and needs my help?"

Del pinched up his shoulders and flung his hands wide. "What about that bear down there!?" he hissed.

Bear? Kat was pretty sure the mysterious guest wasn't a bear. She had seen bears before, and none sounded like the thing that had been in their upstairs hallway.

"It's not a bear, Dad," she said simply and crossed to the door.

"I don't care what it is," whispered Del through clenched teeth. "Don't go down there!"

Kat had already made up her mind. She scooted the dresser back, slowly turned the doorknob, and cracked the door. Behind her, Del stood and leveled his shotgun barrel.

"Then I'm coming with you," he said.

Wooden and ceramic debris littered the hallway, with no sign of an agent or his opponent. No shadows, or any hint of movement. She eased her head through the doorway and got a better look. Nobody was upstairs.

"It's ok," she said quietly.

Stepping quickly into the hall with her shotgun at the ready, she did a quick check of all the doorways. Still no movement. Del crept into the hall, crouching, shotgun pointing down the stairwell. He turned to Kat and nodded.

She stiffened and held up a hand for Del to stand still. He flared his hand out in a *"what is it?"* gesture. Kat put a finger to her lips and listened. *There it is again.* A wheezing rumble like a congested snore, or an asthmatic lion. The sound's source was their living room. Whoever was making it was still alive, but sounded weak. Kat pointed to the stairs and moved toward them.

Del barred her with a strong arm. He pointed to himself, then moved ahead of her. With his shotgun pointed down the stairs, he slowly descended, gingerly putting weight on his injured leg. Kat followed one step behind. Del crouched lower to peek below the top floor edge, froze for a second, then lurched up one stair.

"Jesus!" he hissed. "It's… It's like a giant, mutant wolf."

Kat swallowed hard. "Is he – it alive?"

Del nodded. "Hurt and bleeding, but breathing. Looks like they tranked it a bunch of times."

"Anybody else down there?"

Del held up two fingers. "One guy next to the door – dead I think. Facedown, hard to tell. Lotta blood. The other guy, near the living room, ain't got a head."

Kat nodded. "Good enough. Let's go."

Del held her back with his arm again and shot her a tense look. "It's still alive and probably dangerous. We have no idea what that thing is, or what it might do."

Kat shook her head. "Dad – I – I think it's Merrick."

"It's… What?!"

Del's arm relaxed, probably from numb confusion, and Kat pushed past him. She involuntarily paused once she could fully see the downstairs, shocked at all the blood despite Del's warning. It was everywhere. Red streaks and slick pools along the entire hallway from front door to kitchen, leading up to the rug in the living room, and even smeared on several walls. Blood also matted the fur of the enormous creature lying on the floor, facing away from Kat.

Its back looked human, but twice the size and covered in long, stiff, almost needle-like hair. The legs were canine, with backward knees, and what she could see of its ears were triangular and pointed. The face wasn't visible. As Kat crept further down the stairs, the lower vantage point became harder to determine any further details.

She stepped over the face-down agent on the ground, noticing that his neck had been severed almost completely. Only the back patch of skin and muscle held the head to the body. If the agent could heal, he would need to reattach his head first. But the man appeared dead: no breathing, no movement, substantial blood loss.

Mere seconds had elapsed while Kat examined the dead agent, yet when she looked at the creature's body again, it had changed. Still large, still hairy, but some of the hair had receded. Patches of pale skin showed through the hair like the creature had mange. The backward knees looked slightly straighter.

As Kat stretched a foot over the dead agent's arms, she slipped in a blood puddle and lost her balance. Her hands braced against the corpse's torso, then she carefully stood again. Cautiously navigating the less bloody areas of the floorboards, she reached the edge of the living room. When she looked again at the creature, it was barely a creature anymore. It was visibly shrinking at the rate of a snail's journey across a hot sidewalk. Sparse hair was retreating into the pale skin of a nearly naked human. Once Kat got around to his head, there was no doubt it was Merrick.

He was shivering, shirtless and barefoot, with shredded, bloody pants. *He's gonna need another pair of Dad's old pants*. The thick sheen of sweat on his body resembled clumpy Vaseline. Seven darts hung off his skin, all of which Kat yanked out. Merrick made no reaction to the needles being pulled, he just continued shivering. Kat brushed back some of his wet hair from his forehead.

"Can you understand me?" she asked.

"Y-y-y-ysss," he said with a quavering voice.

"Is there more agents alive?"

"D-d-d-d-dooonnnt thhhiiink so."

Kat nodded, then looked around her living room for her throw blanket. She found what she was looking for draped across her sofa. She retrieved the blanket and draped it over Merrick.

"Better?" she asked.

"Thhhank you."

"What can I do? Is this normal for – uh, when this happens?"

"Nnn – no," he said, clenching his teeth in an effort to be clear.

"Then what can I do?"

"Ddd – don't know," he said clearly, swallowing hard between words. "Can't move. Nnnot rrright."

Del surprised Kat briefly when he blurted, "Dear God! What...? What...?"

"It's ok, Dad," said Kat. "It's just Merrick. He's hurt. Block the doors and watch for other agents, just in case. I think they're all dead, but –."

Del nodded slowly though he didn't move. He stood numbly, regarding Merrick's shivering body like it was an unexploded bomb.

"Dad!"

Del nodded again and this time moved toward the kitchen.

Kat tucked the blanket around Merrick, unsure of what she was supposed to be doing to help. She brushed his forehead again, noticing his sweat seemed to have dried.

"I don't know what to do, Merrick," she said.

Merrick moved his head a little, lifting it an inch off the rug. "Don't know either," he said, his voice clearer but weak. "It's the tranks. Something in them – makes me numb – blocks the other one." His head fell to the rug again.

"Do you want to sit up?" asked Kat.

"Yes."

Kat scooped up Merrick's torso, lifting him enough to lean him against the sofa. She propped his lolling head with a throw pillow.

"Thank you," he said.

His eyes struggled to focus on her, but were at least clear and lucid.

"I – uh, guess you really are a monster boy, huh?" said Kat with an apologetic expression.

Merrick coughed, either as a failed laugh or just still recovering.

From the hall, Del called, "I barred the doors for now. I don't see anyone outside at the moment."

"Kay, Dad," said Kat. She looked at Del and smiled. "You ok? How's the leg?"

He cocked his head and scrunched his mouth. "Hurts, but I got the bleeding stopped. Might need to change the tourniquet soon though." He looked around the bloody floor and broken stair railing, then at the corpse next to the front door. "I assume these were the, uh – men Merrick was afraid would show up?"

Kat nodded. "Yeah, looks like."

"So, Merrick wasn't really running from mobsters, was he?"

"No."

Del raised his brows, pointed his chin at Merrick, then shot Kat an under-lidded gaze. "You wanna explain what, uh – *that* was about?"

Kat smiled ruefully and shook her head. "I don't understand it, Dad. But…" She turned to Merrick. "You feel up to explaining?"

"Not enough time," said Merrick. "More agents may come. And sheriff."

The sheriff! Damn it. She forgot about him. "He can't move, Dad. We gotta get him outta here before anyone else shows up."

Del grimaced and shook his head slightly. "I've gone along with everything so far, but – I need somebody to tell me something I can understand before I go any further. My house is destroyed, our lives have been put in jeopardy – well, more jeopardy than they already were, and – and…" He slapped his thigh with his hand. "I just wanna know what the hell is going on."

Kat took a deep breath. "You told me when you were on the mountain, you felt like you had two people inside you? Well, there's something else inside Merrick too."

Merrick lifted a hand briefly before it fell to his lap. "Mr. Seavers," he said. "Someone made me this way. I don't know why. But I escaped, and they keep sending these men to kill me, or maybe bring me back to experiment more on me. Is that enough for now?"

Del sighed. "For now." He offered a defeated smile to Kat. "Ok. What do you want me to do?"

"We need to get Merrick out of here. When the sheriff comes, God knows what he'll do to him. Maybe to all of us."

"What about these dead men?"

"What about them?"

Del pushed his boot toe into one of the corpses and got no response. "The sheriff won't know they attacked us, or that their IDs are fake. It'll look like we murdered government agents."

"I…" Kat was ready to scream from all the insane, yet vital, decisions she was having to make. "I have no clue, Dad. I'm out of ideas."

"I can load them into the incinerator," he suggested.

"Will it work for that?" asked Kat.

"It's what it was built for." Del had answered quickly and clearly, then suddenly look ashamed and hung his head.

"You'll need help. Do we have time?" she asked.

Del put his hands on his hips and looked back and forth at the two corpses on his floor. Suddenly, he spun around and pointed his gun at the door.

"What?" said Kat.

"Outside. A car just pulled up. Someone's here."

223

Kat pumped a shell into her shotgun and readied herself with Del. Both their guns were pointed at the door as Kat listened to the car outside turn its engine off, the doors open and shut, and shoes crunch on gravel. Casual voices talking. Friendly banter. She thought she recognized one of the voices.

"I think it's Zeus," whispered Kat.

Shoes thumped on the outside porch steps.

"You sure?" asked Del.

Kat's attempt to nod ended up being a kind of neck spasm. She didn't lower her gun despite her assurance.

"Jefe?" called someone from outside. "Miss Kat? Anybody in there? You ok?"

God, it sounds like Zeus. "Yeah!" answered Kat.

The least bloody path to the door was nearest to her, so she scrambled over to open it.

Zeus and Javier stood on the front porch, Zeus's head was turned to his left, examining the bullet holes in their exterior wall. "What the hell made these? Are you guys ohhh...?" His question jammed in his throat like a crooked bullet in a chamber. He was now staring at the blood-slicked floor and corpses. "Kaaay," he finished. "Mierda! What happened?!"

"It's a long, weird explanation," said Kat. "But – uh, these were the guys trying to kill Merrick."

Zeus's jaw was slack as he backed up a half step. "These – were gangsters?"

"Sort of," said Merrick, still leaning up against the sofa. "More dangerous than that."

"Ay, Dios mio."

Javier peeked around Zeus's shoulder. His face was stretched in an expression of extreme disgust. "Man, that's gross! And they smell."

Zeus spun around and swiveled his head, searching the pasture and hills. "Any more coming?"

"Eventually," said Merrick.

"Yeah, but the sheriff definitely will be soon," said Kat. "We took off Merrick's anklet."

"What?!" said Zeus.

Del took a step forward. "It's part of the long story. Parts of it I was involved in a long time ago. But the short of it is the sheriff is planning to kill Merrick, and maybe us too. We all know too much now, and we can't stay here anymore."

Zeus's eyes went wide. "The sheriff is planning...? What the hell did you do?"

"It's not what you think," hurriedly explained Del. "The sheriff's a member of a secret circle here that's been kidnapping and hunting people for years. It's hard to explain."

"A secret what?" Zeus's mouth was open as wide as a bear trap. "Hunting people? How do you know all this?"

Del hung his head and sighed. "Because they tried to recruit me a long time ago. Made me stay quiet. He's let me alone all these years, but – I don't think he'll let any of it go now." Del rested a hand on Zeus's shoulder. "It's ok, my friend. You don't need to be involved, and you're probably safe for now, but I'd recommend going back home, packing, and finding somewhere new to live. Even if the sheriff doesn't try to associate you with us, Templeton is a death trap. I'm just sorry I didn't say anything sooner. I didn't think it would... Would..." Whatever Del was trying to say wouldn't come out. He turned away and busied himself wrangling the headless man's legs.

Zeus wasn't letting it go. "So some secret group here has been kidnapping and hunting people? For years?"

Del nodded, never turning to face Zeus.

"People like maybe – my sister?" asked Zeus.

Del nodded again.

Kat stepped in. "We don't know who actually killed her, but – we know Sheriff Kind covered it up and framed Saunders. Then killed Saunders to keep him from talking. I'm sorry, Zeus. We only just figured it all out or we would've told you."

Del faced Zeus. "Kind may be here any minute. Go home, Zeus. Don't get any further involved in this. Keep Javi safe." Turning to

Kat, Del said, "I've gotta get these men to the incinerator. You need to get Merrick and get the hell outta here. Now."

Kat wasn't accepting that Del needed to stay behind. "No, Dad, forget the ranch. It doesn't matter. We need to leave together, or else the sheriff will…"

"I can take care of Quinton," said Del. "Get your asses out of here, you and Merrick, and I'll catch up later."

"Daddy, no. I'm not going to go without…"

"Goddamnit, Katheryn!" Del's eyes were wild and intense. Any burst of anger was uncommon for him. His typically placid demeanor, governed by his *"no swearing, no yelling in the house"* rule, had been replaced by an unfamiliar personality. Kat understood there were layers to her father, but hadn't thought about him doing anything illegal or immoral until he had surprised her by admitting to hunting and killing a man. Whatever person Del might have been in the past, he had apparently concealed it for her protection, and it was now sneaking through in little pieces. "Do as I say! Get you and Merrick somewhere safe. I need to take care of these bodies. I'll catch up. I'll call you when I leave."

"Daddy, no."

"Go! Now! I'm not arguing with you."

Kat wasn't used to this version of her father, and didn't know how to react other than to do as he said. She bent down to lift Merrick, having no idea how she was supposed to get a limp, full-grown man to her car.

"Can you stand?" she asked Merrick.

"Don't think so," said Merrick.

"It's ok," said Zeus who had walked up beside her. "I'll help you." He gave her a warm smile, then called back at his son. "Javi!? Go get the wheelbarrow that's around back. Help Mr. Seavers with the bodies. I'll join you when I'm done." He turned back to Kat. "You get his legs, I'll get his shoulders."

"But, Dad said you should go…"

"He's not the boss of me," said Zeus with a smirk.

"He kinda is," said Kat returning the smirk and moving toward Merrick's feet.

"Nah. I quit," said Zeus. "Ready? One, two, three, lift!"

Kat was puffing by the time she got behind the wheel. After helping carry Merrick to her car, then gathering up Merrick's duffel bag (he had left it next to the big tree out front), she couldn't remember where her keys were, then her purse, jacket, all hurriedly found and scooped up before collecting her envelope of life savings and climbing into the driver's seat. The Jeep cranked up with no protest (not always a guarantee) and she spun tires in the dirt heading toward the main road.

"You ok back there?" she asked.

Merrick was laid flat on her back seat, knees up. Del had tossed a shirt and shoes to him before he left, so at least he wasn't barefoot or naked from the waist up anymore. He nodded, gave a thumbs-up, and eventually replied, "As I can be."

Left was toward Idaho and an Indian reservation, right was toward town. There were no road forks or turn-offs either way for miles. With any luck, the sheriff hadn't already noticed the house arrest anklet being off, and wouldn't be chasing them yet. She turned left. Every bend in the road heading to town was memorized, but the other direction was unfamiliar, so she clicked the maps app on her phone and mounted it on her dash. Her destination wasn't hard to navigate: stay on this road for 22 miles, then look for the signs at the intersection. However, in case she needed a quick place to duck or turn around, the map may come in handy. She knew there were a few ranches with dirt driveways like hers, or other access paths, but no real roads.

Merrick's attempt to sit up in the back seat caught her attention in the rearview. He was able to brace his torso with an elbow against the seat, then lift his head to look around.

"Where are we?" he asked.

"Not far from home yet," answered Kat. "Can you move your legs?"

Merrick grunted for a moment, then said, "Not much." He slowly turned his head to look through each window of the Jeep. "Where's my bag?"

"In the back. I found your bow and quiver, but couldn't find your shoes."

Merrick nodded, wincing afterward.

"Sorry," said Kat. "We were in a hurry. A pair of Dad's old sneakers are in the footwell. They're coming apart, but – it's better than barefoot."

"They're fine. Thank you."

"When we get somewhere safe, I'll buy you a new pair." she offered.

"Where are we going?"

I don't know. "I guess the Flathead Reservation is close enough. Or we can just hide in Glacier Park somewhere. Or maybe Canada."

Merrick chuckled. "You wanna try to explain me to the Canadian border authority? I haven't had an ID since – well, ever."

"Right," sighed Kat.

Discounting the Canadian border, either of the other choices would take a bunch of miles before they got to a turnoff to decide on. There was plenty of time until then, which was fine with Kat because her mind wasn't in a good place to make a rational decision at the moment. Her worry over her father was hijacking her ability to think straight.

As if Merrick could sense it, he asked, "What's going to happen with your father?"

"I don't know," she said, which came out as the beginning of a sob. Seconds later, tears were streaming down her cheeks.

"Uh oh," said Merrick. "I'm sorry, I didn't mean to…"

"It's alright," she whimpered.

"No, it's not," said Merrick.

"No, it's not!" she cried.

She bawled uncontrollably for a dozen seconds until her pride squashed the victim vibe and she yelled at herself as a signal to stop.

"Shit!" said Merrick, staring at the rearview.

"It's – ok," she stammered. "I just needed to get a grip on my…"

"No!" said Merrick, pointing to her mirror. "Behind us. I think someone's following."

Kat looked in the mirror for a second, then said, "I don't see any… Wait."

They were on a long bend in the road with trees obscuring most of the asphalt behind them, but she caught the glint of white painted metal.

"Yeah, I see them," she said. "About a quarter-mile back."

"A sheriff's car?"

"Maybe. Too hard to say. Something white though."

Kat put aside her emotional venting and started calculating. She knew she hadn't passed any parked patrol cars. When they left her ranch, the immediate road section was a winding bend around a hill, then a long stretch afterward that was as straight as an arrow for several miles. If someone was following them there, they had been way far back, so to reach this point, they must've been driving at NASCAR speed. That meant whoever was back there was gunning for her. Her 4x4 wasn't built for racing, and the pursuer would catch up long before there was another road to turn off. *Not good.*

Somewhere up ahead, if she remembered correctly, was an old hermit named Harold. She had only passed his house twice in her life. Her dad had told her the old man was afraid of people and rarely left his property other than to hunt game to eat. He tended to shoot at trespassers, hence the warning from Del. But it was the only place she could think of to duck away from her pursuer.

Risky. Her memory recalled a short, upward-sloped drive and an unlit, covered carport. If he had taken his truck hunting, the carport would be empty and dark enough to back her Jeep into, then wait as their pursuer passed by. If the old man's truck was there, she'd have to improvise and park behind the carport and hope the pursuer didn't notice them. And additionally hope she didn't get shot at by Harold.

"Any other roads around here?" said Merrick.

"No," said Kat. "But maybe a place to give them the slip."

A sharp turn was ahead, and her gut alerted her that this might be the place. She slowed for the bend and prepared a sharp left, hoping her memory was accurate.

I'm right! Old Harold's overgrown driveway was immediately on her left. She braked, skidded, and banked hard.

"Hang on!" she announced, already into the steep turn.

Merrick crumpled against the door, barely managing to keep from sliding into the footwell.

Kat got full tread on Harold's dirt driveway and started the steep climb upward. Her 4x4 may not be a racecar, but it came in handy on steep grades and unpaved ground. The knobby tires gripped the dirt and hauled the sturdy vehicle up to the level "yard" of Harold's property.

A few weeds, rusted hulls of things, and more dirt made up the front yard of Harold's shack-like home. His covered carport on the left was surprisingly empty. *Thank God.* She skidded to a stop just past the carport, then did a hard wheel crank to quickly back into the dark recess of the structure. The Jeep was halted mere inches from the rear wall, satisfactorily blanketing the car in shadow. Miraculously, she was straight too. Almost dead center of the carport. She chuckled internally, recalling her instructor's complaints about her backing-up skills when she took her driver's test a decade ago.

"Wow," said Merrick. "Nice flying, Maverick."

Kat smirked. "Well, we're here in one piece. Just gotta sit here and wait for our follower to go by." She knew Merrick's quip was from Top Gun, and she suddenly recalled that this drifter claimed not to watch TV or movies. "So how come you have nerdy comments all of a sudden, smart ass? I thought you hadn't seen any movies or TV."

"Only saw a couple things. There was a drive-in I hung around for a little while. They played old movies."

"Like what?"

Merrick scratched his chin for a moment. "Top Gun, The Shining, Ghostbusters, Indiana Jones. And some teenage werewolf love story I couldn't stand. Don't recall the name."

Kat smiled. "Aww. Come on, werewolves deserve love too, don't they?"

"Not from that whiny girl," said Merrick making a sour face. "If I'm a werewolf, I'd rather slit my wrists with a silver knife dipped in garlic than be stuck with her."

"Garlic's only for vampires."

"It's only for cooking, actually. It's just pungent, so people figured it must ward off all monsters, including vampires."

Kat shook her head, then caught the fact that he had referred to vampires like they were real. "Hey, you're not saying that vampires are really…"

"No. Kidding. I'm not a werewolf either."

"Well, you looked like one."

Merrick stiffened. "I did? Did you, you know, see me in my, uh – my full...?"

"Kinda," said Kat.

She briefly described what she had seen, the fur, pointed ears, canine legs.

"Wow," said Merrick. "I've never seen myself. Jeez. Sounds like I sorta do look like a werewolf, but – that's not what I really am. I have no idea what I am."

Kat turned her head to look at Merrick. "Alive. And a decent man." She waggled her head. "And not a half-bad lover."

"Oh, you just say that to all the stray werewolves you drag home."

"True."

A car raced by on the street below. Judging by the glance she got, it was a sheriff's car. She listened for about ten seconds to see if the car screeched to a stop or made any kind of noises like turning around. *Probably too hard to hear that.*

"Think they'll figure it out?" asked Merrick.

"Only one way to find out," said Kat. "Ready?"

"Not much choice, is there?"

Kat gently pressed the gas pedal and rolled out of the shadows. She eased down the steep drive, then held her breath, listening for anything suspicious like a car heading her way. No sounds. She pulled onto the road and turned right.

It had occurred to her that she couldn't continue to the reservation since she may encounter the sheriff's car that had just passed. Heading back to the other way, there was only one turn-off before she hit town: her own ranch. As risky as it was to head back that way, she could take the narrow back road on the other side of her property that led to the old residential area where the Fosses lived. Driving would be slow there, stop signs and one-lane streets with multiple driveways, and no stretch of open road until they got far east of town. The maze-like street schemes were the reason she took the longer, faster road to town on workdays. The back roads eventually hit an open highway that led east towards other towns, which might give them places to hide. There was also the chance that Sheriff Kind could alert the other sheriff stations in the nearby towns, so she'd be as nervous as a mouse in a cobra pit driving through the little townships until she could get to another lonely highway. It was that or just take her chances continuing straight on this road, past her ranch, until she hit town center, hoping like hell there weren't roadblocks (which she assumed there would be). There was no good option. Their route had taken a massive detour and it was no good moaning about it. Besides, she could at least see her dad again and maybe convince him to get in the car.

The rearview didn't show any sheriff cars following her. Maybe she really had outsmarted them. She was on the long straightaway now where any pursuers would be noticeable behind...

Oh, no. A tiny flash of sunlight reflected off metal or glass way back there. A moment later, red and blue lights started cycling. *You son of a bitch.*

"Leave us the fuck alone!" she screamed.

Merrick jerked up and bumped his head on something. "What!?"

"He's following again. Lights are flashing."

"Son of a bitch."

Kat floored it and was doing 90 within a mile. The Jeep's suspension was built for off-roading not speed, and it bucked and shimmied in complaint. The gentle bend came up and temporarily hid the trailing car in the distance. There was a slim chance the pursuer wouldn't expect Kat to turn back into her ranch, and might fly by once she was already at her house. However, her luck hadn't been stellar so far today. She slowed only enough not to hit a tree as she slid into the ranch entrance drive.

Racing down the bumpy dirt path at highway speeds was bouncing her brain inside her skull and rattling her teeth, despite tensing her jaw to lessen the abuse. Even with all the jarring, she could recognize Del's truck in its usual spot. Zeus's truck was gone at least. However, two other vehicles were on her property.

A silver Range Rover and a white cargo van were blocking the pathway that separated the two pastures. Kat knew both vehicles well. The van belonged to the lumber mill, used for hauling equipment and sometimes people. The Range Rover belonged to Arthur Fosse. And Fosse was standing on her porch along with three other men. One was her father, head down, sitting on a step, and the two other men had rifles pointed at his back.

"Fuck!" she blurted.

232

"What?" asked Merrick. He was struggling to straighten up and peer through the windows.

She did a power slide in front of the porch, not sure if she should get out and confront Fosse (*and accomplish what? You gonna shoot him?*), or sling gravel and head back the way she just came. Where was there left to go? Her best path out of town had been cut off moments ago, the main road would probably lead her into a sheriff's roadblock, and her back way through town was now blocked.

And her father was a hostage. *Fuck, fuck, fuck.*

Del leaped up from the porch and shouted at her. "Go! Leave me! Go!"

Fosse reared back a fist and smashed it against the side of Del's head. Del slumped onto the steps.

"Daddy!" she wailed from behind closed windows. Her teeth ground, the tenseness in her jaw threatening to burst blood vessels.

Merrick had pulled himself up far enough to look out and was focused on the vehicles blocking their way through the pastures.

"Can we get past 'em?" he asked.

"No," grumbled Kat. And they were out of time to consider the question.

She reached for the shotgun on the passenger seat. Though she was never afraid of defending herself, she wasn't sure she could commit outright murder. Or suicide. Fosse's thugs didn't exactly seem like helpless victims. On the contrary, they looked like professional gunmen. Would she even get a shot off before they killed her? A lump grew in her throat as she abandoned her gun and reached for the door handle. The lump grew bigger when she turned to see the movement on her left.

Coming down the drive was a sheriff's car.

CHAPTER 27

Merrick shoved the Jeep's door open and fell out of it. He had enough control over his body now to fumble his hands and knees underneath him to at least view the situation like a dog. In front of him, Sheriff Kind had stopped his car and was getting out. Deputy Simon Pooler emerged from the passenger side door. At first, Merrick assumed Simon had betrayed them to the sheriff, but the drawn and dismayed look on Simon's face said otherwise.

"What are you doing!?" Kat snapped at Merrick.

"Maybe they'll take me and let you go," said Merrick. To the approaching sheriff, Merrick called out, "It's me you want! Let them go!"

Sheriff Kind withdrew his revolver and aimed it at Merrick with a steady two-hand grip. "Don't move! Merrick Hull, you're under arrest for multiple counts of murder and resisting arrest."

Kat flung her door open and stepped out, leaving her shotgun on the seat. Her expression was caught between distress and boiling mad. "You can't! God damn it, Quinton, you're the one who…!"

"Enough!" shouted the sheriff. "You and your father are under arrest too." Kind looked toward the porch steps where Del was sitting under threat of a shotgun barrel. "Delroy Seavers?!" said Kind, "And Katheryn Seavers? You are both under arrest for aiding and abetting a known fugitive, and for conspiracy against a law enforcement officer."

Kind turned his head to Simon. "Deputy Pooler, please handcuff Miss Seavers." The sheriff approached Merrick and commanded, "Stand up."

Merrick drug himself up using the Jeep door for leverage. Once standing, Sheriff Kind roughly spun him around to lock on the cuffs.

"Let them go, Sheriff," pleaded Merrick. "Do whatever you want with me, but the Seavers were just kind people helping out a homeless man. They don't understand any of this. You should let them…"

"You don't make the rules here," said the sheriff. "And I'm done playing games."

Simon approached Kat with his head down and his handcuffs open.

"Don't you dare, Simon Pooler!" scolded Kat. "You know damned well that the sheriff ordered the hit on Saunders." She twisted around to shout in the direction of the white-haired man. "Ya hear that, Fosse?! Your own sheriff ordered those thugs to kill Mr. Saunders!"

Fosse, aka the white-haired man, smiled, then nodded. "I know, Miss Seavers." The smile approximated a snake bearing its fangs to a trapped mouse. "I told him to."

Simon slipped one of the cuffs on Kat's wrist. "Kind found out everything," he whispered, loud enough that Merrick could hear. "There's nothing I could do. He made me come with him."

Kat cast a poisonous glare that, if manifested, would've stabbed Simon through his eyeballs. "You're a goddamned coward. There's a special place in Hell for you, Simon Pooler," she said in a tone intimating that she may be the one who sends him there personally.

Simon's face looked panicked and pale. "I'm – so sorry, Kat," he whispered. "So, so sorry."

"Bring Del over here so I can handcuff him," said the sheriff to Fosse's men.

The man with the shotgun nudged Del to get up and start walking toward the sheriff. Del slouched forward, limping, arms tucked at his sides, the picture of a defeated man, his captors trailing close by. He was ordered to halt a few feet from Kind.

The sheriff unclipped another set of handcuffs from his belt. "You screwed up, Del," said Kind. "You shoulda kept your mouth shut and your daughter's nose out of our business. This is all on you."

"Lies to keep the demons from claiming your soul," said Del in a slow, chilling tone, "All the blood that's been spilled, and will be spilled, is on you and Arthur's hands. It will never, ever wash away."

Sheriff Kind smirked, acting like Del's words were insignificant, but there was a twitch of uncertainty in the corner of his lips. "Turn around," said Kind, lifting the open handcuffs.

Del began a slow, somber turn, positioning his hands to be cuffed, and only too late did Sheriff Kind notice that a rock was held in one of them. Del moved with surprising quickness and cracked the rock on the shotgun man's temple. The man shuddered and clutched his wounded head, losing his grip on the shotgun. With the same motion and speed, Del snatched the shotgun away and whipped the butt of it around to club Sheriff Kind's forehead. The sheriff "umphed" and staggered, as shocked as everyone else that Del had gone from defeated captive to aggressor in seconds. Del pressed the barrel of the shotgun into Kind's back, keeping the sheriff between him and Fosse's men.

The uninjured rifleman raised his barrel to site Del's head.

"Don't!" shouted Del. "Twitch a finger and I blow Quinton's guts out on the ground!"

Fosse slowly reached under his jacket. Sheriff Kind raised a palm of restraint to Fosse.

Del leaned a little closer to Kind and said softly, "No moves, Quinton, or so help me God, I will do it."

"I'm just backin' 'em off, Del," said Kind calmly. To Fosse, he said, "Arthur? Everybody needs to lower their weapon."

The rifleman lowered his site, however, Fosse not only brought out a pistol but began slowly walking toward Del and Kind.

"Arthur!?" snarled Del. He shuffled so that Quinton was blocking Arthur's line of fire. "God damn it, you have no authority here! Pack up your goons and get the hell off my property!"

Fosse shook his head. "That's not going to happen, Del. You broke the rules. It's the way it has to be."

Merrick had no idea what he should or could be doing to help the situation. His hands were literally tied behind his back and he was in no position to do much. At least, not as plain ol' Merrick.

A nearby movement drew his attention. It was Simon slowly unsnapping his gun flap.

Kat whispered, "You think good and hard about what's really going on here, Simon."

Simon's hand stiffened as it hovered above his gun handle.

Del made another surprisingly quick move, wrenching the shotgun in Fosse's direction and firing a shot into the ground near Arthur's feet. Sand and pebbles exploded up and pelted the crowd. Arthur leaped back, covering his eyes. Without losing more than a second of time, Del already had the shotgun against Kind's back again, another round pumped into the chamber.

"Don't test me, Arthur!" said Del. "I'm not afraid of you."

"This isn't going to accomplish anything, Del," said Kind.

"Wrong," said Del. "You're going to let my daughter go. That's what's going to happen. Do what you want with me, throw me in jail, put me in your Godforsaken hunt. I'll surrender, but she goes free. Got it?!" Del poked Kind's spine with the barrel for emphasis.

"It doesn't work that way," said Kind, still calm.

"This is you and Arthur's mess, Quinton," growled Del. "And she ain't gonna be caught in it. That was the deal a long time ago, and I'm holding you to it. If you have a shred of decency left in your warped skull, you – let – her – go!"

"You're gonna get yourself killed, Del," said Kind.

"You think I'm a fuckin' idiot!?" snapped Del, jamming the rifle hard enough into Kind's back, the sheriff grunted in pain. "You'd kill us all anyway! Bring us to the fire, then play Arthur's fucked-up, *Lord of the Flies* fantasy like we're hogs to hunt. I shoulda never kept my mouth shut! Shoulda told the whole world the twisted, sick shit you do, sacrificing people so the demons'll let you live just a few years longer, just to murder more people. Then even more people! No, Quinton. No! I'm not doing this anymore. My daughter stays out of it. She goes free and I'll surrender, or else I kill you and Arthur right here. If you don't think I can get you both before your goons shoot me dead, you are gravely mistaken. Try me and there ain't no ancient spirits nowhere gonna resurrect your sorry carcasses!"

Arthur Fosse strolled casually toward Del and Quinton, unconcerned. The pistol he carried dangled heavily, no attempt to raise it. The gun itself was huge, a chrome Desert Eagle that was nearly twice the size of a typical handgun.

"Ease back, Arthur," said Kind. "Ok, Del. Listen. I understand what you want, but it isn't that easy. Unfortunately, she knows too much to be…"

"I don't give a fuck about your secrets, Quinton!" said Del. "I'd be doin' her a service to kill you and her both before I die rather than let you take her out there, torture her, and rip off pieces of her while she screams. You know I mean it."

"I know you do," said Kind. "But…"

"If there's a shred of decency left in you…" Del noticed Fosse wasn't stopping a comfortable distance away. "Don't fuckin' move another step, Arthur!" He returned his attention to Kind. "You used to be…. Before you started lickin' Fosse's ass, you were a decent man. What would you do if you were in my shoes, huh?" Del started to sob and sniffle. The shotgun was pushed harder against Quinton's spine. "She's my daughter, Quinton. God damn it! My daughter!"

Sheriff Kind held up a palm toward Fosse to signal him that everything was under control. "Ok, Del. I hear you. We—we won't do… I'll make sure she gets a fair trial. I swear she'll get…"

"No, Quinton!" snapped Del. "Every judge in this county is owned by Arthur, and you know it. She goes free. No trial, no fire, no bullshit. She leaves the state and you don't follow. Promise me, or I pull the trigger. Now!"

Sheriff Kind squeezed his eyes. "Alright, Del. Alright." He lifted his hand and motioned once again for Fosse to back off. "We'll let her go."

"Swear it, Quinton!" said Del.

Quinton nodded. "Ok. There has to be provisions," he added hastily. "But I swear."

Fosse interjected, "I'm afraid you don't make the rules here either, sheriff."

"Arthur," said Kind with clenched teeth. "This is not the time. It's ok. We'll work something out."

Merrick couldn't see the sheriff's eyes to check for a wink or some other kind of conspiratorial gesture.

"No, Quinton," said Fosse. His plastic smile flickered between mockery and malevolence. The heavy pistol bumped against his thigh as he spoke. "I'm not going to lie to our old friend Del. After all, he's seen what happens to people who threaten us." Fosse came forward another leisurely step. "Yes, Del. Your daughter has to die. But if it's a consolation, whoever eats from her flesh will absorb her life essence, and a piece of her will live with them forever."

"In Hell, Arthur," said Del. "And over my dead body. The only person here that should die is you. I might just shoot you cuz you deserve it."

"Feel free to try, Del," said Fosse. "I'm right here. And as you know, I enjoy a challenge."

"Arthur!" scolded Kind. "This isn't time for a cockfight! We can argue about whatever you want later. Right now – we need to calmly end this situation and keep my promise to Del. There doesn't need to be blood spilled here today."

"That's not up to you, Quinton," said Fosse.

The sheriff visibly quivered with anger. "God damn it, Arthur! All these years, I abided by your rules and your obsessive ritual because it kept the peace, and that's my fucking job. But right now, you're screwing with my life, and seriously pissing me off! Shut the fuck up, put away that fucking gun, or I'll shoot you myself." To Del, Merrick could plainly hear Kind whisper, "Please trust me. I'm gonna do something. Don't shoot."

That was the only warning Del got. With gunfighter speed, the sheriff snatched his revolver from his holster and aimed it at Fosse's chest. Del didn't fire.

"Put it away, Arthur," said Kind. To Del, he said, "Thank you. I'll keep my promise once Arthur and his men are subdued. Ok? I swear, Del. I can't make any further promises, but I'll keep that one."

Del sucked back a sob then regained his composure. "It's my daughter's life. She's all I've got. I'm trusting you, Quinton. Be a decent man for once."

"I will," said Kind.

Fosse's gun was still lowered, either surprised by Kind's sudden draw or unconcerned about it. After a curious smile from Fosse, the chrome gun slowly raised.

Kind jerked his aim down and fired a round into the dirt at Fosse's feet. Fosse leaped away, once again throwing up his hands to cover his face, this time laden with a gun. When he was done being surprised, he leveled the giant pistol at Sheriff Kind.

"Lower it, Arthur," said Kind, his own revolver aimed at Fosse's chest. "I gave my word."

"This isn't a game, Quinton," said Fosse. "And I don't grant the demands of those who must be sacrificed."

Kind's eyes stayed on Fosse as he spoke to Del. "Cover me. I got Arthur, you get his gunmen." Kind stepped cautiously forward. When Del didn't blow a hole in his back, Kind took another step.

His .357 revolver was still held firmly pointed at Arthur's chest. Del's shotgun swung toward the riflemen.

"I'm not giving you a choice, Arthur," said Kind. "We're going to do the right thing here." Quinton slowly shook his head. "This one isn't yours."

Fosse made an almost imperceptible grin and inched his pistol down.

Sheriff Kind nodded.

Then he spun quickly and fired. The round hit Del in the sternum, knocking him off balance and sending him crashing to the ground. The shotgun in his hand bounced away and tumbled underneath Kat's Jeep.

Kat screamed. Del convulsed and floundered, unable to find any control of his arms or legs. His wide eyes stared at the sky in disbelief. Streams of blood flowed from under Del's back, pooling on the surface of the hard-packed dirt.

"Nooo!" shrieked Kat. Merrick had rarely seen her tear up, much less cry, but the cork that normally bottled everything up in her popped free, with nothing left to hold back the emotional torrent. She fell to her knees, hands still cuffed behind her back, wailing at her lungs' capacity. Tears pelted the ground, making little mini craters. "Daddy!" was the only coherent word she could muster.

Slivers of smoke ascended from the barrel of Sheriff Kind's gun, held in the exact position he fired it for several seconds before he lowered the revolver. "Goodbye, old friend," he murmured.

Kat scrambled over to Del's side. Turning backward to get her hands to his chest, she fumbled with his shirt, seeking some avenue to stop the bleeding.

In a hoarse voice, Del muttered, "Love you, baby girl. You're my…" He couldn't finish the utterance. His eyes fixed permanently on something far away, his mouth locked open in a frozen question. A gargled breath exited his throat, then nothing more. Del Seavers was gone.

Merrick had no idea what to do. He had rarely been afraid for his own life, but he was truly afraid for those around him. These good people were suffering for others' crimes. Everything wrong in this town was the byproduct of Fosse and Kind's vile infection, destroying others' lives to spare their own, and satiate their bloodlust.

And perhaps the days' quota of blood wasn't done being filled. Deputy Simon Pooler had his revolver drawn and aimed at Sheriff Kind's head.

"F-f-freeze!" stuttered Deputy Pooler. "Drop the gun, Sheriff! I – I'm sorry, but I can't let you get away with this. You can't... You are under arrest, sir. Drop the gun." Simon's aim briefly shifted to Arthur Fosse. "You too, Mr. Fosse. You're all under arrest!"

Sheriff Kind scrunched his face and held up his free palm. "Easy, son," said Kind. He slowly rotated his revolver nose down, pinched between two fingers, then hovered it above his holster. "I'm putting it away, ok? We don't need more shooting here."

"Hands up, sir!" demanded Simon.

"Easy, Simon," said Kind. His revolver slid into the holster. "Lower the gun. I shot in self-defense. Ok? Just self-defense. You understand?"

"No, sir!" said Simon. He clicked the hammer back. "No more cover-ups. No more deaths. No more bullshit. It ends here." His eyes darted to Kat, then back to the sheriff. "Kat, get behind me!"

Kat was oblivious to Simon. Her cheek was pressed against her father's bloody chest, shoulders heaving in despair, eyes closed. Like a mantra, she softly repeated the word, "No."

The sheriff stayed focused on his deputy. "Son, you're going to get yourself killed with this stupid stunt," said Kind. "You're not thinking clearly. And I can't afford to lose another deputy because you..." Sheriff Kind flinched and halted himself from saying more. Too late. Simon apparently wasn't too flustered to notice the slip-up.

"Another...?" stuttered Simon. "Another deputy? Who...? What have you done? Is it Max? You did something to Max?"

Sheriff Kind sighed and pinched the bridge of his nose. "Nothing, Simon. I misspoke. I was trying to say..."

"That's enough!" said Simon. His finger tensed on the trigger. "You're under arrest for the murder of Del Seavers, and – uh, you're all under arrest for the murder of Errol Saunders, Jeremiah Gunn, conspiracy to commit multiple murders, the – the – the obstruction of justice, kidnapping, extortion, unlawful imprisonment, and..."

One of Fosse's henchmen flipped his rifle sight up and aimed it at Simon.

Simon responded by twitching his revolver's aim toward the henchman. "Don't move!"

Fosse quickly raised his Desert Eagle. Though Simon noticed Fosse's sudden movement, his reaction wasn't fast enough. Before Simon's revolver could aim at Fosse, the chrome-plated pistol blasted its massive .50 caliber round into Simon's upper right chest. The impact spun Simon completely around and lifted him off his feet. He hit the ground with surprising control, rolling like a stuntman, and coming up with his own revolver aimed at Fosse. Poorly. He fired once, the shot harmlessly disappearing into the sky. Fosse's henchman fired a precise shot that hit Simon's gun hand, mangling the hand and propelling the revolver out of reach. Simon screeched and cradled his hand, but seemed unable to do anything more. The chest shot had caught up with him. Besides his quivering grip on his injured hand, the rest of his body went limp. Despite the lack of threat, Fosse leveled the hand-canon at Simon and fired again. This time, the huge round blew Simon's ribs apart. He bucked and twisted once, with his trembling fingers in a clawed pose, then flopped flat on the blood-stained dirt. Fosse didn't stop firing. Three more bullets mangled Simon's corpse, this time with no reaction other than the force of the shot shifting the corpse's position on the ground.

Kat snapped out of her trance, screamed, and swapped her tears for vein-popping anger. "I'll kill you!" she roared at Fosse.

Merrick hadn't realized how much rage he had held in while Fosse and Kind killed his friends. His hope had been to keep tempers down and bad fate focused on him by staying silent at the beginning. He had remained silent from sheer shock. All the contained anger exploded from him like a burst balloon.

"Motherfuckers!" he roared. "Fuckin' cowards! Do that to me! Do it! I dare you! You're big shit, huh?! Come on! Come on, shoot me too! See what happens! Fuckers! Shoot me!"

Arthur Fosse lowered his pistol and strolled toward Merrick. "No, I don't think so. I have something else much better in store for you."

"Scared of me?" spat Merrick. "Scared of a guy in handcuffs? Fuckin' shoot me, ya pussy!"

"In such a hurry to die too? Hmm?"

Sheriff Kind marched up to Arthur and wrenched the giant pistol from his grip. "What the fuck, Arthur? God damn it! Now I have to invent some bullshit explanation about *two* deputies going missing. Fuck! You don't give a shit about anyone but yourself, do ya?!"

Fosse stared intently at Merrick, shaking his head in response to Kind's verbal abuse. "I'm not interested in your problems, Quinton. But I am interested in what's so special about this strange man."

"You a pussy too, Sherriff?" taunted Merrick. "You afraid of me? Huh? Come on! Shoot me!"

Kind paused for a moment, as if he was going to respond, then seemed to think better of it. "Maybe we should, Arthur," he said. "Instead of taking him to the fire. We don't know his story. He could be dangerous to underestimate."

"Oh, I know he's dangerous," said Fosse, reaching behind his back to withdraw a different pistol.

Merrick recognized it immediately as one of the agents' trank guns.

"You don't like this, do you?" Fosse said with a cat's grin to Merrick. "You are a delectable mystery. I will enjoy killing you slowly and absorbing your life force."

"Where'd you get that?" asked Kind.

"Inside Del's house." Fosse handed the gun to Kind. "Lying on a bloodstained carpet. Somebody wasn't very welcome at the Seavers' home today."

Kind examined the gun and looked at the cartridges. "Looks like tranks. I wonder if it belonged to those agents who came by asking about Mr. Hull. Whoever they were, Hull probably killed 'em. And those thugs Jimenez sent up here too. I'm telling you, Arthur, this punk is bad news. Best to kill him right here. We can use the incinerator to get rid of the bodies like we used to. Looks like it's running already."

"No, Mr. Hull is exactly who I want at the fire. Finally, a real challenge."

Sheriff Kind shook his head subtly and mumbled, "That'll be your epitaph." He walked toward Kat, trank gun still in hand.

Kat's face was red from both crying and seething anger. "Son of a bitch," she said with menace, yet almost no volume. Like all energy had drained from her vocal cords. "I'll kill you. I'll kill you both."

Sheriff Kind made an amused shrug. "You'll get your chance. But really, you should thank me. I kept my promise and did the decent thing. Killing your father here was a mercy compared to what waits for you, my dear. Honestly, I did him a favor."

"You're gonna burn in Hell."

"Someday. Eventually," said Kind.

He raised the trank gun and shot Kat in the neck. She shuddered and convulsed for a few seconds, then crumpled on top of her dead father.

Sheriff Kind raised one brow. "But it'll be a while before I get there, so – save me a place. Sweet dreams." He whistled to the two henchmen and waved them over. "Get the two bodies to the incinerator over there. And put Miss Seavers in the van with the others. I'll handle Hull."

Fosse said to Kind, "Find Hull some warm clothing from the house. I want him to be in good shape when we take him to the mountain."

"Later," replied Kind. "Listen, we still have to collect the two people that worked here."

"The two Mexicans?" said Fosse. "Already in the van. I took the liberty earlier."

Kind audibly huffed. "Arthur? You can't just... Jesus Christ. Why do you even bother with the pretense of having an actual sheriff here?"

"It doesn't sound like you're very thankful to have your job," gibed Fosse. "You think I'm some kind of dictator?"

"Yes. And dictators don't live very long, Arthur. You should watch yourself."

"Oh? Planning a coup?"

"Don't have to," said Kind. "You keep this up, you'll kill yourself."

"I've lived a long time without your help, Quinton. A very long time. And if you ever shoot at me again, even for a ruse, you'll be prey instead of a predator at the next fire. Are we clear?"

Kind just shook his head, refusing further banter. He walked toward Merrick.

"I'm gonna kill him," offered Merrick with a psycho's grin. "You too. Rip both your heads off."

Kind gripped Merrick's shoulders and pointed him toward the white cargo van. "Save your strength, hero. You've still got another battle coming. Your last one ever. Let's go."

Merrick tried to turn around despite Kind's solid grasp. "Why wait, asshole? You want me? Come at me right now. Both of you. Right here! You don't even need to remove my handcuffs. Let's go!"

"Not yet," said Kind, giving a quick side-eye to Fosse who didn't see it. "But we will see what you're made of very soon. Sweet dreams to you too."

The sheriff raised the trank gun at Merrick's neck and it coughed three times.

Merrick's view went black.

CHAPTER 28

When Kat awoke, she was in a bleak, windowless room made of concrete block walls, dimly lit by bare, low wattage bulbs. On one side of the room, steel shelves were stocked with canned goods and dry foodstuffs, obscured by years of dust and cobwebs that made their precise identity unknown. On Kat's side of the room were evenly spaced prison cells, one of which she was inside. Iron bars in front and steel mesh between each cell. There were other people in the cells too.

As she sat up straighter, Kat swiveled her head to look behind her. In the next cell, Merrick slumped against the steel mesh divider. His chest was moving consistently, so Kat knew he was alive, just unconscious. Inside her own cell was Deputy Yellow Feather. He steadied her as she began to wobble.

"Hey," he said softly. "Good to see you awake. Easy – don't sit up too quick. Those tranks were pretty powerful. Messed up all our heads."

"How long have I been out," asked Kat groggily.

Max shrugged. "Hard to say. I think we've been out for hours. Maybe half a day. Maybe more. Hard to tell time down here."

"Down...? Where are we?"

"I think under the old, torn down water tower. When they dragged me out of the van, they musta cracked my head on something because I woke up in pain. Didn't last long, I went unconscious again, but not before I got a glimpse of the old water tower ruins. The high school kids like to hang out here, drink and stuff, so I've been here before, just – not underneath it. Looks like someone built a bunker here, like for nuclear war or something. Guess it's been modified for kidnapping people."

Kat rubbed her temples. Her skull felt like it was in a vise. It aggravated the nausea she felt from the overall situation. Though she had expected to wake up behind bars, these cells weren't a legitimate jailhouse. It meant that everything she was led to believe was true and she was being held for some secret event that would likely end in her death. "The fire," she supposed, based on what Fosse and Kind had divulged. There was no use denying it, or crying about it. A better use of her remaining time on earth should be to assess the situation, then work on the best action. She was all cried out anyway from snapping after her father's murder. And now was not the time to revisit that.

"Who's here?" she asked. "And is everybody ok?"

"Everybody seems ok, other than dizziness and headaches," said Max. "As for who's here? A few of them you know, a few you don't. The farthest from us is some mobster types. Not sure from where, but – scary guys if they weren't locked up here. I don't know any of them. A couple cells over is someone we arrested a few months ago for rape, and in the same cell with him is one of Tanner's buddies."

In that just-mentioned cell, a long-haired man raised his head and turned to them. "I'm not his buddy," he said. "The guy's a dick."

It took a few seconds, but Kat recognized the man. "You were there that night. The bonfire on my property," she said.

He nodded. "Yeah. Really sorry. I was new at the mill and I was told to try and impress Tanner if I wanted the good shifts. It was a bad call."

"You tried to coax him back to the truck," said Kat.

"Yeah. He didn't give a shit what I said. He wanted us to be in some weird-ass cult where they played at being wolves, or whatever. So, I quit. And now…" he gestured grandly to his cell, "I'm here. Name's Denny by the way."

"Shut the fuck up," said a man on the other side of Denny's cell. "Annoying asshole."

Denny rolled his eyes. "That's Cyril. He says 'Hi.'"

Cyril mumbled something and slumped down onto the floor.

"Nice to meet you both," said Kat with a hint of sarcasm. She squinted to see who was in the adjacent cell behind Max. "Is that…?" Her mind answered her own question before she finished it.

Max nodded. "They woke up around the same time I did. Just napping now. We figured we should save our strength for whatever's next." He rapped on the mesh divider. "Hey, Javi?" he said, his voice still soft. "Look who's awake. Get your dad up."

Javi awoke with a start. He blinked to focus on Max, then turned to see Kat. "Hey," he said. His voice was spiritless. "I mean, good to see you Miss Seavers, but…" He waggled his head as the *"you know what I mean"* gesture.

Kat smiled ruefully and nodded. "I know."

"Dad!" said Javi in a forcible whisper.

Zeus blinked and sat up, rubbing his eyes. "Wha?" Javi pointed at Kat with his chin and a few seconds later, Zeus clued in. "Oh… Miss Kat, you're awake? Sucks to see you here – um, well, you know."

"I get it," said Kat. "And thanks, Zeus. I'm really sorry you're here too. Looks like anyone who bothered Fosse or the sheriff is in here. I was hoping you'd get away."

Zeus shook his head. "Son of a bitch Fosse tracked us down. Think he has some cell phone tracking thing. Hijo de puta. He had no right. None. Asshole. If I get outta here, I'll kill 'im."

"I'm guessing we all would. Probably why we're in here," said Kat.

"Where's Del?" asked Zeus. "Haven't seen him yet. He get away? Maybe he got in touch with the feds?"

Kat took a deep breath, not quite ready to respond. She hadn't prepared what to say, and the thought about constructing an anesthetized answer made her want to scream and put her fist into the iron bars of her cage.

Zeus seemed to pick up on the reason for the hesitation. "Oh. Jesus. I – ah, shit, Miss Kat."

Kat nodded slowly, trying to calm herself. She wanted to reassure Zeus with *"It's ok,"* but it wasn't ok. Nothing about this was remotely ok. "We need to focus on our situation. Not panic. Keep our minds sharp for whatever's next."

"Yeah. Sure," said Zeus. "Of course. We're with ya."

"Ok, so, has anybody got any ideas?"

Zeus snorted. "Like what? There's no lawyers, no legal process, they're just gonna kill us. They got guns, we got squat. The bars are iron, so unless you know Superman, I got nuthin'."

Kat glanced at the room and located a dark set of concrete stairs. "Those go to the surface?"

Max nodded. "Yeah. I'm not sure how deep we are. Last time they came down here, I could see light come in pretty clearly, so we might only be one level down."

"They came down?" asked Kat. "Who? Anyone we might be able to, you know, talk to? Bargain with?"

"Don't think so," said Max. "Last time it was Tanner and one of his cronies. They came down to pick us out." Max's jaw tensed and his eyes hardened. "He picked me. Like I was a freakin' lobster in a restaurant tank."

Kat scrunched her face in both disgust and bewilderment. "Huh?"

"They each claim one of us before they take us to the fire," said Max. "Tanner wanted you, but someone already claimed you before. One of the higher-ups. Not sure who."

Kat shook her head, face still scrunched. "What?"

Zeus said, "Hey, man, she probably doesn't know the stuff you told us."

Max nodded. "Right. I guess I should explain." The tenseness in his face faded and he met Kat's eyes. "I've been unknowingly studying this group for years. I told you some of this already, I forget how much. Ya know, the myths of the wolf-men in the mountains, horror stories that seemed like monsters rather than real men, but are actually men in wolf suits? I knew Fosse and Kind were involved, I just didn't know they were the leaders. All the councilmen of the town at the very least are part of it. It makes sense now why Sheriff Kind was covering up all the evidence. I had all these weird pieces that wouldn't fit, and I guess I just couldn't see past my job. Ya know? Everything was complicating my…"

"Max?" prodded Kat. "Can we get to the point?"

"Sorry. Just been an obsession of mine for a while, and… Doesn't matter. Fosse is apparently the leader of a cult of lycanthropes – uh, not the fictional monster kind, but the traditional kind from Greek mythology. Men who pretended to be wolves, did a ritual around a fire on Mount Lykaia, hunted people, and ate their flesh. It all came from a legend about a king, Lycaon, who tricked Zeus into eating human flesh, then was cursed as a wolf. It spawned other weird cults which were probably the origin of all the stories about werewolves and…"

"Max?" chided Kat.

"Right. Sorry. Anyway, that's what they're planning to do to us. Build a big fire on some out-of-the-way mountain, drag us out there, and hunt us. And – eat us. Or parts of us."

"Jesus," murmured Kat. Not all this information was new, of course, but it felt so much more terrifying since they were stuck in a cage awaiting that very fate.

Max continued, "They've been doing this for years and everyone just thought it was a silly myth. The original lycanthrope legend centered around the new moon, once a month, but I guess it's too hard to hide a bunch of murders that many times a year. So, it looks like they do this once a year. And I guess that's why they needed this hidden place to store their victims until it's time. People go missing here and there, not all at once. Doesn't ring alarm bells. Some people like me got a little suspicious, but – we didn't figure it out. Now it's too late."

"Holy fucking shit," said Kat. "I mean. I assumed they were going to kill me, but… What the fuck are they…? How fuckin' sick are these people? I mean – eat us?"

Max hung his head and nodded. "That's what I meant about picking us out. They each pick one of us to hunt and eat."

Even though her father had told her some of this, a lot of it flew by from bewilderment. The confirmation of it, and subsequently becoming the subject of it, was swelling her tranquilized brain, and she rubbed her scalp with her fingertips to massage away the overload. "I'm not sure I care why they wanna eat me, but – why?"

Max shook his head. "There is some kind of result—something that happened to Fosse, and maybe Sheriff Kind too, that makes them think that doing this cannibalistic ritual is vital to continue. They seem to believe that the ritual grants them longer life, or some kind of supernatural power, but I don't see how cannibalism helps. Makes no sense."

"Like any of it does?" said Kat.

"Well, no, none of it does. Except… I guess some part of it works. I saw a newspaper article a while back when I was doing research. It said Fosse and Kind had been Army buddies in Vietnam."

"I read that too. Was an error though. He couldn't be that old. They retracted it and said their dads had the same name."

Max cocked an eyebrow. "You think if Fosse can have half the town kidnapped and killed, he couldn't make a local paper retract a statement?"

Good point. "Ok, so what's it mean?"

"I think they **are** that old. Maybe older. Whatever secret Fosse found to make himself stay younger, he kept it guarded, known to only a select few, and it has something to do with the ritual, or the mountain. Or, actually, I don't know for sure, but it has to be something he needs here or he wouldn't have stuck around all this time. Maybe he believes there's gods or demons on the mountain he has to appease, make sacrifices to. Like the Zeus, Lycaon thing."

"Hmm?" said Zeus, hearing his name.

"Sorry," said Max. "Other Zeus. Greek Zeus."

"This is insane," said Kat. "My dad said something similar. Except, there just isn't magic spirits on mountains that makes people live super long."

"It may not be magic," said Max. "Fosse owns a biomedical lab in another town that's been doing stuff on regeneration therapy for wounded soldiers and amputees. Maybe he found something, some formula that he kept to himself. Could be part of the ritual."

"Secret formulas, spirits, demons, or whatever, doesn't matter. It's all bullcrap." *You sure, honey? Your boyfriend turns into a chemically altered, magic beast. And somebody made him that way.* "Anyway, like I said – I don't care why he wants to kill me. I just want to keep him from doing it. To all of us."

"Now, **that** I understand," said Zeus.

"What are we gonna do, Miss Seavers?" whined Javi.

She wanted to say, *"Why ask me? I just woke up,"* but she had been acting bossy since she opened her eyes, so they probably were seeing her as the leader. "I'm thinking," she said. "And I'm open to suggestions."

Nobody seemed to have one to give her. She stayed silent to give them opportunity, taking time to finally scratch something irritating on her back shoulder. The silence did not breed new suggestions. Max scratched at something behind his back too, though it could have been a ploy to pretend distraction rather than cluelessness. As she poked her fingers through the tight mesh to try and wake

Merrick, an idea dawned on her. A dangerous one. But their situation was already dire, so…

"Anyone got something sharp?" she asked. "Like a knife? A nail? Pin? Anything."

Max looked embarrassed. "I, uh – actually have a knife in my boot. I always keep it there. They never bothered to check."

"Dios mio," said Zeus. "Why didn't you say so?"

"What good would it be?" replied Max. "Best I could hope for is to try and stab one of them when they come down here to take me, but how would that help? They have guns and they'd just shoot me."

"Give me the knife," said Kat.

"Why?"

"I need to try and stab Merrick with it."

"What?!"

"Just give it to me," demanded Kat.

Though Max shook his head, he rolled up his cuff and slid out the knife. He reluctantly handed it over.

Kat took it, then shuffled behind Merrick's slumped form to find the best position to get to him. There just wasn't one. When she tested the width of the mesh holes, the knife was too wide to fit through. No attempted angle improved the situation, and pushing it harder also didn't help. Kat swore in frustration and threw the knife onto the concrete floor.

"Hey!" said Max, seeing his knife abused. He snatched it back up.

"Sorry," mumbled Kat, drawing her knees up to her chin and wrapping her arms around them. She was hoping Merrick could turn into beast form and smash his way out of the cell. Even if the knife could reach him, the tranks might keep the transformation from occurring. Either way, the hope was dashed. She wondered if their captors understood the importance of the tranks on Merrick.

"What the hell were you doing?" asked Max.

She shook her head, wobbling her knees against her chin. "Doesn't matter. Isn't going to work."

Max tucked the knife back in his boot. "Alright. So, now what?"

"Yeah, what're we gonna do?" moaned Zeus.

"Jesus, guys!" groaned Kat. "Doesn't anyone here have a brain besides me?"

Zeus clamped his mouth shut and narrowed his eyelids. Max gave Kat an offended, under-lid stare.

Kat raised her palms in appeasement. "Sorry. Sorry, guys. I'm just pissed off at the world right now."

Max waggled his head. "It's ok. We all are."

"There's a lot to process," said Kat, "and I'm not exactly in the best frame of mind right now, considering…"

She couldn't finish the sentence. Trying to describe the trouble of suppressing her grief unfortunately reminded her of the very pain she was holding back, which defeated the purpose of doing it. There was no other course but to put her father and Simon completely out of her mind until she could find a way out of this. Which seemed impossible. "Come on, guys. Help me. Think!" she said.

Max let out a long sigh. "I, uh – always thought I was a smart guy, but…"

"You are a smart guy," said Kat.

"Just smart in figuring out clues, doing research, knowing what it means," said Max. "Not so smart is coming up with solutions."

Kat shuffled over to where Max sat. She placed an arm around his shoulder. "Listen," she said. "We need someone exactly like you to know things, give us the knowledge we need so we can think of something to do about it. Ok? You gave us a lot to start with. You knew stuff nobody else does."

Max nodded somberly. "I guess. And a lot of it I told to Simon. Even though he didn't believe all of it, maybe he believed enough to tell someone. I know the sheriff was watching him, but maybe there was a chance he could've…"

Ah, shit. He doesn't know. Max met Kat's eyes which probably weren't doing a good job of hiding Simon's demise.

The deputy squeezed his eyes closed. "He didn't get away, did he?"

Though Kat didn't want to think about this anymore, she had to answer Max. She closed her stinging eyes and slowly shook her head.

The deep breath Max took rattled in his throat. "Right. Ok. I understand," he said with forced stoicism.

Kat blew out a cleansing breath. "There's no one on the outside to help us. We're on our own down here. So we need to keep it together and come up with a plan to somehow stay alive. Ok?"

"We're with ya, girly," said a man in one of the far cells. "Though I doubt you'd like me very much outside of here," said the man, "I want to stay alive as much as you do. So, whatever it takes, count on my help."

Kat nodded. "Alright. Thank you. For starters, my name is Kat, not girly." She was trying to gain respect from the obvious mobster, but realized she came off as uppity. If she survived this nightmare, she'd have to work on her social attitude.

The man smiled politely. "My apologies, Kat. I'm Ernesto. Several of these men are my associates. "This one is Sacha, that one is…"

A noise interrupted Ernesto. The grating squeak of a heavy metal door came from above the staircase. Light spilled over the steps, followed by moving shadows. Legs wearing black jeans and work boots appeared in the opening, culminating in a tall, middle-aged man with white hair. Arthur Fosse. Behind him came Quinton Kind, dressed in an all-black, military-looking ensemble.

As Fosse walked toward the center of the room, Ernesto started in.

"You will pay for this, gringo," said Ernesto. "My people will find you. Your family, your business, everything you love in this town will be destroyed. Those you love will be tortured, killed slowly. You will never feel another day of happiness and safety again. Not one. Unless you let me out of here."

Fosse darted his eyes toward Ernesto, only for a moment. "You will be let out soon. All of you," said Fosse. "Then we will see what your threats amount to."

Fosse walked past Kat's cell to Merrick. The smell of his aftershave was pungent and nauseating. Fosse knelt near the barred door, staring curiously at the unconscious man. After a few seconds, he rubbed his chin and gently shook his head.

"What is so special about you, Mr. Hull?" mused Fosse in a near-whispered voice.

Kat had the urge to reach through her bars and strangle Fosse, though she knew it was fruitless. However, hearing his contemplation gave her a new idea.

"I know," said Kat. "I've seen what he can do." Her smile was feline as Fosse shifted his eyes to her.

"Oh?" said Fosse. "Are you going to enlighten me?"

"Nope," said Kat, maintaining her enigmatic grin. "Looks like it may be the one advantage we have that you don't."

"I see," said Fosse, sounding amused. "Forgive me if I don't believe you. It would be easy to say you know something that you don't, and refuse to prove it."

"Maybe," said Kat, not taking the bait. "And maybe I don't have to. You saw all those agent men dead at our house. You think me and my – father did that?" It was a herculean effort to mention her father and get past the lump in her throat considering the two men in this room were directly responsible.

Fosse looked perplexed for a moment. "The, uh – agents were gone when we got there. Incinerated I assume. But – I did see the blood. How many were there?"

Kat hesitated to answer, wondering if doing so gave away anything. "Not sure," she said, which was partially honest. "They didn't all die inside the house."

"And you saw Mr. Hull fighting some of them?"

"Wasn't much of a fight. Slaughter."

"I see." Fosse's expression was calm, but there was a noticeable flicker of worry he was biting back. "Do you think this little conversation will frighten me into letting you or Mr. Hull go? Hmm?" He shook his head and smirked. "I wanted him here, Miss Seavers. You see, I picked him for myself. I welcome the challenge."

"And what happens when you lose?" said Kat.

"I don't lose," said Fosse. "Ever."

"Only takes one. And then I won't get to say I told ya so because – you'll be dead."

A scoffing snort came from Fosse's throat. "So, I should reconsider? Perhaps pick you instead?" Fosse turned to Kind who had remained standing near the staircase. "Would that be alright with you, Quinton?"

Why's he asking...? Oh, dear God. Kind picked me for himself, didn't he? To do what? Eat? Kat was starting to commiserate with Max on feeling like a lobster in a tank.

She got a grip and held her cool. "Doesn't matter who you pick. Merrick will kill you all anyway. If I don't first. Starting with you, Quinton." She tried to shoot burning, poisonous lasers with shrapnel through her eyes at Kind. He seemed uninterested in the conversation altogether.

Fosse gave her a patronizing grin. "I'm sure you are very formidable with a gun, Miss Seavers. But alas, none of you will have weapons out there. Unless you count sticks and rocks."

"Won't matter," said Kat. She was acting a whole lot more sure of herself than she felt, and was pleased she hadn't revealed her fear.

"Won't it?" Fosse examined Merrick again. "So, perhaps I should just kill him now? Save us the trouble?"

"I don't care. Go ahead," said Kat. *Yes!* It was finally circling around to where she wanted this sickening chat to go. "Shoot 'im. He's unconscious. Should be easy, even for you."

Fosse's shit-eating façade was being corroded by uncertainty. This stupid banter was a long shot, but maybe, just maybe, the asshole would take the bait. He glanced at Merrick, then Kat, then Merrick, undecided.

"You're amusing, Miss Seavers," said Fosse. "However, killing him here would ruin the ritual. Lessen the power of consuming his life energy. No, I can wait. As will you. I like your moxie. It's almost too bad you will die, but unlike your poor father, a piece of you will live on inside us." The snaky grin reappeared on Fosse's face. "Or more specifically, inside our dear sheriff."

Kat wanted to throw up. She refused to react by looking over at Kind.

As Fosse got up to walk back to the stairs, Kat's last hope to force Merrick into beast-mode was blowing away like the retreating smell of Fosse's awful aftershave. The heat in her skull felt like it was boiling her brain. But once this ritual thing started, maybe she'd have another chance.

A loud voice interrupted her internal rage. "You want a fight? Let me outta here and I'll give you a fight!" roared Cyril, the rapist. "I won't need a weapon. I'll kill you with my bare hands!"

Fosse's smugness was back in full force. "You'll all get your chance. But it won't be how you imagine it." He gave the row of cells a once over and briefly met Kat's eyes. "Be careful what you wish for."

CHAPTER 29

"Hey."

Kat heard the voice, but couldn't figure out where it was coming from. She was desperately trying to grasp her father who was coated in blood and falling endlessly through darkness. She was also falling, unable to catch up with him. No matter how she tried to grab him, he slipped away

"Kat. Wake up."

No one was around her, and everything was dark.

A noise popped in her head, then she opened her eyes, waking from her nightmare. Max was next to her. Apparently, it was his voice she had heard and they were both still in their cell. Reality came crashing back.

Hours after Fosse and Kind left, and still with no good plan to get themselves free, Max and Zeus had agreed that they should start napping to calm nerves and conserve strength, with one person to remain on watch, switching every few hours. Max had been the first on watch. Now it was Kat's turn.

"Right," said Kat rubbing her eyes. "I'm up."

The watch plan they had constructed was only between the friends. The other inmates hadn't asked, so they were on their own until this ritual thing happened, then everyone could reevaluate their group bonds under survivor mentality. She peered around and saw that only Ernesto and Cyril were awake. All of Ernesto's "associates" were asleep along with Denny, Zeus, and Javier.

Max gave Kat a weak smile. "You good for a while?" he asked.

"Yep. Get some rest." Kat still had some cobwebs to clear, but she'd be fine in a few minutes.

"Kay." Max drew up his knees and wiggled his shoulders searching for a comfortable position against the cell wall.

Kat stretched her cramped legs and scratched at that odd, itchy spot on her back shoulder. Probably some spider down in this hell hole had bitten her as insult to injury. Maybe Max too since he had been scratching at something. She looked behind her to see if Merrick was awake yet.

At first, it didn't appear so since he hadn't moved and he was facing away from her. Then a moment later, he spoke.

"Kat?" he asked. "That you?"

His voice was as fragile as a man on his death bed. It scared Kat a little, though she didn't think tranquilizers could actually kill Merrick. Then again, he had been pumped with about 10 of them in the last half a day. Each of the other captives only had one dart knocking them out, and even those could've killed them if not dosed correctly (she doubted any such care was taken by their captors). So, with that in mind, what could 10 (or maybe more) do to Merrick despite his supernatural ability to ward off fatalities?

"It's me," said Kat. "You ok?"

"Just chillin'," said Merrick. "Enjoying the scenery."

Though it was a sad attempt at a joke, Kat almost chuckled anyway. Anything other than misery down here was welcome.

Merrick coughed softly. He still hadn't turned his head. "Since I can't move, pretty much all I can do."

"Back to that again?"

"I was getting better 'til they shot me up some more," said Merrick. "Where are we?"

"An underground bunker. In cages."

"Everybody's in cages? Not just me? Don't suppose we're being sold to a zoo?"

Again, the lame joke was enough to make Kat want to laugh. A little chirp-like chuckle slipped out of her lips. "No. Unless you count being fed to the wolves? Then – maybe."

"Who else is here?"

"Me, Max, Zeus, Javi, a bunch of gangsters, and a couple other people you don't know."

"Oh, no," said Merrick. "They got Javi and Zeus? And Max too?"

Kat nodded, forgetting Merrick couldn't see her. "Yeah."

"Damn it." Merrick took a deep, labored breath. "All my fault. I shoulda never done anything other than pass through your town."

"How's it your fault? Fosse and Sheriff Kind, and Tanner, and all them assholes – it's their fault. They're responsible for all this."

"Yeah, I know but… Doesn't matter. I'm just sorry."

Kat sighed. "Well, we all had our separate cries about it. Now we need to get past that and make a plan to survive whatever horror they're gonna do to us."

"Yep. You're right. Ok, so – anyone had any ideas?"

"Not good ones. My best plan was to stab you with a knife, but I couldn't fit it through the mesh."

"Gee. Love you too," said Merrick.

Though Kat knew it was just a dumb joke, the words *"love you too"* sent a subtle buzz through her spine. She chose to ignore the comment. "Since you're up, I don't suppose there's another way to bring out in the beast in you?"

"No. And may not be a good idea anyway. I can't control it. I might kill all of you."

"It's a better chance than we'll have with Fosse and his cronies."

Merrick was quiet for a moment. She assumed he was considering the issue. When he spoke, his already weak voice sounded even more strained. "There's too much risk that I'll kill you."

"I'm definitely gonna die if you don't. We all will. I don't see any better options."

Merrick was quiet again for a few seconds before his head moved. The nod was subtle but clear. "Ok," he confirmed. "We'll have to wait a while though. The drugs are still affecting me. The other one can't come out. When they take us to wherever this ritual is, we can assess the situation and…" He paused and didn't finish the statement. Kat got the full message anyway.

"Yes. We'll assess everything then. Assuming we're together." As she said it, it hadn't dawned on her that they may not be together. She had just assumed Fosse and crew would dump them somewhere as a group and then start the terror all at once. What if it wasn't that way?

The question would have to be pondered later because the doorway opened above the stairs and voices could be heard. Many voices. *That can't be good.*

"Here we go," mumbled Kat.

"What?" asked Merrick unable to turn and see what was coming.

"Shhh. Pretend to be asleep or they might shoot you with more tranks."

He didn't respond, so she hoped he was already mimicking sleep. Kat poked Max's leg with her shoe. "Get up!" she hissed.

"Hnnh?" mumbled Max.

"Zeus! Javier!" Kat rattled the mesh between them to get their attention.

"What?" Zeus blurted while snapping awake. His transition from sleep to fully awake was much quicker than Max.

Several men in all black, carrying assault rifles, came down the stairs along with Sheriff Kind, also dressed in black. They surrounded the two first cells, then a two-man team opened Ernesto's cell. Ernesto's associate (Sacha, if Kat remembered correctly) leaped at the man opening the door and received a rifle butt to the forehead for his effort. Ernesto raised his hands and stood back, understanding the consequences of resistance. Another black-clad man stepped into the cell and jammed a syringe into Ernesto's neck, then plunged another into Sacha's neck. Both men slumped to the ground, no longer conscious.

Oh, man. The men-in-black drug out the now unconscious prisoners, threw Ernesto over one's shoulder like a fireman carrying a victim, and hauled him up the stairs. Assuming they went one cell at a time, Kat assumed she still had a few minutes.

She was wrong. Sheriff Kind walked all the way to her cell, skipping the others. Her temporary relief drained along with the blood from her face.

Max stood and retreated to the rear of the cell.

"Relax, Mr. Yellow Feather," said Kind. "It's not your turn." He put his hands on his hips and appraised Kat. "Miss Seavers and I have something to discuss first." He unlocked the cell door, hesitating before he fully opened it. The man behind Kind gripped what looked like an M-16. "Don't do anything stupid," said Kind. "I'm not here to hurt you. Yet."

Kat had no idea what was going on and she didn't like being separated from the others, especially Merrick, but what else could she do? Jump the rifle-carrying brute and pelt him with her puny fists?

Kind opened the door and came in with handcuffs open. Without a better counteroffensive, Kat let herself be cuffed again. Though she was expecting to be drugged like the others, Kind simply guided her out of the cell walking. She looked back at Max and Zeus, feeling like she should say something as a hurried goodbye, hoping like hell it wasn't goodbye yet. Zeus waved with doe-eyes that made Kat want to cry again. Her eyes shifted to Merrick, still facing away from her, unable to even turn around and watch her leave. She wanted – no, **needed** to say something to him, but what? Everything that occurred to her to say was inappropriate, or inadequate. She was at the stairs before she had decided what to say. Too late. *Everything is too late.*

The stairwell was only one level, leading to a landing that ended in a short vertical climb up hand rungs. They were hauling up Ernesto's body through the surface portal as she and Kind approached. They waited for the team in front of them to clear, then went up themselves.

Standing above the portal, breathing the fresh air, Kat had the urge to run for it. It would mean abandoning everyone down there, and miraculously escaping the goons with rifles, running pell-mell in a section of the forest she had never been while sober, all the while hand-cuffed. She doused her panic and decided to go with Kind for now. Merrick was still everyone's best option.

Sheriff Kind led Kat to his patrol car and sat her in the back seat. He closed the door then got in the driver's seat.

"Ok, listen," said Kind. "I know you hate me, and I'm not going to try to explain again why what I did was a better ending for your dad than what is about to happen for you – but if you can get over your anger at me for a minute, I think we can help each other."

Get over my Anger? Get over my Anger?! Kat wanted to leap over the seat, crash through the security mesh, and pummel Kind with his own handcuffs. She took a deep breath thinking that whatever ridiculous scheme Kind had in mind, it might open a new, unexpected door if she could keep calm enough to listen to it.

Kat tensed her jaw and made one forced nod.

"Ok," said Kind. "You stand a better chance than me at convincing your boyfriend, so that's why I'm asking you. I don't know what he can do, or what specific skills he has, I'm just judging by the results I've seen – which make it seem like he has a real chance of turning the tables on Arthur out there. And I know you think I'm a monster, but Arthur is the real monster here. He's made everyone in this town his personal playthings, and anyone who gets caught crossways in his path becomes the victim of this ritual obsession of his. I'd have been dead a long time ago if I hadn't played it Arthur's way, and it's too late for me to get out of it, but – not too late to eliminate Arthur. You follow me?"

First of all – my boyfriend? Why does everyone assume... Never mind. Second of all, you killed my father in cold blood and now you want me to team up with you to kill Fosse? This is like the crap that happens in some twisted movie thriller, not real life. And why the hell would I let you live? You both need to die.

Kat's inner dialogue probably made a disgusted look on her face because Kind seemed frustrated. "I'm gonna make this simple," he said. "You get Merrick to kill Fosse and then keep him off me, I'll do what I can to keep everyone else off of you. That's why I picked you. After it's done, you two disappear. How would I know where to find you, huh? You go off and live your merry lives, and this town gets free of Fosse. We clear?"

As if the situation wasn't crazy enough, warning bells were ringing in Kat's head from Kind's offer. Even in her dazed, terrified, and panicked state, she could see there was a giant hole in the promise to let her and Merrick go free. Kind had either killed or lined up for slaughter every person that had a shred of evidence on his misdoings. Yet, the two people that know the whole sick truth about him would be allowed to wander free, and risk them telling whoever they meet? *Fat chance.* Kat wasn't that stupid.

Sheriff Kind probably really did want to stage a coup, and he supposed Merrick doing some kind of Rambo act in the secluded woods would be his best chance to hide it from a public inquiry. Or maybe just blame Merrick and Kat for it. Kind could take control of the town, or at least be rid of Fosse's leash. Meanwhile, Merrick and Kat would be genuine fugitives, with a legitimate arrest record, and Quinton could legally hunt them down and arrest, try, and convict them. Or if possible, just kill them as soon as Fosse was dead. In everyone else's mind, he would've done justice to Fosse's murderers. The scheme was obvious, did nothing but benefit Quinton Kind, and would buy Merrick and Kat only a little more time before death came for them. If Kind could get by Merrick, that is. Killing Fosse was probably a necessity for escaping this

263

nightmare regardless of an agreement with Kind. Kat had no illusions that Kind would keep any portion of his word after Fosse was dead, but – up until then, it would indeed buy them a little bit of time. There was also the sticky point of whether Merrick could control who he killed. However, Kind didn't know that. And since Kind was lying to get what he wanted, she could lie too.

Kind was smart enough to know Kat couldn't abandon her friends for a deal that only benefited her and Merrick, and a straight-up agreement would be suspicious, so he'd expect her to bargain. "If you promise me you'll let Zeus, Javier, and Max go too, I'll do it," she said.

Kind shook his head. "That's too many. I can't. The deal has to be for just you two."

Expected. He can't give in right away or that would also be suspicious.

"No deal," said Kat. "If you want me to hold Merrick off you and only kill Fosse, then me, Merrick, Max, Zeus, and Javier go free. All or nothing. I'd rather die with my dignity than let my…"

"Alright. Alright," said Kind, with a fair acting job of looking reluctant. "Then Merrick has to get to Fosse first thing. It's too hard holding off the – uh, hunters on everyone all at once."

Kat had to give Kind an *"I don't trust you"* look to sell it, then she nodded and said, "Ok."

Kind nodded back. He got out of the car, then opened her door. As he leaned in to pull Kat up, she said, "If you go back on your promise, Merrick will kill you."

Kind froze just for a second then met her eyes with a dark stare. "Not going to do it yourself?"

Be careful what you wish for, you son of a bitch. She hoped her glare looked venomous.

Kind waggled his head, then produced a folding knife. He raised the cuff of her pants and tucked it in her boot. "Now you have two. For what it's worth. Satisfied I'm not bullshitting you?" His little cockeyed eyebrow raise suggested he wanted to know if she got his meaning.

Two? He knows about Max's knife? How…?

So, Sheriff Kind was both aware and unconcerned that Max kept a lethal knife in his boot. She guessed Kind let it slide so Max could help in this little coup. Proof Kind planned to acquiesce to her friends-go-free demand all along. It was also frightening that even though Max was a trained law enforcement officer with a lethal weapon, and now Kat had one too, the sheriff didn't view the knives as legitimate threats. What assurance did the "hunters" have that Max, or her, couldn't sneak up on someone and cut their throat?

As she considered the implications, she unconsciously dug her nails into the spider bite on her back.

Kind helped her stand and she got a good look at the cargo van they were being put into. Ernesto was already lying flat inside. His associate, Sacha, was being dumped next to him. It all too much resembled a meat wagon being loaded with beef or pork carcasses. That chilling thought was the last thing on her mind when Kind pricked her neck with a needle.

"See you out there," said Kind, like they were about to have a picnic.

Perhaps they were. A smorgasbord of helpless humans being hunted like boar.

CHAPTER 30

Merrick had been drugged so many times recently, he wondered if his system might have developed a tolerance. At least enough to remain conscious, however bleary-eyed and soupy-brained he may be, after yet another trank dart. He remembered being hauled out of the bunker, driven in the back of a van with other unconscious people lying next to (and partially on top of) him, carted up a bumpy mountain by some kind of utility vehicle, then deposited on the ground next to a pile of gasoline-soaked wood. It had been early evening when all the prisoners had been taken from the bunker, and mid-evening by the time they were delivered to their destination. After so much traveling and movement, it was unexpected when they stopped and were just left alone.

The evening air was chilly and crisp, and lying on the frigid pine needle-strewn ground permeated his jacket. Merrick was used to such things, even at mountain elevations, though not everyone was going to handle the temperatures as well. At least the wind was calm at the moment.

Despite the new tolerance for the tranks, he was still unable to move his arms or legs, and couldn't take full advantage of being unshackled and uncaged. Rotating his head was the sum total of his extreme efforts, and through bleary vision, he could make out a large moonlit rock shape that might resemble a skull if someone was imaginative. A wide-mouthed skull with the maw as a cave or deep recess. If it really did look like that, it seemed more like a Hollywood set than a real rock formation. Maybe that's why their captors chose this place. They believed in demons, or specters, or supernatural energies, and a skull-like rock cave would seem like an ideal place to worship those things. That, or it was just a coincidence that whatever secret power the mountain possessed just happened to reside near a spooky Halloween attraction.

All of the people from the bunker had been deposited nearby, most still unconscious. Some of the gangsters moaned softly as they stirred, taking a lengthy effort to sit all the way up. Merrick suspected the captors didn't know he had been partially cognizant during the journey since he made sure he never fully opened his eyes until he was left alone. Unfortunately, that meant he couldn't fixate on any landmarks during his trip. He might as well have been asleep for all the good it did. And since most of his body was immobile during the ride, he couldn't have attacked anyone with his meager Merrick Hull muscles. His "other" self would have to wait for a better moment.

For the time being, he could acquaint himself with the rest of his surroundings which were difficult to determine in the dark. Starting with the obvious, they were high up on a mountain. The rest was uncertain. Which mountain? How far from a road, or any kind of civilization? If he had a guess, it was a long way from either since he doubted the captors would allow their prey to be near help if they escaped. There weren't any lights that could be seen, no manmade line of a road, or boxy shape of a building anywhere visible.

The breeze increased in strength, making the chilly air feel colder. Merrick's adrenaline was keeping him plenty warm for the time being and hoped the others were ok as well. The bright ¾ moon peeked through the looming pine trees, which were tall enough to deny the moon's full effect on the clearing around them. Overall, it was dark near the ground and the ready-to-light bonfire was still unlit. That seemed creepier than having the thing ablaze. They resembled bones stacked in a funeral pyre, preparing to send their ashes to the heavens to soothe the restless spirits of the dead, yet left undone.

He hadn't seen anyone besides his comrades for a while and was curious why the captors were so confident that no one might come-to quick enough to run away. Or perhaps, they wanted them to run away? A hunt couldn't start until the prey took flight. But how in the world, on this vast mountainside, could the hunters be so sure they could find and catch everyone in the dark?

A while ago, when he was sure the captors weren't around, Merrick had squirmed, flopped, and inched his way next to Kat. It took a quarter-hour to get to her, and when he got there, he couldn't reach his hand up to stroke her hair. Brushing his fingers against her hand was as much physical comfort as he could offer at that time. After about twenty minutes of examining his surroundings, and pondering what came next, he had regained enough body control to sit up and place her head in his lap. He suspected he could walk if he concentrated extremely hard, but he wasn't leaving Kat, Zeus, Javier, and Max. The others he could care less about. Though he didn't wish them harm, whenever the shit finally hit the fan, he knew what his priorities were. If time allowed, he'd help the rest.

If I can get him to come out. The tranks from the agents' guns apparently had been designed to inhibit his transformation. There was an all too real chance that he couldn't transform at all, regardless of the catalyst. *And just when I actually wanted him to come out.*

The drugs will eventually wear off and you'll get your chance.

Maybe. If everyone isn't dead by then.

The head he was stroking moved under his fingers. Kat groaned and tried to sit up. "Whaaa…" she murmured.

"Shhh," said Merrick. "It's ok. We're all safe. For now."

She struggled to brace her arms under her body to get upright. "Whhoooff," she muttered. "Head's spinning."

"Yeah. Very sporting that they make all their victims dizzy before they hunt them."

Kat shook her head and winced, seeming to regret the action. Through gritted teeth, she said, "I've been drunker than this and still fought off assholes."

She turned in all directions, then met Merrick's eyes. Her smile, though timid, was genuine, warm, and very welcome. For the briefest of moments, Merrick had the urge to tell her he loved her. Before his mouth could open to spout that bad idea, he squashed the notion and simply smiled back.

"Really good to see your face, pretty lady," he said.

She snorted in amusement. "God, you must be hard up if I still look good after being locked in a dirty cell, drugged, dragged up a mountain, and tossed on the ground."

Yep. The real Kat is awake.

"Who's here?" she asked.

"Everyone from the bunker. Haven't seen any bad guys yet."

She stood up, wobbly, found her balance, and looked around again. Then she offered a hand to him.

"Can you move well enough to run outta here?" she asked.

"Run? No. Walk, maybe. But…" he wasn't sure how to put the next statement.

"But what? If there's no one around, maybe now's our chance."

Merrick shook his head. "I can't be certain, but I feel like they're waiting for us to run before they start the – you know, show."

Kat scanned the area again, then slowly nodded. "Yeah. Damn it, you're probably right. Why leave us alone at all? It's all just part of the mind fuck." She placed her hands on her hips and ground her teeth. "God damn them!"

"Shhh," said Merrick. "Let's wait 'til everyone's up and fully mobile before we call attention to ourselves."

"Right," said Kat, listening, though distracted.

Merrick knew she was adept at multitasking. She was probably absorbing information about her immediate environment, searching for the best path to take once the running started, along with paying attention to whatever he said.

The clearing where they had been deposited was more level than the rest of the mountain, with steep grades below and beside them. Some rock formations and dense clusters of trees surrounded them in every direction but down, which was the only viable downward path away from this spot. Once they started running, they would be herded in a specific direction, which likely fit the captors' plan. After they got a considerable distance down the mountain, perhaps they could try to shake up the expected path.

Merrick stood up next to Kat and suggested they rouse their friends. The gangsters and other inmates were all awake now, some of them standing, and Merrick didn't want Zeus, Javi, and Max to be the weak links whenever the terror started. Merrick considered grabbing a rock or club-like branch in preparation for a surprise assault, but everything their captors had done so far suggested they were dutifully following strict rules of the ritual, which apparently included giving the hunted group enough time to gather themselves before the killing began.

Javier took Merrick's hand and stood up. He blinked like he couldn't see well. "Where are we?" he asked.

"A mountain," said Merrick. "Somewhere North West. Can't tell you more than that."

"I can," said Max. He waved off Kat's hand and stood on his own. He too blinked away the drug-induced vision impairment. "I can't see well yet, but I know these trees. They only grow like this at the higher altitudes, and the taller mountains are just over the border of the Flathead reservation."

"You been here before?" asked Kat.

"Not on foot," said Max. "Flew over in a helicopter once looking for lost hikers. These mountains are off-limits to anyone that doesn't have permission from the Flathead nation. No hikers, no hunting. People do it anyway, but if they get stuck or lost, they're in trouble. Plus, there's a mountain chain here that frightens people so much, they stay away. Myths about spirit creatures that stalk and eat stray humans."

"I think we know where that comes from now," said Merrick.

Max nodded. "Most people think it was just made up to keep tourists away from the mountains. But..." he shrugged and gave a rueful smile. "I always thought there was something to it. Kinda sucks now that I was right."

"Yeah, well, they're gonna have to catch me first," said Javier. "And I'm not letting them do nothing without a serious fight."

Regardless of the bravado from Javier, of the five friends, he and Max had the best chance of fending off their attackers. Javier was young, athletic, and could probably maneuver better than any of them. Max was still a young man, in shape, and professionally trained in defense. Though Kat was a tough cookie, facing men armed with God knows what (assault rifles, arrows, knives, swords?) her toughness would only get her so far without a solid plan. Maybe together, with a decent strategy, the group could mount a legitimate defense.

They won't need to if I can get the "other one" to show up.

And expect him to kill only the bad guys? You really confident in that plan? Merrick rubbed his head from the stress of the conundrum.

"Merrick?" someone asked.

"Hmm?" He hadn't realized he had been lost in his thoughts.

"I said the gangster guy is starting to walk away," repeated Kat.

Shit. It wasn't time yet. Even though Zeus was sitting upright, he couldn't stand. If their captors saw the gangsters leaving...

Ernesto turned to Kat as he and his associates walked past. "Time to go, mis amigos. Before they come back. Good luck to you."

"No, wait!" said Merrick, much louder than he had planned. "As soon as any of us leave, they'll think it's time to start the hunt. That's what they're waiting for. We need to all be fully capable of running. Some of us can't see well yet."

Ernesto shook his head. "I'm not waiting for these pendejos to fuck around with me any longer. No, mis amigos. It's time for me to take my life into my own hands." He made a brief wave then focused ahead as he descended the slope.

"Coward," said Kat, to herself, but loud enough for Ernesto to hear.

The head gangster made only the slightest hesitation before continuing to walk down the slope, never turning to acknowledge whether he heard the insult.

"Yeah, that's right," she said. "You know it too."

They pulled Zeus to his feet and steadied him.

The other inmates, Denny and the grouchy rapist, Cyril, stood next to Kat, not following Ernesto's men.

"I'm sticking with you guys," said Denny.

Cyril said nothing and merely looked sullen.

Merrick hadn't seen movement anywhere else, so maybe he had been wrong. "Then, I guess we better get moving too before they..." he started.

Something flashed through the air, briefly painting the night landscape orange as it passed. A flaming arrow flew toward the unlit bonfire pile, which happened to be near Merrick and company. They all leaped back, some of them gripping others' arms for balance. The missile smacked into one of the gasoline-soaked logs and immediately started the whole thing ablaze. The resulting sudden whoosh of heat, and whump of the fire spreading, was enough to make them all stumble several more steps backward. Even Ernesto's crew halted on their trek down slope to look back up at the spectacle. In any other instance, the powerful blaze and surprising way it was lit would've been a cool thing to see, inspiring an "Oh, wow. How pretty," remark instead of what Merrick was thinking: *Oh, shit. It's starting.*

As suddenly as the arrow had appeared, a strange shape emerged behind the blaze. Only his head, torso, and arms were visible, the remainder was blocked by the edge of the fire. Despite knowing the beings who threatened them were just men in disguises, the sight of this "wolf-man" made Kat gasp. She clutched Merrick's arm like it was an emergency handle on a train. The being had a wolf's head, long pricked ears, broad chest, and stiletto-like claws that glinted in the flickering firelight. Its fur was stiff and long, and its lupine snout showed rows of shiny, sneering teeth. A grotesque mashup of Marvel's Wolverine and a werewolf. The most chilling aspect was a set of glowing green eyes, glaring at its prey.

The demonic apparition had a voice to match its frightening appearance. When it spoke, it was as if an animal was speaking English.

"Sacrifices!" it bellowed in a canine howl, raising its clawed hands to the night sky. "Your souls will be welcomed by the spirits of the mountain. We have lit Lycaon's Fire and will commence the hunt soon. Make no mistake, you will all die. There is no escape. And we shall consume your flesh to honor the spirits that dwell here, and through us, share with them your life energy. We encourage you to fight well. There is no dishonor in fighting and dying. No one has survived the hunt, and no one ever will. Yet, the challenge is yours to try. You will have a thirty-minute head start to get as far away as you can."

The wolf-man paused and Merrick looked at Kat, who likely had the same question: *Should we start running now?*

As the wolf-man lowered its gaze to Merrick, its eyes seemed to get brighter. "Your thirty minutes has started. I wish you a good death."

Yep. Start running.

Kat didn't bother with a parting insult. She just gripped Merrick's arm and called out, "Let's move!" Within seconds, they had caught up to Ernesto's men, becoming a mob of twelve terrified people careening down the mountainside. Most everyone fell at least once, some more than once, sliding down steep patches of pine needles, or wobbling on loose rocks. Merrick caught himself after a slip and ended up facing the top of the hill where the fire raged. The green-eyed wolf-man peered down at them as they ran, not bothering to follow, and not using anything like binoculars to observe them.

They're confident they'll find us regardless where we run, even in the dark, and giving us a huge head start. Though Merrick knew this was important, his brain wasn't good at solving mysteries while stampeding down a treacherous mountain in bare moonlight. *Maybe they won't have to kill us. We'll die trying to run away, fall over some cliff, or impale ourselves on sharp branches or rocks.*

"Come on!" shouted Kat.

At first, Merrick thought she was impatient with his pace, but he quickly realized she was calling to Zeus who was further behind and being helped by Javier. Of all of them, Zeus was the least adept at running, especially since he might also be the least recovered from the effects of the drugs. Merrick decided to keep a few lengths ahead of Zeus and Javier and find the easiest path for them to tread.

A few minutes later they were all in a dense section of forest that made their going slower. The trees blocked their view of the wolf-man and the fire burning above them. Which meant the wolf-man couldn't see them either.

Or can he?

Fifteen minutes of running, weaving, slipping, stumbling, and crashing through low-hanging pine limbs had taken its toll. Zeus fell hard and didn't have the strength to get back up immediately. When Kat circled back to him, her own lack of breath made the words come out in several second intervals. She bent down and clutched at her stomach.

To Max and Merrick, she said between deep huffs, "Let's stop – and catch—our breath."

Ernesto, who had fallen significantly behind, caught up and was on his way past them as he wheezed, "Furthest behind – first to die."

"And we'll – run by you in – couple minutes when – we've caught our breath and – you're gassed."

Ernesto took about one second to consider that argument and agree. He held up a palm to his men and gathered his breath to speak clearly. "Stop here – for minute."

273

Zeus propped himself on an elbow and worked at calming his breathing. "You should leave me," he said after a good exhale. "I'm slowing you down."

"Not a chance," said Kat. "We're all getting out of here alive."

Zeus looked perplexed. "How?"

Kat looked at Merrick with an unspoken question. He shook his head. *Not here. Not now.*

"Because we're smarter than them and we'll think of a way," said Kat. "Just don't give up, ok?"

Zeus nodded unenthusiastically.

Max stood and peered over Kat's head. A few yards to their right was a drop-off that was traversable but treacherous. Going left or straight down was the most reasonable.

"I think I know where we are," said Max.

"You do?" said Ernesto. "You've been here before?"

Max rolled his eyes a little since Ernesto had ignored their previous meeting near the fire. "Just in a helicopter. I know the shape of that valley. If I was someone unfamiliar with these mountains, that valley would look like the best place to go, the easiest path. Once you get there, it becomes narrow and uneven. No road, no nothing. It's just a dip on route to the next mountain. And there's a little stream there that makes the ground soft and mucky. Swampy. Hard to run. In essence, a kill box if they have men on either side. The likeliest place they would expect everyone would run to." Max turned to his right. "This other direction has a lot of rocks and steep sides, a harder hike, but – it's also a more unexpected route, and just happens to be the shortest distance to a road if I remember right. Tiny, dirt access road for rangers to get through in an emergency, with a ranger's emergency station a few miles down the road. It's just hell to get there." He gave Kat a hopeful look. "It'll be harder for the hunters too."

"I'm in," said Kat. "I prefer to play hard to get."

"Denny?" asked Max.

Denny nodded. "I said I'm sticking with you guys."

Max nodded, then reached back to scratch an itch on his shoulder blade. "Cyril?"

The inmate shrugged.

"Merrick?"

"Of course," said Merrick.

Kat interrupted the next question. "Why did you scratch your back?"

"What?" Max looked dumbfounded. "I have an itch. Must be all these pine branches."

"No," said Kat. "You had it before we left the cages. I have one too."

Max shrugged.

Zeus said, "Yeah, me too."

Merrick suddenly noticed his itch returning as well. "Come 'ere," he said to Kat since she was closest. "Let me see it."

Kat pulled her shirt over her shoulder and turned her back to Merrick. Even in the dark, he could see a swollen red dot the size of a nail head. He touched his finger to it.

"Feel that?" he asked.

"Yes," said Kat with a harsh tone. "It hurts and itches."

Javier announced from behind them, "My dad has one too. Same thing."

Merrick tensed his jaw. "I know what this is."

Ernesto waved his arms for his men to stand. "Why does it matter?" he scoffed. "We have to get moving before those – werewolf things come. We're running out of time."

Merrick shook his head. "You can run if you want to, but they'll find you, unless… damn it! If I only had a knife."

Max reached into his boot and unsheathed his six-inch knife. He offered it to Merrick. "For what?"

Merrick snatched the blade and roughly grabbed Kat's shoulder. "Hold still," he demanded.

"Hey, gringo!" said Ernesto to Max. "You've been hiding a weapon from us all this time? Doncha think that might be important information to tell us?"

"I'm not a gringo!" said Max in an unusual rush of temper for him. "I'm Cheyenne. And I don't recall you helping worth a shit a little while ago when we needed to plan together."

"Alright, alright, Cheyenne." Ernesto declined his head as if an abbreviated bow should mollify Max.

"Ow!" cried Kat as Merrick flicked the blade under her skin and pinched the sore area with his fingertips. "Jesus, Merrick!"

275

Merrick looked at the little bloody object in his hand. A tiny puck of round metal, flatter than a BB. Heat rose to his cheeks. "I was curious how they were so confident they'd find us in the dark, with no map of this mountain, and no way to know which way we'd go."

"What is it?" asked Ernesto.

"It's a locator chip. I'm pretty sure we all have one. Those werewolves of yours are tracking us with GPS technology."

CHAPTER 31

Ten shapes gathered along a cliff edge of the mountainside, wolf-like in appearance, though standing on two legs. Their glowing amber eyes peered down into the dark, focusing on something invisible to normal human sight. Most of the ten wolf-men stood still, only a few shifting their stance in anticipation.

An eleventh and twelfth wolf-man came from the cave and joined the others gazing into the darkness. Quinton Kind knew that the leader, Arthur Fosse, had green glowing eyes in his mask rather than everyone else's amber, though he couldn't see colors through his own lenses. The mask eyepieces saw muted grey landscape, no distinguishable color other than lighter and darker grays. The unique lenses separated vision into contrast and shade except for one exceptional feature: heat. That showed up as bright white. He had watched the twelve white shapes of humans descend the mountain, stop briefly, then continue to descend, surely never believing they could be spotted so easily in the dark. Heat vision had limits, however, and currently, at the considerable distance they had traveled, the humans were no longer visible.

Vision was not the wolves' only device to hunt.

One of the wolves abruptly turned away to pace behind the others. He scraped his claws against the cave entrance, sending sparks into the frigid air.

"Relax. It's not time," said Wolf Fosse. His voice was low in timbre with a lupine growling noise rumbling under the vowels.

"They're getting away," said the pacing wolf.

"No," said Wolf Fosse. "I've explained this. They are all marked."

"Yeah, yeah. I see 'em all," said the anxious wolf. "I see 'em all getting away."

"Shut the fuck up and stand still," said Kind to the anxious wolf. The strange sound of his own voice through the electronic filter never ceased to amaze him.

"Or what? What're you gonna do to me, huh?"

"I'm gonna laugh my ass off when you run around reckless, fall off a cliff, and die," said Kind. "And feed the fuckin' crows with your carcass."

The young, anxious wolf was not fazed. He leaned closer to Kind. "Yeah, maybe I oughta find your prey first, huh? Why'd you pick Kat anyway? You wanna fuck 'er before you kill 'er? Maybe you thought eating her meant eating out her pussy? That get you hard, old man?"

Kind swung a stronger-than-human backhand at the annoying wolf's head, slamming him against the cave entrance. A moment later, a vicious backhand from Wolf Fosse propelled Kind against a tree trunk.

Kind shook off the collision and stood up to full height. "He deserved it, Arthur. I didn't. Do that again and it'll go very differently."

"You forget your place!" said Fosse.

"I know exactly who I am and where I belong," said Kind. "Do you, Arthur? Tanner sure as hell doesn't."

The head wolf glowered at Kind, his glowing eyes appearing even more intense despite having no luminance control. "We do *not* use our names here. And whatever my son deserves or doesn't deserve will be dealt with by me. Are we clear?"

Kind said nothing. A non-argument was acquiescence enough.

"Uh, sir," said a different wolf. "Sorry to interrupt, but – I think there's something wrong with the locator chips."

Fosse Wolf turned around to address the speaker. "What?"

"They're still working," explained the other. "But they're not moving. There's no way they've sat there that long."

Fosse Wolf turned to Kind, addressing him in an even tone as if no argument had previously occurred. "You think they're staying still to set up an ambush?"

Kind took a long deliberate step toward the others. "No. There's a couple of smart ones in there. They probably figured out the chips."

Wolf Fosse growled, not a garbled word but a genuine growl.

"See?" said the Tanner-wolf. "They're gonna get away. Let me go after 'em!"

"No," said Fosse. "It isn't time. Besides, I have a hidden tracker on them."

"Gimme the frequency!" said Tanner. "Let me go after 'em!"

"Fuckin' moron," grumbled Kind, dismissing Fosse's decree not to insult Tanner. "Where is it hidden?" he asked to Fosse.

"The Indian's knife," said Fosse. "I assumed they would never allow their secret weapon to be lost. It's why I didn't take it from him."

"Genius," said Kind, acting as if he wasn't aware before, and hadn't done his own version of it with Kat's pocket knife.

"Flattery from you?" asked Fosse. "I know you did the same thing with the knife you gave Miss Seavers."

Kind felt a chill go through his spine.

Fosse continued. "I assume it was for the same reason as mine. False sense of hope to make it more challenging? I see its frequency too."

Sure, that. "So, we're both geniuses."

Fosse ignored the congratulations and turned to Tanner. "The frequencies show up in your display. Just look further east. They kept moving after the shoulder tracking chips stopped."

Tanner scanned around. "There! I see 'em. Kat and the Indian have 'em, huh?"

"Yes," said Fosse.

"Good," said Tanner. "I'm gonna get 'em both. Then I'm gonna fuck Kat before I kill 'er."

"She's mine," said Kind.

"Fuck you, old man," said Tanner. "You can eat 'er if you want, but I'm gonna kill 'er. And the Indian."

Kind stepped further away to discourage himself from reaching back and throttling Tanner. Once the hunt started, how easy it would be to kill Tanner and Fosse both with no one knowing. And even if someone did know, they couldn't tell. It also meant, should someone seek revenge on him, no one would report that either.

To Fosse, Kind said, "You really think they'll keep the knives? They won't figure it out?"

"They're not as smart as you think," said Fosse. "Besides, their strategy of heading east will get them stuck, and then they'll be trapped. They probably thought they were on the other side of the mountain, going west to the access road. Their direction is flipped. See? Not so smart."

"Smarter than the last group,' said Kind. "One of these days, one may actually escape."

"They won't. You keep forgetting that I don't lose. Ever."

*Believing **that's** not so smart.*

Besides his freedom, the captors took one other thing from Merrick: his watch. Only a small crime in the scheme of things, but it would've really come in handy at that moment. No one knew how long they had been traversing the rock slopes of the mountain, sliding down flat faces, stumbling over jagged rock piles, balancing over craggy terrain, all in the dark. So, guesses were all anyone had of how much time was left before the werewolf things came after them.

On the bottom of a steep rock face was a flat ledge that led into a level section of forest, dense with trees. As good a place as any to once again catch their breath. They had been heading sideways across the mountain, a much harder hike, instead of going down the easier path toward the valley. The terrain was exactly as Max had predicted, slow and treacherous for the fugitives, and hopefully the same for their pursuers. Whatever the wolf guises did for the hunters, it was doubtful they made it easier to race across steep rock cliffs and jagged narrow fissures. Perhaps it was even harder for them.

Merrick caught Zeus as he slipped down the rock face, waited for Javi to also descend, though the boy had no trouble, then they caught up with Kat and Denny in the dense tree area. They all stopped and sat down. This time Ernesto made no complaint.

"Since they can't track us anymore, do you think we've gone far enough that they won't find us?" asked one of Ernesto's men: a once well-dressed, Asian man named Kino, his silk suit now torn and dirty.

"No," said Kat. "But we've thrown a couple of monkey wrenches in their plan, and maybe bought ourselves some more time."

"Here waste time?" asked another of Ernesto's men named Sacha: flattop haircut, Russian accent.

"We need time to recharge," said Kat. "And more importantly, get our plan straight for when those things finally do catch us."

"They can't track us anymore," said Cyril. "Fuck 'em. I say we just keep walking that way. They'll never find us."

Merrick replied, "We'll keep going that way, sure, but bet on at least some of them finding us. They wouldn't risk their prey escaping to tell authorities without solid backup plans."

"Like what?" asked Denny.

"I don't know," said Merrick. "Just don't underestimate them. They've supposedly been doing this for a couple of decades and nobody has lived to tell about it. And I'm pretty sure at least some of the victims were as smart, if not smarter, than us."

"Fair points," said Ernesto. "Did you have something in mind?"

"I think our best bet is to keep together," said Kat. "Although we'll be more obvious targets, at least we can mount a stronger defense if they don't come all at once. And I'm not sure, but I think they plan to hunt us one at a time. They did that 'pick us out' thing, made a big deal about it, so maybe it's part of the plan to attack us separately. Sticking together may make that more difficult."

"Very smart, girly – uh, Kat," said Ernesto. "I'm glad you're our ally."

Kat smiled at the man, though Merrick could plainly see it was forced and thin.

Merrick offered, "We keep moving for now, and when we're sure they're coming, we should find a spot, feel it out, settle in, then defend it. Familiar territory makes it easier to turn the tables on your enemies."

"Also smart. Agreed," said Ernesto.

"Screw that," said Cyril. "Those werewolf things are going to slaughter us if we stay in one spot. Better to split up and keep moving. You wanna hunker down together somewhere? Fine. When I make it to the road, I'll say a prayer for your mangled carcasses."

"Well then, bye. Hope somebody cries at your funeral," said Kat.

Cyril gave her a murderous glare but he didn't walk away.

"Ok, so here's what I plan to start doing as we walk," said Kat. She removed the folding knife Sheriff Kind gave her. "I've got one and Max has one, and if we find some straight sticks along our path, we can sharpen the tips. It ain't much, but they'll work like a spear."

"My associates are – uh, specially trained in the use of blades," said Ernesto. "Don't you think those knives would be better off in their hands instead of a woman's?"

"Nope," said Kat. "But they can have sharp sticks if they're nice."

Ernesto balled up his hands and tensed to stand.

"Easy guys," said Merrick. "We're all under a lot of pressure here. We just need to work things out."

Zeus raised his hand like a schoolboy. "I'm nice. I'd like a sharp stick, please."

Javier raised his hand too.

Denny tentatively raised his.

Cyril cracked two medium-sized rocks together and glowered at Kat.

Ernesto stood up and waggled fingers at his men. "Let's move." To Kat, he said, "We'll find our own weapons along the way. Thank you for the kind offer." His tone did not match the respectful words.

They had taken only a few steps when a haunting noise filtered through the trees and echoed in the valley. As chilling as a banshee's wail, as alarming as a police siren, and as heart-stopping as a gunshot, every member of the group knew what it was and what it meant. It was the howling of wolves, amplified from the acoustics of the mountain, and it meant that the hunt had started.

Ernesto and his men took off running with no word to anyone else. *So much for agreeing to stick together.* Cyril made one short glance at Kat before following the gangsters. Denny stood and looked anxious, hopping a few steps in the gangsters' direction.

Kat flashed a concerned eye at Merrick who couldn't do much more than return her concerned stare and shake his head.

"Not yet," he whispered.

"Why?" she mouthed.

Merrick tried to ignore the question and bent down to pat Zeus on the shoulder. "It's ok. We should go too."

Kat grumbled, reached down to heft a fallen pine limb, then walked past Merrick without saying another word.

Max came up behind Merrick. "What's that about?"

"It's complicated," said Merrick.

With no further explanation coming, Max sighed and gave up. He picked up a smaller branch, removed his knife from his boot, and walked away.

Kat had pushed her pace to get some distance between her and Merrick. She wasn't angry at him so much as she was frustrated. It wouldn't even help to argue her logic with him because what she was feeling didn't have anything to do with logic. She was scared. The group seemed to be counting on her wits and savvy to keep them safe, and she was scared she was leading them nowhere except to their death. She was scared she wouldn't be able to avenge her father, or give him the funeral he deserved, and was scared that her own funeral would be attended by no one. Would her mother bother to make the trip? Would anyone even hold a funeral for her? Like Zeus's sister, Esperanza, would they just say she was missing for years until it was academic? And she was scared to watch her friends die. One by one. Then possibly be eaten? She was scared that after all these years of saving money and waiting for the right moment to begin her real life, traveling through Europe, exploring culture and history, she would never get the chance. Everything she had done up until now would be just wasted time. She had never really lived.

Kat slid down a hill slick with dried leaves and pine needles. Surprisingly, at the bottom was Max. She didn't remember anyone outpacing her. He was kneeling and turned only partway to her as she approached.

"Hey," she said coming up to his side.

"Hey," he replied. He waved a finger at a crevasse he knelt next to. "I hadn't counted on this."

The divide was steep, a dangerous climb in or out, and led only two ways: uphill and downhill.

"I don't suppose going down into it is a good idea?" she asked.

He shook his head. "If we walk along the bottom of it, it'll be difficult to get back out if and when the wolf things show up. It'd be a slaughter."

"Uh huh," said Kat, looking down the mountain, then back up the mountain. "Where d'you suppose it leads?"

"Probably all the way to the valley," said Max. "The pressure of the land would force the crack downward. If we walk down along the edge of it, we'd be going right where we said they'd expect us to go."

"And if we go up?"

"Anyone's guess. The crevasse starts somewhere up there. The only question is how far we'd have to go to find the origin. And up takes us back toward the fire."

Kat squeezed her eyes shut and rubbed them with stiff fingers. "So, go down and we play into their hands, go up and we might run into them."

"Yep. Sums it up."

"I like our chances going up. Maybe they wouldn't expect it. They'll be heading where they think we'll be and not where we're actually going."

"Maybe," said Max. "And maybe they have other ways to track us."

Kat sighed. "We have to pick something."

"You're right. Ok. Up. We'll go up." His eyes suddenly looked panicked and he hurriedly added, "I mean I suggest we should go up. I'm not trying to be in charge."

Kat smirked. "Like anyone is."

"They're following you."

"Only cuz no one else said anything."

"Well, I trust you," said Max. "You're smart and you – you…" Max's face flushed, noticeable even in the moonlight.

"Max?" said Kat, leaning to catch his eyes as he diverted them away.

He swallowed hard and met her searching gaze. "I just think you're amazing, that's all. I've known you since we were kids, and I've – uh, had a crush on you pretty much since then."

Kat smiled and patted his cheek. "I've known for a long time, Max. Even before you said it the other day. You told me when we were teenagers."

His eyes narrowed. "When did I...? Wait – was it at a party in Mr. Erickson's barn?"

Kat nodded and raised an eyebrow. "You don't remember, do you?"

"Not really. I was pretty drunk. I don't remember much of what I did that night."

"Well, lessee, you, uh – tried to make me dance with you even though there wasn't any music, then you told me you always loved me, then licked my face, then threw up on my shirt."

"Oh. Oh, God."

She nodded and chuckled. "It was gross. Sweet, but gross."

"I'm – I'm so sorry."

"Ancient history."

"Well," he said, his smile returning, though clearly embarrassed. "My feelings aren't history. I still really care for you."

"I know, Max. You're sweet. Really. And maybe if I hadn't been stuck on the things I planned to do, I'd have taken you up on your offer for a date, but – I had my plans. Plans I'm probably never going to get to do now. And if we get out of here somehow, I'm going to do immediately."

"Traveling across Europe?"

"You remembered? Yeah. I'm not even sure why I want to do it so much, but – yeah, that's what I'm going to do. No attachments, just living free for a while."

Max shook his head and smiled warmly. "You were always your own person. Knew what you wanted outta life."

"So did you. Working hard to be a police chief, or whatever."

"Yeah, well, that may be shot now considering everything that's happened. If we kill Sheriff Kind, how'm I gonna explain that? And if he kills us, then game over anyway."

Kat reached up and kissed Max on the forehead. "Don't give up. On anything. We're not done yet."

She turned away and made the pretense of searching for another branch to whittle on (she had already given Zeus her first attempt at a spear), hoping Max would be discouraged from saying anything awkward like, "I love you," if their eyes had remained locked.

Behind her, Max said, "I'm going to scout uphill for a little ways, see if I can see where the crevasse starts."

Good idea. Kat watched Max disappear through thick brush, then she busied herself looking for straight branches that may have fallen. She found one, yet when she picked it up, it broke in her hand. The one next to it looked solid, although not quite as straight, and would do fine. As she reached for it, a pair of dress shoes stepped on it. *What the...?*

Rising to see what idiot was standing on her branch, she felt a sickening crack on her skull, then heard the crunch a microsecond after. The pain shot through her neck and spine like a ripple in a pond, washing blackness over her as the pain traveled to her toes. She never felt her body hit the ground, though she heard it.

CHAPTER 32

Merrick heard Denny yell, though the words were indistinguishable. The rest of the group was far behind him. Zeus had fallen after slipping on a sharp rock, and when Javier reached for his father's hand, Zeus accidentally pulled him into the sharp rocks as well. Merrick had pulled both of them free and was in process of checking their injuries when Denny shouted.

"Go," said Zeus. "We're fine. We'll catch up."

Merrick began to jog in the direction he last heard Denny's voice. When Denny shouted again, Merrick clearly heard the words, "Kat's hurt!" and began to run faster. He slid down a leaf-covered slope to see Denny holding Kat's head as she sat up. A splotch of red dripped past her ear.

"What happened?" demanded Merrick.

"Son of a bitch!" cursed Kat. "I'll kill 'im!"

"What? Who?" stuttered Merrick.

"I don't know," said Kat. "One of Ernesto's guys I think. Had on dress shoes. That's all I... Ow! Jeez, man," Kat snapped at Denny who was examining the wound. "All I saw was his shoes before he cracked me on the head."

"With this?" asked Denny holding up a scuffed rock with a smear of blood.

She shrugged and winced from the action. "Probably," she said through gritted teeth.

Denny and Merrick helped her stand as she continued to curse under her breath. She brushed off her pants, cursed again, and slapped her back pocket.

"Bastard!" she snarled. "He took the knife."

She dug in her pockets but produced no knife.

"Probably what he was after," said Denny.

All three people turned toward the sudden crunch of leaves and snapping of twigs nearby. Expecting it could be wolf-men coming, Merrick searched the ground for something to defend against them, seeing only the rock that conked out Kat. A moment later, Max squeezed through a narrow space between thick bushes.

He noticed Kat and grimaced. "They took my knife too," he said, rubbing the back of his head and scrunching his face.

"You ok?" asked Merrick

Max nodded, then winced. "Everyone else ok?"

"I'll live," said Kat. "They won't."

Zeus clambered down the slope to where the remainder of the non-gangster group stood. "Who won't live?"

"Ernesto's men," said Merrick. "They took Kat and Max's knives, hit 'em with rocks."

"Dios!" said Zeus.

"They're probably pretty far ahead of us by now. Looks like they went uphill like I was suggesting. We might eventually run into them."

Kat angrily brushed off a few clinging pine needles. "They better hope not. If the wolves don't get 'em, I will."

"With what?" asked Denny. "They took your knife."

Zeus held his sharpened stick out to Kat and grinned. "In case you see one of 'em first," he said.

Kat kept checking the sore spot on her head as she hiked. It didn't seem to be leaking new blood, though every time she stumbled over a rock in the dark, she thought she had reopened it.

The journey up the slope was more tiresome than the horizontal trek across the mountain which they had been doing so far. That said, the mood of the group was much lighter. Now that the gangsters had shown their true colors, stolen the only real weapons, and broke away from the others, there was far less tension other than the standard *"hope we don't die"* concern. They were all friends except for Denny who seemed to be a decent enough guy, just caught up in the wrong circumstance. In a way, that was the same story for all of them.

The darkness from the tree cover made it impossible to move quickly, but they had made decent time anyway, and were still in fair shape. Only a few scrapes and bruises from bumping into solid things, or tripping over unexpected things, or slipping on wobbly things. It was too cold for snakes, so that wasn't a real concern. However, the cold itself was becoming a problem. Kat hadn't expected to be night-hiking at altitude when she had originally jumped in her car and eventually got arrested by Kind. Luckily, the wind was mild tonight, otherwise, she would be shivering her ass off. As it was, she was only shivering a little.

As if she had projected the thought, a jacket whooshed in front of her, then draped over her shoulders. It was one of her father's jackets, apparently supplied to Merrick by Kind.

"Wha…?"

Merrick leaned his face in front of her and smiled. "You were shivering," he said.

She rolled her eyes at him. "Come on, I don't need a guy to just give me his…"

"Shut up and take it, ok?"

Shut up? He had never told her to do that before. It didn't bother her, it was just curious. "Ok," she said. "Not the shut up part, just the taking the coat part."

"That'll do," said Merrick smiling back.

"Hey," said someone in shadow further ahead. "I think I found the origin of the crevasse."

"Can we cross?" asked Kat.

"Yeah. Just a little jump or a long stretch."

Good. Finally, something's going our way.

Max had apparently been the one who had alerted the group since a moment later he emerged into the clear moonlight in front of everyone, waving at the others. He hopped over something Kat couldn't see, assumedly the narrowed crevasse, and beckoned for Denny to follow him. After Denny came Zeus, then Javi, then Kat, and finally Merrick.

The rise they were on was bare for a few yards before hitting a line of tall trees. Kat felt better when they got into the trees and were once again hidden. It had been a while since they had heard the howling that signified the hunt starting, and if her guesses had been correct, with the loss of the tracking chips and unexpected route, the wolf things would be on a wild goose chase and may not fully find their path until they were long gone.

"How much further to the access road," asked Kat anxiously.

Everyone seemed a little jumpier once they started traveling upslope.

"A few miles I think," said Max. "Hard to say."

"Flat terrain?" asked Zeus.

"No," said Max. "But no more big cliffs."

The answer was satisfactory enough to hold them for a while, and they walked in silence.

A few minutes later, Merrick abruptly grabbed Kat's arm and whispered, "Stop."

"What?" she asked.

"Thought I saw something."

"Like what?"

"Movement. Running. I couldn't make it out, but something big."

"Where?"

Merrick stared silently up the hill for five or six seconds before he finally said, "Never mind. I don't know. I'm probably just spooked."

That didn't mollify Kat. Even if it wasn't the wolf things, it could be any number of other predators in these mountains. There were real wolves that lived here, plus bears who might see the humans as invaders. So far, the only wildlife they had stumbled onto were small things that scurried away as they encroached, or birds squawking in annoyance as the humans passed by.

Kat was distracted by these thoughts when Merrick put a hand on her shoulder.

"Something's wrong," he said, pointing ahead.

She looked at the front of the group and saw Max animatedly discussing something with Denny and Zeus. The words weren't distinguishable, but the helpless and confused arm gestures were indicative enough. They were lost.

Kat made her way to the front and joined in.

"Maybe it doesn't go far," said Zeus.

Max shook his head. "It shouldn't be there. I think we're going the wrong way."

"What's the matter?" asked Kat.

Max turned to her, plainly embarrassed and depressed. "There's a cliff here. If this is the mountain I thought it was, it shouldn't be here. That crevasse we just skirted and this cliff are things I hadn't counted on. I – I don't think this is the same mountain I said it was. Or, maybe – I don't know, we're on some different part of it than I thought. There's no sun to gauge which direction we're going and I'm not used to using stars."

"Can we climb down the cliff?" asked Merrick.

Max shook his head. "We'd need rope. In the dark, with no idea where the handholds are? We'd kill ourselves."

"Wait a sec," muttered Kat, the realization hitting her, "So, even if we get around it, we may not find a road where we thought it was?"

"Yeah," Max said flatly. He sighed and hung his head. "We're lost. Plain and simple."

"Awesome. So, we're fucked," said Denny.

"Ok. Listen, guys," said Kat. "We need to stay alive. Doesn't matter that we're lost. We pick a direction and keep going. If we stay alive 'til morning, we can maybe see how to get outta here."

"Yeah, and maybe those werewolf guys will go away when the sun comes up," said Zeus.

"That's vampires," said Denny with undisguised mockery.

Zeus darted his eyes to the ground. "Well, they still might not like the sun."

Merrick put an arm around Zeus's shoulder and gave him the male side-hug.

"We keep moving," said Kat with authority she didn't believe was her right to hold. "Up or down?"

Javier suggested, "Maybe that valley isn't what we think either. Maybe it's a road."

Max shook his head. "All these valleys are streams in the rainy season, rest of the year, it's mucky. I don't think so. I know I led us wrong, but – I still think up is the more unexpected route."

"I agree," said Kat.

"I think we should go down," said Denny.

"We'd be mostly back where we were," said Max.

"I'm going up," said Kat. "I'm not going to make anyone follow me. Good luck."

She reached down to pick up a solid branch, snapped off a few side limbs, then jabbed it into the ground as a walking stick and headed up the mountain. Max followed, as did Zeus and Javier. Merrick trailed, preoccupied with scanning the open area above, assumedly looking for whatever caught his attention earlier.

"Ah, Jesus. I'm coming," said Denny making up the rear.

They hadn't gone more than fifty yards before Max stooped to look at something.

"What is it?" asked Kat.

"Wet ground," said Max. "Water doesn't pool up here. Seeps downward." He swiped a finger on the spot and held it to his nose. "Blood," he said.

"What's going on?" asked Denny from the back.

"Dead animal," said Kat.

Max gave her a questioning look.

"We don't know anything," whispered Kat. "There's predators and prey everywhere up here. I don't want to panic anyone."

Max stood up and nodded. "Hope you're right."

A few yards further up the slope, the next discovery proved she wasn't right. More blood on the ground, plus a shredded dress jacket and a single shoe.

"What's that?" asked Denny.

Kat rummaged through the jacket, looking for anything useful, and surprisingly found Max's knife. She handed it to him.

"Well, at least we know he got what he deserved," said Kat.

"And it means they still found us. Even after everything," said Max.

"They found them, not us," said Kat.

Max gave her a *"stop coddling me"* look.

"Ok, ok," said Kat. "You're right. They're close. We need to be alert, find places to hide, and defend ourselves."

"What's going on?" demanded Denny.

Max began to walk toward the others, "They'll trust you to say it. I'll back you up."

Kat shook her head. "No, Max. You're the one who wants to be police chief. You have the uniform. Be in charge."

"But I'm the one who got us lost."

"Doesn't matter. You made the best decision you could. Now go tell them what we're going to do now."

Merrick gathered with the rest of the group as Max explained the situation. It didn't surprise him that the wolf hunters caught up with the gangsters first. Though they probably all knew deep down they weren't going to escape that easily, seeing the bloody reminder of reality made the group collectively twitchy. Heads darted around, expecting to see the glowing eyes of impending death.

"Fuck," said Denny. "Well – maybe I can take that piece of shit Tanner with me when I go."

"You think he's here?" asked Zeus.

"Werewolf or not, that fucker is here somewhere," said Denny. "Ruined my life. I should be drinking whiskey and making love to a beautiful woman right now in some other town. But no, I'm up on a goddamned freezing cold mountain, being chased by fuckin' werewolves who wanna chew my face off." He bent down and picked up several prune-sized rocks. "Well, fuck 'em. Come and get me."

Zeus took a step toward Denny and held out a grapefruit-sized rock with a sharp edge. "I'm with ya. But use this instead. You stand a better chance of killin' one."

Denny shook his head. "Nah, this size is fine." He reared back and threw one of his smaller rocks at a tree, impacting it hard enough to burst pieces of bark off its trunk. "Used to pitch in high school. I can hit em with these."

"We'll all get our chance," said Max. "But first we need to find a spot we can defend, then separate into teams."

Without being prompted, Kat offered, "Merrick and I will do a preliminary scout over that way. And – uh, I'll need to borrow your knife for a sec. Promise I'll bring it right back."

Max hesitantly gave her the knife, then forced a smile reminiscent of a hand-drawn smiley face on paper, smoldering on top of lava.

Merrick knew Max's mood had nothing to do with the wolves or their dire situation. It had everything to do with Merrick and Kat being alone together. To his credit, Max nodded and turned to the others.

"Ok," he said. "Then Zeus, you and Javi search that area, and Denny, you're with me."

Kat pulled Merrick away from the group and ducked behind a cluster of trees. "You ready?" she asked.

"I don't know," said Merrick. "I guess there's not much choice, but – those tranks are specially designed to suppress my transforming. And they shot me up with a lot. I feel ok, but…"

"Merrick, you said it – there's not much choice. They're close. Somewhere. Could be any second."

He took a deep breath and shook his head. "I know. Alright."

She smiled, a warm look on her moonlit face that made him want to swallow her in his arms and make love to her like it was the last thing he would ever get to do. Which might be true.

She held up Max's knife. "Where? The leg?"

He nodded. "Uh, I guess. Thickest thing without a major organ. As good a spot as any." Merrick reached to grasp her arms. "Listen, whether the other guy comes out or not, I will protect you with my life. It's all I have to offer."

"That's sweet, but no offense, we all really need the other you to protect everybody."

"He might actually kill them. And you."

She shook her head. "He won't."

"How can you be so sure?"

"Look – you didn't hurt me or my dad at the house. And you didn't hurt anyone else at the diner. Somewhere in there, the other you knows who the bad guys are."

"There's no evidence all that stuff you said was anything more than luck."

Kat gave him a sorrowful smile. "I'm betting my life on it."

"And theirs too?"

She sighed. "No one will survive if we don't."

Merrick nodded. "You're right. I just don't like it. God help me if I hurt you." He took a cleansing breath wishing he could kiss her before he turned into the thing that might kill her. "Ok. Go ahead, I'm ready."

She adjusted her grip on the knife. Merrick took another deep breath, closed his eyes, and braced for the coming pain. Instead of a knife penetrating his flesh, soft, wet lips touched his. He opened his eyes and looked at her closed eyelids. Her arms embraced him and he drew her in. Their mouths sucked, pinched, licked, and searched hungrily. For a tiny moment, Merrick didn't care about anything other than her lips. No werewolves, no cold mountain, no imminent death, just her.

When she finally pulled away from him, he smiled in warm satisfaction. "God, I want to do that some more. All day, every…"

Her knife hand flashed upward, then down. The knife bit into his leg and shot a jolt of pain through him like an electric shock.

"Shit!" he cried. Even though his superhuman system wouldn't let him die from a knife wound, nothing suppressed the pain. He trembled with an extreme effort not to flail around and react like a baby.

"Figured a kiss would lessen the pain," said Kat.

Merrick clutched his leg and ground his teeth. "Didn't work. Need another one."

"Wimp," teased Kat. She kissed his forehead. "You're a good man, Merrick Hull."

Something other than pain was beginning to happen. A familiar chill, followed by shivers, surged through his body. He fell to the ground.

"Oh, God," he muttered.

Kat took a step back. "It's happening?"

Merrick tucked into a ball, his whole body a paradox of burning fire and freezing cold. His bones felt like they were splintering.

"Get – away!" he snarled.

"Oh," said Kat. "Right." She backed up several more steps. "I, uh – I'm…"

Merrick groaned as loud as a bear roar and gripped his head in claw-like fingers.

Kat began to move faster. "Remember us. Ok? Merrick? I – I…"

Whatever she was struggling to say went unsaid as she spun and ran out of the tree cluster.

Merrick was left to himself. Though he was never truly alone.

CHAPTER 33

Kat found Max and Denny snapping low branches from a massive tree. She stopped in front of them, out of breath from running. Without explanation, she handed back the knife she borrowed, wiped clean on the back of her jeans.

Max absently accepted the knife as he spoke to Zeus. "I don't know which way they'll come from. Maybe the north? We can hide behind here and jump out and…" he paused, ruefully examining the puny branch he was wielding. "…And give them an owie before they tear our throats out. God, this is useless."

Despite his pessimism, he smiled at Kat, then said, "You and Merrick find a good spot?"

She shook her head emphatically, talking faster than her mind could think. "No. Um, not good over there. And – um, Merrick has something he wants to try to – do. He'll be right back. Let's go over here. I'll – I'll hide with you guys. You know, from the wolf-people. Who else would we be hiding from, right? Cuz any minute they could…"

The sounds of multiple twig snaps and leaves crunching came from behind her.

"Shh," said Max. He raised his crooked stick.

Kat assumed it would be Merrick, already transformed and coming out of the hiding spot, but when she looked back where the noise came from, it wasn't the same place she had left him. Whatever was coming wasn't Merrick. *Oh, no.*

"What?" said Denny. "It's probably just Zeus or Javier."

Max shook his head, put a finger to his lips, then pointed behind Denny. "They went that way," he whispered.

The snapping sounds again. Max pulled at Kat's sleeve and she didn't argue. They both ducked behind the massive pine. Kat held her sharpened branch in both hands.

Denny stood his ground and plucked a rock from his pocket. "Fuck 'em," he said. "Go ahead! Try me, fuckers. I'm re…"

A dark shape streaked through the clearing, sprinting low on four legs. It hit Denny before he could release the rock, driving him backward, completely off his feet. The beast and victim rolled down the slope, tumbling over one another before impacting a tree trunk. A clawed paw reached up and came down on Denny's chest, followed by a spray of blood. A brief cry escaped Denny's throat before it changed to a gargling noise. The head of a wolf was clear in the dim light, rising above its victim, opening its huge jaws, then driving its teeth into Denny's neck. A wet squish was followed by a muted crunch. More blood sprayed, glistening on the dark fur of the wolf-beast. As it shook Denny's neck, the man's head flopped side to side as dead weight, no longer having any muscle control. The rock in Denny's right hand dribbled from his limp fingers.

"Jesus," whispered Max.

The beast turned its glowing amber eyes on the onlookers, making no move to come at them, just glaring as if it wished to kill them with anticipatory terror. Its back bristled with stiff, blood-encrusted hair as it lifted its snout and let out a long howl.

A second dark shape pounded through the clearing, bursting through low bushes as it ran. Kat held her breath, expecting the second beast to kill someone else in the mere seconds it took to tear Denny apart, but it flew by, either unaware or interested in them. It slid to a stop in front of the other wolf, scattering rocks and dirt as its claws scarred the ground. The two growled at each other, then bit down on opposites sides of Denny's corpse. They lifted it, held it tight in their jaws, and suddenly they were running upslope on all fours. Within seconds, the two wolves and their dead prize were gone.

Holy. Fuck. Kat swallowed a wad of spit big enough to bruise her esophagus on its way down. She thought she had known what they were facing (*just psychopathic men in wolf outfits, right?*), but she wasn't prepared for the reality of their speed, strength, lethal claws, and teeth. *How the hell are they using their teeth? How the hell are they doing any of this?* Cold nausea gripped her stomach after watching the wolf-man slice Denny open and crush his throat in its jaws. The bravado she had felt before was washing away like the blood draining from Denny's long gone corpse.

Max twisted to one side and wretched. He slapped his hand over his mouth, too late to stop the vomit splashing against the pine needles on the ground. He lurched once more, then caught his breath.

"Oh, God. Sorry," he whispered.

"Shh. S'ok."

She was about to suggest they start running – somewhere, anywhere, when more snapping, crunching sounds came near where the wolf-men had exited.

No. I can't handle... Where's Merrick?

She hadn't seen him since she stabbed him. This new intruder probably wasn't him either since the sounds were near the same place the wolves had just come from. *Oh, God, please no.*

Another shape ran out of the shadowed copse. This one ran on two legs. Instead of a wolf disguise, he just wore dirty, blood-stained clothes. It was Cyril.

"Help – me!" he wheezed.

Kat wasn't about to risk her safety for that dickhead, but Max wasn't as discerning. He raced forward and held up the weak man before he collapsed.

"What's happened?" asked Max, his head swiveling for more wolves.

"Attacked," said Cyril, the single word being all he could muster between heavy breaths.

Max led him where he and Kat had been hiding and propped the man against the tree.

"Wolves?"

Cyril nodded, still hyperventilating. "Bunch of 'em. Everywhere. Killed two – Ernesto's guys."

"Where?" said Max.

Cyril waved a hand in the direction he had come. "We kept going up. Thought that's – what you said. Didn't find..." He stopped for a moment, gulping air. "Got stuck. Didn't have a chance to figure anything out when – they came. Like demons. Like real demon wolves. Biting, tearing. Friggin' metal claws. Fuck!"

"Shh," said Kat. "Whisper please."

He gave her a flicker of a glare, then closed his eyes and continued. "We never saw 'em coming. Just these kinda orange eyes, then – boom. On us. I hit one of them with a rock. Big rock. Shoulda cracked his skull. But he got right back up. Like his head is armor."

Cyril sat up and swiveled his head. Kat hadn't heard anything suspicious, though there was no telling what was coming.

"I gotta get outta here," said Cyril. "The mob guys were moving this way. Wolves probably following." He knelt and scrubbed the ground with his hands. "Need a rock."

"We should probably all move somewhere else," said Kat, addressing both Max and Cyril. "I guess just start running downhill. We can find some rocks on our…"

Cyril leaped up, waffle-sized rock in his hand, then he sprinted down the mountain. *So much for sticking together and helping us, huh?*

Max shook his head. "Let him go. He's not really…"

More bodies crashed through the distant brush. Less of a surprise than Cyril, these could be seen and heard twenty yards away, cursing as they ran, heedless of the noise they created. Two of Ernesto's men lead the way, trailed by Ernesto himself. The Asian man had bloody, shredded pants, and the other man, Sacha, look unharmed, just dirty. When Max stood up with his hands raised to show he was an ally, Sacha raised a knife in Max's direction. Kat's knife.

"Hey, hey, hey, whoa," said Max. "Friend."

Sacha didn't lunge at Max, but didn't look friendly either. "I kill anyone who touches me!" he sneered.

"Fine," said Max, then slumped down next to Kat.

"Only person who'd touch him is himself," muttered Kat.

"This is your fault!" shouted Ernesto as he approached them. "Your fault!"

What? Who?

Ernesto seemed oblivious to the ruckus and alarm he was raising. Kat decided to lean out from behind the tree to tell Ernesto to shut the fuck up and fuck off. As she shifted her weight, she was momentarily surprised to see Zeus and Javier leaning against a nearby tree, partially hidden by a weedy bush. Zeus met her gaze and started making gestures. First was the finger to the mouth to symbolize "shhh." The next was two clawed hands opening and closing like monster jaws, followed by jabbing a finger in Ernesto's direction. Then a hand across the throat, stuck out tongue, and crossed eyes to symbolize Ernesto dying. *Right. Let him doom himself.*

Except he'd still be drawing the wolves here. *And where the hell is Merrick?*

As if on cue, something moved quietly but noticeably in the brush just west of them. If it **was** west. They had gotten lost, so perhaps their compass was spun around. The thing crept low through the brush closest to the Asian man. *Kino?*

Kat wanted to yell "Watch out!" but didn't dare make a peep and expose herself. Though her conscience felt guilty about preferring the beast take Kino instead of her, Kat's survivor conscience was fine with it.

Kino turned too late to get into a good defensive posture when the wolf-thing sprang from the brush. It tackled the man and lifted him off his feet. Its claws shot forward, burying themselves in Kino's upper chest. The victim got his feet up and managed to catapult the wolf-man off, a usually effective martial arts move. Unless your opponent has four legs. Kino was swift getting to his feet, shirt soaked with blood, but his opponent was faster, having landed already on its feet. It flashed its lethal fangs and leaped again, this time slamming its chest into the man's ribs and spearing Kino's neck in its jaws. Both bodies hit the ground, and when Kino's head snapped back from the force, the jugular severed. Blood spurted like a garden hose for two seconds before it became a simple flow. The wolf-man shook its head against the ripped neck, then stood over its defeated foe. As a macabre finale to the shocking spectacle, it lifted its blood-soaked nose to the sky and howled. Within seconds, another wolf stopped next to the victor and did what the previous ones had done. They gripped opposite sides of the dead Asian man in their teeth, then bounded off, disappearing like they had been ghosts.

Max nudged Kat out of her stupefied trance watching the slaughter. "Run," he whispered.

Kat thoroughly agreed. She waved at Zeus and Javier. "Run!" she relayed, afraid they might not understand the hand gestures. She saw them nod before she turned her attention where she was planning to sprint – *in the friggin' dark.*

301

Max was barely ahead of her and she was following close by, hoping he wasn't going to lead both of them into a tree trunk or off a cliff. She risked a quick head turn and saw virtually everybody running behind her. Zeus, Javi, Sacha, even Ernesto. Cyril was God knows where. And still no Merrick. Or at least, no human Merrick. Had he transformed and looked like one of the wolf beasts? *No, he's bigger.* And his face looked more like a hairy crocodile than a wolf. *Holy shit, I can't believe this is real.*

A dense line of trees made them bob and weave to keep their footing and not be bashed by an unseen branch. At altitudes, trees like pines grew tall and developed most of their branches closer to their ultimate height because the lower area received less sunlight and less need for leaves or needles to absorb it down there. That said, lower branches still existed in sparse amounts and it would be their luck to hit one at full speed.

Max had to dodge something that surprised him, and unfortunately, Kat couldn't catch her balance. As Max passed a small sapling, he clutched it to hold himself back, then reached a hand out to Kat. She couldn't grasp it fast enough and flew off the edge of what seemed like a cliff.

Dear God, I'm going to die from falling off a cliff. A fucking cliff!

But it wasn't a cliff. Just a trough dug by water runoff during a downpour that long ago dried up. Kat fell face-first into the trough, cracking her chin on a rock. It wasn't enough to knock her out, just another pain she didn't need. All her limbs seemed to be unbroken, and luckily her ankle wasn't sprained, despite the twinge of pain. Only twisted.

"Twisted ain't sprained, bitch. Stop moaning and get up," she heard a voice in her head say. It was the memory of the captain of her high school soccer team who had walked over to help Kat up after a vicious spill on the field. Kat soldiered through the remainder of the game, but that was the one and only season she played a sport. She didn't need that crap. Her teammates weren't friendly to her beyond the playing field anyway, and plenty of other means girls in school would be willing to call her a bitch without requiring Kat to bust her ass practicing to receive that privilege. She got back at the captain by sleeping with her boyfriend. "He wasn't even good," Kat taunted the girl before she sauntered away.

"Kat!" called Max, snapping her out of her delirium.

"Yeah! I'm ok."

"There might be a shallow shoulder a little further down. I'll meet you down there."

Why? She could find it herself and climb out. "Just go!" she said, standing up and beginning to jog downhill in the trough. "Get yourself safe!"

Max didn't answer and disappeared over the edge. She hoped he took her advice, though she doubted it. Max was sweet, and a straight-up good guy, but he had always been a bit like a puppy dog around her. Slavish admiration from men wasn't her goal. She just wanted… *what do I want?* She didn't know. Max was nice, there just had never been a spark. *And yet you hopped on top of a homeless guy instead?* Merrick was no normal homeless guy, and not a normal anything else. He was something that couldn't be explained and she was utterly intrigued by him. Not in love. But – something.

Get a grip, chick! Remember the bloodthirsty werewolf things? People dying?

A shallow ledge was up ahead on her left and she veered toward it. As she expected, Max slid to stop next to it.

"Give me your hand," he said.

She vaulted up past him. "I got it, thanks."

"Okay," said Max with just a hint of hurt feelings in his tone.

She knew she needed to work on her attitude with people who really were friends. "Sorry, Max," she said. "Don't mind me. I get a little…"

Something swung at Max like a baseball bat, tumbling him completely heels over head. He rolled into the trough she had just climbed out of. Her shock of what just happened gave way to gut instinct and she reared back to jab her puny spear at whatever the thing was that just hit her friend. She looked up into the blazing amber eyes of a wolf-man. Her thrust never struck. The wolf-man swung the same devastating arm at her head and crushed her against a tree trunk. She slumped to the base and tried to gather her wits when the wolf-man pressed a heavy boot on her chest.

A boot. It reminded her calculating mind that the wolf-thing was human.

"I could've killed him, but I'm keeping my promise," said the wolf-man in a deep, growling voice.

Promise? What the f...? Sheriff Kind?

Though she didn't say it aloud, it seemed like the only explanation. If this was Quinton Kind, and he was still pretending they had a mutual agreement, she'd keep playing the game. Looking up at his massive, hairy chest shining with fresh blood, fur-covered arms, and metal claws, and especially the razor-looking teeth in his open, wolf-like mouth, it was hard to keep her cool and remember this was just plain ol' Sheriff Quinton Kind.

Human.

She nodded. "Thank you," she said.

"You're stalling," said Wolf Kind. "Where's Hull?"

The question of the day. She thought up an answer quick. "Looking for Fosse. Haven't seen him yet."

Wolf Kind glared down at her with those unnerving orange eyes. He neither nodded nor made any threatening move toward her. Just stared. She had to keep reminding herself this was someone she knew in disguise and not a real werewolf. Otherwise, she would've peed her pants right then.

Finally, he said. "Arthur has green eyes."

"Ok. I'll – uh, tell Merrick."

Wolf Kind glared at Kat for another few seconds, then said, "Fail and you both die."

Then Wolf Kind leaped away at unnatural speed. Only the lingering musk of the blood on his fur remained to testify that he hadn't been an illusion.

Kat realized she had been tensing and holding her breath, and let out a sudden rushed exhale. She calmed herself for a few seconds before she was ready to sit up. Her body had barely shifted in process of sitting upright when metal blades wrapped around her throat from behind.

Oh, God, now what?!

The clawed hand threw her back against the tree trunk. "Well, if it isn't my favorite pussy – cat," said the feral voice.

A different wolf-man appeared in front of her, thumped a boot onto her chest, then fell on top of her with all its weight.

"Unmph!" she coughed.

304

The claws raked her throat again, the tip of one pressing into the soft area under her jaw.

"Scream and this goes through your brain," said the wolf voice through the snarling mouthful of curved X-Acto blades. "Quinton may be too dickless to fuck you, but I'm not."

The other clawed hand traced the valley of her chest, plucking up the buttons and snapping them open.

What – the – fuck? It wasn't bad enough these sick, psycho, cannibal, wolf-men wanted to kill her and eat her. This one needed to rape her as well? If God existed, where the hell was he when she needed him to knock this Hell-sent, demon rapist off her and disintegrate him with a lightning bolt?

She tried to wrench herself into a position to bite or kick this wolf-thing, but he held her firm, then punched a knee into her abdomen.

"Auggh!" she grunted.

"Don't worry, Kitty Kat," the wolf-man said, tucking one claw under her pants button. "You won't be in pain for long. After I fuck you, I'll kill you. It'll be a mercy. You just need a good, long dick first."

It didn't matter that the voice sounded like a wolf speaking English, she knew that vocabulary anywhere. The same talk that she had heard for years.

"I know it's you, Tanner!" she blurted out. "You fuckin' prick!"

Wolf Tanner smashed a fist into her forehead, rattling her head against the hard tree roots. "You won't remember me, or anything else, in a few minutes," he said.

I can't believe this. I'm going to be killed, raped, and eaten by an insane man I went to high school with, dressed as a werewolf.

"Just a man," her brain reiterated, as if it was a guardian angel floating outside her body. *"Men can be hurt."*

She bucked once, hoping like hell the claw at her throat didn't penetrate. It didn't. The sudden move only bought her a smidgeon of space between them, yet that was enough. She had been gripping her sharpened stick since he held her down and she now rammed that into his side, eliciting a yelp from Wolf Tanner. Whatever the wolf suit's armor covered, it wasn't the side. Wolf Tanner twisted away to paw at the embedded stick, which gave Kat the exact opportunity she had hoped for. With every ounce of strength she could muster, she shot her knee into his groin. His very human groin.

Wolf Tanner shrieked and fumbled to get his feet under him to stand up. Kat aimed another kick at his groin, this time blocked by his hand. The claws from that same hand punctured her leg. She wanted to scream, but didn't have time.

Though Tanner's legs shouldn't have been fully stable yet, he lurched forward with unexpected force and once again pummeled her into the tree roots.

She didn't have any more tricks. And Wolf Tanner wouldn't bother to undress her anymore. She fully expected to be impaled by either his claws or teeth any moment. *I'm sorry, Daddy. I tried. I love you. See you soon.*

Death did not come. Something else did.

CHAPTER 34

Kat heard the sound of crashing bodies before she saw it. Expecting her flesh to be ripped from her bones by Tanner, she had squeezed her eyes shut, preferring not to witness her own death. The whump of lung air being expelled above her surprised her enough to risk opening her eyelids.

Another man, shirtless and coated in slimy sweat, had steamrolled Wolf Tanner. The sweaty man drove her antagonizer into the ground several yards away, then rolled free. Wolf Tanner was quick to get to his feet, but stopped there. He had an additional branch shaft, as thick as the diameter of a fifty-cent piece, protruding from his abdomen, not far from the spot Kat had stabbed him. Even with his expression hidden behind the wolf-head mask, Kat could tell he was in severe pain. His furry arms quivered as he grasped the branch, perhaps unsure if pulling it out would cause more pain than he was already in. Tanner's clawed fingers curled around the branch near the base of his abdomen and snipped the branch off, leaving a stump stuck in his furred flesh.

Kat's instinct was to run, yet she knew it wouldn't matter. The wolf-men could run on all fours, faster than any human, were stronger than any of them, and had Katana sharp claws and saw blade teeth to tear her into cubes. It seemed pointless to fight the wolf-man. Yet… she was still alive and she had help.

Merrick was regaining his feet behind Wolf Tanner. He had saved her – for the moment. Just plain ol' Merrick, not yet transformed into anything other than a shirtless, sweaty human. Stabbing his leg apparently hadn't worked. And despite whatever trauma his body seemed to be experiencing, he had summoned enough courage and strength to tackle Tanner and give her a few extra seconds of life. She was determined not to waste it.

Kat rose with strength she didn't think she owned and did a jump kick into Wolf Tanner's chest. He raised his strong arms to block her, but her momentum made him tumble backward. His awkward recovery combined with the abdominal injuries might give her enough time to get a running start to kick him again.

As it turned out, she didn't need it. A rock shaped like a deflated football hit Wolf Tanner in the head, knocking his mask askew. A hint of neck flesh peeked out from underneath. Tanner gripped his mask, desperately trying to reorient it, perhaps because he couldn't see through his amber eyepieces.

"Hey! Try *me* you stupid asshole!" taunted Javier, hefting another rock.

When Tanner did fix his mask, his focus went to the newest assaulter.

Kat scrambled behind the closest tree. She wasn't going to leave her friend alone to face Wolf Tanner, but she had no weapon to contribute to the fight. A rock, stick, anything was better than trying another kick which he would see coming well in advance. She pawed at the ground looking for something useful. As she did, she saw Javi take several steps back. Tanner stalked toward him, then dug in for a full-power leap.

Come on, Javi, move!

Javier merely backed up another step. Wolf Tanner crouched for a cat-like lunge, gripping the dirt with his hooked fore-claws, then pounding the ground with his back legs as he leaped. At that moment, Zeus jumped out from behind the tree Javi had just stepped past, slid butt-first on the ground, and held a sharpened branch toward the lunging Tanner. It was the spear she had already used and Tanner had tossed aside. Like spiked defenses on a dark-ages battlement, made for impaling attackers as they rode too fast into its midst, the spear worked to perfection. Wolf Tanner's stomach hit the sharp tip, his momentum driving the point into and past his body so that the bloody tip stuck out from his back. He landed heavily, punching air from his lungs, too caught up in pawing at the spear to catch his balance. As he lay sideways, his clawed hands wrapped around the shaft, this time, lacking the strength to snap it off. He rolled and squirmed on the leafy floor, stuck in a loop of gargled utterances and whimpering.

With menace that Kat had never seen from Zeus before, he grasped the shaft of the makeshift spear and cocked it upright, pulling Tanner's broken body with it into a flat-on-his-back position.

Then Zeus drove the protruding tip into the ground with startling fury and gave another tug for good measure.

Jesus, Zeus.

"That's for Espy!" shouted Zeus.

Wolf Tanner was bleeding from multiple wounds, and staked to the forest floor by a pine tree limb rammed through his stomach. Dying. His gargled whimpers became choking cries.

At this point, the crowd of fugitives gathered. All those who had been running for their lives needed to witness the defeat and death of one of their antagonists. Even Ernesto had nothing condescending to say as he stared, dumbstruck. Javier's shoe pinned one of Wolf Tanner's wrists, while Sacha stepped on the other wrist. Sacha was fingering a knife in his hand. Kat's knife.

As Kat looked at the wolf-man helplessly pinned to the ground, the heat of the rage she had felt earlier was rising again. Everything that had ever been wrong with her life in Templeton was personified by one word: Fosse. And here was half of that word lying before her, finally receiving justice for all the hurt he caused, all the hate he spawned, all the women – no, *girls* he raped and were too afraid to prosecute him (or died trying to), and all the lives he condemned because his father couldn't accept that Tanner should be responsible for his crimes. Esperanza, Merrick, her father, her. Better other people die than Arthur's son be prosecuted. Well, justice wasn't quite finished. Kat walked over to Tanner with a regal carriage. She stared down at the hateful thing that treated her as nothing more than a bug to play with and squish at his convenience.

Without looking at Sacha, she demanded, "Give me the knife."

Its handle was pressed into her palm. At the moment, she was too consumed by vengeance to realize how inconceivable it was that Sacha simply handed it to her. She strangled the handle in her fist, squeezing the life from the inanimate object like it was Tanner's throat.

Tanner spat up a gob of bloody phlegm. "No," he said. "Please." Another gob bubbled up and was spit out. "I'm sorry. Sorry. Sor…" he coughed a spray of blood. "I didn't mean… Daddy. Daddy!"

Kat knelt and gripped the edge of the mask that was now visible. Popping and tearing noises resembling Velcro preceded the mask coming off. She met Tanner's real eyes. They were pink from weeping.

"I don't wanna die," he whined. "Please. Don't make me die."

She shook her head. "You're already dying. This is a mercy. Like you were going to show me."

Without risking the time to change her mind, she thrust the knife deep into Tanner's throat, feeling the knife tip pierce his spine. He bucked and twitched for two seconds, one last gasp escaped him, and then he was quiet. His open, blank eyes focused on nothing.

As the crowd became engrossed in Tanner's final moments, Merrick had crawled unnoticed behind a tight grouping of young trees, hoping to get distance between himself and everyone else. It probably wasn't far enough. He could see them through a gap in the tree trunks, which meant they could see him if they were looking. But they weren't.

He did a soldier crawl to gain more distance, then found a sturdy sapling to haul himself up. Unfortunately, the sapling was not as alive as he had thought and it snapped. His balance was poor and he fell hard to the ground, eliciting a grunt from the impact.

Though the leg wound hadn't transformed him, it had brought the initial state to the surface, literally. Sweat and milky slime coated his body, soaking his now discarded shirt. His muscles were on fire, and his bones felt like they were made from glued-together glass shards. Everything on him signified something that was about to explode or break, and all he wanted to do was curl up and scream until he blacked out. That was the usual beginning. The process would start, he would feel like this for less than a minute, then he would pass out. This time, he had stayed in this condition for the last – God knows how long. Much longer than a minute. Half an hour? It had to be the tranquilizers corrupting his system, keeping him from fully transforming. His body wanted to do its thing, but the catalyst just hadn't been strong enough.

"Merrick?" someone called from behind him.

He turned to see Kat running to him, the bloody knife still in her hand. She knelt next to him and tried to pull his head to her. He twisted away.

"It didn't work," said Merrick. "Not severe enough wound."

"I see that," said Kat. "Are you ok?"

Am I...? "No," snapped Merrick. "I'm useless. I can't help anyone."

"You just helped me," she countered.

"For a second."

"It was enough."

Merrick shook his head. "It won't be enough the next time. They're coming back."

"I know. Maybe there's some other way to tweak the wound so..."

"No. Needs to be more extreme." He examined the bloody knife, a smaller blade than the one that had come close, but not quite, to transforming him before. "The only way is to force it out through severe injury, and those goddamned tranks are messing with my system."

"Ok, so what can we do?" asked Kat. "There's no time for wishing anymore, we just gotta take our best chance."

Best chance. Right. If he couldn't keep Kat alive, he might as well be dead. His life was pathetic anyway. So – their best chance was his death. Or as close to death as he could get.

"Kill me," he said. "Put that knife right in my heart and kill me. I'm serious."

"What? No. I can't do..."

"I just saw you stick that knife into a man's throat up to your fist. Yes, you can do this."

"But not to someone I – I, uh..." she stammered. "I care about."

Merrick pulled the knife tip to his chest. "You have to." His eyes darted to the others bending over Tanner's dead body. "And hurry. Before anyone sees us."

Her eyes began to water. "Damn it, Merrick! Why's it gotta be me?" she cried.

"I'm glad it is. The last thing I'll see is your face before I go. In case it doesn't work."

311

"Damn you," said Kat smearing tears on her cheeks with her forearm.

"Already been damned. Thanks."

Kat convulsed once in what might have been a laugh attempting to overwrite her distress. She put her other hand on the knife to steady her shaking. "Don't you dare die," she said. "Or I'll find you in Hell and haunt you."

"I'd like that." He nodded. "Do it. Now."

She sniffled one more time, then closed her eyes and shoved hard against the knife handle. The blade sank into Merrick's chest up to the handle guard, then she yanked it out.

Merrick's chest was now a bonfire of pain. Everything on him locked up. He wanted to say something, anything, to tell Kat she had done the right thing, but he was in unfathomable agony, unable to do anything at all except pass out. His vision went black and all he could feel was the heat from his bones as they shattered in every part of his body. The "other one's" hand had to be forced, and it was finally happening.

Kat said something to him which he couldn't hear. Everything in Merrick's world was muted. The "other one" had awakened.

Kat watched Merrick twitch, then go still. A squeak and a bubble of wet air escaped from his mouth. His eyelids remained peeled back in wide shock, framing eyeballs that didn't roll or move at all, as if they were sewn into his sockets like a doll.

"Oh, God," muttered Kat. "Don't you dare die. Don't you dare!"

"Kat?" someone called from the distant group.

Merrick's body began to tremble, then shudder, like he was being electrocuted. Little blobs of something yellow oozed from his already slimy skin. His chest warped into moving shapes like some creature was underneath trying to escape. She supposed there was.

"Ok," said Kat, swiping her cheeks again with her arm. "Ok, you're still there. And, uh, now – so is someone else, right? Right. Ok, it's gotta be working."

Merrick's face made an audible crack, then began to deform into something unidentifiable.

"Oh, wow. Gross," said Kat nervously. "I guess the other guy's coming now, so, uh – Hello! Nice to meet you."

Merrick's torso was being encased in a thick, scab-like substance. His whole body seemed bigger than it was seconds ago.

Kat stood and backed through the tree gap. "Remember us, ok? Remember? We're the good guys." She took one last look, muttered "Oh, boy," then ran to the rest of the group.

They were further from her than she thought (probably a good thing), and she was at a full sprint before she slid to a stop next to Zeus.

"Oh, hey! There you are," said Zeus. "You had me worried for a sec."

"I'm fine," she said flatly. "Listen, we need to move. Now."

Max shook his head. He was kneeling next to Tanner's corpse, examining the suit. "I've gotta get a longer look at this thing and…"

"Yeah, yeah, we will," Kat rambled. "It's just – that, uh, I heard something in the bushes behind me."

On cue, something shook and rattled the brush she had just come from.

"Shit," whispered Max. "Uh, where – where…? Everyone duck down into the ditch. Hurry!"

Kat didn't see how that would be more protection, but there wasn't time to argue. They all jumped into the ditch that she had been in just a little while ago.

Above, and about twenty yards away, whatever had been moving in the bushes was now breaking branches in those bushes. Kat heard a base growl, a much different sound than the wolf-men, closer to a massive alien bear. She had heard that same sound before, and knew exactly what was coming. It was Merrick. The other Merrick. *It worked!*

The unseen Beast Merrick cracked something that sounded like a medium-sized tree. He wasn't exactly being stealthy. She hoped that wouldn't matter against the wolf-men. He growled again, almost like he was searching for something instead of rampaging.

Maybe he **was** searching for something. *Can it be?* Kat considered doing something that every instinct told her was a bad idea. But her inquisitive nature also needed to know the answer to the crazy question. *Holy shit, I'm gonna do this, aren't I?*

Kat pulled herself to the lip of the ditch, digging her nails into hard ground.

"Jesus! Kat!" hissed Max. "What are you…?"

Kat wasn't listening. She was praying her intuition wasn't betraying her. She threw a leg onto the ditch lip and got her head above it.

The creature that stood before her was huge. Much bigger than the wolf-men. The moonlight highlighting its back gave it a ghostly gleam. Hair covered its entire body, most of it spiny and thick like a wolfish porcupine. Its legs had canine-esque, backward knees, and shiny gray claws extending from both its feet and hands – or paws. She knew those claws weren't manufactured steel like the wolf-men's, yet they looked just as deadly and as sharp. Its back was almost as tall as its forward-mounted head, surpassed only by the pointed, stalk-like ears that stood up similar to the spikes on Batman's mask. In most ways, it resembled a werewolf, as massive and as powerful as any comic book beast, with clearly defined muscles that looked as indestructible as stones underneath hardened leather. The muzzle was the only exception to the wolf resemblance. Longer and flatter, a more reptilian shape, with rows of tangled, gray teeth, hooked and wicked like the claws. The short fur on the muzzle quivered as the creature snarled at Kat. Unlike the wolf-men, its eyes weren't glowing. They were wild and hungry, shining like a mirror.

As scary as the wolf-men were, this thing in front of her was more terrifying, both from appearance and implied invulnerability. No sharp stick or clumsy rock would discourage it. It was an agent of death, a corporeal nightmare whose only purpose was to tear living things into carrion. Hell would've expelled this demon for terrorizing the other demons. Whatever trick Kat could think of, whatever weapon she could finagle, would not beat this thing. It was a juggernaut designed for destruction, and would not be bothered by puny human efforts to defeat it.

Kat swallowed hard and slowly stood. The giant werewolf took two steps toward her. She froze. *Nice doggy?* She wanted to say something so that – *God help me* – it might recognize her. That was the point of standing up and facing it. *Right? Then do it.* She worked spit into her throat to make the sound come out.

"Merrick," she squeaked. *Come on, Kat!* "Merrick!" the word came out better this time. "It's me, Merrick. Kat. It's Kat. You hear me? You in there?"

The werewolf growled low and menacingly. But it didn't approach her.

She lifted a hand and waved. "It's ok. It's ok. It's just me. Just your Kat. And, uh – and I need your help, Merrick. Remember? You told me to turn you into, um, you know... Um, cuz those other wolf-things are gonna kill us, Merrick, if you don't help. Please give me a sign that you hear me."

The Merrick Creature didn't move. It just glared at her and drooled like she was a piece of pork on a spit.

"Please, Merrick. Please. I know you're in there. Don't hurt us. Help us."

The tears she had wiped clean earlier were welling again. *No, no, no. Even if he kills me, I'm not going like that.* It made her more mad than frightened.

"Damn it, Merrick!" she shouted. "I need your help! Stop those wolf bastards from killing us! Please!"

The creature stared at her for two more seconds, then suddenly tore off to its right, crashing through a thicket of bushes and saplings, flattening them as it bounded through. It was gone.

Kat let out a deep exhale, not able to produce one smooth breath, but rather a ratcheted, hyperventilating exhale.

He heard her. It had to. She got through. And even if she didn't, he knew she wasn't an enemy.

"Jesus, Kat!" griped someone behind her.

She nearly jumped out of her skin. It was Zeus. He looked both confused and frightened.

"What the hell was that?" he demanded.

She had planned a lie, a simple cover like the beast was a unique mechanical wolf-man suit from someone they hadn't seen before. A secret confederate that only she knew about. But instead of that fabrication, from her lips, out came, "It was Merrick."

CHAPTER 35

Though Kat was still shaken by her confrontation with Beast Merrick, and everyone else was probably confused by her explanation, once they climbed up from the trough, they were all focused on studying Tanner's wolf suit.

While they alternated shifts on guard, Max stripped the corpse of its possessions which included only 3 things: a set of car keys, a pocket knife, and a pistol. Max took the keys, handed Zeus the pocket knife, and he gave Kat the pistol.

"You earned it," he said.

Ernesto grumbled from behind the group, but didn't officially protest. Kat examined the gun, a 9mm Colt with a full magazine, then tucked it into her waistband. On an impulse, she turned to Sacha.

"Were you the one that hit me with a rock?" she asked with an edge to her voice.

He shook his head vehemently. "No. Is Tyson." His accent was thick Russian, close to stereotype. "I take knife from him when he is killed."

She held out the bloody knife to Sacha. He met her eyes briefly, then accepted the gift.

"Thank you," he said.

"Don't make me regret it."

Max held up the wolf head, examining the complex array of electronics inside. "Looks like the eyes are a combination of heads-up display and night vision. There's moving indicators on the lenses."

He placed the mask on his own head and suddenly the eyes brightened to their usual amber color. Several people took a step back. The jaws snapped shut, then opened again, then snapped shut.

"Holy crap!" said Max in an animal-like growl. "This thing's got sensors that react to my jaw opening wide like I'm trying to bite..." The jaw opened and snapped quicker. The clang of metal teeth colliding made Kat's skin crawl. "…Something. Like that," said Max.

Zeus was plucking at the blades on the hairy wolf-paw gloves still attached to Tanner's hands. "I don't suppose we can use these? You know, like Freddy Kruger style?"

"Why not?" said Kat. "Do they come off?"

Javier was on the other side of Tanner and after a snap, pop, and a Velcro tear, he held up a clawed glove for everyone to see.

"Yep," he said proudly.

Javi put the glove on, which seemed a little big for his hand, but once he pulled the strap around his wrist, it seemed stable. He walked over to a nearby tree and took a swipe at it. Chunks of bark flew off and four half-inch deep scars appeared in the tree.

"Ay, Dios!" said Zeus.

"Super sharp!" said Javi, staring amorously at the blades.

Tanner's other glove was removed and Sacha tried it on. It fit his hand better than Javi. He wiggled the shiny claws.

"Now maybe we even things up," said Zeus.

Max handed Kat the wolf mask and turned his attention to the leg prosthetics of the suit. As he bent them back and forth, they made air-hissing noises.

"Hydraulics," he said. "Mounted on springs. Same with the arms. All mechanically engineered to push off with more force than regular legs. It's probably how they can run around on four legs better than two."

"Where did they get this?" asked Ernesto.

Max thought a moment. "Fosse owns a biomechanical company. Out of state. Makes all sorts of prosthetics, like for wounded vets and stuff. He probably had these made special. I don't know why he did it. Coulda been some experiment for the military that got canned and he adapted it, or… Hell, I don't know. But it seems to legitimately work."

"Why would someone who owns a biomechanical lab want to run a lumber mill?" asked Kat.

"I don't know," said Max. "The mill's always been here. Like a hundred years I think. He just took it over."

"It's this mountain," said Zeus. "The hijo de puta wanted to be here so he could be around this mountain."

Kat nodded. "Fosse thinks this place gives him special powers. Strength, long life, and stuff. And maybe it does. We, uh – think Fosse and Kind are a lot older than they look."

"Dios mio," said Zeus. "Like werewolves weren't bad enough. They're immortal too?"

"No, normal humans, just – extended," said Max.

"Not immortal," said Javi. "They die." He waggled the blades on his fingers.

Kat looked down at Tanner's pale and lifeless face. *Yes, they do die.*

Though trying on the suit was briefly considered, nobody wanted to bet their life on being able to maneuver it well enough to not be a stumbling, flailing, uncoordinated, easy target when the wolf-men returned. It and Tanner's corpse were left alone while everyone discussed strategy for the next onslaught.

The wait wasn't long. Within a few minutes of the discussion, accomplishing only the agreement that they were no longer going to run, the faint sound of twigs snapping and ground debris crunching pricked their ears.

"Hide," said Max.

Everyone did.

Kat used the same tree she had used before because it had a wide trunk. She was still holding the wolf head mask, honestly forgetting she had it in the sudden panic to get to her tree. When she got to her spot, she found it occupied by Zeus.

"Oh!" she blurted. "Sorry, I…"

Zeus shook his head. "It's ok. I knew you'd come here, so…" he shrugged. "Javi kinda wants to do his own thing."

"Ohhhkay," said Kat.

"I – don't wanna die alone," said Zeus.

"You're not gonna die," stated Kat with confidence she didn't feel. "Come on, you were a badass just a few minutes ago."

Zeus shook his head. "I was just angry."

"We all are."

"No," Zeus hung his head. "It's more than that. In my cell – in the bunker, I found some writing on the wall. In dried blood. It was from Espy. Her name and year. And said 'Murdered by Fosses.' Fosses plural."

"Wow. I'm – so sorry, Zeus."

"It's ok. At least I know. I always thought she was dead even though Javi denied it. And I figured, after the stuff about Saunders, that Tanner was the one who raped her. So – they covered it up like every other thing that Tanner ever did. She was just another problem to get rid of."

"God, I'm so…"

"No," said Zeus with a strange new confident tone. "No more. Tanner's dead. And we're going to get rid of the real problem."

Kat grinned. "Yes, we are."

The sound of movement in multiple directions got slightly louder.

Zeus swallowed hard. "Right. So – how do we do it?"

"I have no fucking clue."

Kat looked at the mask in her hands. She lifted the mask over her head and slowly lowered it. Several metallic plates pressed against her temples. Immediately, the lenses in front of her eyes lit up, displaying a few small white dots with numbers next to them. When she turned toward Zeus, he looked bright white, like an angel seen in blown-out exposure.

"Whoa," she said.

"Yeah," said Zeus. "Those eyes are creepy as hell."

Past Zeus's head, she saw the bright form of Max crouching near another tree, a numbered dot floating next to him. There was also something behind him – walking on four legs.

"Max!" she hissed. "Behind you."

Max reacted quickly, taking the spear Zeus had used to impale Tanner and swinging it quickly to jab at the unseen thing that had crept up behind him. Kat saw the spear impact something, and then the canine-shaped thing flail and stumble backward. It seemed to disappear, which confused Kat until she remembered that Max had crouched near the ditch. There was no telling how easy or hard it would be for the wolf-man to climb out of the ditch. Max wisely decided not to find out and ran for another tree. Nothing chased him.

I can see them in the dark! She quickly scanned her immediate surroundings, saw nothing coming toward her, then leaned around the other side of the tree to look for other heat-signatures. About ten yards away were the crouching forms of what she believed were Ernesto and Sacha. Two wolf shapes were stalking from opposite sides. Ernesto and Sacha were too far away to tell them to watch out without shouting and giving away her own position. She had no good way to warn them.

It appeared that Sacha was already hyperaware of something approaching. He balanced on his toes, ready to spring. At least he had the clawed glove. She felt a little guilty she couldn't warn him, then she suddenly remembered what could really help. *The gun.*

Tugging it from her waistband and gripping it in two hands, she looked down what should be the barrel. From inside the wolf mask, all she could see was her white hands. *Damn it!* The wolf mask was pulled off and laid on the ground. She sighted down the barrel with her human eyes, guessing where the targets were based on where she last saw them in night vision. The dim light shone off Sacha's scalp through his short-cropped hair. He twisted right and left, scouring the shadows for what he could hear but apparently couldn't see. Neither could Kat, until... *There!* Two amber eyes flashed through a mass of leaves. Kat lined up the pistol's sight. *Come on, come on. Show yourself.*

It did. Too fast for Kat to aim, the wolf shape leaped at Sacha. He was ready for it and met the creature with his clawed hand. The wolf-man crushed Sacha backward, rolling away. Taking advantage of the wolf's occupation, Ernesto dove behind a different tree. Sacha and his opponent were too close together to try a shot from Kat. But as soon as the wolf-man rolled free, then crouched for another spring, Kat fired.

The flash and sound made Kat jump. She had fired plenty of guns at night before, just not while being hunted by lunatic wolf-men and trying to remain hidden – exposing the hell out of herself.

But she hit the wolf-man. It jerked and fell backward, kicking and flailing. Sacha found his feet and plunged the claws into the wolf-man's neck. *Sacha learns quick.* The wolf-man's kicking and flailing ceased.

Another pair of amber eyes appeared behind Ernesto's new tree. Kat swung her pistol in that direction until she noticed several pairs of amber eyes much closer to her, and moving her way. *Oh, boy.*

Apparently, Zeus had seen the same thing because he slapped her on the back and shouted, "Run!"

She did, followed by Zeus, pushing his less-than-agile legs to their stride limit. Ernesto broke cover and was also sprinting, grunting indistinguishable Spanish swears as he ran. He hadn't gotten level with her when he was overtaken by a wolf-man. It seemed to soar above Ernesto before it rammed its metal jaws into the mobster's spine, making the man scream like a toddler. He hit the ground face first, and as the wolf-man landed, it ripped through Ernesto's back with its mechanical jaws, taking a hunk of Ernesto's vertebrae with it. Blood squirted momentarily, coating the wolf mask in sparkling blood. The wolf-man stood above its victim howling as Kat and Zeus ran away.

Bye, Ernesto.

Max appeared on the other side of Kat, closely followed by Javi. Two wolf-men were gaining fast. Kat wasn't practiced at firing on the run with any accuracy, and was too afraid to stop and take the time to aim, so she did the best she could and pointed the pistol behind her and fired. The bullet splintered a clump of rocks on the ground that exploded shards of stone and bullet, hitting none of the wolves directly. However, as they twisted away, their pace slowed momentarily. Both sets of amber eyes subsequently centered on her.

Shit. "*Run faster, sweetheart!*" She imagined her father yelling at her which somehow added motivation. The wolves were still faster than her. Much faster. There was nothing between her and them except scattered trees, and not enough time to turn and aim accurately.

A sobering thought came to her. If the wolves were focused on her, the others might be able to escape if she were to lead the wolves away. *Shit. Why me?*

Her father's voice said, "*Because you're my baby girl. And I raised you to do the right thing.*"

Fuck.

"*Don't you cuss.*"

To Max, Kat shouted, "Split up!"

322

"What?!" said Max.

There wasn't time to explain. She slapped a hand on Max's back, then banked hard right. As expected, the two wolf-men followed her.

The only place to hide was the trough on her right. Maybe it was deep enough to confuse the wolves if she could just distract their vision long enough so that it would seem like she disappeared once she jumped into the trough. She reached blindly behind her and fired twice at the following wolves, blowing up dirt, leaves, and pebbles. Then she dove into the ditch.

She rolled to a stop at the bottom, slicing up her arms on the sharp rubble that had collected at the bottom of the long dried-up stream. Coming up on one knee, pistol still in hand, she swept it side to side, searching for her pursuers. Nothing. Had she actually outmaneuvered them?

A dark shape of a wolf-man leaped into the ditch, its glowing eyes fixed on her. *Guess not.* An instant later, the other one landed behind her. One on each side. No way out except to climb, which she wouldn't have enough time to do before either wolf jumped on her. And only one pistol to point in one direction while the other would overtake her as soon as she fired. *Fuck it.* If she was going to die, one of them was too. She leveled the pistol at the wolf-man in front of her, but didn't have the chance to pull the trigger. Instead, she was surprised by a savage snarl from something that wasn't a wolf.

Or more accurately, not a mechanical one. The massive form of Beast Merrick descended through the air, pile-driving the wolf-man behind her, and flattening it under clawed feet. Powerful hands lifted the wolf-man by its throat, then a clawed hand swept over the wolf-man's waist several times, ripping away a shiny belt buckle as Merrick's hand sliced past. The wolf-man's pants fell off. *No.* The whole bottom of his body fell off. *Jesus!*

Suddenly remembering the wolf-man in front of her, she prepared to fire at it. It had already moved – further away, desperately trying to climb out of the ditch. Beast Merrick noticed the fleeing wolf-man, dropped the half of the victim still in its claws, then was upon the other wolf-man in two bounds. The wolf-man attempted a claw strike on Beast Merrick, who seemed unconcerned with the effort. His own clawed fists battered the wolf-man, turning the wolf-head mask into a crushed, twisted, bloody mess with only three blows. For measure, Beast Merrick speared the wolf-man with his hand, piercing the body up to his hairy elbow, then pulled out a bloody organ and tossed it aside.

The frightening, mirror-like eyes looked at Kat, regarding her silently for several seconds. For that frozen moment, Kat feared that the mutual understanding between them was just her imagination, and the beast would shred her without further thought. Beast Merrick made no move other than stare at her, then he bounded to the top of the ditch and disappeared.

Kat blew out a huge, held breath, then calmed herself. Twice she had stood before Beast Merrick, and twice he left her unharmed. And this time, he had saved her life. It had to be confirmation that she was right. *Right?* Her boyf... her friend was doing exactly what she hoped he would do. Turning the tide.

She climbed out of the ditch.

Max had barely escaped a lunging wolf's claws by diving behind a boulder. Once he regained his balance, he saw that the wolf-man was already preparing for another lunge. The piercing amber eyes bore into Max as the wolf-man snarled. Max gripped the knife in his white-knuckled fist. The wolf-man crept toward him on all fours, crouching for a spring, yet didn't spring. Instead, it suddenly rose up on two legs and began to step backward. *What the...?* Max looked at the knife in his hand, but there was no way it had worried the wolf-man.

A strange growl came from behind Max. The haunting sound was unlike any of the wolf-men. More like some imaginary creature from a horror film. Max cocked his head to see the thing that was looming above him. Despite Max being directly below, the beast ignored him and glowered at the wolf-man in front of them both.

It was an astounding "it." Werewolf-shaped like the other hunters, but this one was much bigger, visibly stronger. Hulk-like muscles, a reptilian snout covered in fur, and backward knees like a dog.

Whatever this beast was, it was most definitely not a human in a wolf-suit. It snarled again at the wolf-man ahead, then without further regard to Max, it ran at the wolf-man. Whoever was in the wolf costume was stumbling over his black tactical boots, waving his arms in a surrender gesture. "Please, don't…" he said frantically. Though the words were deep and guttural, altered by the wolf mask to sound sinister, they were plainly desperate pleas.

The bigger wolf-beast reacted by smashing its huge shoulder into the fake wolf-man, driving the man into the ground hard enough to create a crater. The wolf mask tore away, revealing one of Fosse's gunmen. A final plea from the pinned man was cut off as his skull was crushed in the beast's massive jaws. Like a nut being cracked, the skull split and gushed blood and pink matter onto the pine straw ground. The wolf beast wasted no time on the dead man, turning its head only enough for Max to see its intense, mirror-like eyes, then the beast tore off into the dark, leaving behind the oozing pulp of what used to be the gunman's head.

Max was left alone to try and quiet his thundering heart.

Kat found Javi hiding under an overturned tree that had pulled up its root ball. Dirt was caked on his face giving him pretty good camouflage within the tangle of roots. The boy had been so brave minutes earlier, but was now shivering and clenching his knees to his chin in terror. Kat couldn't blame him. The lines separating bravery, shock, and paralyzing fear could be tenuous in extreme situations. If she had time to consider what was going on, she may curl up in a ball and go catatonic. But survival instincts were still controlling Kat at the moment.

"Hey," she said as she slid up to him.

"Hey," he said, distant and toneless.

"We need to find your dad," she said. "You willing to come with me?"

He shook his head. "I'm afraid to move."

Kat nodded. "I understand. I'm scared too. But – can I let you in on a secret?"

He shrugged.

Kat continued. "We got a special weapon you ain't seen before."

"What?" he said, still toneless.

"Well, it's – um, it's hard to explain. Do you remember when I disappeared with Merrick for a few minutes, and we…"

The overturned tree creaked. The dangling roots wiggled. Something was on top of the tree, heavy enough to cause it to teeter.

Kat held a finger to her lips. Javier needed no such encouragement to be silent. His eyes were as wide as golf balls. A group of four curved blades appeared above them, curling around the shaft of a large root. The amplified growl from its wolf mask was immediately recognizable as one of Fosse's wolf-men.

Kat yanked her pistol up and fired, hoping to put a bullet through the wolf head. The bullet hit something metal and the wolf-man jerked back and out of sight.

"Run!" ordered Kat.

Javier was on his feet sooner than her, but neither could take a step because a pair of canine legs jumped in front of them. Real canine legs, long and muscular, that belonged to the person she most wished to see. Beast Merrick moved within clearer view, gripping the wolf-man in two hands like he was holding a sack of flour. He slammed the wolf-man into the ground, causing a spark from the mask and a garbled grunt that started as an amplified wolf sound and ended up as a human cry. Beast Merrick's fist rose and smashed into the wolf head, rose and fell, again and again until the wolf head looked like nothing more than pummeled roadkill. Blood dripped from Beast Merrick's fist as he stood and once again looked at Kat with his haunting eyes.

"Thank you," she said, more whispered than she planned.

At that moment, another wolf-man crashed into Merrick like a football player trying to de-cleat its opponent. Merrick was slung off his feet. He rolled to a stop and righted himself quickly. So did his attacker. Merrick had a gushing wound on his shoulder that drizzled blood over his heaving chest. The wolf-man stalked Merrick, likely looking for a weak spot. Kat didn't think there was one. Beast Merrick faced its stalker, seeming more curious than concerned. The wolf-man finally sprang at Merrick's head. Like a sword thrust, Beast Merrick shot out a clawed hand and skewered the flying attacker's neck, the claws protruding from the wolf-man's back, spine clutched in his fist. The mechanical wolf-man flopped forward from his momentum, then dangled from Merrick's arm. Beast Merrick slashed with his left hand, spraying blood several feet, then the dead wolf-man was tossed to the ground like a gross thing to be discarded and washed off. Tangles of bloody fur and flesh slapped against the ground with a sickly splat.

Beast Merrick did what it had done before, meeting Kat's eyes, then bounding off and utterly disappearing.

Kat's heartbeat was faster than normal, and even though this wasn't her first sighting, she still couldn't help but be astonished by what she was witnessing. As if God himself had materialized, smote the evil hunters, and then vanished.

When she looked at Javier, he was wide-eyed, shivering, and breathing rapidly like her. "*That* – was – Merrick?" he sputtered.

Kat smiled, more prideful than warm. "Yes. He's, um – our protector now."

Javi swallowed once, his shivering subsided, then a smile slowly grew on his lips. "Cool."

Kat wanted to laugh at Javi's simple acceptance. "Let's go find your dad," she said.

"Yeah."

"Kat? That you?" hissed a low voice.

Kat and Javi crept behind a cluster of boulders in a fruitless attempt at stealth. The wolf-men could see their bodies in both heat and night vision, so creeping and whispering wouldn't really make a difference at all. However, not taking extreme caution felt insanely reckless. They had been searching for Zeus, whispering his name as they moved. Now someone finally responded to their calls. Was it really Zeus? Anybody could sound like someone else whispering.

"Dad?" called Javi.

The voice groaned and whispered, "It's me."

"Prove it?" said Javi, uncertain he should ask.

Another groan. "Homerun power," said the voice.

"Dad!" cried Javi and raced around the rock cluster. When he got around the edge, he leaped back in fright.

"What?" asked Kat, running with gun outstretched.

Javi backed up, pointing at the ground. When Kat got there, she saw a man's body, decapitated, with what looked like the face ripped off. She honestly couldn't tell if a wolf-man did this or Beast Merrick. Either way, she knew who the corpse was by his clothes. It was Cyril.

Pebbles originating from above the boulders skittered down at Kat and Javi. Kat snapped her pistol's aim at the disturbance. Zeus peeked over the ledge and stared at her barrel.

"It's just me," he said, hands raised.

Javi climbed up and embraced his father.

"You ok?' asked Kat.

Zeus shook his head. "Cut bad. One of those werewolf guys got me."

He shuffled his sitting position until Kat could see his filleted leg. It was bleeding profusely.

While Kat stripped Cyril of his shirt to bind up Zeus's wound, he continued his explanation. "The wolf-guy slipped on some loose rocks or he woulda gutted me. Cyril sacrificed himself to draw it away."

Kat gave Zeus a questioning look. *Our Cyril?*

Zeus nodded to the unasked question. "He accidentally found my hiding spot. Was running from a wolf-guy. Musta felt guilty for leading him to me. Said to tell everyone he never raped anybody. He was framed cuz he found out something and tried to blackmail Fosse. Cyril wanted us to think better of him before he died." Zeus took a second to gather himself, before resuming. "He ran out from this spot and yelled at the wolf guy, hoping to lead him away. It came outta nowhere, slipped as it hit me, and wound up near Cyril. He hit the wolf with a big rock, but it wasn't enough. The wolf guy killed him right there. Then it came after me again."

Kat cocked a brow, waiting for the finale of how Zeus escaped the second attack. Zeus seemed hesitant.

Finally, he met Kat's eyes. "That thing that you said was – you know, Merrick? He came back." Zeus shook his head. "Tore up the wolf guy like he was tissue paper. Then threw him down the hill like a Frisbee. I never saw anything like... It was crazy."

Javi nodded. "I saw him too, Dad. It's ok. He's helping us."

Zeus looked incredulous. "Where'd he get that wolf suit then?"

Kat didn't bother to correct him. Instead, she produced a white lie to cover. "It's what those agent guys were chasing him for."

"Oohhh. Makes sense then."

Kat wanted to laugh again. With everything so utterly bizarre, Zeus's imaginative guess somehow made more sense to him than the truth.

"Can you walk?" she asked.

"Hobble," he said. "I'll use that broken limb to lean on."

They helped him up, then they all slowly descended the rise.

"So, did we win yet?" asked Zeus.

This time Kat actually did laugh. She slapped a hand over her mouth to stifle it. "I doubt it, but – Merrick did kill a bunch of 'em. Maybe – maybe if we can survive a little longer, he'll get the rest?"

They made slow progress down the hill, looking for better cover to hopefully outlast the remaining wolf-men. She believed what she said, especially after seeing Beast Merrick in action, if they could just keep safe and hidden for a little while longer, maybe Merrick could finish the rest. As far as she knew, Merrick could've been fighting all the remaining wolf-men right then and everyone was already safe.

Before Kat had finished the hopeful thought, she found out she was dead wrong.

CHAPTER 36

Kat saw it from the corner of her eye a moment before a dark blur streaked past, knocked her over, and slammed into Zeus, sending him tumbling down the mountain. A hint of pungent aftershave wafted to Kat as the wolf-man stood to his full height, aiming his blazing green eyes at Javier. *Green eyes? Aftershave? Fosse?* As it charged again, Javi swung a right cross with his clawed hand at the wolf-man, but got back-handed into a tree trunk, knocking the boy unconscious.

Kat crab-crawled backward, not daring to turn her back on the wolf-man she assumed was Fosse. She had shoved a knife through his son's throat. If he knew, there would be zero chance of mercy from him. He may torture her before he gutted her. *And then eat my guts?*

Wolf Fosse slammed a boot heel into her chest.

"Where's Merrick?" he growled in that eerie, manufactured wolf voice.

Kat could barely breathe from the pressure on her chest, much less answer. "I don't know," she coughed.

Wolf Fosse leaned down and pressed a claw blade under her chin. "Call to him," said Wolf Fosse.

She swallowed air instead of saliva. "I can't," she grunted.

The green eyes came even closer. "Will he come if you scream in pain? I think he might."

So close to finally coming out of their nightmare, this hell-spawned asshole was about to make all their miraculous accomplishments moot. The claws pushed into her throat and she felt the sting of one of them drawing blood. Of all the things to feel, she felt mad. Mad of being robbed the victory she thought was so near. Mad about her father's murder, mad at Fosse for making this town the shithole that it became, and mad that he was trying to kill everyone she cared about. Fucking mad.

"Merrick'll fucking slaughter you!" she roared, surprising herself with her reckless bravery. "You won't even be a challenge."

That apparently pissed off Wolf Fosse. He swung a steel toe into her chin, knocking her further backward. The coppery taste of blood pooled in her mouth. For a moment, she thought she'd have a chance to get her gun from her back, but the claws were at her throat again before she could try.

"He'll die like all the others," said Fosse. "And so will you right now unless you call him."

So, Kat did. "Meeeerrrriiick!" she shouted, then sneered at Fosse despite the blades to her neck. "Your funeral. If anyone cares to give your sorry ass one when you're dead."

"You think your boyfriend is special?" said Wolf Fosse. "He's nobody. You're less than nobody. I have never lost, you pathetic bitch. Not in eighty-two years. Dozens of men thought they were bigger, stronger, and faster than me, and I killed them all. Easily. Pieces of their souls are trapped in me, making me stronger with every one I kill. Your boyfriend is just another…"

Somebody in a gray suit sprang from behind the tree and jabbed two clawed hands into Fosse's torso. Wolf Fosse stumbled, then spun fast and met the roundhouse kick from his attacker, blocking it with a mechanically enhanced arm, then smashing that same arm against the gray-suited foe. The man in the suit tumbled, recovered, and got into a martial arts stance. *Sacha?*

It seemed that Ernesto's main man discovered a moral core and decided to help Kat. Or perhaps he was more like the hunters and sought a fighting challenge. Either way, he had fitted himself with an additional clawed hand from a dead wolf-man, and now Sacha was armed with double-fisted Freddy Kruger gloves. Blood streaked his formally expensive suit from some other previous battle.

Wolf Fosse stayed in his stance, unmoving. Surprisingly, he was bleeding from both his shoulder and side where Sacha had surprised him. An old movie quote came to Kat's mind: *"If it bleeds, we can kill it."*

"Come! Mudak!" roared Sacha.

Wolf Fosse feinted to his left and Sacha dove the other way, right into Fosse's haymaker swing. Fosse's claws went through Sacha's head. The Gangster's eyes froze wide and blood dribbled from his mouth onto the rocky ground. With no respect for his brave foe, Fosse flung Sacha aside like he was scum to be cleaned off.

His blazing green eyes turned back to Kat. "I will handle your boyfriend as easily," he said. "It will be…"

Fosse twitched and became statue still. Kat was aiming her pistol at his chest. His son's pistol.

"Surprise, fucker!" she yelled.

She fired twice. On the third trigger pull, the gun froze with an open chamber. Both shots had hit where she aimed: the middle of his chest.

Fosse scrambled back, caroming off one tree trunk, then smacking into another. He slumped against it, his arms trembling and flailing like he was a malfunctioning robot. Gagging and choking sounds were being amplified by the mask. He limply swiped twice at his chest, then seemed to lose all muscle control and just leaned against the tree, struggling to breathe. Kat hopped to her feet, wishing she could put another round in the man's skull. Popping out the magazine confirmed it was as empty as she feared. However, when she looked at the chamber, it was stuck open by a crookedly loaded round. *It jammed!* Still one round left, just needing to be reoriented. Once the bullet was pressed correctly into the chamber, the slide snapped shut.

Kat tensed her jaw and approached the dying Fosse. He was still choking, though more subtle than before. Considering there were two 9mm bullets in his chest, she was amazed he was still alive at all. Maybe all that mysterious chemical and spiritual enhancement was inhibiting death just like Merrick's mysterious agents. The agents seemed to die just fine once their brain was separated from their body. Kat stretched on tiptoes and stared inside the green eyes.

"You couldn't handle Merrick," she said. "You couldn't even handle a pathetic bitch." She lifted the gun to the glowing eyes. "I already killed your son. Recognize the gun? He wasn't supposed to have it, was he? None of your other dead pals had guns, so I'm guessing Tanner lied and snuck it in. He fucked up everyone else's lives in this town, and now he fucked up yours. By the way, he cried for you like a baby."

"Bitch! You're fucking dead!" gargled Fosse, the strangled words barely audible from the liquid in his throat. He swung a weak clawed hand at Kat who easily dodged and slammed a kick into Fosse's groin. As the dying man doubled over, Kat caught his masked head and slammed it back against the tree.

She placed the gun muzzle between his dimming eyes.

Fosse wheezed desperate cries. "No! You can't...! How...? You're... You're nobody. Just – a girl."

Kat grinned. "That's right. When you get to Hell and they wanna know who the infamous Fosse boys finally lost to, that's what you tell 'em: Just a plain ol' girl. Nobody."

She pulled the trigger. The wolf head shuddered. A brief spark caught on the fur which sizzled and sent a slither of smoke lifting from the blackened hole. Fosse's body slid to the ground. His eyes stopped glowing.

There was one more thing she needed to do to make sure. *No surprises.* Kat looked at the inert clawed hand. *It'll do.* She hurriedly removed it before she lost her nerve.

When Kat was done with the detestable task of severing Fosse's spinal cord, Javi had awakened. They went in search of Zeus and found Max leading him up the hill in a wide-open clearing. Just the fact that they weren't hiding behind bushes or rocks suggested the status quo had changed. That, and the strange sight of Max wearing one of the undamaged wolf masks. He took it off as Kat approached.

"See any more of 'em?" she asked, assuming that's what he was doing.

"No, actually," he said. "I've scanned the area three times and haven't seen anyone but us."

Kat's brows went up. "Is that it then? We actually won?"

Max pinched up his shoulders in a slow nervous shrug. "Maybe. I don't wanna get caught with our guard down though."

"That's just what happens in horror movies," said Zeus. "The final girl feels like she's safe, then all a' sudden – boom! The bad guy jumps out."

"We're not in a horror movie, Zeus," said Kat.

"Says you," quipped Zeus. "This whole thing is worse than any movie I ever saw. And Javi's got a Freddy Kruger glove to prove it's real."

"That's not a…" Kat sighed. "It don't matter. I get it. We need to be cautious until we're safe."

"There's a couple more things," said Max. "Good news, bad news, and more bad news. The good news is I've located the van in this wolf mask. It's labeled with GPS location. Three miles opposite the way we'd been heading."

"Ok," said Kat. "I assume the keys we got from Tanner might be to that, so – yay."

"Yeah," said Max. "I never found any more keys or guns on the other dead wolf guys, so probably it."

"Was that the bad news?" asked Kat.

"No. Bad news is I can't see Merrick in the mask. Whether he's inside that big wolf contraption, or just plain ol' human now, can't see him either way."

The makeshift explanation Zeus had voiced about Merrick being in a different wolf outfit seemed to be spreading. Kat wasn't going to correct it.

"I understand," said Kat. "Well, we can wait around for a while and see if he turns up, or – since he lives in the woods anyway, maybe he'll be ok on his own. Maybe he just took off." *And left all his possessions at my house? Nope.* She'd figure that out later.

"So – then the more bad news," said Max. "There's no sign of Sheriff Kind either. Not dead, not alive. Just gone. At least, nowhere this mask can see."

That worried Kat more than Merrick being missing. If Kind made it back to town somehow, he could concoct a crazy story about how the group killed Fosse and Tanner, and maybe add Simon and her father to the mix and get them all arrested on his word. Who, in Templeton, would know the sheriff was the real bad guy?

"Well then, come on," said Kat. "We need to get to the van while it's still there. Before Kind does."

The trek to the opposite side of the mountain was exhausting to the tired friends who had already redlined from literally running for their lives. Max and Javi took turns supporting Zeus, and Kat traded off times wearing the helmet with Max, keeping an eye on their destination and also continuing to probe the darkness for pursuers. They were all weak, some from dehydration, some from blood loss, all from fatigue.

When they found ATV tracks in the dirt, they perked up a degree. This side of the mountain looked as daunting as the opposite side, but there was a snaking trail hidden behind a hillock of rock and tree clusters. Once they rounded the edge, they found the false barrier, a trellis of vines covering plaster rocks, hiding the trail that wound around and down, wide and flat enough to drive ATVs up here. *Sneaky bastards.* Without worrying about shorter, straighter lines, they followed the windy ATV trail, knowing it would lead them true.

Kat and Max kept themselves from falling asleep while walking, chatting about what was going to happen after they got back. Assuming Kind wouldn't beat them home and have them arrested again, Max knew he'd have hellacious reports to file, explanations to give, and hearings to attend, testifying as to exactly what happened to nearly twenty people on this mountain. Twenty-two counting Del Seavers and Simon Pooler. They still weren't sure how to address the dead assassins behind the diner. And weren't going to mention the dead agents that had no known organizational affiliation. Those, at least, had disappeared in flames in her dad's incinerator. She shivered thinking how her grandfather had been caught up in all this years and years ago.

Fosse alluded that he was at least eighty-two. Either he was lying to shock her or he really had found some combination of chemicals and supernatural energy that had prolonged his life. Maybe this mountain really did have powers that could be cultivated and turned into a fountain of youth. Kat was curious what that could be in reality, but didn't think she'd ever be willing to come back here to find out. As far as she was concerned, the fountain of youth should stay a mystery, or at least be someone else's problem.

As they trekked down the trail, they spun around every minute or so, walking backward at times to scan for wolf-men they might have missed, or just Sheriff Kind sneaking up on them. Based on the GPS signal, the van was still parked, so he hadn't stolen it yet. And perhaps he was dead somewhere on the mountain, just another of Merrick's victims.

Speaking of which, still no Merrick either. And as they dragged further on, their sapped energy allowed for only the occasional glance around. Most of their reserve energy was spent keeping them from falling face-first into the dirt.

It was either approaching sunrise or was just lighter at the base of the mountain. Or perhaps their brains were lacking oxygen and everything seemed brighter because they were getting ready to faint. Whatever the reason, they could clearly see the van at the bottom of the last slope. Everybody wanted to run, nobody could. Max had enough magical energy to resemble a jog (upright downhill stumbling).

Though she had scoffed at Zeus before with his comparison to horror movies, in such movies, the heroes would be ignorant of the terrible surprise hiding behind the van, and since everything in this world was wacky enough to feel like fiction – she withdrew her pistol and let it hang by her side as she approached the van. Only after a few steps did she remember there weren't any more rounds in the gun.

Max got to the van first and seemed to have the same idea as Kat as he inched around the vehicle, knife drawn, peeking around corners and through windows. After two circumnavigations of the vehicle, he shrugged. *"Seems clear,"* was the silently conveyed message.

So, it isn't going to be like a movie? We really made it? And yet, still no Merrick. Though Kat knew he would be fine on his own, leaving without him felt like abandoning him. What else was she supposed to do? Hike around a massive mountain in the dark, searching uncountable square miles until she just happened to run into him? She had the feeling he had been watching over them ever since he transformed, and if he wanted to leave with them, he would've followed. It was just a feeling, but a strong one.

Since Kat had the gun (she hadn't told anyone it was unloaded), Max waited until she got to the cargo doors. Zeus and Javi gathered on the other side. After a moment of worry that Tanner's keys were to something else besides the van, the key fit and the lock opened. The last worry dissipated.

"I'm driving," said Kat grinning.

"Shotgun," said Javi.

Max tossed Kat the keys. "All aboard for the 'Get the Hell Outta Here' Express," he said, opening the rear doors.

The cargo area wasn't completely clear. There were boxes containing God knows what, some spare wires and cable rolled up on the floor, and a tarp covering a pile of something. Both the boxes and tarp blocked the space in front of the doors, so Max shoved the boxes forward, and the tarp-covered lump to the side.

A hand shot out from underneath and grabbed Max's wrist. His knife clattered to the ground. The tarp flipped up and Quinton Kind pointed a large caliber revolver at Max's head.

"Everybody freeze!" said Kind. "Or I blow Max's head off."

No one knew what to do. Even Kat, who had been expecting this kind of scenario minutes before, had relaxed her guard just at the wrong time. And the gun she still held in her hand was empty even if she wanted to try something risky.

Kind didn't know the gun was unloaded, however, and his eyes darted to it. "Put it down, Seavers," said Kind. "Slowly place the gun on the ground. Then throw over the keys."

Kat was dazed. Despite all the warning bells about a movie end-twist going off in her head, she had ignored them. She was more angry than afraid. That seemed to be a recent pattern with her, and even in the hazy moment of panic, she noticed it.

Kind hooked an arm around Max's neck and wrenched the deputy around to face Kat. The revolver was pressed to Max's ear.

"Seavers!" barked Kind. "Put down the gun now or your friend is the first to die from your stupidity. Now! Slowly!"

Kat shook her head. "No," she said. *What am I doing?*

Kind's eyes narrowed to make his glare more intimidating, however, the rest of Kind's body was trembling as he spoke. "Katheryn, I know you have the keys, and I don't want to spill any more blood, but I'm getting out of here, and if I have to kill all of you to do it – that's what's going to happen. So, I'll say it for the last time – put the gun down. Then throw me the keys."

Kat raised the pistol and sighted it on Kind's chest. *What in the hell am I doing?* It was like some "other" Kat was pulling the strings now. She wondered how similar it was for Merrick.

Merrick! The revelation hit her. *That's what Kind's worried about. That's why he hasn't shot us yet.* Quinton knew Merrick had

337

been protecting her, and maybe all of them. Maybe Kind had been watching all this from somewhere, knew they had the keys, and knew that things had gone south for his buddies, so he ran here. But couldn't drive away. And since he didn't see the human Merrick, he assumed Beast Merrick was still lurking and might attack if Kat or her friends were in danger. What would it take to constitute danger? A gunshot might be enough. That possibility made Kind afraid to shoot anyone, yet it was the only weapon he had to make them all back-off and do what he wanted.

Kat's aim stayed on Quinton's chest. "You're not leaving in the van, Quinton," she said. "And if you shoot, Merrick will hear it." She grinned unconsciously. "So, I'd suggest running before I shoot first." Whatever movie this had become apparently had a script where she acted like Clint Eastwood. She knew her anger at herself was really the culprit, but *damn!* – she was pushing everything to the edge of disaster.

Quinton looked torn. His expression portrayed confusion more than rage. Probably because his supposedly simple plan had been turned upside down, and he didn't know what to fear most. He continued to tremble as he calculated his next move.

Max took advantage of Kind's hesitancy and slammed an elbow into Kind's groin. The sheriff bucked, then doubled over and Max wrenched himself free. Max lurched and stumbled, reaching for his dropped knife. Kind's previously indecisive mind made a quick decision and fired at Max. The deputy grunted, arched his back, then spun and dove headfirst over a clump of rock and tall grass.

Zeus and Javier took cover behind a low-lying bush, the only thing close to them.

Kat went cold. Her first reaction was to pull the trigger of her pistol, but that would net her nothing. There didn't seem to be anything she could do that would be helpful. She even considered throwing the gun at Kind, which would also buy her nothing and probably get her shot. Only one thing made an inkling of sense in her head. She ran.

Fast-moving humans at a distance aren't easy targets, and Kind was still wobbly from the groin punch. His first shot hit the dirt behind her. If she could make it behind a copse of trees on her right before he got off another shot, she stood a good chance of staying unharmed. She crashed through the densely spaced saplings without a shot following her, then risked a quick look back while continuing to run. Kind had done exactly what she thought he would: gave chase. After all, she still had the keys to his getaway vehicle. As soon as she saw him clearly following her, she reached in her pocket (not as easy as she hoped while running) and yanked out the keys. Another gunshot hit something near her.

She flung the keys far to her right, making a purposeful show of it to make sure he saw. Apparently, he did because he slowed, then changed course to where the keys landed.

Kat had weighed the chances of Kind letting them all go free and she didn't like it. If, by a miracle, he let them live, he would likely drive back to Templeton and spin a yarn about how these crazed prisoners kidnapped a bunch of people, ambushed him, drove them all out to the mountains, and killed most everyone while he alone escaped. Or some other bizarre fabricated excuse to his advantage. One way or other, she couldn't let Kind leave here. For the sake of her friends, and for her father, even if it took her death to do it, Quinton Kind needed to die right here, right now. Like the other hunters, his fate should be to stay here as a permanent addition to the forest and let the fauna take care of his corpse.

She didn't have a good plan to accomplish that, or even a bad plan. Zero plans. As she considered this, she glanced through the bushes she was passing and noticed the white metal of the van several yards away. Her panicked run had circled her around to the front of the van.

A bad plan popped into her head. Was it better than no plan? *Oh, dear God, what am I about to do?*

CHAPTER 37

Kind jingled the keys in his hand. It was the sweetest sound he had heard in several hours.

At the beginning of the evening, all he could think about was the inevitable mess Fosse was once again creating, this one bigger than anything Quinton had dealt with before. By early morning, eleven of the hunters who had taken part in the Lycaon's Fire ritual were dead on the mountain. Though seven of the sacrifices did at least die, several more had survived and were further complicating Fosse's dumpster fire. This time, Quinton's solution had one colossal advantage: Fosse was dead. Not just Arthur, but his piece-of-shit son too. As well as all the paramilitary goons Fosse hired as his personal Gestapo. There was nothing left to keep Quinton from enjoying the peace and quiet of being a small-town sheriff, and keeping the spirit cave on this mountain to himself without Fosse's interference.

This ridiculous ritual had nothing to do with their health and longevity. Years ago, it had served the purpose of executing those that cheated the justice system, but in recent years, it had become just an eccentric excuse for satiating bloodlust and cleaning up messes made by the Fosse men. Kind had taken part in the cannibalistic aspects at first like everyone else, but the last few years, he'd been faking it. It simply didn't matter. The energy surge he received from the combination of the cave and Fosse's chemical cocktail felt the same regardless of whether he consumed a piece of human flesh or a barbequed pulled-pork sandwich. Just another of Fosse's baseless ideological obsessions. The drug Arthur had supplied (or stolen if Kind's guess was correct) combined with the energy inside Lycaon's cave produced the desired effect all by themselves. There weren't spirits in there needing appeasement. Unexplained energy, yes, but spirits? *Well,* – maybe, but they still didn't need human sacrifices. *Fuck Fosse.* Unfortunately, Quinton had no way of getting the health formula Fosse kept hidden, but – *oh well.* He'd prolonged his life by about forty years already, and the peace he'd gain without the Fosses was worth the price of limiting his remaining years.

Kind came up to the van and did a sweep around its perimeter. Seavers, the two Morenos, and the Indian were probably keeping their heads down, not wanting a .357 slug in their craniums. *Oh right.* He forgot he shot the Indian. *Dead?* Hard to say. Everything happened faster and crazier than he was prepared for. If the deputy was dead, that was another lie he needed to create. He really hated losing his deputies. Other than being nosy, they were good deputies, and Kind really didn't want either of them to be a part of Fosse's mess.

Kind multitasked about what story he'd have to invent to explain all this. Something like how Kat and Del and the Morenos, etc. were all involved in this cult activity, and were explicit in the Fosse's murders – *I might have to blame them for Del and Simon's murder too.* Assuming he didn't kill Kat and her accomplices before he left. Should he hunt them down? Seavers was probably out of bullets or she would have shot at him. And the thing that Hull had become, or the contraption he wore (Kind still didn't know or understand it), didn't seem to be around here or he would've already come to the rescue when Quinton shot at both Kat and Max. Maybe Hull had died up there somewhere. Regardless of how Quinton spun it, the paperwork and excuses he needed in order to write it all off to the authorities were going to be insanely tough. But he had done it for years. Just once more. *Last time ever.*

Two cautious loops around the van satisfied Kind that no one was around. The survivors were probably hiding, or just ran away. That was fine. There were contingency plans. He unlocked the driver's door and hopped into the van. His gun stayed ready as he gave a long look at the cargo area, half-expecting to see Hull's monstrous form waiting there. *Nope. Not here.* Just the same boxes and tarp he had hidden under himself. Both were too small to hide the beast form Hull had adopted. That thing was enormous.

Kind placed his revolver on the center console and turned the ignition. He steered the van onto the bumpy little path that had been expressly cleared by Fosse's men to get to and from the Lycaon ritual. This road existed on no map. *If you could even call it a road.*

His mind was preoccupied, juggling several questions, like how to officially explain everything, and whether anyone was secretly following him. He glanced in the rearview. Something blocked his view of the back windows. In the mirror, he saw vengeful eyes staring back.

Too late, he reached for the gun. One of the arrows they stored for the bonfire lighting ceremony speared his shoulder, rammed in by the person belonging to the murderous face in the mirror. It was Seavers.

Quinton's hand tightened on the revolver, attempting to twist it to point at Kat, but his injured arm was weak and shaking with spasms, unable to accurately aim the gun. He fired and hit the roof, nowhere close to Kat. Lucky for him, she ducked anyway.

The arrow wound was shooting bolts of searing pain through him as the shaft bumped against everything in the cramped driver's space – the seat, the console, the dash – as he maneuvered himself into a better position to fire at Kat again. He gritted through it, knowing he had an easy target who was out of weapons to use against him and also stuck in an enclosed space. There was just another important thing he needed to do first, and – he couldn't remember…

Shit! He snapped his eyes back to the road ahead. His left hand snatched the wheel, ready to turn whatever way was needed. Not quick enough. A slender tree, painted bright white by the headlight, impacted the front grill at the same moment he yanked the wheel right.

The rear of the van rose and dropped to the ground, violently bouncing the vehicle on its shocks. Something big and white punched Kind in the face. His stunned mind took several seconds to realize that the airbag had deployed. Although he didn't pass out, he felt like he was drunk, needing to shake himself sober.

He did a quick check of his immediate situation. All parts of his body responded, nothing was broken or severed. His injured arm was weak, though not paralyzed. The gun remained in his right hand. The van had ceased moving but was still running, so likely drivable. And Kat was lying on the cargo floor, unconscious and bleeding from a gash on her head. *No airbags in the cargo area, ya dumb cunt. Nice plan.* Though he had always considered Kat a smart woman, albeit exceptionally troublesome, there was no substitute in battle for experience. Book smarts be damned, he was the only person that was going to survive the night. Kat would've been allowed a few extra hours, maybe days, of life if she hadn't tried this stupid stunt. She and her friends would've all stayed alive for the time it took to do things by the official law enforcement book: post an APB; mount a statewide sweep; possibly cheat and track the tracking chips in their knives if any of the survivors still carried them. His pride couldn't let Kat go now.

When he tried to aim the revolver, the arrow was obstructing his shoulder joint and sparked a surge of excruciating pain when he moved it. He gritted his teeth, snapped off the shaft, and yanked the arrow out. That agony was worse than the previous pain, though he knew he'd only need to do it once. A few cleansing breaths later to gather his calm and he aimed the revolver at Kat again.

Kat being dead (or just missing perhaps) was a lie he had expected to tell anyway, and there were plenty of places to dump the body before he got back to town. That said, Kind was beginning to reconsider leaving the other live bodies behind. Should he drive back now, find them all and kill them, even in his weakened state? Or should he just drive away and make up the complicated lies he had been planning, then hunt them down later with deputy help and full legal authority? There was also the problem of Hull running around in that beast outfit (he hoped it was an outfit), who Kind might encounter if he went back. The safer play was probably to just drive home and regroup there.

One thing at a time, Quinton. Kind looked down the sight of his revolver at Kat's prostrate body. He put pressure on the trigger.

The driver's door was suddenly opened and ripped off its hinges. The whole door, including twisted bolts and severed hinges, was inexplicably removed and thrown several yards into the woods. *What the fuck...?* A hairy arm shot through the opening, its claws puncturing Kind in the previously undamaged shoulder. The claws went through his back and stuck out the front. The pain from the arrow wound was nothing compared to the overload of torturous agony from being impaled by a beast's claws. Before he could overcome the incapacitating pain to accomplish the mission of getting his revolver around to point at the thing attacking him, the creature had yanked him through the open door and hauled him onto the ground.

Quinton thought fast. *Ignore the pain!* He still had the gun, if he could just get it up and...

The tip of a snarling muzzle touched Kind's cheek. Hot saliva drizzled down his jaw and neck. The creature's snout was long, like a crocodile, yet hairy, displaying rows of hooked, gray teeth that could easily strip the flesh from his bones. Horrible eyes fixed on him, shiny and impenetrable, reflecting his pale, terrified face at himself. This creature wasn't some mechanical suit like his had been. This was a beast from horror fiction, immense and incredible, with strength like a superhero, and claws and teeth that could turn Kind into filleted carrion that would be consumed by the predators of the forest in less than a day. A search party wouldn't find him, no one would ever know how he died, and probably no one would care. Quinton Kind was about to disappear from the world and all he had to stop it was his revolver. The .357 magnum he carried looked like it would be more of an annoyance to this nightmarish monster rather than a legitimate threat.

Kind raised the gun. The beast reared back with a flared hand of long claws and struck before Kind could pull the trigger. No shot happened. All Quinton could understand is that he had fallen to the ground and was rolling away from the beast as it watched him. Except... why was his body still in the grip of the beast? Torso, arms, legs – even the gun in his hand were visible, but – where was his head? *Oh.* He rolled to a stop three yards away from his body. Such an odd, naked feeling it was to see himself that way. Though he never expected to be immortal, he at least assumed his body would be whole at his death. *Not like this.* As the lights dimmed, he watched the beast shred his headless body open, filleting it like a slaughterhouse worker, then tossing the remains toward his head. *I can be together before I go! If I can just reach out and touch...* But heads have nothing to reach with.

The lights went dark. He wished his life would flash before him so at least he could recall the better memories before death came. But no memory montage happened. Even trying to recall one, he drew a blank. All he felt was a bottomless pit of despair and loneliness. Whatever Quinton Kind had been, he was no more.

Kat had no idea how long she had been knocked out. When she came to, the first thing she noticed was that she was still alive. *Genius deduction.* A cut on her head seemed to be the only casualty from her unconsciousness. *He didn't shoot me?*

When she exited the van, she found out why. What used to be Sheriff Quinton Kind was a mess of pink, red, and brown material, along with shredded black clothing, heaped beside the van. Only Quinton's head was recognizable, and that was separate from his body. She thought for a moment about hiding the remains, but knew in this part of the forest, scavengers would clean it up in very short order if she left it alone.

As much of a relief as it was to find her last oppressor dead, an equal relief was that Merrick was also next to the van. He was half-naked and shivering, with icky skin and deflating lumps on his body indicating he was still coming down from his transformation. The same freaky show she saw in her living room not long ago. Remembering what she did then, she did the same thing now. She retrieved the tarp from the van and draped it over Merrick. As his eyes finally met hers, his words came out haltingly due to his trembling, but were nevertheless clear. "Thank – you – Kaaat. Is it – over?"

She nodded. "It's over."

"Don't let them – sssee me this way," he stuttered.

Them? A moment later she heard the distant voices of her friends. It sounded like three people were calling her. Was Max still alive?

"Here!" Kat called back, then waited. She couldn't lift Merrick, and she wasn't about to leave him alone in case some other crazy movie twist happened. The van hadn't driven far. Maybe a quarter-mile. They'd find her soon.

Within five minutes, three people came hobbling up the path. Zeus leaning against his walking stick on one side, Max clutching his ribs on the other, both their arms around Javier in the middle.

Merrick was fully human now, and stable, though still shivering. It was time to pack everyone up in the busted van and get the hell out of this nightmare.

CHAPTER 38

Ambient late morning sun filtered through the sheer kitchen curtains as Kat sat at her dining table, lost in thought. There were numerous reasons why. One reason would be the events of last night, during which a dozen bloodthirsty lunatics tried to kill her and her friends, and instead, the lunatics all died. Another reason was the death of her father by one of the men she had helped kill last night. Further reasons included: her boyf... no, *friend (with benefits)* who turned into a real supernatural beast; and a group of mysterious, sinister agents who were killed by said beast, then turned to ash in her father's incinerator. Added to the mix was an experience from late last night intended to wash away the foul taste of the last two days: a love-making session with Merrick that started as just a comforting cuddle for both of them, then turned into a desperate, hungry, tension release exercise.

All those were good candidates for brain occupation, but the thing forefront on her mind at the moment was her future. For years, she had debated when the right time was to start the first step on her European experience. When the nightmarish recent events began, and she had recklessly raced off with Merrick in her Jeep, it had necessitated a hurried decision to pack her things, grab up her savings, and begin her new future immediately. Now, with the pressure of running for her life over, and her father gone, and her boyf... *Oh, hell. Yes, he's your boyfriend...* going God knows where indefinitely, there was nothing left to hold her here. The primary question was how to move forward and what to move forward to.

The ranch was hers. A box in Del's closet contained his will which left everything to her. Her father had told her there were things in his closet that would help her whenever he was gone (not expecting it would be so soon), and things in the secret niche in his closet that would answer her questions.

Inside the niche were parts of a wolf suit that had long ago deteriorated. Proof of the terrors she had just endured if it was ever needed in court, or as evidence for Max's report. Next to that was a stack of documents Del wrote to explain, or perhaps testify to, everything he was aware of that Quinton Kind and Arthur Fosse had done. It was bizarrely interesting reading, even though she lived through part of it. A strongbox of cash was also in the niche with a note rubber-banded to the wad, addressed to her.

"To my sweet Kat. I don't know how much will be here when I finally give it to you, but on the day you announce your intention to step out into the vast world and explore what it has to offer, this money is yours to do with as you please. A few dollars here and there, a windfall saved instead of spent, whatever comes my way that isn't earmarked for bills went into this box to help you live your dreams and begin your future. I hope you didn't take too long to start it. I love you. I always will. You are the best thing that ever happened to my life and I have cherished every minute of being your father. – Dad."

Her own savings from working at the diner added up to ten thousand, barely enough in her estimate to do what she wanted to do if she was very careful once she got to Europe. Del's box tripled that. There was also the house, but that was her guarantee that once she got back to the states, she had the equity to buy a residence elsewhere. She would never live here again.

Kat took a sip from her coffee and absent-mindedly examined her kitchen. A kitchen she had known for twenty years and had no interest in seeing anymore. Everything in the house was a reminder of her father. And thinking about her father made her want to cry. If she stayed here, she'd be living with a ghost, either metaphorically or actually, and bawling every day.

Outside, she heard the commotion of Zeus and Javier getting ready to start their day. Or to be more precise, Zeus telling Javier all the things he needed to do to start their day. Since Zeus's leg was going to be healing for a while, he would have to monitor things from a little motorized cart. They would also be training a new ranch hand since they would be the sole people on the ranch once she left.

Zeus wanted to buy the ranch, but wasn't sure about his finances. He'd been living in a trailer for years to save money. Kat was in no hurry to sell anything, so she promised to let Zeus stay on the ranch, keep all the proceeds from it, and buy it at his convenience. In a few years, however long she spent abroad, he might be in a more comfortable position to purchase the place at the friends-and-family discount she planned to offer. The only thing she cherished here was her father's memory.

A knock came at the front door.

"Kat" called a familiar voice. "It's me. Max."

"Door's open. I'm in the kitchen."

The door had been torn from the hinges during the sinister agent melee, and Kat temporarily leaned it up, braced with a piece of furniture until she could get it fixed.

Several seconds later, Max hobbled in. His jacket bulged over the clump of bandages on his side from his gunshot wound. The bullet had miraculously hit nothing vital, and besides a long recovery time, he was going to be fine. Just maybe stiff on cold days. He was dressed in his sheriff's deputy outfit which surprised Kat.

Max answered the unspoken question. "There isn't many of us left at the station," said Max. "Even injured, I had to be on call, and it's a pain to dress, so – I'll just keep these on."

"I didn't say anything," said Kat. "But yeah, I figured you'd be taking it easy for a week or two."

"Pfbbbt," mocked Max. "You kiddin'? I got mountains of paperwork to create, explanations to file for the main office. Court dates, interviews. Hell, I've already got some reporter who wants to make his Pulitzer dreams come true writing the story of our harrowing adventures on werewolf mountain."

"That *is* a joke, right? They ain't gonna call the place werewolf mountain?"

"It's a joke. But – God knows what they'll call it when they know the whole story. Maybe Mount Lykaia since that was the place where the cult followers of King Lycaon created their festival, and where they…"

"Max," said Kat with a pointed stare. "Let's not talk about this stuff right now, please."

"Sorry. I understand."

"And we're clear that we're not going to talk to anyone about…"

"…To anyone about Merrick. Yeah, I know," said Max, finishing her sentence. "He never existed. Don't worry. I mean, Frank Chaney was fingerprinted an' all, but there's not much I can do about that.

349

Well, unless… maybe I could kinda alter a record or two – it would hafta be gradual, so they won't…"

"No, Max," said Kat. "You're the good-guy cop. You don't alter records and start becoming Quinton Kind even with good intentions. It always starts that way before it goes bad."

Max hung his head and nodded. "Yeah. You're right. Merrick'll be hard to find anyway. Hope he'll be ok."

Kat offered a more confident smile than she felt. "He will. So, why'd you come over?"

"Oh, right." He held up a satchel and pulled several papers from it. "Speaking of falsifying records – I need your signature on a few things as an eyewitness to the bullshit I just made up a couple of hours ago. One and only time, I promise." He placed the papers on her table. "Feel free to read it to make sure you agree with my, uh – recollection of events." He made air quotes.

"Does it paint me in a good light?"

"Yep. You're a badass. Saved us all. I helped a little."

Kat gave him a grin and a doubtful look. "You seriously didn't make yourself out to be Rambo? You really want me to read this and see?"

Max grimaced, more from comedic effect than true embarrassment. "Ok, I, uh – did have to give myself credit for a few things you and Merrick did to make the deaths easier to write off as necessary acts for a law enforcement officer in the performance of his duty in the... Hey, come on, don't roll your eyes. It's the only way."

Kat nodded, keeping the same enigmatic smile. "Relax, Deputy Yellow Feather. I'm just teasing. I don't want credit for crap." She signed one document and started on another. "I'm nobody. Just a girl."

"What's *that* mean?"

"Nothing. Never mind." She signed another document. "Honestly, I'd rather not be mentioned at all in this report. I know you can't but – I'd rather pretend like I was never there." She made a comical magic wave. "You never saw me."

"You wanna turn into Merrick now?"

"Not the same way," she said. "But I'm going to go experience world history in person, up close, with my eyes and ears, hands and feet. Not a television or the internet."

"To each their own."

She finished the papers and handed them back to Max.

"Speaking of Merrick," said Max, "Where is he?"

"Went back to sleep. Last comfy bed he may get for a while."

"Couldn't convince him to stick around?"

Kat held her breath for a moment, then shook her head. "Doesn't work that way. But we did talk about it."

In a moment of weakness and passion, Merrick had changed his mind and took her up on her previous offer to come with him. And in a moment of unexpected responsibility, Kat told him no. She regretted nothing concerning her time with Merrick, and knew full well he needed to be on his own. *For now.* Danger followed him, the people he cared about would get hurt, and he would remain in constant anxiety trying to protect her if she stayed with him. She was less worried for herself than she was for him. It was unfair to ask him to bear that weight, and she never wanted anyone to think they needed to protect her. Until whoever or whatever was after him gave up, died, or were incarcerated, Merrick would need to do exactly what he had been doing. Living like a man who was his own country, invisible and alone. That's the thing that bothered her the most. Even if he couldn't have her, he deserved love, friendship, and human contact, the same as everyone else. It was what kept most humans truly alive, and yet he had to deny it to himself. Something she could never do.

Really? You're denying yourself Merrick. No, the agents were doing that. She would continue to blame the right people for the wrongs in her life instead of building up unfocused angst until it manifested as outward anger at the ones who cared about her. The façade she put up to keep people at a distance was the first thing she was going to alter.

She stood up, wrapped her arms around Max, and gave him a much-too-long hug. Then kissed his forehead.

"I never thanked you properly for what you did out there," she said.

Max was struggling not to turn pink, but he managed to almost look nonchalant. "Just doing my duty, ma'am," he said in a TV cop voice.

She reached around and swatted Max on his rear. "Now get going. You've got mountains of paperwork to create, and I've got things to do."

He chuckled. "Yes, ma'am. Except – uh, does Merrick need a ride anywhere? You know, to help him get started?"

She shook her head. "No. When he leaves my door, he wants to be completely on his own again. Don't ask me. Just what he said."

"Ok, then. See you later. You – aren't leaving for a few days, right?"

"Yeah," she answered. "Dad deserves a proper funeral."

"I'll come. I'd like to say goodbye to him too."

"Thanks. Is there going to be a funeral for Simon?"

Max shook his head. "Not here. He had family in Illinois. Sister's coming down tomorrow to take custody of his body and pack up his stuff."

Kat nodded somberly. "I've got a few of Dad's things to pack and store somewhere. I never collected much for myself, so –. Anyway, I'll see you at Dad's funeral, and I'll say goodbye before I go."

"Kay."

Max left the kitchen, squeezed past the leaning front door, then went out to his patrol car.

Kat followed with her coffee cup in hand. She watched Max's taillights disappear behind the trees that bordered her entry road.

Zeus waved at Kat from his scooter. "Morning!" he said.

Kat smiled and lifted her cup in salute.

"What'cha gonna do with your dad's truck," asked Zeus.

She shrugged. The 3 axle truck had been bought for ranch business, and though it served as Del's personal vehicle, he rarely went anywhere in it for pleasure. "It'll be the ranch truck. Utility for whatever."

"Thanks! Appreciate it."

She looked at the treetops below the sunrise. Recent events had altered her outlook on life, and with it, a new appreciation for the view outside her door she had seen for twenty years. This really was majestic country, and with the Fosses and Sheriff Kind gone,

Templeton would probably be a nice, quiet place to live. Max would make a good sheriff if the main office let him. A real-life Andy Taylor that everyone assumes exists in small towns. In a way, it was a shame that she was leaving now just when everything was about to improve. But her heart wasn't here. This was her dad's place. Actually, her grandfather's place. Their spirits would always rest here. She had a new life to start and wasn't waiting any longer than necessary.

A hand rested on her shoulder and warm lips kissed the back of her neck.

"Hey, stud," she said as she turned toward him. She met his lips and they held each other for a full minute.

Merrick had his duffel bag stuffed with his usual possessions, some extra clothes, and ziplocked food. Del's analog watch (Kat insisted) was on his wrist, and an envelope with several hundred dollars in cash was secretly placed in his jacket pocket. Wherever life was about to take him, he'd be in good shape for a while.

"I don't know if I can make it to the end of the driveway without turning around," said Merrick.

She smiled. "And I'm not sure I won't lose my nerve and follow you." She patted his butt. "But you're not getting rid of me that easily."

She held out a slip of paper to him.

"What's this?" he asked.

Printed on the paper were two lines: "studwolf1800@gmail.com," and "pass = MonsterBoy01."

"It's something called email," she said.

"I know what email is, smartass," he chuckled. "But I don't have anything to read it with."

"Yes, you do. Most any library has public-use computers, and you're always hanging around libraries. Just log on and check your email there. No one knows who the address belongs to. I obviously didn't use your real name."

Merrick shrugged. "Ok, but – why?"

"Cuz we're going to talk to each other on it, ya bonehead. You're cute, but you're dumb sometimes."

Merrick nodded. "They can't trace me with this?"

"Not unless they do a search for every email everywhere and just happen to get lucky and read ours. I'm going to use a different email with a fake name and buy a prepaid phone to send it on when I get where I'm going. Can't trace those. See? I got your back. And like I said, you ain't getting rid of me."

"You're amazing. Truly."

"And when you get in trouble, it'll be easy to reach me."

"And if you ever get in trouble, I'll find a way to get to you."

"I can take care of myself. But – I kinda like havin' you around, anyway." She grinned. "So, when you finally get these asss…" She suddenly remembered her father's rule of no swearing in the house. "…Agents off your back, you can come claim your prize." She cocked her hip in a coquettish pose.

Merrick made a scoffing face. "You'll be married or dating a dozen male models by then. I don't think you'll want me back as much as you think."

She reached down and cupped his crotch in her hand, then grinned wickedly. "Where am I gonna find another animal in bed like you, huh? A sexual wolf in sheep's clothing? A boudoir beast?"

"Dear Lord, have you been saving those puns?"

"I got more."

"Not necessary." He lifted her hand and kissed the back of it. "I'd rather you think of me as a swashbuckling gentleman."

Kat laughed. "I'll swash your buckle, monster boy."

Merrick chuckled as well. "Is that punishment or sexual innuendo?"

"Not sure," said Kat. "Guess you'll have to wait to find out."

Merrick shook his head. "Damn, you're making it hard to leave."

Kat smirked and sipped her coffee. "Just making it so you'll pine away for me for as long as we're apart and never love another woman."

"Done and done."

They stayed silent for a few minutes, then Merrick asked, "Where are you going to start?"

"Portugal," said Kat. "Then work my way northeast. Spain, France, Germany. Take a detour south to Italy. How 'bout you? Gonna find the agency that's after you? Take the fight to them?"

"Don't know where to look. And I'm not prepared yet. Need to dig around, come up with something that'll help me. They'll probably find me whether I'm ready or not though. I need to get far away from anyone I – care about."

"Got somewhere in mind?"

Merrick shrugged. "I went as far north in the U.S. as I could go this time. Caused a lot of trouble. Maybe I'll try south."

"I came from there. Specifically, Texas. Just so you know, they have guns and sheriffs there too."

"Hopefully not people in werewolf suits."

"Who knows? Their werewolves probably wear cowboy hats."

Merrick smiled. "I'm really gonna miss the hell out of you."

"Good," said Kat. "Cuz I'm gonna miss you, and I'm punishing you for it."

"I can survive anything you can dish out. I'm pretty resilient."

"Yeah, well, I'll still shoot you if you don't email me constantly."

He fought back a laugh. "Every town I get to, first thing I'll do."

Merrick gave her a gentle kiss on the cheek.

Kat smiled knowing that the kiss was the last thing she was going to get from him for a long time. *How long?* She leaned into the kiss, then took a good cleansing breath. "I want you back in one piece, ya hear? You take care of yourself, Merrick Hull."

"If I don't, someone else will," said Merrick.

He picked up his duffel and descended the stairs. After hugging Zeus and Javi, then chatting for a moment, he turned and waved at Kat. Once he began his walk down the long, dirt driveway, he never looked back.

It took every ounce of mental fortitude Merrick had to keep his eyes straight as he walked. If he looked back and saw her, his feet would run in her direction and he wouldn't be able to turn them away again. He had the email code she made and could talk to her whenever he wanted. It wasn't her wonderful, warm, sensuous body, but – it was something. More than he ever had before. *I'm not alone.* He tried to block Kat from his mind and concentrate ahead.

As he approached the main road, he was admiring the view of the mountain chain he had escaped from only hours ago. From this distance, it was beautiful. It always intrigued him how the surface of something could be so different than what was underneath.

Days ago, when he got off the bus in Templeton, it had seemed like the picturesque, quintessential, Small Town U.S.A. He didn't expect to be hunted by demented cannibals with a werewolf fetish. He also wasn't expecting to make love (multiple times) with a gorgeous and amazing woman. And maybe fall in love.

And can't have her. Ever? A "normal" life hadn't been an option before, so he had embraced this lonely, nomadic one, despite never being close to someone because the people that continued to hunt him would destroy anyone and anything to get to him. It was the way it had to be for his safety and everyone else's. Unless things changed.

"Gonna find the agency that's after you? Take the fight to them?" What if he could? Hunt them down and destroy them first? It wasn't a new concept, and he had always considered the possibility, but – to actually do it? How?

And where to start? He had already examined the agents' abandoned vehicle this morning before Max impounded it. According to the public VIN report, the car itself belonged to a state senate pool in Helena. Stolen, most likely. The plates were faked, no registration, and not even a McDonald's receipt under the seat. There was probably a tracker in the engine block, but tracking chips didn't track two ways. Untraceable occupants. A ghost car.

Find somewhere safe on your terms, then capture one of them and get information from him.

Maybe. Maybe. Kat was expecting that once he solved his agent troubles, he'd come back to her. Even if he could, was she safe from the other him? His continual worry was that his other self couldn't distinguish between friend or foe, and the chances were just as good that he'd do as much harm to her as the agents would, yet the trials on the mountain proved otherwise. His beast-self had stood in front of her multiple times and not only didn't harm her – he protected her. Days ago, having control over his alter ego was a pipe dream. But now?

As with the mountain and the town, underneath the surface of his own skin lurked something greater than his meek frame. Even in human form, he had been more heroic than he thought. If there was a chance to control his other self, maybe he could be a real hero. *Or at least end my nightmare.*

The road in front of him ran left and right. He had to pick a direction. Though he knew there was little significance to going either way, in his mind, the choice symbolized something more philosophical. Neither direction led to safety. His life, and everyone around him, was in jeopardy regardless if he ran from his antagonists or toward them. Facing them meant a much greater risk to himself, yet it might bring him back sooner to those he cared about. Behind him were an extraordinary woman and genuine friends that he had to leave for their safety. Temporarily? Hard to know for sure. He couldn't be around them, or anyone, until he was no longer hunted.

The hunt may be over for them, but not for him. For a long time now, he had been the prey. Just like on the mountain, perhaps it was time the hunted became the hunter. He had a new reason to try, and she was in that house behind him. Getting further away with each step.

He picked a direction and began to walk.

THE END